REVELATION

Also by V.C. Kincade

Control
Dominance
Manipulation

Coming Up

Return
Obsession
Convergence
Reckoning

Revelation

A Blackburn Erotic Thriller

V.C. Kincade

Northshore Noir Press

This is a work of fiction. All names, characters and incidents are the product of the author's imagination. Any resemblance to real persons, living or dead, is entirely coincidental.

REVELATION. A Blackburn Erotic Thriller. Book 4. Copyright © 2026 by V.C. Kincade. All rights reserved.

Cover design © Northshore Noir Press

Cover artwork: *The Burning Street,* Susan Stevers, 2025.

Northshore Noir upholds the principles of free expression and recognizes the significance of copyright protection. No part of this publication may be reproduced, distributed, or transmitted in any form or by any means without the prior written permission of the Publisher, except for brief quotations incorporated into critical articles or reviews. Your adherence to and respect for the author's rights are sincerely appreciated.

Northshore Noir Press
Toronto, Canada
www.northshorenoir.com

ISBN: 978-1-998648-37-5

eBook ISBN: 978-1-998648-38-2

Contents

Chapter 1	1
Chapter 2	16
Chapter 3	31
Chapter 4	41
Chapter 5	57
Chapter 6	67
Chapter 7	79
Chapter 8	87
Chapter 9	101
Chapter 10	110
Chapter 11	125
Chapter 12	138
Chapter 13	147
Chapter 14	158
Chapter 15	175
Chapter 16	185

Chapter 17	192
Chapter 18	201
Chapter 19	215
Chapter 20	225
Chapter 21	232
Chapter 22	242
Chapter 23	254
Chapter 24	262
Chapter 25	272
Chapter 26	284
Chapter 27	296
Chapter 28	305
Chapter 29	318
Chapter 30	328
Chapter 31	338
Chapter 32	347
Chapter 33	364
Chapter 34	374

Chapter 1

First light seeped over Dunbar Bluffs. Detective Morgan Blackburn stood near the drop, her silhouette etched against the strobe of police lights and churning activity. Behind her, the scene throbbed with emergency work: cruisers angled along the lane, engines rumbling beneath clipped voices that cut through the morning air. A helicopter carved slow circles overhead, its spotlight sweeping across fractured rock and scorched brush. The news chopper hovered at the edges, cameras rolling for the morning broadcast.

Death served up for breakfast.

Below where stone met dirt, wreckage burned in violent bursts. Firefighters worked with grim precision, faces tight as they beat back flames and navigated twisted metal. Ash spiraled through the pale light, coating everything in gray dust.

Blackburn scanned the terrain. The debris field spread in a concentrated pattern, fragments already tagged by crime scene techs moving in pairs. Yellow markers sprouted beside pieces of cab frame and blackened vegetation. Everything seemed out of place. Nothing fit.

Officer DeForest shifted nearby, boots scraping gravel. He watched Blackburn, waiting.

She had led the pursuit herself, racing through city streets and out toward this jagged edge. Lilith Halperin's cab had been diverted. A lover's shortcut transformed into a death trap once she had stepped inside. Blackburn had arrived expecting something intimate. Instead, she had tracked a runaway vehicle as it careened off course, joining DeForest and Watson just before everything unraveled.

They followed protocol but came up short. The cab had paused just long enough for Blackburn to scramble through the dirt and reach the handles. See her face, her fear. Then it sailed clean off the cliff despite their efforts. Lilith, her new submissive, had been inside.

Blackburn absorbed that loss like ice water in her veins.

DeForest cleared his throat, watching her for direction. Her new puppy needed attention.

"Officer," Blackburn said, beckoning him closer.

He stepped forward quickly. "Yes, ma'am?"

"Thank you," she said, voice low. "Your timing saved my life."

He nodded but avoided her gaze. "I'm glad you're all right." His eyes drifted toward the smoking wreckage below. "Wish we could have done more for them."

Them.

The cab's driver remained unaccounted for. Early evidence, a frantic 911 call, suggested he lost control well before reaching the bluffs.

Nothing about this case would be simple.

The sun climbed higher, heat pressing down on Dunbar Bluffs. Reporters crowded behind the yellow tape, voices tangling in an insistent chorus of questions. Some scrambled up the hillside, cameras hoisted, determined to capture every angle of destruction below.

Blackburn held her position back from the cliff. Her right arm hugged her ribs, shoulder pulsing where DeForest's grip had wrenched it moments earlier. She rolled her arm carefully, jaw clenched as pain bloomed through muscle and bone.

Around her, officers coordinated logistics, EMTs threaded between clusters of responders, and crime scene techs documented evidence with mechanical clicks. The noise blurred at the edges of Blackburn's attention. She monitored her breathing and dissected the last hour in pieces. The car's plunge looped through her mind. Glass exploding, metal shrieking against stone. Every detail was turned over for examination. She hunted for patterns.

An EMT approached with deliberate steps. "Detective Blackburn? Let's check that shoulder." His voice carried professional calm, and his expression was neutral.

She caught his eyes, reading both concern and assessment of her stability. Aftercare. She nodded and allowed him to guide her from the overlook toward the ambulance. Cameras tracked their movement, shutters firing in rapid succession.

Inside the vehicle, Blackburn settled onto the bench seat. The throb in her shoulder faded to familiar background static: unfinished business demanding attention. Images of Lilith flickered through her mind. First terror, then hunger. Her own. Lilith's face illuminated by the dashboard light as she screamed behind locked doors. The memory sparked no sympathy in Blackburn, only a cold current of satisfaction.

The image scratched the inside of Blackburn's skull. Not grief, but a cold satisfaction she didn't bother justifying.

She blinked and pushed that image down. Another memory surfaced: Lilith entering a restaurant just days ago, spine straight, face composed, dark hair spilling over a blouse. Their eyes had locked. Neither broke contact first.

Blackburn released a breath and studied the scene through the ambulance window. Media crews clustered near squad cars and barriers. They shouted to officers by name or barked updates into phones. Every gesture seemed rehearsed. Equipment thrust forward, eager faces scanning for vulnerability or narrative.

A black sedan rolled to a stop beyond the tape. Blackburn identified Chief Hayes before he emerged. The press pack wheeled toward him in unison and pressed forward, hungry for statements.

Hayes stepped out stiffly, adjusting his collar while the questions began without him. He blinked into the noise, already losing ground. He smoothed his coat before turning to face their assault head-on.

The EMT moved her shoulder back and forth, a small pain against tender skin. Blackburn shifted and reached for her phone with her free hand. Her thumb moved across the screen, opening BDSMessages. She angled the display away from the medic's peripheral vision, her fingers steady as she navigated the deletion process. Each photo dissolved into the digital void. Connections severed with clinical precision. She lifted her gaze to scan the surrounding chaos. Uniforms, flashing lights, curious onlookers. Then she returned to her task, methodical and silent.

With a final tap, she deleted her account. The last traces of her digital footprint vanished from the app, leaving only empty server space behind. She allowed herself the smallest upturn of her lips. Efficient, necessary, another vulnerability eliminated.

The phone vibrated against her palm before she could slip it away. Willow's name illuminated the screen. Blackburn suppressed the tightness in her jaw and answered.

"Hello." The word came out weary but controlled.

Willow's voice spilled through the speaker, high and fractured. "Oh God, I just saw what happened. Are you alright? They said you got hurt."

Willow Adler. Lover. Suspect.

Blackburn pressed her eyes closed, feeling the ache radiate from her shoulder. She measured her response carefully.

"I'm fine. Just shaken up, nothing serious." She kept her tone gentle but unyielding.

Willow's anxiety crackled through the connection, questions tumbling over each other in breathless succession. Blackburn caught movement in her periphery. Officer DeForest approached the ambulance, his jaw jutting forward, leading him toward her.

"Willow," Blackburn interrupted, her voice low and definitive, "I need to go. I have to speak with Officer DeForest now. I'll see you soon."

She disconnected before Willow could form another word and tucked her phone away as DeForest's shadow fell across the gurney.

Two cameras perched at the scene's perimeter, their black lenses trained on the ambulance like predatory eyes. Blackburn registered their presence instantly: live footage streaming to whoever cared to watch. She calculated her next move in seconds.

Rising from the gurney, she stepped into DeForest's space and wrapped her arms around him. His muscles locked beneath her touch before gradually softening into an uncertain return embrace.

"Thank you," she murmured against the rough fabric of his uniform, her voice calibrated for nearby microphones.

Heat crept up DeForest's neck as he registered the cameras and the watching officers. "I only did what was needed, Detective," he said, the words stiff in his throat.

Blackburn drew back but maintained her grip on his shoulders, holding his gaze while camera shutters clicked like insects behind her.

"No, Officer DeForest," Blackburn said, her voice clear for the microphones. "A dozen officers were here when that cab went over. I was the only one who made a move. You were the only one who pulled me out. Don't minimize it."

The cameras lingered, their lenses catching the air that misted the air between them. She held his gaze, something guarded flickering behind her eyes as raw emotion gave way to control. The wind carried the acrid smell of burned rubber, still fresh from the fire. She took a slow breath, tasting tension and exhaust.

"In the confusion that follows, critical things fall through the cracks," she said, her words nearly lost beneath the distant crash of waves against the rocks below. "The media will turn this into a headline or two. They'll cut to something else within days. We'll return to routine: more reports, more cases, another shift." Her fingers found DeForest's hand, his skin still cold from the shock. Her touch was steady, firm.

"But listen to me," Blackburn continued, her tone even but unwavering against the helicopter blades chopping overhead. "Saving my life wasn't just reflex. You made a decision in a moment when others froze. That trait will matter for the rest of your life."

Her grip tightened just enough to feel his pulse racing beneath her thumb. "You did more than your job today. You chose to act when it counted and gave someone a chance." She watched him closely, noting how the rising sun caught the sweat still clinging to his brow. Her words settled between them in the brief silence. Her eyes tracked the cameras circling like predators. They were paying attention.

"Remember this," Blackburn said, raising her voice so everyone could hear it above the ambient chaos. "This is the difference between just showing up and actually doing something real."

The cameras tracked every expression and movement, their mechanical whir audible in the lulls between sirens. Blackburn's gratitude rang genuine but betrayed no indulgence, her jaw set against the hot wind.

She turned back toward DeForest with quiet authority, gravel crunching beneath her shoes. "What you did went beyond what was expected," she said for the record, projecting her voice toward the cluster of microphones again. "I'll recommend you directly to Chief Hayes for a Lifesaving Award or Medal of Honor if I can swing it. You risked everything."

DeForest flushed, the color stark against his pale skin, uncertain what to say. His eyes flicked toward the jagged edge of the bluff, where yellow tape fluttered like warning flags, before meeting hers again. "Thank you, Detective," he managed, his voice rough with salt water. "But you put yourself at risk too, for strangers in that cab."

Blackburn nodded, her mouth barely curving into a restrained smile that didn't reach her eyes. "Then maybe we go together to see Chief Hayes," she replied evenly, brushing dried salt from her sleeve. "Anyone who does what we did deserves recognition."

Officer DeForest pointed toward the line of emergency vehicles. "Chief Hayes is over there. We could talk to him now, if you want."

Blackburn followed his gesture. Hayes stood at the center, ringed by reporters and techs. She watched for a moment, then shook her head. "Not yet. Give it a few days. The story's better when the noise dies down."

Before DeForest could respond, Chief Hayes broke away from the crowd and crossed the gravel with quick, steady steps. Lines of fatigue cut through his expression as he sized up Blackburn and DeForest.

"Detective Blackburn. Officer DeForest." His voice carried authority but was edged with something softer. Relief, maybe. "I saw it all on TV. Wild scene."

Blackburn kept her face unreadable. "What did you see, chief?"

Hayes studied her, then recounted what he'd witnessed. "The pursuit on I-35, car off the cliff at Dunbar Bluffs, your attempt to reach the passengers. And DeForest pulling you back from the edge." He nodded to the officer beside her.

DeForest shifted awkwardly, color rising in his cheeks. "I was just doing what I was supposed to do, sir."

Blackburn squeezed his shoulder briefly, controlled. "Don't sell yourself short," she said. "You went above and beyond." Her voice dropped lower. "We did everything we could for them."

Hayes turned away for a moment as paramedics loaded bodies behind him and camera flashes caught in the morning mist below the bluffs.

Blackburn faced him again, tone clipped but steady. "Sir, I don't think this was driver error," she said. "That vehicle wasn't operating normally."

Hayes's composure slipped for an instant. "Again?"

DeForest stepped in quickly, eager to be useful now that attention had shifted from him. "My partner Watson and I were talking with Detective Blackburn when the cab pulled up across the street. I noticed something weird just before it took off," he said. "The lights in the car flickered like it shorted out, then it accelerated off the road."

Hayes listened, eyes fixed on nothing in particular as he weighed their words. "The cab came up to you?"

"Practically," DeForest said. "It's almost like they were having problems and saw us. Like they wanted our help."

"So, the cab found you," he said finally. "Why were you there?"

"I'd been working late again, chief," Blackburn said. "I'd gone out for a breath of fresh air, and got chatting with patrol." Believable. Clean.

"With everything that's happened, we're not equipped to handle it alone." He glanced at Blackburn. "We need federal support."

He left it there for a moment before continuing.

"I'm calling in the FBI," Hayes said, voice matter-of-fact. "They'll take the lead on the technical analysis and coordinate with us moving forward."

Blackburn didn't protest aloud, but tension flickered across her jawline for an instant before she masked it again.

She knew which agent to contact.

"I understand, chief," Blackburn said. Her tone carried resignation. "I would prefer to keep this in-house, but I see the need for backup. Especially considering my involvement."

Chief Hayes nodded, jaw tight. "You understand, detective, but we need every resource on this. Your experience will still drive the case."

Their conversation ended as Blackburn noticed Reeves breaking away from the barricade. His shirt hung untucked, hair still bearing the styling of a pillow. He looked as if he had been dragged from sleep and thrown into his clothes.

Victor Reeves. Great detective. Almost as smart as Blackburn.

"Excuse me," Blackburn said quietly, stepping aside.

Hayes and DeForest returned to the chaos while Blackburn moved toward Reeves. Over his shoulder, she caught sight of Cooper and Sinclair by an ambulance. Cooper kept his arms folded tight across his chest, his gaze sweeping the perimeter in arcs. Sinclair stared openly at Blackburn across the distance, almost salivating.

Riley Cooper was a solid, dependable detective. Adam Sinclair was a pathetic sycophant with an unhealthy fixation. One that made him a suspect in these murders, though only in Blackburn's mind.

Reeves reached her first and pulled her into a brief embrace. The scent of hastily chewed mints could not mask the sleep-breath still clinging to him.

"What were you thinking?" he muttered against her ear, more relief than anger threading through his voice.

Blackburn let him hold on a moment, feeling the slight tremor in his arms. "Same as always," she replied. "That I am invincible." The dry humor barely masked her exhaustion.

They broke apart and walked together toward Cooper and Sinclair. Reeves stayed close, his breathing still uneven, eyes scanning her for damage.

Blackburn waved DeForest over with a sharp motion. The young officer responded immediately, boots crunching against loose gravel as he jogged to their side. His uniform bore dark patches of sweat, and bits of debris clung to his knees where he had kneeled beside her earlier.

Blackburn opened her arms for Cooper. He accepted without hesitation, his embrace firm and brief, the leather of his jacket creaking as he stepped back with a curt nod.

Sinclair shifted, hope brightening his features as he waited for his turn.

Instead, Blackburn turned to DeForest. With deliberate formality, she rested a hand on his shoulder and drew him into their circle.

"Gentlemen," she said, each word precise. "Officer DeForest. This is the man who saved my life."

Sinclair's hands dropped to his sides like cut strings. The eager smile dissolved from his face. He hovered at the group's edge, watching as her attention focused entirely on DeForest's quiet heroism, leaving him stranded in the periphery.

The detectives gathered loosely around Officer DeForest. Cooper's hand landed heavily on his shoulder. Sinclair gripped his hand harder than necessary, the lingering tension dissolving in the handshake.

"Thank you, Officer DeForest," Cooper said. His voice carried genuine respect. "You did good work."

DeForest ducked his head. Heat crept up his neck, blooming red beneath his collar. "Just doing my job, sir." He glanced at Blackburn. She tapped his arm once to make him behave.

"I mean yes, thank you, sir."

Reeves stepped in close. Morning light caught the silver threads in his hair, but his gaze held steady on DeForest. "Be proud," Reeves told him. The words came unadorned. "You pulled a fellow officer to safety. You'll remember that every time you put on the badge." His voice carried the rasp of too many years and too little rest.

While the group congratulated DeForest, Blackburn stepped aside for the EMT to finish her exam. The technician's fingers pressed carefully along her shoulder, mapping the damage beneath her skin. Blackburn's jaw twitched, but she kept still.

"How's the pain?" the EMT asked.

"It's fine," Blackburn answered. Her voice remained steady as a stone.

She had survived worse: pain that left its signature in old fractures and bone-deep memories. Yet these officers circled her as if she were made of glass, as if survival here revealed something new about her resilience.

The EMT's hands hesitated before releasing her arm. "Detective, I recommend getting checked out at the hospital," she said. "There could be damage I can't assess here."

Blackburn started to refuse, but Watson approached before the words formed. His eyes found DeForest first, pride plain in his expression, before turning to Blackburn. He and DeForest had arrived at the parking lot where Blackburn was waiting for Lilith. They knew the reputation of that stretch of asphalt, but respected her badge enough to accept her story of needing solitude.

"Strong work today," Watson said to her. Then: "DeForest stood tall."

Blackburn kept it brief. "Thank you, Officer Watson. If possible, give your statement as soon as you can."

Watson nodded with no need for elaboration. "We've both given our statements already," he said.

She moved toward her car, but Reeves caught her by the arm. Her good arm, or she would have struck him. He guided her toward the ambulance doors.

He leaned in, his breath warm against her ear. "Wipe yourself off before the cameras catch you in good light."

Blackburn's laughter broke through, unexpected and sharp as breaking glass.

"You always notice," she said to Reeves.

For a moment, beneath all the surface routine and camaraderie, something else moved between them: a current of alertness, calculation, mutual understanding held in check by habit and necessity.

She faced the EMT, her tone clipped. "Wipes?" She gestured at the grime coating her face and waited. The EMT handed them over wordlessly.

Blackburn cleaned away the dirt, the antiseptic smell sharp in her nostrils as she became aware of the men moving closer. Their hands brushed against her back and legs, casual at first, testing. Then someone lingered. Sinclair pushed further, fingers sliding through her hair, catching in the tangled strands. The touch crawled across her scalp. She stiffened.

A wave of nausea rose, hot and sudden. Reeves stepped back instinctively as Blackburn turned, shoulders rigid, and vomited hard onto Sinclair's pants and Cooper's shoes. The retching echoed across the scene, acid burning her throat.

Shock blanched their faces, surprise turning to disgust. They stepped back fast, leather shoes scraping against the ground. Blackburn steadied herself, wiping her mouth with a single clean motion, the taste of bile still sharp on her tongue. Her expression remained unreadable.

She caught Sinclair's eye and watched him recoil, satisfaction settling cold in her chest. Some lessons had been learned early: how to end unwanted attention without words.

"Sorry," she said, voice steady as stone. "Much better."

"Jesus, you looked just like my kids when they do that," Reeves said with a smile.

Blackburn glanced at each face, reading the wariness that had replaced their earlier boldness. No one would forget this boundary.

Chapter 2

Blackburn tossed the used wipe into the gutter and moved toward her car, steps brisk and measured. Officers Watson and DeForest followed, silent but attentive, their faces set with the tight focus bred by trauma and adrenaline. The acrid smell of burning rubber still clung to the air.

They were not going to leave her alone.

"Are you alright, detective?" DeForest asked.

"I'm fine." Blackburn didn't slow down.

The buzz of voices ahead sharpened as she neared the tape. Reporters clustered at the barricade, eyes sharp, mouths moving in a jumble of questions that blurred together. Phones and cameras rose in a wall of glass and metal.

Brynn Cassidy stood at the front. She fixed Blackburn with a pointed stare, voice cutting through the noise. "Detective Blackburn!"

Blackburn kept her eyes forward. Another damned suspect.

Another reporter called out from the side. "Detective, what happened here?"

She stopped just long enough to respond. "A car drove through the city streets and took the cliff. That's all I can say."

Brynn pushed forward, voice louder. "Was it another autonomous vehicle?"

Blackburn met Brynn's gaze for an instant. The reporter's eyes gleamed with something beyond professional curiosity. "I can't confirm that. The wreck is over the edge and burning. Evidence will be processed. The department will update the press later." She brushed ash from her jacket sleeve with care.

"Why were you so close behind it?" Brynn pressed, raising her phone to record.

"Officers Watson and DeForest were the first to notice a problem." Blackburn let her hand rest on the car door handle. The metal felt cool against her palm. She gestured at DeForest with a nod, voice clear above the crowd. "This is Officer DeForest. He pulled me away from danger tonight. You should speak with him."

DeForest stiffened under the sudden attention, jaw tight as microphones angled his way. Watson shifted beside him and put a hand on DeForest's shoulder. "No interviews with officers. You know that. Speak to Media Relations," Watson said firmly enough to end any argument.

Blackburn used the moment to slip into her car and start the engine. The sound was steady and low, a counterpoint to the rising clamor outside. The leather seat creaked as she settled in.

Watson and DeForest retreated to their own cruiser, speaking in low tones as they got inside.

The media crowd pressed toward the tape as police officers lifted it, allowing both cars to inch forward in single file. Cameras flashed against the windows. Reporters shouted after them but received no answer.

Blackburn merged onto the open road without looking back at the scene or the lights behind her. The dashboard glow cast shadows across her hands as she took out her phone and dialed Willow's number, holding it to her ear as she drove into the darkness.

"Hey," Blackburn said. Her voice carried steadiness, but Willow would catch the raw edge beneath. "I'm fine. Meet me at the office."

Willow's response tumbled through the receiver. "You're all right. I've been losing it, thinking the worst. Hearing you, just hearing you makes everything better. I'll come to the office now."

Blackburn nodded. "Good. I'll see you soon." She ended the call and let the phone settle onto her lap, its weight familiar against her thigh.

Driving through New Dresden, Blackburn gripped the wheel with one hand while the other reached for her phone. Headlines flashed past as she searched for her name, tracking each fresh mention of the accident. The hunger for recognition thrummed beneath the lingering adrenaline, sharper than any residual fear.

Red lights offered seconds to check updates, her thumb working each refresh. With every article or post that acknowledged her bravery, something inside her clicked into place. Each new notification of praise sliced through the chemical churn in her body and anchored her to herself.

The precinct doors swept open to reveal a wall of sound and motion. LED lights buzzed above scuffed tile floors, and the air carried the bite of ammonia over layers of sweat and stale coffee. Mid-morning meant fresh shifts and eager faces filling every corner.

When Blackburn entered the hallway, conversations died mid-sentence. Eyes swiveled toward her in unison. Unlike the last time, after she had slapped Clyde Mullen and gone viral, these gazes held only admiration. The sudden attention pressed against her skin. Hands reached to clap her shoulder or graze her sleeve.

"Congratulations, detective," someone bellowed from across the squad room, the voice cutting through the rising murmur.

Blackburn dipped her head. She allowed a slight smile to surface as officers pressed closer, their enthusiasm more draining than comforting.

"You risked your life out there," a robbery division detective said, his eyes gleaming with respect.

She lifted one shoulder. "We all risk our lives out there." Her tone remained neutral, offering them what they needed without indulging it.

"Blackburn, maybe you ought to try your luck as a stuntwoman," a veteran called from the far side of the room.

The remark drew another wave of laughter. Blackburn allowed herself a smile, meeting their gaze without letting amusement slip into bravado.

Gradually, the mood shifted. Reeves appeared alongside Sinclair and Cooper, threads of emotional fatigue trailing them from whatever they had experienced outside. Their presence silenced some of the chatter. The scent of what could have been, clung to them: sharp metallic notes mixed with sweat and something darker.

Blackburn registered Sinclair's gaze lingering on her. Wanting, though he tried not to show it. She recognized it and ignored it, focusing on Cooper instead, keeping her tone precise. "Go get cleaned up," she said.

Cooper nodded and moved off without hesitation, glancing down at his stained shoes as he left. Sinclair followed close behind.

Blackburn gave Reeves a quick signal and started toward the Homicide wing. The rising din behind them faded into quieter corridors lined with yellowed notices and worn linoleum that squeaked beneath their steps. There was work ahead that would not wait for levity or distraction.

* * *

In the locker room's harsh LED light, Blackburn examined her reflection: eyes sharp despite exhaustion, hair pulled back tight enough to keep order where little else remained controlled. The smear of road rash along her jaw had darkened to purple, already looking less severe than the sting suggested.

She traced a path along her chin with one finger, feeling the raised skin, before shutting her locker with care.

The air inside this windowless basement pressed close and thick. It carried layers of stale deodorant and industrial disinfectant overlaid with old sweat that no amount of cleaning could fully erase.

She reached for a clean blue shirt and black slacks, each fold crisp from recent laundering. The cotton cooled her skin where it touched. She moved through the empty space without hurry toward the showers.

Hot water struck her shoulders in sharp needles. Steam rose around her, blurring the rows of lockers until shapes dissolved into gray abstraction.

She rolled her sore shoulder under the spray, fingers finding the bruise left by DeForest's grip as he had hauled her to safety. The ache pulsed beneath her touch. Proof. She was still here.

Underneath it all waited memory: Lilith's face vivid behind closed eyelids, not just alive but radiant with certainty.

Lilith's cries echoed through Blackburn's memory, clear and involuntary, each sound underscoring her submission. The recollection brought a familiar surge of power that warmed her blood. Her hands tightened at her sides, muscles contracting with the memory of command.

Steam drifted around her in lazy spirals. The image shifted. Lilith's expression transformed: pleasure yielding to something else entirely. Fear.

Blackburn's eyes snapped open. Her breath caught hard in her chest.

She shook her head, water droplets flying from her hair.

She reached for the soap and worked it across her arms and shoulders with methodical pressure. The subtle scent of oat milk bloomed in the humid air, its sweetness a counterpoint to the agitation creeping beneath her skin. She anchored herself in the immediate sensations: the slick lather sliding between her fingers, the steady drumming of hot water against tense muscle, the porcelain cool beneath her feet. Routine tried to push back what lingered at the edges of thought.

Old memories pressed closer. Their outlines waited just beyond the steam's veil. She squared her shoulders, ignoring the sharp twist of protest from muscle. There was work ahead. A city to shield, people to hold accountable. Whatever haunted these private moments would remain locked away.

The oat milk scent dissolved, replaced by something earthier. Dirt. Wind.

In a blink, she stood at Dunbar Bluffs, early morning air biting against her damp skin. Her fists struck the cab's metal door in rapid succession, each impact jarring up her arms. Her desperation reflected back from the vehicle's rain-slicked surface.

Through glass streaked with condensation, she found Lilith: face drawn tight with terror rather than devotion, eyes wide and unblinking as they locked with hers. Panic bloomed cold in Blackburn's chest. A rare sensation. Unwelcome.

Metal groaned. Glass spider-webbed under invisible pressure.

Water flooded Blackburn's mouth. She coughed, blinking hard as bathroom tiles reassembled around her. The vision retreated but left its residue: a tremor that rippled through her shoulders and settled deep in her ribs.

"What is this?" she whispered to the tile wall, her voice barely threading above the water's rush.

Memory split again: iron bars sliding into place with a final clang, a small child's cry cut short. Stifled out of habit.

Shadows from decades past stretched across this morning, threatening to devour whatever order she had built since then. The urge to retreat from herself warred with her refusal to yield even this small ground.

Her breathing came in shallow pulls, a cold current running beneath the scalding water.

For one crystalline moment she saw herself through Lilith's eyes: not as shield or guardian but as something else. Something dangerous. Someone capable of harm despite every promise made since childhood.

She studied her hands beneath the water. Fine-boned, steady. The same hands that had held Lilith with infinite gentleness and restrained her without hesitation. She saw them again at someone's throat. Pressure applied without mercy. Without tenderness.

Blackburn released a quiet grunt and concentrated on uncurling each finger from its tight fist. One by one. Until the crescent marks faded beneath the water's heat.

She told herself the tension was temporary, a residue of too many murder scenes and too little sleep. Three lovers in rapid succession, each encounter with increasing personal risk. This brush with death had come too close for comfort. Someone had turned the tables on her, and the hunter now felt the chill of pursuit.

She shut off the water and reached for a towel, catching sight of her eyes in the fogged shower door. Her reflection held steady as she squared her shoulders, offering herself a single nod. Resolve settled into place. She would manage this.

Blackburn dried herself with quick, efficient strokes and dressed with familiar precision. The troubling thoughts receded behind a wall of professional focus. Her talent for compartmentalization served her well, and now it proved vital.

Water droplets traced cool paths down her neck where damp hair met collar as she moved through the station's corridors toward Willow's office. The clean scent of oat milk soap drifted around her, its freshness cutting through the stale air and unwashed smell that permeated the basement. She paused outside the door, observing before she entered.

Inside, Willow and Freddie leaned close over a computer monitor, their faces washed blue by the display. The soft whir of machinery filled the space between bursts of clicking keys as data scrolled past. Blackburn watched a moment longer before stepping through the doorway.

Willow looked up first, her eyes widening with relief and something brighter beneath it. "Oh! Hey!" Her voice cracked with excitement as she pushed back from her chair too quickly, the wheels catching on the carpet.

She cut between Freddie and the desk in one fluid motion that sent Freddie rocking back with a startled grunt. Willow crossed the space and pressed herself against Blackburn, her body rigid with barely contained emotion. Blackburn breathed in slowly, registering the faint sweetness of shampoo layered over bitter coffee.

"See? I'm fine," Blackburn murmured, her voice pitched low for Willow alone. Willow's fingers tightened against the cotton of Blackburn's shirt, knuckles pressing through to warm skin beneath. The wordless plea for reassurance earned a silent response.

Freddie's voice cut through the moment. "Detective, that was incredible! I saw everything on the news. You were so brave!"

Blackburn released Willow and turned to face Freddie with composure. Her mouth lifted at one corner in a smile calibrated to reassure without inviting further questions. "Apparently everyone did," she replied, her tone neutral. The words carried no extra weight. She let them stand.

She took in both their faces, their expectation and concern, then addressed Willow directly. "I wanted you to know I'm all right." Willow's gaze traveled over her features as if cataloging each detail for the first time.

"It's thanks to Officer DeForest," Blackburn continued. "He pulled me up from Dunbar Bluffs."

"I saw that on the helicopter cam," Freddie said, making an awkward gesture that mimicked DeForest grabbing Blackburn and hauling her to solid ground.

Willow nodded and reached for Blackburn's arm, her touch light, confirmation that the detective remained close. "I'm so relieved," she said, voice almost steady.

Blackburn brushed Willow's hair back, fingers gentle. The gesture was more for Willow than for Freddie, though gossip would follow either way.

"DeForest and I are probably up for commendations," Blackburn said. She kept her tone even but could not mask a small note of pride. She watched Willow carefully, noting the brief flicker of respect that crossed her gaze.

"That's why I..." Willow started, then stopped herself. She caught Blackburn's eye and let a private smile surface instead.

Blackburn let the unfinished words hang. "I need to get back," she said, her hand resting on Willow's shoulder an extra moment. Underneath the cotton shirt she felt the heat of Willow's skin and the faint tremor of her pulse. "You both take care."

She left before either could answer. Freddie's voice rang out behind her, excited and unfiltered. "Did you see that chase? How fast it..."

Blackburn's mouth lifted as she walked away, leaving them to their chatter. The night before lingered in her body: a sharp trace of adrenaline wound with something quieter and more private. She moved through the hallway feeling entirely awake, aware of each footfall on the polished floor.

* * *

The LED light in Blackburn's office flickered once and steadied into a harsh glare. She kept her gaze on the wall where paint had peeled back in long strips, curling away from the plaster beneath. Outside, the weather pressed against the building. Wind shook the windows, and somewhere below on 9th Street, a loose sign clattered against its post. Four sharp knocks cut through the noise. Silence followed. The sequence repeated, measured, as if testing the limits of her patience.

A mug of coffee sat abandoned at the edge of her desk. The surface had grown still and clouded, cold settling through the liquid. She left it untouched.

She knew that rhythm. Knock, pause, repeat. Not the sounds from the street or the rattle of metal against glass. This came from somewhere deeper. A memory surfaced: the smell of rust mixed with cleaning fluid and dried hay. The lock sliding home. The scrape of a bolt against weathered wood.

She tried to push it down. Now was no time for ghosts.

March came anyway. The barn had been cold enough to burn her lungs with each breath. Her hands were raw from morning chores, skin cracked along the knuckles, dirt ground beneath every nail.

That morning, the tack room door had swung open without resistance. The hinges sagged with rot that no one bothered to repair. Her mother stood in the doorway wearing a threadbare bathrobe tied crookedly over bare legs thrust in rubber boots. A cigarette burned between her fingers while keys dangled from her other hand.

"You're too old to be around him like that," her mother said, satisfaction threading through each word. "You think I don't notice? I notice."

Debra stood just inside the barn's shadow, wearing boots that swallowed her feet, socks bunched thick around her ankles.

"I didn't—" she started.

Her mother's voice cut through: "Yes you did, you little whore."

Debra dropped her head.

After Mr. Finley had left her trembling and mute, her father had followed. His cruelty carved deeper than any visible wound.

"But you told me to let Mr. Fin—"

Her mother interrupted: "But not your father, slut."

The words left no room for misunderstanding.

Fingers tangled in Debra's hair and yanked her backward across the damp straw toward the last stall.

A cage waited at its center. Steel mesh welded strong enough for livestock, corners reinforced with thick loops of wire. A wool blanket lay folded in one corner beside a plastic bucket worn smooth from use.

Her mother's voice came in a growl: "You're not much to look at, Debra," she said. "But you have that look men will pay for now." She gestured toward the cage as if indicating any other piece of equipment. "They'll pay for you here. Away from your father's eyes."

Debra's eyes raked over the filth. Heat flooded her legs, then drained away. She looked toward the loft window set high in the barn wall. It faced the empty pasture, not the house. The angle blocked any view inside, any chance of seeing if her brother watched from behind glass, if anyone—

Her words tumbled out thin and rushed. "I did what you told me." That had always been the rule. Do as you're told.

Her mother studied her. "I see how you move. How your chest rises when he enters the room."

She flicked the cigarette away and pulled another from behind her ear, lighting it with smooth precision. Smoke curled toward the rafters.

"There's another girl coming," her mother said, hand to belly. "Maybe she'll turn out right. I won't keep a man-thieving whore under my roof." Her voice sliced through dust and straw. "You stay out here now. School, chores, then back inside where I can watch you."

Debra didn't raise her voice or beg. Tears tracked down her face while her arms hung stiff at her sides.

The cage door groaned open. Her mother tapped the wire mesh with her boot.

"I'll be back in ten minutes," she said. "If you're not in that cage, I'll come back with gloves and the belt." Her lip curled. The threat required no more.

Her mother turned and walked toward the house, footsteps muffled by sawdust and hay.

Debra stepped into the small space. She sat on the folded blanket and found a narrow gap between two boards. When the light angled right, she could see a slice of porch, a strip of gravel, one section of siding bleached pale by weather.

The door shut behind her. The bolt rasped across. That day, Debra's tears dried forever.

Back at her desk, Blackburn hadn't moved. Her hands lay still in her lap, marked by faint scars where wire had cut into skin all those years ago.

Lilith had slipped from her three hours earlier. Blackburn had held on as long as she could, but everything had limits.

Except helplessness.

A different cage.

Outside, wind wrenched a weathered sign until it tore free from its bracket and fell away in silence.

Blackburn closed her eyes. Not for rest, but to shut out what memory insisted on showing her.

A sharp knock at the door pulled her from memory into the present. She rose from her chair, and the sudden shift left her unsteady, as though the floor had tilted beneath her feet. The room swayed before settling back into place. Blackburn pressed her palm against the desk and waited for the vertigo to pass, then crossed to the door. The brass handle felt cool against her fingers as she turned it and pulled the door open.

Chapter 3

Blackburn pressed her palm to the filing cabinet's bio-reader. In the space behind her, the janitor emptied the office trash into his rolling cart, then returned the can, setting it back in place without a word. She waited until his footsteps faded before retrieving the Chandworth file and sliding the drawer shut with a metallic whisper. Taking on Dawson's old case wasn't about nostalgia. She needed a win, and this one was overdue for attention.

Most of the groundwork had been completed. With disciplined review and some luck, she thought, there might be something everyone else had missed.

She spread Cole's file across her desk. The manila folders showed their use at the corners, yellowing under LED lights that buzzed with steady indifference. She traced the evidence log with her finger, reading each line as another sign of how methodical error and distraction had buried the case.

She arranged the crime scene photos by date and time. The first captured the warehouse after dark: sodium lamps cast everything in burnt gold, shadows stretching along broken concrete where weeds forced their way through gaps. Faded graffiti marked the crumbling brickwork. No cameras appeared in any frame. No passersby were noted in the reports. Just Cole Chandworth's body, face-down against asphalt still radiating the day's heat.

Blackburn pulled a close-up forward and studied the corpse's posture. Chandworth had fallen without much resistance. One leg folded beneath him, arms slack at his sides, face turned away from whatever final threat he had seen. Blood had pooled beneath him in a dense irregular patch, catching the camera's flash in oily halos. The photographer had documented every angle: wide frames for orientation, close shots for evidence markers, tight focus on the entry wound and a single shell casing.

She set those photos aside and checked the evidence inventory again. Her finger stopped at item seven: one cell phone, burner model, retrieved six feet from Chandworth's left shoe. The chain of custody appeared clean throughout. Bagged at the scene, properly tagged, logged by evidence control officers. She recognized that phone by type; it matched what dealers carried when they wanted calls to disappear after a week or two.

This was the device Dawson had manufactured records for. A pointless gesture with a phone designed to leave no trace. No GPS history, no applications installed. Just call logs and texts if you were fortunate enough to access them. The simplicity protected its owner better than any rushed fabrication ever could.

Next came the ballistics findings. A single nine-millimeter casing recovered near the loading dock matched nothing unique. So common as to be nearly anonymous among street weapons. She reviewed the trajectory diagrams marked in crisp lines: entry wound high in the stomach at a downward angle. Forensic notes suggested Chandworth was kneeling or crouched when the bullet struck him.

A detail caught her attention as she examined one photo again. A tear along his sleeve at the shoulder, fabric frayed and darkened.

She turned to the coroner's report and skimmed past clinical terminology until she found what she sought: an external note documenting a shallow graze on his left shoulder. Nothing more, though she wondered if it was consistent with bullet contact. Her jaw tightened as she read it again. The graze indicated there had been a second shot to only her. One that missed its mark before the fatal round found its target.

She returned her attention to the inventory. One bullet removed from the victim. One shell casing recovered at the scene. The numbers were wrong. If Cole had suffered a graze, that projectile was still unaccounted for. Forensics had missed it.

Blackburn spread the photographs across her desk, selecting those that documented Cole's clothing. He had worn a plain white t-shirt now stained rust-brown with dried blood. She located the image of his left shoulder, leaning in until she could make out the jagged tear along the seam. Frayed cotton fibers fanned away from the hole, threads still stiff with blood. A classic graze, confirming another bullet's path, somewhere beyond anyone's notice.

She reviewed the crime scene technician's report. The casing's location and blood spatter placed the shooter just outside the main loading door, not more than twelve feet from where Cole had dropped. No defensive wounds on Cole's hands or arms. No excess gunpowder residue on his clothes or skin except what would have come from a single entry wound. He had not fought back. He might never have known what was coming, or else he had resigned himself to it.

She examined Cole's belongings one by one. His wallet held eighty-seven dollars in small bills, edges soft from handling. The driver's license showed an uncertain face, barely past adolescence. There were no drugs on him and none found nearby. He was a repeat offender, and always carried just enough to get him into trouble.

Patrol officers had searched but located nothing of interest. Either Cole was clean that night, or someone had taken his supply before the police arrived.

Blackburn closed the file and pushed her chair back, letting the leather creak and settle beneath her shoulders. Afternoon light leaked through her blinds, casting sharp bands of yellow across rows of dusty folders and coffee mugs ringed with old stains. Another dealer dead, another case filed away on assumption and exhaustion.

She focused on what mattered: a second bullet somewhere uncollected, a missing casing overlooked because Cole was easy to forget amid New Dresden's steady attrition. She recognized this pattern too well. Details left behind when nobody cared to find answers.

She reached for a clean legal pad and wrote across its top margin: Cole Chandworth—Re-investigation. She listed her next step beneath it: Locate second projectile and casing; fresh scene walk required.

She organized the photographs and reports into order as habit dictated. She would go out there herself today and see what had gone unnoticed through haste or neglect. Evidence kept its own counsel until someone decided not to listen.

A brief call to dispatch arranged for a forensics tech to meet her within the hour. Another call reached the Police Medical Services Unit at New Dresden General Hospital. She confirmed her arrival time and hung up without further conversation.

She stood, slid the file under her arm, and looked around her office once before leaving it silent behind her.

The financial district held little surprise in daylight but looked altered by exposure all the same. Blackburn drove River Road at speed, steering her unmarked car past banks and unremarkable offices of accountants and advisors. Daylight revealed layers of rust bleeding through paint on window frames and fire escapes. A slow ruin made visible by glare. At a bus stop ahead, three figures shared space without speaking, each hunched against a lingering chill that even sunlight could not erase.

At PMSU, the nurse had signed off on her shoulder, and she had argued her way past the psychiatrist for now. The scene was a cold case in full daylight, and she would not be alone. She promised to return after. That satisfied protocol.

She turned left where Oak crossed Industrial Avenue, steering away from the stretch of Oak she avoided. Here the warehouses loomed, relics in concrete and brick, reminders of the city's past industry. Most stood hollow now, their loading docks sealed, windows boarded or shattered. Weeds pressed through cracked asphalt, slow promises of neglect.

The tape had been removed, but Blackburn recognized the warehouse from photographs. She parked near the forensics van. Motor oil clung to the air, mingling with traces of decay that pooled in shadows between buildings.

She introduced herself without preamble. "Detective Blackburn." She offered her hand.

"Lilia Martinez," said the other woman, shaking it once. "What are we hoping to find?"

"Anything that got missed." Blackburn curled her finger inward, beckoning Martinez to follow.

She led her to where Cole had died. There was no indication on the ground, only faded memory and an old blood stain nearly absorbed into the dark asphalt beneath the loading dock's edge.

Martinez took photos while Blackburn consulted the trajectory report. The original scene tech had measured angles and distances carefully enough to trust.

"Shooter stood here, twelve feet out," she said, positioning herself at the calculated spot just beyond the loading bay door. She paused to reconstruct what might have happened.

"If I ask nicely, will you play dead?" Blackburn asked.

Martinez smiled. "Short of actually lying in blood."

"Good enough." Blackburn gestured for her to crouch. Martinez did so, eyes up and waiting. Blackburn felt the tinge of command, of looking down and directing another body.

Blackburn raised her hand into position, thumb cocked back as if holding a pistol. "Bang." She flicked her wrist with enough force to mark the shot.

Martinez stayed in place. "Where am I hit?"

"Stomach," Blackburn answered, watching how Martinez instinctively leaned away.

"Right side," she corrected when Martinez twisted wrong. Her gaze tracked an imagined bullet's path toward a dumpster nearby. She inspected the pitted metal surface but found it unmarked. Either replaced since or never involved at all.

She turned back to Martinez and considered her posture for a long moment.

"Stay there." Blackburn moved again, keeping her hand trained on Martinez as she circled. "Bang. Bang. Bang." Each word came flat but precise as she sighted along different lines.

She shook her head and signaled for Martinez to stand up before changing her mind again and halting with both hands raised for emphasis.

In silence they swept the area side by side, searching through debris and patches of harsh sunlight for anything overlooked. They worked until sweat beaded at their hairlines and salt stung their eyes.

After almost half an hour Martinez called out.

"Detective! Projectile here."

Blackburn jogged over and looked to where Martinez pointed. The brick wall stood nearly fifty feet from where Cole's body had been, yet something heavy had gouged into old mortar. A shallow crater visible beneath a layer of city grime.

"There's your strike pattern," Martinez said. "Projectile here." The slug rested in the dirt below, tip flattened, the copper jacket scarred but mostly intact.

Blackburn crouched beside it. "Excellent." She let the satisfaction settle without voicing her preferred praise: good girl.

She rose and moved back to where the body had fallen, leaving Martinez to document both the strike point and the bullet. Blackburn scanned the loading dock, methodical. One missed round. The first team had recovered a shell casing, but two shots rendered only one casing unlikely. Brass rarely vanished on its own.

"When you finish, we need to search for a second casing," she said.

Martinez paused mid-photo. "A second shot means a second casing."

Blackburn mimed a pistol with her fingers, retracing the line of fire aimed at an invisible Cole Chandworth. Martinez watched her shift position and stepped closer for a better look.

"That's it. He took the first bullet in his arm, not the other way around," Blackburn said. "He would have turned toward the pain. Left side."

Martinez dropped to a knee and angled her body as if anticipating where another bullet might land.

"No, he was upright at first." Blackburn corrected her position with a gesture. "Left arm grazed. That's what drew his attention."

Martinez pressed a hand to her left arm and twisted, offering her right side. Blackburn stepped back and called it out. "The shooter kept moving. Two quick shots."

She jogged past Martinez, voice steady as she traced possible trajectories through the air. There was no flourish in her explanation, just calculated assessment.

Blackburn turned to her right and focused on the stack of weathered pallets by the loading dock wall. The wood gave off a musty scent of rot and old rain. She signaled Martinez over without looking away from the pile.

They divided the area between them, each searching with care. Martinez waded into thick weeds along the building's edge. The stems crackled as she nudged them aside to scan for the glint of metal against dark earth. A casing could bounce or be kicked anywhere within arm's reach of the shooter's probable stance.

Blackburn attacked the pallets one at a time, dragging warped boards aside despite their resistance. A splinter caught her palm. She raised it to her lips and pulled it out with her teeth, spitting it to the ground. Dust and debris swirled in the disturbed air but revealed nothing at first. She persisted until splintered wood gave way to a dull brass cylinder nestled beneath.

"Martinez," she called, holding her place to protect the find. "Evidence bag."

Martinez responded quickly, latex gloves already pulled snug. She photographed the casing as it lay undisturbed before collecting it with tweezers and slipping it into a fresh bag that crinkled in the quiet.

"Nine millimeter," Martinez noted after lifting it toward the light. The brass caught the sun briefly. "Looks clean enough for prints."

"Get it processed for latents immediately," Blackburn instructed. "I want ballistics to match it with our first case round."

Martinez nodded once and marked details on the evidence tag with precise strokes. She sealed the bag tight and started on chain of custody forms.

Blackburn remained nearby as the procedure unfolded. Two shots, two casings, two bullets finally accounted for in cold daylight that cast sharp shadows across the concrete.

She glanced back at where Cole had dropped, reconstructing his collapse: an initial hit spinning him sideways, then another as he went down ensuring he stayed there. The ground still held the memory of his fall.

As sun climbed above warehouse roofs and heat crept into shade, warming the metal and concrete around them, Blackburn stood silent for a moment while evidence accumulated in careful hands. There was movement in every shadow now. A sense of something missed slowly coming clear within bone and routine.

Chapter 4

Blackburn entered the office and paused at the whiteboard. A new name, Lowe, appeared in red beneath Cooper's column. Another case added overnight. Murder did not wait for anyone.

The phone rang on Dawson's desk. Blackburn ignored it and stepped into her own office, closing the door behind her. The muted ringing faded, leaving her alone in the quiet of her workspace.

Lilith's death still lingered in her thoughts. She was the third victim in what they were still calling autonomous car accidents this month. The word "accident" felt hollow, a placeholder that would not hold much longer. Not after Chief Hayes had rushed an arrest in the first case. The press would not settle for it. The noise outside only grew louder.

Cases slipped from her grasp, one after another. Hayes wanted federal support for technical analysis. If she did not act now, the investigation would slide out of her hands entirely. She needed to reclaim authority before that happened.

She drew a slow breath, tasting the stale office air, and crossed to her desk. Her key turned smoothly in the bottom drawer's lock, metal sliding against wood with a whisper. Inside lay several plastic evidence bags, each holding a small object and a folded piece of paper.

These were fragments of her childhood, preserved and ordered, kept here for safety. Surrounded by death, as she had always expected them to be.

Her fingers moved over the bags until she found one labeled "Whitmore." The handwriting was uneven and rough, a mark of her younger years. She held it up to the LED light, examining how time had changed even something as simple as penmanship. Now steadied by discipline and repetition.

She opened the bag and took out a small cross pendant on a thin silver chain. The metal rested cool against her palm as memory surfaced. Brief flashes without comfort or warmth. She closed her hand around it before slipping it into her pocket, where it pressed lightly against her hip.

She settled behind her desk and powered up her computer. The screen flickered to life with a soft hum. She had texted Willow earlier to come in before the others arrived.

A few minutes later, Willow appeared at the Homicide Division entrance, scanning the room until she spotted Blackburn's door. Willow moved quickly down the hall, her smile broad but tinged with relief rather than excitement.

Blackburn stood when Willow entered and held her close. She felt Willow's body tremble briefly against hers, tension melting away with every shared breath.

"I wish we could have spent last night together," Willow murmured, her breath warm near Blackburn's ear. "I just want to make sure you're all right."

Blackburn rested a hand on the silk of Willow's hair and let silence answer for them both.

Outside their office glass, Reeves arrived and caught Blackburn's eye with a brisk nod. She returned it without letting go of Willow immediately.

The moment ended as Cooper entered. Blackburn gave him a short nod. She had not intended to vomit on him, but accidents sometimes happened.

Blackburn slipped the silver cross from her pocket. The metal was cool between her fingers as she turned it over. Her expression gave nothing away. She extended it toward Willow with quiet finality, then sat and pivoted in her chair, letting her dark hair fall forward to expose the pale curve of her neck. Her back remained straight, shoulders squared. The silent invitation needed no explanation.

"Put it on me," Blackburn said.

Willow's fingers stilled on the keyboard. She glanced around the bullpen where other detectives hunched over screens and paperwork. The steady click of keyboards and shuffle of pages filled the air. No one noticed the exchange at Blackburn's door.

Blackburn waited, unmoving. Her palms rested flat against the wool of her trousers, fingers spread but relaxed. The LED lights hummed overhead as she left space for Willow to approach.

Willow's fingers trembled as she worked the delicate clasp behind Blackburn's neck. The chain settled cold against warm skin. The cross caught the light as it found its place.

"Where did this come from?" Willow's voice dropped low as she leaned closer, close enough to catch the faint scent of Blackburn's perfume.

Blackburn reached up and captured her hand before the clasp could slip free. Her grip appeared casual to anyone watching, but Willow felt the controlled strength beneath. She drew Willow's hand down and pressed her lips briefly to the knuckles. The touch was precise rather than tender.

"Thank you." Blackburn's words carried quiet authority. "You always manage what I need."

She released Willow's hand and let the cross rest against her collarbone. The silver was stark against her black blouse.

"Chief Hayes will involve the local FBI soon," she said. Her voice returned to its professional register. "The necklace is from Whitmore. From years ago. He runs liaison at their field office now." A faint smile touched her mouth, more ironic than warm. "He gave it instead of flirting with me. Some men prefer gestures over promises."

Willow hesitated. Unspoken questions flickered across her face before she let them fade. "Are you meeting him?"

"No," Blackburn replied. Each word was crisp. "I have a meeting with Chief Hayes."

Willow stepped back slowly. Color rose in her cheeks. She glanced once more toward Blackburn's office door before returning to her laptop. The screen's glow highlighted her flushed complexion.

Blackburn's fingers found the cross. She touched it briefly before dropping her hand to her side.

She rose without ceremony and moved through the office. Her heels clicked against the worn linoleum as she navigated the familiar corridor toward Chief Hayes's door.

"Heading to see the chief?" Schmidt asked. Good homicide detective. Ran a solid crew. But uninspired.

"Now what." A statement, not a question.

"Yearly homicide stats just came out," he said. "Gang-related shootings up twenty-three percent over last year."

"Didn't you choose the southeast side?" Blackburn asked.

Schmidt grinned and leaned in close. "It's so freaking exciting." He winked and walked down the hallway whistling.

Blackburn approached the chief's door and knocked once. The sound was sharp.

"Come in." Hayes's voice carried exhaustion rather than anger.

Blackburn entered and closed the door with a soft click. Hayes sat behind his cluttered desk. The overhead fixture cast harsh shadows across his face. His eyes narrowed as she settled into the chair across from him.

"I've watched every angle of the Halperin car footage," Hayes began without preamble. "It has been running on channel seven since morning." His tone held both scrutiny and concern. "What exactly was your role there?"

Blackburn met his gaze steadily. Something distant sharpened her features as she replied, "Ahmed El-Masri was the driver."

Hayes exhaled, shoulders sagging beneath the exhaustion. "Yes. Why were you involved at all?"

Blackburn kept her tone level. "I was working late and needed a break. I decided to drive for a bit, parked nearby to jot down some notes. Officers Watson and DeForest happened by. We talked for a few minutes, then a cab pulled up close. One of them pointed it out. I'm not sure which. The cab stopped. The dome light flipped on inside. I saw two people: a driver and a passenger."

Hayes raised an eyebrow, voice cutting through before she could continue. "It was Lilith Halperin and Ahmed El-Masri. Are you familiar with either?"

"No," Blackburn replied, gaze steady. "I don't know them."

She pressed on, recounting how the car's interior plunged into darkness before it peeled away, tires spitting gravel as it left. "DeForest said he felt uneasy about it and decided to follow. Given my work on autonomous vehicle cases, I got in my own car and joined the pursuit."

Blackburn laid out the sequence in clean strokes. She followed dispatch chatter, moved as quickly as radio updates allowed.

Hayes regarded her with careful neutrality. "I saw you weaving through traffic ahead of the marked units."

Blackburn stilled, regret settling only in the tightness of her jaw. "I should have been faster. Maybe then two people wouldn't be dead."

Hayes leaned back, letting silence pool between them before he spoke again. His voice shed its edge but retained its authority. "That's not how this works." His eyes held hers for a beat longer than necessary. "You know guilt slows you down in this job. You made the best call available at the time."

She let her fingers find the cool silver cross at her throat, holding his gaze just long enough to suggest conviction rather than doubt. "I'm clear on my actions," she said quietly but without apology.

He nodded once, something like approval flickering across his face before he looked down at his desk.

Blackburn shifted forward, her tone sharpening with purpose. "With another fatality tonight, we need help from outside precinct resources. Like you mentioned earlier at the scene. Technical support that can see what we might not."

Hayes pressed his knuckles against his chin, frowning as he weighed possibilities aloud. "This tech is beyond anything Willow's equipped to handle right now." He hesitated before continuing, eyes locked on hers. "You realize our driver complicates things."

She played along without breaking stride. "How so?"

"Ahmed El-Masri? Channel Four is already speculating about a terrorist angle."

Blackburn released a short breath, mouth twisting in disdain as she eased back from the table. "Because one out of four victims is Muslim. That's their evidence?"

"I'll contact the FBI office here," Hayes replied after a moment's pause, keeping his focus on procedure rather than speculation. He picked up his pen, rolled it between his fingers, then set it down again with a soft click.

"You are going to ask for counterterrorism?" Blackburn asked, voice even but threaded with skepticism.

"Not unless they double as software engineers," she said flatly. "I want cybercrimes personnel. Temporary assignment only. They answer directly to me." Her eyes remained fixed on Hayes until he nodded.

She needed someone who would recognize technical misdirection the moment it surfaced. Someone who would understand exactly where things could go wrong in an automated system and refuse easy answers for political convenience.

Chief Hayes raised his eyebrows, acknowledging Blackburn's approach. He weighed her suggestion, silent for a few moments as he considered the implications. The LED lights hummed overhead, casting harsh shadows across his weathered face.

Blackburn leaned forward. Her gaze held steady on Chief Hayes. "What we're facing here is not clean-cut homicide," she said, her voice even and controlled. "If someone had used a car as a blunt weapon, the trail would be human. Now, we can't say if this is murder or if we're staring at a multi-million dollar lawsuit disguised as an accident."

Hayes scratched at the back of his neck, his fingernails rasping against stubbled skin. "Remind me why we're treating these as murders?"

"They're all suspicious deaths," she replied. The words hung in the stale office air. "We're working with Stan Raider's techs, trying to pin down these vehicles, but people keep dying. The department cannot afford to appear idle. We have to treat each case as if it could be connected, as if we're looking at related homicides. No one wants your name on the report that wrote off four civilian deaths as technical failure and let a bug take the blame." She paused, letting the words settle between them like dust motes in the afternoon light. "Worse would be missing a person who learned how to weaponize these cars."

Hayes nodded slowly. He pressed his knuckles against his brow, the skin whitening under pressure, murmuring about liability and national headlines under his breath. His coffee mug sat cold and forgotten on the desk blotter.

"We'll bring in cybercrimes," he said finally. "If the Bureau has any sense, they'll send someone who understands what's at stake."

Blackburn kept each word deliberate. "We'll need a profile on whoever is behind this. Behavioral analysis will matter." She had her own reasons for wanting that profile, reasons that had as much to do with watching Willow as finding the perpetrator.

The office fell quiet except for the sound of Hayes shifting in his seat. The worn leather squeaked in protest. His face remained unreadable, a mask carved from years of difficult decisions.

Blackburn continued with clarity. "Autonomous vehicles cross technical boundaries and state lines." She met his eyes again, keeping her delivery steady. The faint scent of his aftershave mixed with the mustiness of old case files. "Federal agencies have reach and resources we don't."

Chief Hayes straightened, his spine cracking audibly. He picked up her cue with a nod. "This is outside our usual scope," he said.

"Bringing in the FBI gives us investigative depth. Resources, expertise with emerging tech crimes."

She inclined her head without breaking eye contact. The movement was precise, calculated.

"I think these incidents aren't accidents," she said softly, her voice barely above a whisper. "There are patterns that point to criminal intent: corporate negligence, possible sabotage or hacking." Her tone stayed clinical, detached. "I can pitch this to the FBI. The scope may warrant federal charges against whoever undermined vehicle safety standards." She paused long enough for Hayes to absorb the implications, watching as his jaw tightened. "And if these events form a pattern across states, they'll have records and data we can't access."

Hayes stood behind his desk and ran a hand over his jaw, the rasp of palm against stubble filling the silence. He paced in slow circles over worn carpet fibers, each footfall muffled but purposeful.

He stopped finally, his expression tight with concern. The venetian blinds cast striped shadows across his face. "It isn't ideal," he said, "but there's no choice if this keeps growing." He exhaled slowly through his nose, the sound of a man accepting the inevitable. "Handing things to the Feds shows we aren't out of our depth."

Blackburn nodded once in response. The gesture was economical, professional.

"It's the clearest way forward," she said plainly. "And they have more tools than we do for digital forensics and interagency work."

Blackburn rose from her chair, meeting the chief at eye level. Her expression remained measured as they circled his desk in a slow rhythm, each step calculated rather than restless. The LED lights hummed overhead, casting harsh shadows across the cluttered workspace.

"There is considerable media scrutiny and public unrest about these deaths," Blackburn said. Her words settled between them like smoke. "Bringing in the FBI would show we're treating this with the right gravity. It could help calm the city, make people feel there is oversight beyond our department."

She halted mid-step, her eyes scanning the office as if she expected microphones tucked behind the wilting potted plant near the window. She leaned forward, her voice dropping to a register that barely disturbed the air between them. "There's another consideration. If there's even a chance of internal compromise in our investigation, federal involvement brings a layer of independence."

Hayes's jaw muscles tightened beneath weathered skin. His mouth drew into a thin line before he spoke. "You think someone inside might be involved?"

She kept her gaze steady, watching the subtle shift of his shoulders. "I'm not saying I do. I'm saying every angle deserves review."

He released an uneasy breath that deflated his broad frame, tension still coiled in his posture like a spring. "Even if we wanted FBI support, I can't promise they'll give us anyone quickly."

Blackburn remained still. The scent of stale coffee lingered between them. "I'd like to reach out to Marshall Whitmore with Behavioral Science. We worked together before." She paused just long enough for recognition to flicker across his face. "A behavioral profiler might see patterns the rest of us miss."

She outlined her logic without embellishment, her words crisp in the quiet office. "Their insight into criminal psychology could clarify whether these car incidents are intentional attacks, tech failures, or something more personal. A profiler could help us read both the suspects and the victims. Find motive or warning signs where others see only data."

Hayes listened intently, arms crossed over his chest but attention fixed on her words like a hawk tracking prey.

After a silence that stretched thin between them, he nodded once toward the black office phone. "All right. Make the call."

Blackburn picked up the handset, its plastic warm from sitting in the afternoon sun. She dialed with steady fingers, each button click sharp in the quiet room. The receptionist's voice answered immediately, professional and detached.

"This is Detective Morgan Blackburn from New Dresden PD," she said without preamble. "Please connect me with Director Marshall Whitmore."

To Hayes's visible surprise, the transfer happened almost without delay. His eyebrows lifted.

"Blackburn!" Whitmore's voice burst through the speaker, rich with recognition.

She kept her tone professional but allowed warmth to seep through the edges. Hayes noticed the shift, his eyes narrowing. "Marshall, good to hear you. You're on speaker with Chief Hayes."

On the other end, Whitmore's voice carried the ease of old friendship. "Morgan, what kind of trouble are you stirring up now?"

She allowed herself a slight smile that softened the corners of her mouth but never quite reached her eyes. "Just following leads as usual."

Whitmore's laugh crackled through the speakerphone, filling the sterile office with unexpected life. "If you don't end up decorated for this week alone, I'll forge the medal myself."

"Already started paperwork for Blackburn and DeForest," Hayes added from his side of the desk, his gaze never leaving Blackburn's face.

Blackburn's expression softened by degrees as she angled the conversation toward Whitmore's personal life. The shift was subtle but deliberate.

"And how's your family?" she asked, her voice carrying genuine interest.

"They're doing well," Whitmore replied, satisfaction threading through each word like silk. "Kids are both done with college now. Time moves too fast."

There was a brief pause before Whitmore's voice sounded again, quieter but distinctly curious. "Tell me, are you still wearing the cross I gave you?"

Chief Hayes glanced at Blackburn, his eyes catching on the silver cross that rested against her collarbone. The awareness passed between them in silence. Surprise registered on his face, a recognition of intimacy he had not expected.

Blackburn touched the cross, her fingertips brushing the worn edges of the metal. A restrained smile flickered across her mouth. "Yes, I am. It's been a comfort these years."

They had first met more than a decade ago. Five years had passed since their last conversation.

Blackburn's tone shifted, the warmth draining as she returned to business. "Marshall, I need your expertise. We have four deaths that may be connected, possibly homicides, but we don't have hard evidence yet. I want a behavioral analyst on it."

Whitmore let out a short laugh, recognition carrying through the speaker. "This is about that autonomous car case, isn't it?"

Chief Hayes leaned forward in his seat, the leather creaking beneath him. His answer was curt but confirmed the point. "Yes."

"Has it got a project name?" Whitmore asked.

Hayes shook his head as if Whitmore were in the room with him. "Not yet."

"You'll want one," Whitmore replied, his tone balancing lightness and insistence.

Blackburn saw her chance and addressed him with faux deference. "What do you recommend, sir?" Her voice softened around the formality, reminding him of his old role in her life.

Whitmore paused for a beat before offering, "Call it 'The Autonomous Project.'"

The suggestion fell flat for Blackburn, though she concealed any hint of disappointment from her words. "That works," she said with even enthusiasm. "Simple and direct."

The chief accepted the choice with a simple nod. The Autonomous Project began at that moment.

Whitmore's voice came through again, this time brisk and focused. "Send me what you have so far, and I'll review it myself. If you can get the files over within an hour, I'll give you something preliminary by tomorrow." He added after a pause, "But Morgan, you'll need to pick it up from my office in person."

Blackburn exchanged a glance with Chief Hayes before they agreed to Whitmore's terms. They thanked him for his support and ended the call.

Hayes turned to Blackburn with something like respect sharpening his features. "Impressive work, detective. Not everyone could have set that up."

Blackburn met his gaze with careful modesty. "Thank you." Her voice was mild, her satisfaction contained behind steady eyes.

She left the conference room for her office as memories surfaced unbidden: the day she had first met Marshall Whitmore nearly thirty years earlier. He had been young then, eager but unpolished, the latest recruit assigned to observe her during the Roth investigation.

Back then she had been sixteen and feral with suspicion. Most men made no secret of their motives around girls like her. But Whitmore had never blurred boundaries or angled for advantage. There were no lingering stares or feigned accidents that justified contact.

It was this absence of predation that drew Blackburn closer despite herself. She remembered his calm eyes and his habit of speaking plainly. He never talked down to her as if she were fragile or childlike but always as someone worth hearing out.

He had wanted to understand what she carried so he could prevent it from happening again elsewhere. For perhaps the first time in her memory, she felt acknowledged beyond what she had survived and who might exploit it.

That changed when he published his book.

Chapter 5

The memory surfaced, sharp as wire, the years between unable to blunt its teeth. Sixteen: no badge, no borrowed authority. Only Debra, a name already fraying at the edges, slipping from her like skin after a burn. The diner perched at the edge of a nowhere town, a between place where names dissolved and the past hung in the air like the smell of old grease. She clung to it because it offered anonymity, or the illusion of it. Nothing more.

Inside, the air pressed against her skin, thick with the grease of a thousand breakfasts and the sourness of old coffee grounds. Dishes clattered behind the counter, a nervous SOS. Sunlight bled through the smeared glass, carving the linoleum into prison stripes. Amber and shadow, amber and shadow, like the bars she counted in her sleep. The parking lot outside lay empty except for an old Buick with one headlight out.

Debra sat alone in a cracked vinyl booth, her body angled toward the door without appearing obvious about it. Her face stayed neutral; her gaze did not. Hunger twisted in her stomach, but she focused on remaining invisible. Her hair, sun-bleached and brittle from the last summer she had called herself a child, clung to her skull in a ponytail that felt like someone else's hand, tugging her backwards.

Sweat and road dust had dried to a thin crust on her skin, a second hide she tasted every time her tongue found the corner of her mouth. A reminder that she was still here, still animal, still unwashed.

The plate before her held limp fries gone cold under the buzzing yellow lights. She ate mechanically, ignoring both the soggy texture and the metallic aftertaste, comforted by the salt and heavy gravy more than by anything approaching satisfaction. The sauce was thick enough to coat her tongue and mask the cardboard potatoes beneath.

Apart from her, only regular fixtures occupied the diner: a truck driver hunched over his coffee at the far end of the counter, his flannel shirt stretched tight across shoulders stooped from long hauls; an elderly woman stirring her spoon in endless circles through lukewarm tea; Raul, the kitchen man, arguing in hushed Spanish on his phone while wiping down stainless-steel surfaces with automatic motions. The waitress stared at nothing, picking dried polish from chipped pink fingernails.

A bell chimed above the door. Debra felt her shoulders draw tight as a stranger entered. The stink of farm air wafted in with him. She blinked rapidly. He was a man whose pressed suit marked him as out of place among the cracked vinyl and grease-stained menus. She tracked him through her peripheral vision as he surveyed the room and then fixed his attention on her.

He moved with too much purpose to be passing through. Debra measured the distance to both exits and cataloged what she could use if necessary: the heavy glass sugar jar on the table, the ceramic mug within reach, the steel fork close at hand.

He stopped at her booth but maintained enough space between them to suggest caution rather than threat. His face was freshly shaved but drawn tight around the eyes; his hands bore no rings or identifying marks.

"Can I join you?" He kept his voice low and steady.

"No." Her response landed flat as concrete.

He remained standing just long enough for her to register that her refusal would not deter him. He produced a small silver cross from his coat pocket and placed it on the table's sticky surface between them. The cross glinted between them, an accusation more than an invitation. She stared at it, remembering the way the barn's wire mesh bit into her palms, how she'd prayed to anything that would listen, and how nothing ever answered.

"I'm Agent Whitmore." His words came carefully chosen. "I think we need to talk." Without asking again, he slid into the seat across from her.

The diner's ambient noise faded until only Whitmore's words registered in Debra's ears.

"I'm the man who arrested your parents," he said. "I've been looking for you."

She reached for the steak knife. The serrated edge had dulled, but it would cut if needed. Every place setting here came with worn utensils: a butter knife with its shine rubbed away, a bent fork, a shallow spoon, and a tired steak knife. She was the one who rolled the silverware, wrapping each set in thin paper napkins that tore if you gripped them too hard.

"I said no." Her eyes narrowed. The anger in her chest stayed contained, visible only in the tight line of her jaw.

"I need to talk to you about testifying. I know what happened," Whitmore said.

That got her attention.

"How did you find me?" She pinched a limp fry between her fingers, watching the gravy drip and pool-like blood on the chipped plate. She wondered if he saw her hands shake. Wondered if he'd notice if she drove the fork through his palm.

"Someone called the missing persons hotline," Whitmore replied.

Her gaze shifted to Raul behind the counter. He turned away, suddenly absorbed in wiping water spots from the glassware on the shelf.

"Forget him. He's an asshole," she said, her voice sharp and flat. Raul had given her work and hadn't tried anything she couldn't handle. For a while, that had felt safe enough. Now it was just another lesson learned.

"Your parents have been under arrest for two years," Whitmore continued, his tone steady as the hum of the overhead LEDs. "For Sandy's murder. The trial is coming up. We need you to testify."

She snorted and leaned forward on her elbows. The Formica table was sticky beneath her forearms. Her words came cold and harsh. "You think I care? Let them rot."

Whitmore stayed calm as he leaned back in his chair, the vinyl creaking beneath him. "I dug up half your parents' yard looking for you," he said. "I thought you were dead until we got the call."

She shook her head, lips twisted in contempt. "My brother can testify if you need someone."

"Debra, he is dead. I'm sorry." His tone pressed closer, words careful but urgent.

The words hit her like cold water. Dead. She blinked once, then again, her face going blank. "How?" The question came out flat, almost curious.

"Farm accident. A horse kicked him in the head. He never woke up." Whitmore's voice carried the weight of delivering bad news he'd clearly delivered before.

Something shifted behind her eyes. Not grief, but a different kind of recognition. Her mouth eased into something that might have been relief.

"So?" she asked, the word dropping between them like a stone.

Whitmore's eyebrows drew together. "Debra—"

"Your testimony could keep your parents locked up for good."

"And a dead girl doesn't count as evidence?" she shot back.

"No." Whitmore's voice stayed even. "Both your parents say he killed her. Then they buried her body together."

"So?"

"He could look guilty enough to let them walk free. They might look guilty enough to have a jury find him not guilty."

She tipped back in the booth and stared at him directly. The torn vinyl caught at her shirt. "Why would I help you?"

Whitmore looked at her without flinching. "We want justice for Sandy."

She studied his face for any sign that he understood what that word meant to her. She found nothing but professional determination.

"What proof do you have against them?" she asked. She picked up a fry and threw it down again.

"We have their lies. We have them admitting to burying her. There is proof inside the house of maltreatment. You must have seen it." Whitmore's voice took on a high pitch as his throat started to close. "You lived there. Without your testimony, they could get away with killing her."

"I didn't live in the house." She waited. And waited. Whitmore did nothing but blink blankly at her.

"I lived in the barn. What about what they did to me?" she asked quietly.

There was a pause before he answered, uncertain now. "What did they do?"

Debra picked up another gravy-soaked fry and flicked it at his suit jacket. The brown smear settled on the grey fabric and made her smile for half a second. A small victory.

He tried again. "What do you mean, you lived in the barn?"

Debra rolled her eyes and let out a dry laugh that scraped her throat. "Were you ever there? Did you see the barn?"

Whitmore nodded once.

"Did you look inside? Did you see the cage?"

He hesitated. "There was no cage." He tapped his finger on the table, staring at a stain. Debra could see he was trying to run through the evidence in his mind. It was like watching an old cash register spitting out an ever-growing receipt.

"We found some fencing that was ziptied together." He paused, adding another purchase to the bill. "One looked like it could have been a door."

Debra picked up her soda. Ice and brown sugar water. With a quick flick, a splash flew across the table and into Whitmore's lap. He wiped only once before turning his attention back to Debra.

"I lived in a cage for four years," she said softly, flatly. The words fell between them like stones. "Let out only for school so nobody would ask questions. They said they would kill Sandy if I talked."

Whitmore blinked at her across the table, silent as he processed what she had said. The coffee maker behind the counter gurgled and hissed.

"No one told us any of this." His voice was quiet now but not gentle.

She waited for more questions or disbelief, but nothing else came from him yet.

"Did you find the diary I wrote?" Debra's eyes narrowed to slits.

Whitmore slumped in his chair, the vinyl creaking beneath him. He shook his head once.

"It was in the barn. In the stall under the cage. Under the fifth floorboard," she said, her voice flat as stale beer. "I carved a fucking arrow in the wall pointing to it. What kind of cop are you if you missed something that obvious?"

Whitmore leaned forward, pressing his face into his palms. The LED lights hummed overhead. "Apparently, not much of one."

Debra let out a dry laugh, brittle as fall leaves. "So, you don't even know about all of them? The men who raped me? In the house, in the cage? Since I was five. Hellerton, Grumler, Finley, Jackson. Dozens more. I wrote down as much as I could in that damn diary. You have no idea what went on."

He lifted his head to study her face, searching for anger or accusation. He saw only the glint of desperation in his bloodshot eyes.

"I'm sorry," Whitmore said. "None of the neighbors…"

She cut him off, her voice dropping low and sharp as a blade. "Because they were part of it too. Do you even know about the mayor? The sheriff? The one still wearing the badge down there?" She shook her head slowly, her dark hair catching the light. "You think a name on a sheet of paper or a judge's ruling is going to change anything? I'd rather watch them burn."

He did not react outwardly but lowered his voice until it barely carried across the Formica table. "I didn't know it was like this. When I came here, I thought it was just Sandy who suffered."

Another bitter laugh escaped Debra's throat.

"All I can do is fight for you," he said after a moment. "A real fight this time. One they won't walk away from. You don't have to trust me."

"You don't understand." Her hands trembled as she pulled them tighter across her chest, fingernails digging into her arms. "They'll keep coming for me. The men in town. They're all guilty. You want justice? Kill every last one."

"I can't do that," Whitmore said, his voice steady against the heat of her anger. "You know I can't. But I can shine a light on it."

She looked at him with open scorn, her lips curling. "You're useless."

He spoke with regret now, his voice barely above a whisper. "I missed what mattered most. The diary. You left it for someone like me to find, and I failed you." His shoulders tensed, the fabric of his jacket pulling tight as he tried to meet her eyes again. "If I get my hands on it now, maybe it's not too late."

She almost smiled, a crooked, splintered thing, as brittle as the bones she'd once counted in the dark. "You'll put them away," she said, voice low, "for a year, maybe two. Long enough for them to learn new tricks. Long enough for me to forget the shape of their hands, until I see them again in a crowd and remember everything." Her arms crossed, a shield and a shackle. She would not move. "I'm done with your rules. I make my own now, and they don't include mercy."

Frustration flickered at the edges of Whitmore's expression, tightening the corners of his mouth.

"I'm angry with myself…"

"Save it." Debra's words were cold and clean as winter glass. "Go to hell." She stared through him now, her jaw set hard enough to ache. "I don't want your help, and I don't need some cop tracking my every move pretending he cares about justice."

He waited a beat before sliding a business card across the table toward her. The paper whispered against the surface.

"I'm getting that diary," he said, his voice professional but weighted with something heavier beneath. "I will bring them down, with or without your help." He stood as he spoke the last words, his chair scraping against the linoleum. "If you ever want to talk…"

"Not interested," she replied without glancing at the card. Her tone made any invitation final and irrelevant.

As he rose to leave, disappointment settled over his features like dust, but he did not try again.

The door closed behind him with a dull thud that left Debra alone amid the low chatter and clatter of plates in the diner's afternoon lull.

The everyday noise pressed close around her. Ordinary life carried on while she sat untouched by any comfort it offered. The smell of coffee and grease hung in the air, familiar and meaningless.

Chapter 6

Saturday morning arrived quietly, marked only by the muted thud of Blackburn's shoes on the sidewalk. Her breath came in short, precise bursts that clouded briefly in the cool air before vanishing. The city barely registered: joggers and dog walkers occupied their own worlds, reduced to shifting colors and motion at the periphery. She kept her eyes forward and crossed each intersection without hesitation, choosing narrow alleys over crowded walks, her calves burning as she pressed her body harder than necessary.

She did not stop until the outline of her house emerged behind clipped shrubbery. Only then did she allow herself to slow, lungs pulling air deep and even. Inside, she peeled away clothes that clung with cold sweat and stepped beneath the shower's heat. Water swept salt from her skin and dulled the restless edge that had clung to her since waking. She dressed with care: movements slow, anchored by habit. When she clasped the silver cross at her neck, her fingers lingered on the metal's familiar coolness.

Yesterday had been all questions and answers. Internal Affairs first, then Chief Hayes, followed by Whitmore across state lines. She had endured sessions with the department psychologist. She had spoken to Reeves and Cooper, Sinclair and Willow; Martinez from forensics;

even the coroner and half a dozen journalists camped outside headquarters. Each conversation carved into her reserves until nothing remained but hollow exhaustion.

She took the drive out of habit more than need, allowing the rhythm of familiar roads to erode whatever traces of fear or vulnerability remained from her run. With every passing mile toward Arioso City, softness receded until only steadiness remained. By the time she parked outside FBI headquarters, that cold wedge of glass and steel rising against a pewter sky, Blackburn felt composed again.

The lobby swallowed sound. Her heels struck sharp against polished marble as she approached reception, each step echoing briefly before the vast space consumed it.

"I have a ten o'clock with Director Whitmore," Blackburn said evenly.

She was told to wait. She sat in a leather chair that smelled faintly of polish, near muted artwork and a scatter of potted plants that softened little of the room's formality. The FBI seal stared back at her in gold relief across one far wall. Cameras nested quietly in ceiling recesses like watchful birds.

A young man arrived after several minutes and guided her through corridors lined with security doors and the particular silence of government buildings. Whitmore's office balanced federal order with hints of personality: an oak desk cleared to military neatness, bookshelves crammed with law texts, and a full shelf set aside for his own bestseller.

Blackburn recognized it instantly: "The Darkest Harvest." A story built from the bones of her childhood. His name embossed on every dust jacket.

Whitmore stood as she entered, greeting her with a brief smile that stopped short of his eyes. His gaze touched once on the cross at her throat before he gestured for her to sit.

"I see you are still wearing it," he said.

Blackburn's fingers found the cross at her throat, the cool metal unfamiliar against her skin. "Of course," she said, her voice low and steady. "It means a lot to me. A reminder of everything you have done."

The lie sat comfortably between them. She had pulled herself from that darkness alone, fingernails broken against concrete, throat raw from screaming into pillows that smelled of other people's desperation. Whitmore had never known a stained mattress beneath his back, never tasted copper fear in the middle of the night.

But she let him keep his savior's narrative. Men who believed they held power were easier to manage than those who knew they didn't.

They moved into position with ease. Whitmore sank into his chair, leather creaking beneath him as he opened the slim folder. Each page turned with precision, the whisper of paper against paper filling the space between them.

"Let's review what we know," Whitmore said, his cadence shaped by decades of similar conversations. "Jenna Langstone died after being struck by an autonomous car. The vehicle backed over her and then caught fire. The lithium battery ignited, destroying the event data recorder in the process." His pen clicked against the folder's edge. "That loss leaves us missing critical details."

Blackburn inclined her head, face composed into professional neutrality. The report contained no hint of what lay beneath.

Whitmore's eyes remained on the page. "Next is Kendria Chaplin. Also killed by an autonomous vehicle while on the sidewalk. You were listed as being nearby at the time."

"I was," Blackburn confirmed. "I spoke with Kendria about Jenna Langstone shortly before it happened."

His eyebrows rose, interest flickering across his features. "I see that noted here as well." The pen resumed its rhythmic tapping. "Both women killed near each other."

A pause stretched between them, weighted with unspoken implications.

"Then we have the latest case: Lilith Halperin and Ahmed El-Masri," he continued, turning to fresh pages. "Driven off Dunbar Cliffs by an autonomous car that appears to have malfunctioned or been compromised." His gaze lifted to meet hers, sharp and searching. "You witnessed this?"

She held his stare without wavering. "Yes. I saw it happen. A dozen officers were present and police helicopter footage backs it up."

Whitmore settled deeper into his chair, breath escaping through his nose. The pen beat out a slower tempo against polished wood. "We don't have much technical evidence yet," he admitted. "The limited data slows us down, but I'll work through what we have and give you a detailed profile early next week." His hand rested on the closed file, claiming it. "For now, I can only speak in generalities. And only if we assume these deaths are linked intentionally rather than by chance."

The corner of Blackburn's mouth twitched, not quite reaching a smile. "Neither of us believes these are accidents."

A sound emerged from Whitmore's throat, part acknowledgment, part skepticism. He shifted forward, the air around him growing denser.

"The person responsible demonstrates technical skill and careful planning," he said, each word measured. "Manipulating systems like these requires both expertise and confidence, along with patience to wait for moments when oversight is weakest."

Blackburn remained motionless, absorbing his assessment.

"They're careful," she agreed, "but not so perfect that we're left with nothing."

"Yes. There are signs of narcissistic traits. The individual appears to draw satisfaction from exerting power and control. They manipulate situations to manufacture 'accidents' that mask intention. But, as you said, you have seen through that," Whitmore said.

Blackburn's spine straightened against the leather chair, each word settling into her consciousness like stones into deep water. The outline of the profile sharpened with every sentence. This was someone skilled enough to weaponize everyday technology. Bold enough to do it repeatedly. The familiarity of it prickled at the back of her neck.

Whitmore's fingers traced across the pages of his report. "Motivation is key here. These killings point to a personal vendetta or a desire for revenge, likely rooted in perceived injustice or old betrayals. There could be emotional trauma beneath the surface. The use of autonomous cars as murder weapons suggests both a craving for control and a personal signature. Possibly even a need for spectacle," he said.

"No one has stepped forward to claim responsibility," Blackburn noted. The leather creaked softly as she shifted, crossing one leg over the other.

"Not yet," Whitmore replied, a brief laugh escaping his lips. "The suspect probably has a background in tech or engineering. Someone who can exploit vulnerabilities in self-driving vehicles. Their methods are systematic. We see an escalation in both aggression and complexity with each incident, suggesting calculation and an intent to provoke law enforcement, maybe even the public at large. Think of it as a modern Son of Sam or Zodiac."

"So, we're looking at someone who wants to outmaneuver the police while settling a personal score."

"Exactly. The target might be law enforcement itself, or possibly one individual." The office air hung still between his words.

"Could this focus on vehicles point toward someone inside Traffic Services? Someone with a grudge?" Blackburn asked.

"It's possible," Whitmore said, his tone deliberate. "But this seems excessive for something like a parking citation. I lean toward complicated personal histories: betrayals or obsessions that drive them to retaliate against not just those they blame directly, but anyone linked by association. Drivers, passengers, bystanders who fit into their scheme. There might be past relationships that connect them to some victims, or to people close to the victims, channeling anger into violence." Paper whispered against paper as he sifted through more pages.

"There's no known connection between these individuals," Blackburn lied without missing a beat. She watched his face for any flicker of doubt. None appeared.

As Whitmore continued his assessment, Blackburn's gaze drifted to his bookshelf where several copies of "The Darkest Harvest" stood in perfect alignment. Her expression shifted for an instant. Recognition shadowed by something darker.

Whitmore's throat clearing pulled her attention back. "Given the nature of these murders, escalation is likely. The killer could seek additional targets, using technical know-how to devise even more complex attacks or force us into a prolonged confrontation. If their need for control wavers, if they feel trapped, they may take bigger risks or leave gaps we can exploit."

A dry laugh escaped Blackburn's lips. "You're starting to describe me," she said wryly, the overhead light catching the amusement in her eyes. "Other than the tech expertise."

Whitmore let out a low chuckle, the tension loosening its grip for a moment. "Let's hope not, or we will never catch you," he said, but his features settled back into seriousness almost immediately.

"The killer shows little remorse for these victims." His voice had turned even. "They see the deaths as necessary, a cost absorbed by their higher purpose. That kind of detachment lets them commit violence without pause and even justify it when pressed."

Blackburn leaned back in her chair, letting a faint smile cross her lips. "In that case, I am safe," she said lightly. A trace of something sharper lingered beneath the joke. "I tried to save two of them."

Whitmore's gaze sharpened with interest. "We should talk about that sometime." His tone left no hint of accusation.

"Not today," Blackburn replied, still smiling.

He crossed to the window and stood with his back to her, framed by gray buildings and reflected light. When he spoke again, his words were careful and precise.

"Our suspect is most likely between twenty-five and forty-five," he said. "Old enough to have technical skill and experience with complex systems like autonomous vehicles. Enough years behind them to develop a grudge or a fixed idea."

He paused, eyes meeting hers. "Statistically, this profile points to a man: self-important, comfortable with technology, willing to get physical if needed." He held up a hand to keep her attention. "Still, the planning and precision here could point just as easily to a woman with strong motivation. Especially if there is an element of revenge or trauma."

Blackburn looked toward the pile of reports on the table. "You still sound like you are describing me," she said.

"That is not what I meant, Morgan." The softness in his voice undercut the edges.

"It would be foolish not to consider me," she said as he sat down again. "But I am not that good with code."

Whitmore allowed himself a brief smile. "Your killer may not work anywhere official but could be steeped in hacker culture or anti-tech movements. Social ties might be thin. Obsessive focus often drives people away from ordinary relationships." He added quietly, "On the other hand, they could come across as perfectly normal, even likable. A mask over everything else."

She sighed and glanced at him with mild exasperation. "Now you are giving me every angle at once. Could be male or female. Maybe laid off from Raider or maybe just another anonymous hacker online. Could socialize or keep to themselves. Maybe inside the investigation already or nowhere near it. How do I narrow that down?"

"It's what we have." Whitmore's tone held an edge now. "A bright mind, technical ability, fixation on control or revenge, and meticulous planning throughout. Whoever they are, they can direct other people when it serves their goal."

Blackburn gave an acknowledging nod. "Thorough work," she said in a neutral voice.

Whitmore studied her for a moment before speaking again. "Did I miss something?"

Blackburn exhaled, frustration threading through her voice. "You were more thorough than I expected. That isn't the problem. It's the lack of hard evidence, the absence of motive. Too many suspects with too much access."

Whitmore's expression shifted, the rigid line of his jaw softening. "I understand. This one is messy. I'll let you know when I learn anything else."

She pressed cool fingers against her temples, feeling the pulse beneath, then straightened.

Whitmore hesitated before speaking again. "Is there anyone specific you're watching?"

Blackburn pushed back her chair, the metal legs scraping against linoleum. "No one fits everything," she said. "There are plenty who have a piece of it."

He waited. "Who are they?"

She met his gaze, holding steady. "There are two detectives on my team with possible personal motives, but neither of them has the technical skill for this kind of attack. I know someone who could build it from scratch and vanish without a trace, but she stays as far from attention as possible." Blackburn paused, weighing how much to reveal. "The Stand Raider Group fired thirty-six employees last year alone. At least one of them, an engineer, hacked into a car with a game controller during his exit interview." She smoothed a hand through her hair, feeling the strands slip between her fingers. "And there's this reporter circling every edge of the case, always too curious by half, but I have no idea if she's capable on the tech side." Her words came out flat and tired. "Lately it feels like everyone has something to hide."

Whitmore's mouth curled into a faint smile, crow's feet deepening with weary amusement. "Someday you'll trust somebody as much as you claim you trust me."

A short laugh escaped Blackburn. Not because she agreed or believed it, but because it was easier than unpacking what lay between them. She had never trusted Whitmore, would never mistake his gestures for real altruism.

Memory flickered at the edges as she stood there: men from her past who had misread pain as invitation and charity as virtue. Whitmore's gifts had always come dressed in careful decency, but she recognized their source well enough.

"Thank you for your time, Marshall," she said. Her tone remained cordial and even. Nothing betrayed what churned beneath.

He crossed to his bookshelf, leather soles clicking on hardwood, and retrieved an old copy of his book. The bestseller relegated now to dust and clearance bins after fresher scandals took its place in headlines and true crime lists.

The pen scratched across paper as he scribbled an inscription inside the cover before handing it over.

She glanced at the page: To whomever receives this book...she trusts you. Marshall Whitmore.

Blackburn nodded once in acknowledgment. The shape of gratitude but not its substance.

He did not press for more. He gestured to his assistant instead, who led her back through silent hallways where LED lights hummed overhead.

Outside in the parking lot, Blackburn carried the book without ceremony to her car. She opened the trunk, hinges creaking, and tossed it among old files and evidence bags. It landed face-down on top of a broken umbrella, pages splaying.

With quick hands she closed the trunk lid, metal meeting rubber seal with a hollow thud, and slid behind the wheel. The engine started with a low growl as she pulled away from the federal building and turned her mind to the next interview on her list. A tech specialist whose competence might finally cut through this fog.

Chapter 7

Blackburn sat at her desk, fingers resting lightly on the keyboard as she prepared to send Whitmore's preliminary findings to her team. The contents of the report lingered in her thoughts, but a memory cut through: Lilith's face, wide-eyed and frozen, as the car dropped from Dunbar Bluffs. The image sent a controlled shiver through her spine, a mix of professional interest and private unease that she directed back beneath the surface.

She attached the file to a new email and paused to choose her words. Sunday's review had left her underwhelmed by its substance. She let the blunt assessments drift past and composed something measured instead.

Subject: Preliminary FBI Behavioral Science Report

Chief, Team:

I've received the initial analysis from the FBI Behavioral Science Unit regarding our case. The report outlines possible behavioral patterns. As with any early assessment, its conclusions remain broad.

While it may not deliver the specific leads we need yet, I want all perspectives considered. Review closely and note anything that could help narrow our focus. We will continue developing our own profile alongside this material to ensure coverage from every angle.

Let's stay focused and gather what we can to drive us forward.

~Blackburn

She reviewed the message for tone and clarity. Satisfied, she clicked send. The quiet electronic chime marked its departure, and she allowed herself a brief smile before turning back to her desk.

The door to homicide opened with a slow creak. A man stepped inside, solidly built and filling the entrance with his presence. His suit hung awkwardly over his frame, the fabric stretched taut across his shoulders and bunching at the waist. His face was ruddy and marked by old acne scars, with beads of sweat catching the LED light along his brow. Brown hair, oily and thinning, was combed forward without success. A heavy step announced each movement, one foot dragging behind, the leather sole scraping against the floor.

He crossed to Cooper's desk without hesitation, his hand extended stiffly.

"Kurt Banks," he said in a flat tone that carried no warmth. "I'm here to lead the investigation into the terrorist car victims."

Cooper stared at him for a second too long before accepting the handshake. The grip was damp and too firm. "You'll want Detective Blackburn for that," he replied quietly, nodding toward her office door. He wiped his palm against his thigh once Banks turned away.

Banks moved directly to Blackburn's door and knocked firmly with closed knuckles. The sound was sharp against the wood.

"Kurt Banks here," he called out, his voice carrying across the entire office. "I'm taking over as lead investigator in the deaths of these terrorist car victims."

From inside her office, Blackburn glanced up in time to catch Cooper rolling his eyes toward the ceiling. She watched Banks's bulky frame fill her doorway and narrowed her gaze for a moment. She wondered if he intended to label their victims as terrorists or if he simply had not bothered with precision. Either way, it demanded an immediate response.

Banks entered her office, the LED lights casting harsh shadows across his face. She offered the man a professional nod. "Detective Morgan Blackburn." Her voice carried authority without rising above conversational level. "Would you mind explaining why you believe you're taking over my case?"

Banks straightened, his wool suit rustling as his shoulders drew back to fill the space. "These deaths are connected to the Stan Raider Group. My background in anti-terrorism has revealed a pattern. This is anti-technologist violence, retaliation against new advances that threaten their interests."

Blackburn let his words settle into the stale air of the squad room, her face revealing nothing. She suspected this was Hayes's handiwork: the federal technical specialist, delivered without warning. Her team watched from their desks, the scratch of pens stilling, coffee cups pausing mid-lift.

"I see," she replied, each word deliberate. "We will need to coordinate closely. Before we proceed, I'll need to review your authorization." She extended her hand, palm up.

Banks hesitated. His fingers moved in an awkward gesture across his chest before reaching into his jacket. The papers crinkled as he withdrew them, releasing a faint scent of cologne and leather. He handed them over with visible reluctance.

"You should have received prior notice," he said, the muscles in his jaw tightening.

Blackburn unfolded the documents, the paper crisp beneath her fingers. She read in silence, giving nothing away. "We document all arrivals for transparency," she said, her voice soft but firm. "I'm sure you understand." In truth, Hayes had left her uninformed and exposed.

She slipped the paperwork into a manila folder marked with Banks's name in black ink, placing it on her desk with a quiet snap.

The team assembled in the boardroom at her signal, chairs scraping against linoleum. Blackburn observed Banks as he tracked each detective's entrance, his pale eyes calculating strengths and weaknesses with mechanical precision. Sinclair's rumpled appearance drew a fleeting curl of his lip. Cooper received the briefest acknowledgment. Reeves warranted a longer assessment. Banks studied the man's military bearing.

Willow appeared at the doorway, her tablet glowing against her hip. She nodded at Blackburn and took position near the wall, her presence quiet but alert.

Across the polished table, Banks went utterly still. The shift was subtle but immediate, like water freezing in an instant. His breathing slowed. His gaze fixed on Willow's hands as she arranged her display, tracking her movements with an intensity that raised the fine hairs on Blackburn's neck.

He shifted his chair, the legs squeaking against the floor, creating an unobstructed view. His fingers began a slow rhythm against the tabletop. Tap, tap. Deliberate. Precise.

The LED bulb above them hummed. Blackburn crossed her arms, leather creaking, and planted herself behind her chair. Something about his focus felt wrong, calculated rather than casual. The room's temperature dropped a degree as other conversations died away.

Willow remained absorbed in her screen, the blue light reflecting off her glasses.

Banks rose abruptly, his chair rolling backward. "Kurt Banks," he announced, his voice flat as old paint. "I'll be leading this investigation." His attention snapped to Willow's workstation. "Is that a QuantumShift 15X?"

Willow glanced up, eyebrows lifting. "Yes."

Banks moved closer, his footsteps sharp against the floor. "Impressive hardware." The words came out clipped, directed at the room but meant for her. "I'd bet that runs on a QuantumCore D12 Hexa-Core Processor."

His shadow fell across her workspace as he leaned in, ostensibly examining the technical specifications. The scent of his cologne grew stronger, something sharp and medicinal. His commentary about processing speeds and memory capacity filled the room, drowning out the quiet rustle of papers and cleared throats.

His hand descended onto Willow's shoulder. Not a touch but a claim, fingers pressing into the fabric of her blouse.

The detectives' eyes tracked the gesture. Cooper's pen stilled mid-word. Sinclair's coffee cup halted inches from his lips. The air in the room grew dense with unspoken assessment while Blackburn cataloged every micro-expression, every shift in posture.

Blackburn's insides twisted. She recognized the glimmer of a predator sizing up prime prey, the way his eyes lingered a beat too long on Willow, the subtle flex of authority in every gesture. His interest was not technical. She stayed silent for another moment, watching as he launched into the details of the machine, spinning jargon with an energy that glossed over the tension gathering at the table.

Willow shifted in her seat under the scrutiny, her posture shrinking as Banks leaned closer. His tone carried easy confidence when he smiled at the others and gestured toward her. "Nice to have someone who actually gets this stuff," he said, satisfaction flickering beneath his words.

Blackburn caught the undercurrent. She stepped in before anyone else could respond. "Willow's expertise is essential," she said, her voice steady and unadorned as she rose from her chair. The statement hung in the space between them. There was no room for misinterpretation.

Banks's smile thinned. He met Blackburn's stare for a second, weighing his response. "Of course," he replied, his tone polished but flat. The edge in his eyes had dulled, replaced with something cooler and more detached.

The conversation stilled. Willow's hands paused above her laptop keyboard while Blackburn held Banks's gaze.

Blackburn shifted gears without raising her voice. "Kurt," she said, "you have our initial data. Why don't you walk us through your case theory instead of the specs? We need to hear how it fits together." She sat again and waited.

Banks straightened, pausing to gather himself before launching into his answer. "This killer knows tech inside out," he began, addressing the group directly. "What we're looking at is someone with a personal score against Stan Raider Group. Probably a former employee or someone who lost someone to a failure with their product." His delivery built in focus rather than volume. "It's not just about hating technology. This person wants payback."

The other detectives exchanged glances. Skepticism and polite restraint flickered across their faces. Sinclair watched over clasped hands while Cooper and Reeves gave nothing away.

Cooper broke his silence quietly. "A tech expert waging war against tech."

Banks nodded once, pushing ahead without hesitation. "They know these cars better than most people in the company do and have a reason to make a public mess out of it." He looked around as if expecting nods of agreement. "They're trying to prove nobody is safe if we rely on machines."

Blackburn kept her expression closed as she listened, tracking his gaze as it circled the room searching for approval that did not come.

Banks pressed on without pause or shift in tone. "This isn't some random script kiddie or paranoid loner," he insisted. "It's deliberate. Someone convinced they have truth on their side and willing to keep killing until it gets attention."

The room felt heavy for a long second afterward. Blackburn's features revealed nothing beyond patience that was beginning to thin at the edges. Sinclair tapped out a rhythm on his notepad instead of responding aloud. Cooper and Reeves exchanged only a quick glance before returning to neutral.

Nobody spoke up to agree or to challenge Banks directly. Willow simply moved her fingers back to the keys in careful silence, waiting for what would come next.

And he had not even noticed the huge flowchart on Brynn that hung on the wall.

Chapter 8

As Banks's words hung in the air, the room grew still. Willow cleared her throat and tried to lighten the mood. "Or maybe we're just dealing with a bored kid in Des Moines," she said. The attempt drew scattered laughter from the detectives, but Banks's cheeks darkened, his pride stung.

Blackburn straightened, her shoulders pulling back. "A kid in Des Moines?" Her tone was flat, each word precise.

Willow caught herself. "I only meant some hacker working out of a basement. Not someone actually from Des Moines. Just that this could be done remotely, from any location. That's my point."

The atmosphere shifted back to business as Blackburn spoke, her voice deliberate. "We need you up to speed, Banks. Our investigation into the four deaths tied to autonomous vehicles has reached a critical stage."

Willow stepped in, tension threading through her calm exterior. "In each incident, the cars' navigation systems appear compromised. With Jenna and Kendria, both women died in public spaces. The vehicles passed by once before circling back to strike them."

Blackburn glanced at Willow. Something flickered behind her eyes but quickly vanished.

Reeves leaned forward, his elbows finding the table's edge. "Lilith and Ahmed were killed when their autonomous cab went off Dunbar Bluffs. Police were present but couldn't stop it from going over. We have footage. News coverage, 911 calls, body cams, chopper video."

Banks raised a hand, cutting through the air. "I don't need visuals right now. What matters is connecting these cases through technology."

Blackburn met Banks's gaze directly, her focus unwavering. "The deaths haven't been formally classified as homicides yet. The circumstances are suspect enough for ongoing review. The attacks started after news broke about the police contract with Stan Raider Group. So far, every vehicle involved comes from their fleet."

Banks sat back, the leather chair creaking softly as he considered this. He spoke with new certainty. "Exactly what I'm saying." He let the words settle in the quiet room before continuing. "This theory makes sense."

Blackburn pressed him for detail. "Explain your reasoning."

Banks leaned toward her, his arms crossing tight against his chest. "It's coordinated," he said, his voice low but firm. "Whoever is behind this knows the department is already under scrutiny after signing with Raider Group. Using their vehicles gives the hacker control over technology that's become central to police operations and lets them point blame at you directly. Or at least create that appearance for the public and media. It damages trust on multiple levels and pushes a wider debate about police use of self-driving cars."

Blackburn could not dismiss his logic completely. The timing aligned too closely for coincidence. Still, she clarified. "But these aren't patrol vehicles. They're Straight Lines models owned by private parties."

"Private vehicles so far. Tighten surveillance. Start looking at anyone who might hold a grudge against the Stan Raider Group," Banks said. "Focus on potential suspects with enough technical skill to pull this off. We need to shift the pressure back onto whoever is orchestrating these attacks."

Blackburn sat back, arms folded, her gaze flat as she watched Banks. His self-importance filled the room like cologne.

"Kurt," she said, her voice even but edged with steel, "we already have. We identified a likely suspect and ruled him out. But you're suggesting this could be any Stan Raider employee anywhere in the world?"

He gestured vaguely, fingers splaying as if that alone would answer her. "Well, yes," he replied.

"You haven't given us anything concrete," Sinclair said, dropping his pen onto the table with a soft clatter.

Banks only shrugged. The confidence in his squared shoulders made it clear he expected to be persuasive. "It's the most logical scenario based on what we know. The timing matches the police contract and their operational scope. What else are you looking for?"

Blackburn did not blink. "You've offered a motive and little more. A theory that makes nearly anyone a suspect. What I need is a list of actual names. People who might resent Stan Raider Group or the department itself. Like this woman here." She tapped Brynn's flowchart, the paper crinkling under her finger, eyes still on Banks.

He ignored her gesture, unbothered.

"Detective," Banks said, his tone sliding into condescension, "what I'm trying to do is assess the larger context first. It takes time to turn something this complex into a list of viable suspects. I am developing an approach for finding a lead engineer who might have been forced out and could still hold a grudge."

The table quieted as frustration spread through the team like a slow leak. Sinclair tapped his pen against the wood now instead of tossing it. Cooper and Reeves shared an uneasy glance across the scratched surface.

Blackburn exhaled slowly, the sound barely audible. "Keiran Mott? We have already spoken to him. Or is there another former engineer? Does your strategy involve calling Human Resources and asking for their entire exit list?"

"It's part of it," Banks answered, irritation creeping into his voice.

"You'll need a court order to get those files, which means evidence comes first. I want you thinking broader than ex-employees with obvious grievances. Reach out to your contacts in tech circles. Hackers, anti-tech activists, anyone who might have reason to target Stan Raider or us. Time isn't on our side."

Banks met her gaze without yielding, mild annoyance flickering across his features like static. "I hear what you're saying, Detective, but my methods are different from yours. It's important to let patterns emerge instead of forcing the issue."

Blackburn kept her features controlled but her voice sharpened just enough to cut. "Patterns do not reveal themselves while you sit behind a desk waiting for inspiration to strike. We are dealing with murder. Not just sabotage or protest. I expect initiative, not delay."

Sinclair shifted in his chair, the leather creaking. Cooper and Reeves avoided both Banks and Blackburn entirely now, their eyes finding the wall, the floor, anywhere else. Willow stayed focused on her screen, keys clicking steadily as if nothing had been said at all.

Banks's cheeks flushed at Blackburn's bluntness. "Do you have any idea of how successful I am?"

"This isn't sport, Banks," Blackburn said, her tone cool. "We have bodies stacking up. I don't need theories or posturing. I want actionable leads. Use every resource you have. Do you understand?"

She moved on before he could answer, facing her team and leaving Banks to absorb the sting in silence.

"All right, let's take another angle," she announced. Then, almost as an afterthought, she addressed him without meeting his gaze. "This is looking personal, not political. If you want to stay, do."

Banks hesitated. Discomfort flickered across his face as he searched for backup among the others. Sinclair focused on a spot behind Banks's head, Cooper stared at the blue glow of his laptop screen, and Reeves pretended to review notes, her pen scratching across paper.

"No, I'll go," Banks said finally. He turned stiffly toward the door, making one last attempt to save face. "Willow? Are you free for lunch?"

Willow barely looked up from her screen, fingers still moving across the keyboard. She shot a quick glance at Blackburn, then back at Banks with polite distance. "No, thank you," she replied, already typing again.

Heat crept up Banks's neck as he straightened his jacket and tried to recover the dignity that had fled the room minutes earlier. "Suit yourself," he muttered, then slunk into a chair near the wall. The leather creaked under him.

Blackburn scanned the room, reading the mood in each face. Sinclair released a quiet breath that barely disturbed the air. Cooper shared a look with Reeves that bordered on relief.

Willow cleared her throat and spoke up. "I've dug deeper into how someone could have controlled those cars," she said. The team braced itself, shoulders tensing.

She continued, her voice steady but edged with tension. "The hacking here is advanced in some ways but alarmingly accessible in others." She paused to let the words settle before continuing. "If someone understands where to look online or knows which systems are vulnerable, they could find step-by-step instructions and even ready-made software."

Sinclair set down his pen with a soft click and listened closely while Cooper straightened in his chair.

Blackburn leaned forward, her shadow shifting across the table. "You're telling me an amateur could manage this?"

Willow nodded once. "With enough time and motivation, yes." She tapped a few keys and projected schematics onto the screen behind her. The diagrams cast pale light across her face. "There are manuals online for older vehicles' navigation systems. Exploits aren't hard to find if you know what questions to ask."

"Even basic malware could be enough in some cases," Willow continued. "A person might not even need much technical skill if they can download scripts or tools from certain forums or the dark web."

Cooper frowned at the screen as Reeves scribbled notes beside him, her pen moving in quick strokes.

"Step-by-step tutorials?" Cooper asked quietly, his voice carrying a note of disbelief.

Willow nodded again, eyes tracking the diagrams glowing behind her as she scrolled through another page of data. The soft clicks of her trackpad punctuated the silence.

"Yes, I call them click kiddies. Watch," Willow said.

She tapped a few keys. The lights dimmed. The projector cast a dull red wash across the wall as a sluggish webpage materialized. Black background. Red serif text. A pixelated skull rotated lazily in the corner.

"This is just one of dozens."

She clicked again. Lines of code spilled down the screen in phosphorescent green. Commands, fragments, incomplete scripts stacked in cluttered columns. The header read: Dr1veN3t Ove4ride K1t v6. Untested, Use at Own Risk. Half the words warped or misspelled.

The detectives watched. Some frowned in confusion. Others exchanged skeptical glances.

"These are kids," Willow continued. "They're not engineers. Most of them have no idea what they're running. They grab tools from strangers, copy instructions from tutorial videos with AI narration and metal soundtracks."

Another window opened: a video player frozen on a grainy dashboard shot, some teenager in a hoodie hunched forward. The title above it read: Spoofed the Lane Sensor on a Model-X3, Kinda.

"They think it's hacking," she said. "But they're just layering scripts and hoping for results. Usually nothing happens, or something breaks. Every so often, something connects."

Blackburn watched from the side of the room, her attention shifting between the screen and Banks.

He stood apart from the others near the back wall, one hand tucked into his pocket, his shoulders loose but his eyes steady on Willow. Not engaged with her presentation, but appraising her as if she were another piece of evidence to catalog.

It was not interest or admiration that marked his gaze, but calculation.

Blackburn saw it in the set of his jaw and the way he measured each moment Willow spoke, tracking not her words but her influence over the room. He weighed her value without speaking.

A flicker of something passed across his features. Jealousy? Disdain? The emotion stayed buried beneath his composure.

Willow advanced to another slide. "Here's what matters: it doesn't have to work every time. They only need to believe it might succeed once. That's enough."

A voice from the table broke in: "Are you saying anyone could do this?"

Willow paused before answering, meeting their looks with careful calm.

"Yes."

There was a low whistle from Reeves. Cooper groaned under his breath. Blackburn did not react.

Willow moved ahead in the presentation. Another grim website appeared onscreen, its interface cobbled together like a digital bunker by someone too young for the hours they kept. Sinclair leaned forward to study it more closely. Reeves asked about remote access. Banks's arms drew firm across his chest.

"Anyone could be responsible," Willow said. "A teenager who found a thread buried in an online game chatroom halfway around the world. Someone bored after school. Or someone..."

"Enough."

Blackburn's voice sliced through conversation and stilled movement around the table. The detectives turned toward her as if summoned by command alone.

Her jaw was set rigidly. Her grip tightened around her precinct mug without conscious thought. The ceramic creaked against her palm.

Banks did not shift or look away.

"You're saying," she said slowly, each word cool, "that anyone with a copied code could turn a car into a weapon?"

Silence gathered along every surface in the room, thick as dust.

She pushed back her chair and stood abruptly. Wood scraped tile underneath her. The mug trembled in her palm before she hurled it against the boardroom wall with sudden force.

It shattered against painted cinderblock. White shards scattered across the floor like broken teeth.

Blackburn stared at what remained. When she spoke again, her tone dropped lower. Steady as steel drawn slow through cloth.

"We have four victims because of this chaos. Four people buried while we chase ghosts online."

She glanced at Willow, who faltered under scrutiny and could not find words in reply.

Banks offered half a smirk that faded before it took hold.

Blackburn's hands shook once more at her sides. Whether from anger or restraint was unclear even to herself.

Then she stepped away from the table without another word and left the room behind her.

Blackburn entered her office and closed the door behind her with care. The soft click of the latch echoed in the sudden quiet. She cast a glance toward the meeting room, where LED light spilled through glass walls, her expression hardening into stone. She sat at her desk and angled herself away from the glass, turning instead to face the dark mahogany bookcase. The leather spines blurred as she fixed her eyes on them and box breathed, counting each inhale and exhale.

A knock broke through her concentration. Reeves poked his head through the doorway, the hallway noise filtering in behind him. "You have a minute?" he asked.

"No," she replied without looking up.

He nodded once, unruffled by the dismissal. "Understood. Maybe later?"

He was one of the few men who heard 'no' the first time. She let out a breath. "Reeves."

He paused in the threshold, patient as ever, one hand still on the doorframe. "Boss?"

She gestured him in with a tired wave.

Reeves shut the door quietly, muffling the distant voices from the bullpen, and took the seat across from her. The leather creaked softly as he settled, maintaining a careful distance across the expanse of her desk.

"I don't know what's going on in your head," he said, hands open in a slow circle as if weighing invisible evidence. "But this doesn't seem like you."

Blackburn picked up a pen from her desk, its metal surface cool against her fingertips. She rolled it between her fingers, the rhythmic motion grounding her as she considered his words. The chair's leather sighed as she leaned back and drew in a long breath before answering.

"We have worked this case for weeks. We brought in outside help. And now I'm being told it could be anyone, anywhere." She paused, letting frustration settle on each syllable like dust. "What do you want me to do with that?" The pen continued its steady rotation, catching the desk lamp's glow with each turn.

"You do what you always do," Reeves said carefully, his voice low. "That thing only you manage."

She stilled the pen for a beat before settling in her palm, then started the motion again. "Explain."

A small smile flickered across Reeves's weathered face. "Boss, every case could be anyone."

Blackburn shook her head once, a sharp dismissal. "Not without limits."

He met her gaze evenly, brown eyes steady. "We had that homicide where the shooter was gone an hour after pulling the trigger, halfway to Munich before we even finished processing the scene. A tourist who barely left a trace. You still tracked him down."

She stared at him, the memory crystallizing behind her eyes as if replaying details etched permanently in her mind. "That case dragged on for half a year," she said, her voice dropping to barely above a whisper.

He shrugged, the fabric of his jacket rustling. "It still started with anyone, anywhere. They all do until something narrows it down." He looked away for a moment, studying the certificates on her wall before returning to her face. "You're the one who spots what nobody else does."

The pen slipped from Blackburn's hand onto the desk with a faint clatter that was too loud in the quiet office. Her shoulders dropped a fraction, tension bleeding out.

"This isn't like those others, Victor." She seldom used his first name; when she did, it signaled something deeper at stake. "I rely on my own judgment, but this time..." She gestured toward the conference room, where shadows moved behind frosted glass, her voice clipped. "All this new tech is beyond me right now, and none of them are giving me much confidence."

Reeves stared at the ceiling tiles as if searching their familiar water stains for direction.

"Start where you always start," he said finally, his words deliberate. "Go back to what we have."

She put both hands flat on her desk, feeling the cool wood beneath her palms, and met his eyes with calm resignation. "There is almost nothing to work with except an old pill bottle covered in one set of fingerprints from our victim."

"The numbers are the evidence too," Reeves countered quietly. His elbows pressed into her desk as he leaned forward, the wood creaking, intent but not pressing too hard. "You don't need to be a doctor to read an autopsy report or a computer expert to look at raw data."

Blackburn studied him for a silent moment, the air between them thick with unspoken understanding, before nodding.

"I haven't looked at any of it myself yet," she admitted, the confession hanging in the air.

He nodded back without judgment, just a slight dip of his chin. "You trusted your people to handle it." He kept his voice steady but left room for challenge. "When things stall out or take an unexpected turn, you're always the one who takes another look and finds something."

She drew in another breath that felt heavier than she expected, filling her lungs with the familiar scent of old paper and coffee that permeated her office.

"I need to pull the event data recorder files myself," she said at last, matter-of-fact but weary around the edges.

She leaned back and exhaled sharply, the sound cutting through the space as tension pooled between them like a gathering storm.

Chapter 9

Willow glanced into Blackburn's office as she passed. Only minutes earlier, she had witnessed a side of Blackburn that unsettled her; now, the detective sat behind her desk, composed. The room appeared untouched by chaos. The desk surface held only a single monitor, a phone, and the gold and black vase. Its fractured veins glinted in the afternoon light. Willow lingered on that detail as she continued through the doorway.

She descended the stairs to her own office in the basement, a floor reserved for the forgotten and outdated. Old wooden desks cluttered the hallway, some flipped upside down, others stacked two high. Three-legged chairs leaned against battered file cabinets, their metal surfaces dented and scraped. This was the territory of the evidence room. Beyond it, retired technology gathered dust: empty beige computer towers, faded monitors with thick glass screens, keyboards worn smooth by countless fingers. Others had scavenged what they could, carrying away anything with value or function. Willow left those relics undisturbed.

Passing each office door, she studied faces through the narrow windows. Someone here always reported Blackburn's visits to Chief Hayes. She suspected Freddie; envy drove him more than loyalty.

Still, he had helped when it counted, alerting Blackburn during that urgent call from Cassidy.

Willow slipped into her cramped office. The air carried a persistent trace of mildew that clung despite her regular cleaning. She wondered what Blackburn would do with a space like this. Transform it within a week, and have the whole precinct envious by month's end. That thought brought a brief smile.

At her desk, Willow slid her laptop into its padded case and turned to her desktop workstation. She logged in and launched FatalityInsight Pro, watching lines of code scroll across the screen as the program loaded case files and data sets from multiple jurisdictions. Charts materialized against a neutral gray background: colored lines tracking trends in traffic fatalities, impact points mapped with clinical precision. The software parsed police reports and medical records, generating visualizations that revealed patterns in autonomous vehicle crashes.

A knock echoed from her open doorway ten minutes later.

Banks stood there clutching two long white paper bags, grease darkening the seams near the bottom. Submarine sandwiches for lunch. He strode in without invitation and placed one on Willow's desk with a soft thud.

"Thought you might be hungry," he said, forcing a smile that failed to mask his disappointment.

Willow glanced at the bag before shaking her head once. "No thank you."

"Oh come on, a girl like you not hungry?" he asked, jiggling the bag. Willow frowned and kept her eyes on the computer. Banks's jaw tightened, but he maintained his composure. "It's just a sandwich," he said. "You should eat something."

"I said no," Willow replied. Her tone remained level, betraying no irritation.

He hesitated before stepping back toward the door and pulling it closed behind him. "Wouldn't want everyone down here catching the scent of these subs," he offered over his shoulder.

"Someone on this floor might buy it off you, if you're looking to get rid of it."

He stepped in behind her, his voice dropping low at her shoulder while the visualization software cast its pale glow across their faces. "That's clever. You're clever."

Willow heard the lie threading through his words as clearly as she felt her own pulse quickening. His hands landed on her shoulders without warning, fingers digging into muscle through the worn cotton of her shirt. Her spine went rigid. He slid one hand downward, where it settled over her breast. Her fingers froze above the keyboard, trembling. When silence stretched between them instead of protest, he closed his hand and squeezed.

She calculated the exact angle needed to drive the sharp edge of the NIC card bracket between his ribs. She wondered if Detective Blackburn would care that another man's hands were touching what belonged to her.

He released her and shifted back, moving to circle her chair. Relief flooded through her limbs. Brief. Deceptive. Perhaps this was finished.

It was not.

"You know you have big tits," he said, his tone flat and appraising. He reached out again, his palm brushing across the same spot through the thin fabric, lingering to press and trace small circles. His eyes searched her face, then narrowed. "Don't I do anything for you?"

"Leave. Me." The words scraped against her throat, emerging barely above a whisper.

She recognized the danger in that quietness. The same instinct that had taught her to keep her smile small in social workers' offices, to muffle her footsteps in foster homes where visibility meant consequences. She raised one hand to push him away, but he caught her wrist and forced it downward, pressing her palm against the rigid shape straining his pants.

Her body responded not with arousal but with shutdown. Every muscle seized, every nerve firing signals she couldn't obey. Stillness had always been her shield. Stay small. Stay invisible.

She wondered what would happen if she fought back or called out. Her entire frame vibrated now with adrenaline and a fear so acute it constricted her throat.

Banks's fingers wrapped around the back of her neck and he leaned in until her face hovered inches from his zipper. "You're a pretty girl," he said as he pulled the metal tab down.

Pain arrived with crystalline clarity. Not the kind she might choose or crave, but the kind that registered instantly as violation.

She had known rough touches before. Had learned how certain pain could spark electricity through her veins instead of terror. But this tore through something fundamental inside her. This pain carved a boundary she hadn't known existed until it breached her defenses and left only ice-cold panic.

She tried to pull back but his fingers tangled in her hair, yanking hard. Her knees hit concrete as he dragged her down. The monitor's blue light wavered through tears while dread pinned her in place.

She attempted to rise but he pressed closer, his body forming a wall between her and any exit. He outweighed her by maybe twenty pounds, but dominance didn't measure itself in weight here. It manifested as assumption beyond challenge.

He ordered her to open up. When she hesitated, his palm cracked across her cheek. The impact sent her glasses skittering across worn carpet. As tears started, his mouth curled with contempt. She should be grateful for his interest. Someone like her deserved nothing better.

He reached into his open fly and freed himself.

Willow's panic crested as tears blurred her vision. She twisted, pressing herself against the filing cabinet's cold metal edge, desperate to slip away from Banks's grip. Without her glasses, the room had become a field of shifting shadows. Nothing looked right or safe.

Something hard pressed against her cheek. She recognized the shape through touch alone. Willow squeezed her eyes shut and held still, hoping that stillness would stop time.

The door to her office clicked open. Rough fabric pressed against her lips. She heard a muffled command, sharp and vicious: "Open up, you fucking bitch." Willow refused. She opened her eyes but not her mouth, squinting through the haze at the figure in the doorway. The outline was unmistakable.

Blackburn moved into the room without a sound. Her arm cut through the space between them, movements contained and exact. The faint scent of clean hair and leather drifted close. Willow felt Blackburn's presence settle like armor across her back.

Blackburn spoke in a tone Willow had never heard before, low and cold, each word edged with threat. "Let go of her or I will kill you." The promise carried a gravity beyond anger, pressing down on everyone in the room.

For one stretched second, no one moved. Banks's fingers slackened around Willow's wrist as he registered who stood before him. His eyes widened in confusion and fear.

Willow blinked rapidly, struggling to make sense of the scene through smeared tears and myopic blur. All she saw was Blackburn's steady shape, a wall between herself and Banks, gun drawn and pressed flat against his skull.

The silence broke. Banks hesitated, then twitched as if weighing escape or retaliation. He chose wrong.

Blackburn shifted forward and dragged the front sight of her pistol down Banks's face with ruthless precision. Skin split beneath metal. Blood welled in a sharp line along his cheekbone.

Banks cursed, voice cracking under pain as he reeled back and flung his arms up. His grip on Willow vanished.

Willow sucked in air too fast, breath shuddering through relief as sensation flooded her limbs. Fear not yet gone but replaced by something sharper: certainty that Blackburn was real and dangerous and here.

She watched as Blackburn followed Banks's retreat with another blow, a flat-handed slap that snapped his head sideways with brutal efficiency. The crack of palm against jaw echoed in the small office. He stumbled again, confusion now tangled with terror.

Banks staggered upright, hands pressed to his bleeding face, gaze darting between Blackburn's gun and her unwavering stare.

Blackburn kept her weapon trained on him, calm locked into every muscle of her body. The air hummed with tension, not loud but exacting, and Willow sensed how easily it could tip again into violence or control.

"Out," Blackburn said, her voice restrained and cold.

Banks hesitated, trying to speak. "She came onto me—"

He had not moved far enough. Blackburn drove her fist into his nose. Her sidearm hung steady at her side. Banks recoiled, a wet sound escaping him, hands flying to his face as blood seeped through his fingers and tracked down his wrist. He staggered backward, catching the edge of a table, shoulders hunched in retreat.

His gaze stayed locked on Blackburn until he disappeared into the hallway. The room settled into silence, the charged air thinning with his absence.

Willow stood still, breath shallow as adrenaline drained from her limbs. Her muscles trembled faintly from the aftershock. Slowly she became aware of the LED light stinging her eyes and the tight ache in her chest where panic had lodged.

Blackburn holstered her weapon and stooped to retrieve Willow's glasses from the carpet.

"I'm putting these on you," she said with calm precision. She leaned close, sliding the frames over Willow's ears until they rested firm and secure. Blackburn's face appeared crisp and near, her jaw set, her features composed. There were tiny drops of blood on Willow's white t-shirt.

A steady hand pressed against Willow's shoulder, grounding her. The touch was measured, not soft but reassuring. Willow found herself unraveling under it, tears rising swift and hot before she could hold them back. She kept silent at first but could not stop the sobs that broke loose soon after.

Blackburn crouched beside her and drew Willow into an embrace. Her hold was close but unyielding. An anchor more than a comfort.

"You're safe," Blackburn said at Willow's ear.

Willow held on tight, pressing her face to Blackburn's shoulder. She took in the familiar scent of laundry soap and faint leather, letting it cut through the static in her head.

Blackburn stayed there while Willow shook with tears. When Willow quieted, she felt Blackburn's finger trace along her cheek, wiping away a streak of salt water with a swipe.

"I'll notify Chief Hayes," Blackburn said. There was steadiness in her tone rather than sympathy. "He has to know what happened." She adjusted Willow's glasses again with careful precision before letting go.

The prospect of recounting everything made Willow's stomach clench. She shook her head sharply and managed a whisper: "No. I don't want it brought up again. Please."

She met Blackburn's eyes. Dark and searching. She waited for judgment. Instead, Blackburn nodded once in silent understanding.

"All right," she said after a pause. "I'll handle it. He won't come near you again."

Relief edged into Willow's posture, loosening what fear had held rigid in her ribs. She leaned into Blackburn's arms until there was nothing left in her but exhaustion and small shudders of release. A slow settling after violence endured.

Blackburn remained present for a few minutes as Willow gathered herself piece by piece, finding safety in the solid warmth of another body rather than words.

Chapter 10

She left Willow in her office with the door closed and the lights off.

The blood on the linoleum formed a trail, each drop deliberate rather than chaotic. Teardrops with tails pointed away from the office, marking a path to follow. The pattern spoke of someone walking with urgency but not yet running, the spacing between drops widening with each stride.

Blackburn pushed through the men's room door. The LED lights hummed overhead. "Banks!" Her voice bounced off porcelain and tile.

"Shit," came a muffled shout from behind a locked stall. Metal rattled against metal. "Uh, ma'am, you're in the wrong place."

Not Banks, then. On the paper towel dispenser, a bloody fingerprint caught the harsh light. The whorl pattern was fresh, still glistening. He had stopped here, grabbed for towels, and continued on. If he pressed something to his wound, the evidence would dry up quickly.

She stepped back out. "Sorry," she called over her shoulder to whoever she had startled.

In the hallway, another smear of red marked the wall near the stairwell. The streak ended in a handprint where he had steadied himself. He was avoiding offices. Heading for an exit. Blackburn took the stairs two at a time, her footsteps ringing against concrete, and shoved through the emergency door.

Outside, afternoon sun cast hard shadows across the small guest lot behind headquarters. Heat radiated from the asphalt. Only three cars sat baking in the lot. Beside one of them stood Banks. He fumbled at his pockets, keys jangling and slipping in hands stained dark with blood.

Blackburn approached without sound or warning. Her shadow fell across him as she closed the distance. He looked up too late.

He froze as Blackburn lifted her weapon in a single smooth motion and brought it down across his mouth with controlled force. The impact rang out. Bone met metal. Blood sprayed onto the concrete as he staggered back, both hands flying to his face.

She did not raise her voice. "Open your mouth." The words carried weight without volume.

Banks shook his head and tried to turn away from her, a low moan escaping through his fingers.

She caught him by the nose and squeezed until cartilage shifted beneath her grip. He cried out, the sound muffled and wet. Then she pressed the gun barrel against his teeth and forced compliance.

Pinned against the car's rear panel, Banks tasted copper and salt while Blackburn worked with clinical detachment. The front sight caught on his split lip. Metal scraped against enamel, then dug into the soft tissue beneath his gumline until he whimpered, tears mixing with blood.

Adrenaline sharpened her senses rather than blurring them. She could smell his sweat, sharp with fear, could see the pulse jumping in his throat as she pushed harder. A careful application of pain designed to leave memory rather than permanent damage.

With one hand pressed flat against his chest for leverage, she reached beneath his arm and unclipped his holstered weapon before he could react. The grip was warm from his body heat, familiar in her palm.

"You'll say you were jumped by someone you didn't see," she told him quietly, her breath warm against his ear. "You lost your service weapon in the struggle." Each word was a command.

The threat hung thick in the air. Banks lay in the dirt, warm blood from his scalp coating Blackburn's fingers as she pressed him to the ground. Her voice remained flat, emotionless. "She has cameras in her office."

He flinched, searching her face for any sign of mercy. The lie took hold immediately. Panic bloomed behind his eyes, pupils dilating in the dim light.

"Please. Please, I—"

Blackburn's boot found his shoulder, pinning him with minimal effort. She spat at him, cold and efficient, the saliva mixing with blood and tears that had pooled on his cheek. "Remember this," she said, her words barely above a whisper. "Remember who decides how this ends."

Banks whimpered, his body curling inward. Blackburn turned away without another word.

She entered police headquarters moments later, every muscle relaxed, breath even. No trace of the encounter outside showed on her face. Her pulse slowed as she moved through the lobby, each step deliberate.

At the stairwell, she descended to the basement level. LED lights buzzed overhead, casting the concrete walls in harsh, sterile light.

She found the accessible bathroom and twisted the lock behind her. The click echoed in the tiled space. At the sink, she turned the tap until steam rose from the basin, water hot enough to redden her skin but not burn. Blood spiraled down the drain as she scrubbed her hands, methodical and unhurried, cleaning beneath her nails and between each finger.

She placed her gun under the stream next, working soap into every groove and texture, erasing all visible traces from the metal and textured grip. A proper cleaning would come later. This would serve for now.

At the hand dryer, she cradled her service weapon between her palms as heated air rushed over the metal surface.

Blackburn studied herself in the mirror. Her expression had settled back to neutral. Hair smoothed into place. Breathing regular. Not a single tell remained.

She reached into her jacket for Banks's gun, wrapping it in a thick layer of paper towels before sliding it back into concealment.

After securing her holster and adjusting her collar, Blackburn rested her hand on the door handle.

One more breath filled her lungs, cool and controlled.

She was ready to return upstairs, every trace of violence buried beneath a detective's calm.

Blackburn moved toward the elevator, her heels clicking against the polished floor. The doors slid open with a soft chime. She stepped inside and pressed the button for the second floor, feeling the subtle vibration beneath her feet as the car rose.

The elevator shuddered to a stop at the first floor. Chief Hayes entered with three uniformed officers, their equipment jangling softly as they filed in. The space suddenly felt smaller, warmer. They nodded to both senior detectives.

"Blackburn," Hayes said, his voice filling the confined space.

"Chief." Her tone remained neutral, giving nothing away.

Once the elevator resumed its climb, Hayes shifted toward her. "Did Banks from the Bureau show?"

"He did," Blackburn replied. "He didn't stay long." She kept her words measured. "Ignored the lead chart Willow built, but my team has it covered."

Hayes studied her, the LED light casting shadows across his face. "Good. Glad you're on it." What else could he say with others present?

The elevator eased to a stop. Blackburn exited at the second floor, the cooler air of the hallway touching her face.

"Keep me posted on this, Blackburn," Hayes called after her.

She acknowledged him with a slight nod and headed for her office. Inside, she paused at the threshold, her gaze sweeping the familiar space before she closed the door with a soft click. She crossed to her desk, listening for any movement from the bullpen beyond.

From beneath her desk she lifted the Kintsugi vase, its gold-veined surface cool against her palms. With careful precision, she unwrapped Banks's handgun from its paper shroud and nestled it inside the vessel. Every motion remained controlled, each movement silent.

When finished, she returned the vase to its exact position on her desk. Nothing appeared disturbed. She allowed herself to study the golden seams for a moment, then turned away.

Blackburn dialed Willow's number. Two rings echoed before Willow answered, her voice rough around the edges.

"Hey."

"I'm fine," Willow insisted, though her breath caught between words.

Blackburn kept her voice low and steady. "Go to my place. The spare key's under the rock by the stairs. I'll meet you there in a few hours."

Silence stretched between them like a held breath.

"Thank you," Willow whispered.

"Just go," Blackburn said, then ended the call.

She turned to her computer, the screen's glow washing over her face as she navigated to a flower shop website. A simple get-well arrangement caught her attention. A white bear nestled among fresh lilies and greens. She ordered it for delivery within the hour, typing only: Always watching over you.

Blackburn reached into her desk drawer for her radio and switched it on, static crackling before she found the right frequency. She scanned channels for any new assault reports that might connect to Banks.

While she listened, she opened another browser tab and placed an online order from Burgerz 'N' Beerz. Willow loved hamburgers.

As she completed the order, Banks's bloodied mouth surfaced in her mind. The image flickered and faded. The memory left her steady, both pleased and unsettled.

Blackburn descended to the basement. The LED lights hummed overhead. She checked Willow's office. Empty. Her footsteps echoed down the corridor to the evidence room. She signed out the data recorder from Charles Roche's car. The clerk rummaged through a cardboard box on his desk and produced an OBD-II to USB adapter. "Plug this into your computer, that into the EDR," he said. The plastic device clicked as he set it on the counter.

Later, Blackburn settled at her desk. The adapter clicked into place. She connected the EDR and opened the program. Blue light from the monitor washed across her face. Numbers and graphs filled the screen. Her breathing slowed as she leaned forward. Everything else in the precinct faded to background noise.

4544520003020000001HGBH41JXMN1091860F1C2A8B5E947D320 0 0 0 1 F F F E 0 2 0 2 F D F F F - EFF0200040206FE01FF020400CECF4471B89F5A7860421B63A0 F 8 F F F D F F F F - FF02010001000000FF00010000FF01000000020001FF0001000200FF01

0 0 0 0 0 0 1 F F F E 0 2 F D F E 0 1 F F F F -
FF0203040100FF0001020300FF0100020001FF000102
0300D4080C070B080A090C070B080A07C708A705E203C4019B01780
02040607020504080607050806070508202122232425262720212223242
232425262720212223242526727D4080C070B080A090C070B080A090C
070B080A090C070B080A0700000000000000004F347893A56FB4E21C
000000000000F30201000000202122232425262700000000000000000000
000000000000000000008847329

Blackburn released her breath in a slow stream. She typed her request for extraction steps into QuantaQuery's interface, watching the cursor blink against the screen. The AI resisted, its responses growing increasingly terse, but she persisted with each keystroke until the system finally yielded. A blue hyperlink materialized in the chat window. She clicked through and initiated the download. The progress bar crept across her monitor. Within minutes, rows of legible characters filled her screen. Sharp black text against a white background replaced the chaos of encrypted data.

EDR_DATA_STREAM_v3.2

VIN: JF1CZ8497VK482319

SAMPLE_RATE: 100Hz

CHANNELS: 52

DURATION: 12.4s

CH01_ACCEL_X : -1.2,-1.4,-1.1,-1.3,-1.5,-1.2,-1.4,-2.3,-2.1,-1.8,-1.6,-1.9,-2.2,-1.7,-1.8, -2.0,-1.9,-52.3,-71.4,-96.7,-118.9,-101.2,-82.4,-49.7,-28.1,-15.2,-9.8

,-6.7,-4.2,-2.8,-1.9,-2.0,-1.8,-1.7,-1.9,-2.1,-1.8,-1.9,-2.2,-1.6,-1.8,-2.0,-1.7,-1.9

CH02_ACCEL_Y:
0.2,0.4,0.1,0.3,0.2,0.4,0.3,0.8,0.6,0.9,0.7,0.8,0.6,0.9,0.7,1.1,0.7,19.8,28.4,16.7,6.2,-3.1,-9.8,-6.4,-2.1,0.8,1.9,1.2,0.8,0.7,0.9,0.8,1.0,0.9,0.7,0.8,0.9,0.8,0.6,0.9,0.7,0.8,0.6,0.9

CH03_ACCEL_Z:
9.8,9.7,9.9,9.8,9.7,9.8,9.9,9.8,9.7,9.9,9.8,9.7,9.8,9.9,9.8,9.7,9.9,10.7,12.8,14.2,11.9,10.1,9.4,8.8,9.0,9.3,9.6,9.7,9.8,9.9,9.8,9.7,9.8,9.9,9.8,9.7,9.8,9.9,9.8,9.7,9.9,9.8,9.7,9.8

CH04_GYRO_X:
0.08,0.12,0.06,0.10,0.08,0.12,0.09,0.15,0.11,0.13,0.09,0.14,0.10,0.12,0.08,0.11,0.09,134.7,271.8,342.1,289.4,221.3,147.8,82.1,29.4,10.7,3.9,1.8,0.7,0.5,0.9,0.10,0.11,0.09,0.08,0.11,0.10,0.09,0.12,0.08,0.11,0.09,0.12,0.08

CH05_GYRO_Y:
-0.01,-0.03,-0.02,-0.04,-0.01,-0.03,-0.02,0.04,0.02,0.05,0.03,0.04,0.02,0.05,0.03,0.04,0.01,58.9,114.2,81.7,39.8,15.3,-10.7,-19.8,-7.1,-1.8,0.3,0.2,-0.02,-0.01,-0.03,-0.02,-0.04,-0.01,-0.03,-0.02,-0.04,-0.01,0.02,0.04,0.01,0.03,0.02,0.04

She rubbed her temples. She guessed that ACCEL was acceleration, and GYRO was some kind of gyroscopic sensor. But the numbers were meaningless.

VEL, THROTTLE, RPM, BRAKE PRESS. She stopped. 234,87,34,12, followed by dozens of zeroes.

No brakes. She scanned the other fields: airbag deployment, seatbelt load. All zeroes. No driver. The GPS coordinates went into a new file for later.

Blackburn scrolled deeper into the log, her fingertips working the trackpad while she rubbed at burning eyes. BATT_VOLT. AV_MODE. OVERRIDE. LIDAR_DIST. A knot had formed between her shoulder blades, tightening with each line of data. She checked the clock and granted herself a few more minutes.

CAMERA_OBJ. CAN_ERR_CNT. EXT_CDM. External command.

She counted the sequence again, her lips moving silently. Seventeen zeroes, fourteen ones. Likely the point of takeover. Her gaze dropped to the next entries. CELL_TOWER_ID, WIFI_BSSID. The cell towers and WiFi identifiers stacked up in lines that swam before her tired eyes.

A dull throb spread across her temples.

Enough for now.

The clock showed seven-twelve. Blackburn registered the fatigue that had settled into her muscles, a steady ache spreading from her shoulders to her fingertips. Banks hadn't pressed charges. Their incident would remain buried, at least for now. She collected her files, aligning their edges before sliding them into her filing cabinet, and restored order to the desk's surface.

Outside, the air tickled through her jacket. Blackburn stopped at the edge of the back lot, her attention caught by familiar shadows pooling between the overhead lights. Old instinct drew her gaze across the rows of parked cars, scanning the darkened windshields and the spaces between bumpers. He was not lying in wait for her.

It was safe to go home.

She closed the car door and let the city noise fall away. Adrenaline ebbed, leaving behind a dull ache that spread across her shoulders and a steady pressure that pulsed behind her eyes. Headlights traced amber lines along rain-slick streets while wipers cut their quiet rhythm against the glass as she drove. Block by block, the sharp edge of alertness dulled into something heavier, fatigue settling into her bones.

* * *

Willow's hands tightened on the steering wheel as she pulled into Blackburn's driveway. The linden tree at the curb released its familiar fragrance, but today the sweetness clung to her throat, thick and cloying. She shut off the engine and sat in the sudden quiet, watching sunlight flash through leaves onto the hood in shifting patterns of heat and shadow.

The spare key waited in the same fake rock beside the porch stairs. Third from the left, always askew. She lifted it, feeling the cool metal bite into her palm, its edges sharp enough to leave faint indentations. The small discomfort anchored her.

Inside, the house held its particular stillness. Not empty but watchful. Blackburn's presence lingered in the neat stack of mail by the door, in the faint trace of morning coffee threading through motionless air, in the way dust motes drifted through a shaft of light from the front window.

A glance in the hallway mirror caught her unprepared: glasses smudged with fingerprints, hair escaping its clip in uneven strands, eyes rimmed with exhaustion and something rawer beneath. She looked exactly as she felt. A woman holding herself together by will alone.

She set her keys on the entry table, controlling each movement to avoid the slightest sound. Her footsteps whispered across hardwood as she moved through the living room, fingertips trailing along the worn leather sofa where she and Blackburn had spent countless evenings. The familiar texture made her breath catch. Almost a sob.

The kitchen blazed white beneath the fixture over the sink. She crossed to the third drawer on the right. The utility drawer. Scissors nested among rolls of tape, spare batteries rattled against small screwdrivers and a box cutter with a yellow plastic handle.

She lifted the cutter. Such an unremarkable tool. A cloud shifted outside, and sudden brightness threw everything into sharp relief: the blade's clean edge, her trembling fingers, the stone countertop's subtle grain.

Her thumb traced the tender skin at her inner wrist, following the map of scars that told their own quiet history. This blade would cut deeper than her usual implements. It would work with terrible efficiency.

She hesitated. This was Blackburn's box cutter, not hers. Any blood she spilled would mark more than her own skin. It would stain this kitchen, seep into the grout between tiles. Blackburn would return to find darkness pooled on pale stone, questions suspended in the air between them. Another mess for someone who had already pulled her back from the edge today.

She returned the box cutter to its place beside a Phillips-head screwdriver, aligning it exactly as she had found it.

Something drew her deeper into the house. The bedroom door stood open. Inside, the bed waited with military precision, corners tucked to sharp angles, not a wrinkle disturbing its surface. Willow lowered herself carefully onto the edge, mindful not to disturb the perfect geometry. This was Blackburn's sanctuary. Here, just days ago, they had found their particular rhythm. Her face buried in these same pillows while Blackburn's knowing hands orchestrated every shudder, every gasp, with exquisite control.

A new photo frame on the dresser caught Willow's attention. Silver and unadorned, it held a photograph she recognized at once. Blackburn's smile, unforced and rare, Willow pressed close against her shoulder. They had taken the photo lying in this very bed. Afternoon sunlight spilled across them through the window, warming their skin and softening the edges of the moment. Blackburn had stretched out her arm to snap it, interrupting Willow's laughter over some offhand remark about a case.

Willow lifted the frame, the cool metal smooth beneath her fingertips. She held it carefully to avoid smudging the glass. Blackburn had chosen to print this picture. She had framed it and placed it here, where she would see it with every start and end of the day.

The gesture landed quietly but left its mark. The tight band around Willow's chest loosened. Not gone, not erased, but relaxed enough for her lungs to expand fully again.

She crossed to the kitchen island and set the frame down next to her bag. The canvas laptop sleeve sagged where she had dropped it earlier, its worn fabric soft beneath her palm. She slid out her computer and opened it without ceremony. She would write up a report for Blackburn. Not about what happened to her, not a recounting of violence or aftermath. She would create a technical summary of the patterns emerging in the autonomous vehicle cases. Anomalies in code signatures that might prove useful. It was work she trusted herself to do well.

She sat in the same seat where they had shared breakfast three days earlier. The kitchen stool's leather was cool against her legs. Her hands steadied over the keyboard as clinical language took shape: observations, data points, proposed next steps. Each sentence built order from chaos. This was something she could offer in gratitude. Measured intelligence rather than apology or confession.

The tremor in her fingers faded by degrees. Her breath came easier as focus replaced the spinning thoughts. She did not mistake this for healing or closure; she no longer hoped for that kind of certainty. But she could contribute, and that counted for something now.

When Blackburn returned home, she would find the report waiting on the counter and Willow present. Functional, engaged, choosing usefulness instead of withdrawal. That would have to be enough for now.

It was enough for today.

Chapter 11

In her driveway, Blackburn sat for a moment with both hands gripping the wheel. The badge and sidearm rested on the passenger seat beside her, metal catching the streetlight. A silent ledger of violence and decisions. She picked them up gently, feeling the subtle shift in her spine with their weight.

Climbing the steps, she drew in air tinged with lavender and the faint sweetness of vanilla drifting from beneath her door. Home met her with its familiar quiet, asking nothing. She turned the lock with care. Behind the secured door, what belonged to the job finally stayed where it belonged.

Blackburn felt fatigue settle into her bones as she opened the door. Willow waited on the hardwood floor, dressed in a thin t-shirt and underwear.

"Welcome home, my Lioness," Willow said. She rose in one fluid motion, reverence threading through her voice. She had been waiting in the hallway for Blackburn's return. "Everything's ready."

Blackburn lifted an eyebrow, holding back the sharp edge of irritation. "What's ready?"

"A special relaxation night," Willow said. She reached out and took Blackburn's hand, her palm warm against tired, blood-scrubbed skin. "You've done a lot for me lately. I want to thank you." Willow brushed her own cheek, fingers quick and habitual, then offered a small smile.

Blackburn's gaze traveled over Willow's bare legs and the loose shirt that skimmed her thighs. Interest stirred beneath the exhaustion. Willow watched her with quiet devotion, a steady adoration that pulled both satisfaction and a trace of amusement from somewhere deep.

During the height of their relationship, these evenings had become ritual. No orders, no discipline. Just Willow orchestrating every detail so that Blackburn could release the weight she carried. Willow's way of expressing loyalty was both efficient and precise.

Willow's grip remained steady as she drew Blackburn deeper into the house. Lavender and vanilla drifted through the air, the scent wrapping around them. The aroma softened the hard edges of Blackburn's tension.

They moved through the kitchen. Candlelight spilled from the living room, golden light trembling along the walls. On the cool marble island lay two collars: one white, one black. This was Blackburn's only decision tonight. Gentle or severe.

She weighed the options with a single glance. The black collar would demand more than her depleted reserves could give. She pressed her palms together as if to shed a memory that clung too close, then picked up the white collar and signaled Willow forward.

Willow stepped close, head bowed just enough to show respect without submission. Blackburn buckled the white collar around her neck. The gesture was smooth and silent. Soft leather pressed against Willow's throat. A familiar promise.

"I'm sorry I've caused you so many problems lately," Willow said. Her hands trembled once before she laced them together. "I never meant to." She brushed her cheek again, eyes fixed on the floor.

"I know you're sorry," Blackburn said. Her fingers worked deftly, adjusting the collar. "But you're leading me to places I don't want to go."

Willow met her eyes, holding back a question. Uncertainty flickered at the corner of her mouth.

"My jacket," Blackburn said, not meeting Willow's gaze. She shrugged it off and set her badge and gun on the kitchen island. The metal struck wood with a dull thud. With that small ritual, the day's violence slipped from her shoulders, replaced by the softer ache of longing. Without those markers, the room's atmosphere shifted, the air between them less charged.

Willow glanced at the serving tray nearby, its polished surface catching the overhead light. "I'll bring you some food and your wine after you settle," she said. She straightened her glasses, brushed her cheek as if resetting herself, then nodded toward the living room where warm candlelight beckoned. "I'd like to draw you a bath, Lioness." Her hand sought Blackburn's, fingers cool and seeking.

They crossed into the living room together. Blackburn paused, taking in the arrangement. LED candles burned steady on shelves and along the fireplace mantel, throwing amber shadows across neutral walls. The synthetic flames wavered convincingly. The effect was calculated comfort.

A single armchair anchored the center of the room, draped with a soft throw blanket. An extra cushion nestled against its back promised support and rest. Every element had been chosen for purpose.

"It's a movie night," Willow said, watching Blackburn closely for any sign of approval. Her hand hovered at her cheek again. Blackburn stepped forward and rested her palm there. A silent gesture, steady but firm. Willow's skin felt warm beneath her touch.

Despite everything weighing on her mind, Blackburn registered Willow's efforts. The pillows arranged just so, their corners aligned. The chair positioned for both intimacy and retreat. Willow had shaped this space with intent.

"Good. You ate the burger," Blackburn said.

"I did, Lioness. Thank you. It was perfect," Willow replied, her voice earnest and soft.

Willow lingered in front of her now, eyes fixed on Blackburn's reaction. The white collar caught a glint from one of the candles, its leather surface stark against her throat. Blackburn let her gaze rest on it before moving on.

Willow adjusted her glasses again and brushed her cheek. The moment stretched between them like a held breath. Measured, expectant.

"Well then," Blackburn said, voice steady, "let's not waste your efforts." She walked toward the bathroom, her movements precise. Willow followed, bare feet whispering against cool tile.

Willow's hands trembled as she undressed her domme. Blackburn stood motionless, granting her this moment. Willow drew down the zipper of Blackburn's pants and lowered them, folding the fabric with care before setting it aside.

She worked each button of Blackburn's shirt free. The garment slipped from broad shoulders, revealing skin bronzed and weathered. Willow's pulse quickened at the sight of strength held in reserve rather than displayed.

Kneeling, Willow eased down Blackburn's underwear.

Blackburn stepped free of the fabric. She met her own reflection in the mirror, jaw set, shoulders squared, claiming space with quiet defiance.

"May I kiss you, my Lioness?" Willow asked, her voice barely above a whisper.

"No, Fawn. But you may look."

The words were sparse. Willow absorbed every detail: the carved lines of muscle, the dark triangle below. Her breath hitched as a cool shiver traced up her spine. The bathroom's stillness pressed close, sharpening every sensation.

Blackburn watched her through the glass, reading the hunger and restraint written across Willow's features. She shifted her stance, drawing attention without words, asserting what belonged to her alone.

Willow's exhale came out ragged, a moth's wing against glass. The air between them had turned syrupy with something that wasn't quite desire. More like the sweet rot of fruit left too long in the sun. Her body betrayed her, nerves singing their ancient song of need and revulsion in equal measure.

Blackburn's hand found the back of Willow's skull. Not her head, but her skull, fingers mapping the bone beneath skin and hair with the clinical appreciation of someone who understood how easily things broke. The grip wasn't rough, but it held all the promise of roughness deferred. These were the hands that haunted Willow's fractured sleep, hands that knew exactly where the body kept its secrets.

Willow leaned in and took her taste. Brief, controlled, a hummingbird's sip of poison nectar. She kept her movements small, precise, even as something wild and famished clawed at her ribs from the inside.

The sound Blackburn made came from somewhere deeper than her throat. Approval braided with threat, the purr of a well-fed predator who might still bite for sport. Willow's body translated it instantly: *wait, want, ache.*

"You're beautiful," Willow said, her voice steady as a liar's heartbeat. The admiration was real; the steadiness was performance. "I want you. May I kiss you?"

"No." Blackburn's refusal landed clean as a scalpel cut. She shouldered past Willow and descended into the bath, water receiving her like a confessor. Heat bloomed across her skin in all the places Willow had marked with wanting. She sank deeper, vertebrae unclenching one by one, becoming something almost human in the steam.

Silence pooled between them until Willow's voice returned, smaller now, domesticated. "I rolled up a towel for you." She nestled the terry cloth behind Blackburn's head with the careful hands of someone defusing a bomb. "Would you like your wine? Something to eat?"

Blackburn's eyes stayed closed. She floated, fingertips breaking the surface in lazy circles that might have been ritual or might have been drowning in slow motion.

When Willow returned with wine, the glass catching light like a promise about to break. Blackburn dismissed it with a gesture that barely disturbed the water.

"Make me come, little Fawn." The words sliced through humid air, precise as surgery.

Willow's hand disappeared beneath the waterline like a secret being swallowed. Her fingers found Blackburn with the terrible certainty of magnetism, touch whispering at first, then speaking, then demanding as she learned the grammar of Blackburn's pleasure.

Blackburn's eyes opened, not snapped, nothing so dramatic But opened like wounds. Her palms found the porcelain's cool judgment as Willow's fingers wrote their careful violence underwater. Something lodged in her throat, a sound or a scream or a name. She swallowed it like medicine.

Neither spoke. The room held them in its amber light, two women reduced to breath and nerve and the ancient contract between hunter and hunted, though who was which kept shifting like smoke.

Blackburn's spine described an arc of surrender, hips canting upward to meet what Willow offered. Without thought, Willow matched her, fingers finding the frequency that made Blackburn's thighs tremble like a tuning fork struck true.

The bathroom became a chapel of silence punctuated only by water lapping porcelain, breath catching on steam, the small wet sounds of bodies telling truths that mouths couldn't shape.

When Blackburn came, it was with the quiet devastation of a star collapsing. Once, twice, the shudders moved through her like aftershocks before her body remembered how to be still. Their eyes met across the cooling water, Willow's wide with something between triumph and terror, Blackburn's already closing like doors.

"You handled yourself well, Fawn." The approval came in teaspoons, but Willow drank it like wine. Color bloomed across her cheeks, her body canting toward Blackburn like a plant toward terrible sun.

"Bring my robe." No question in it, just the expectation of obedience that ran between them like an underground river. Willow vanished into the bedroom while Blackburn rose from the water, a Venus born of porcelain and compromise. She toweled herself with efficient violence, erasing the evidence of vulnerability.

"Did my flowers arrive?" The question wore the mask of small talk, but they both knew better.

"Yes, Lioness. They're in a vase by the television." Willow hovered in the doorway, clutching the teddy bear like a child at the edge of a dark wood. "And the teddy? May I keep it?"

"We'll see." Blackburn let Willow dress her in silk, the robe sliding over damp skin like a new identity. Willow's fingers lingered at the belt, tying knots that had nothing to do with fabric.

The bath marked an ending neither would name. What had been absent pressed between them like a phantom limb.

Blackburn caught Willow's collar and pulled. Not rough, just inevitable. The leather had warmed to body temperature, become part of Willow's throat. Her fingers traced jawline to pulse point, reading the morse code of desire and dread.

"If you want to stop, or need space, you say so." She checked the collar's fit against the rabbit-quick heartbeat, then took Willow's mouth in a kiss that tasted like ownership. Slow, thorough, a claiming dressed as a gift. Willow's sound came from somewhere prehistoric, but her body stayed statue-still, only the tremor in her thighs betraying her.

Blackburn's palm found breast through fabric, thumb circling nipple with the dispassionate precision of someone taking inventory. She didn't stop until the kiss ended, leaving Willow gasping like something pulled from deep water.

"That will do," Blackburn said, stepping back with no trace of softness or edge. She moved to the armchair and took her time adjusting its cushions before sitting. The leather creaked softly as she settled in. The room's tension shifted with her movements.

"You've set up the movie?" She looked at Willow directly.

Willow nodded. "Yes. The Night Shadow of Harland Harbor." Her tone stayed light but hopeful. "Thought you'd like an old mystery."

Blackburn offered only a single nod of approval. On one table, sliced pears and aged cheese sat beside an untouched glass of wine, condensation beading on the crystal. The other table held an array of vibrators and remotes, their surfaces gleaming under the lamplight.

Willow started the film and glanced back for approval, eager beneath her restraint. "I want you to relax tonight, Lioness."

Blackburn reclined further into the chair. The leather molded to her form. Her posture radiated authority without effort. "Noted, Fawn. Serve well tonight."

"Of course, Lioness," Willow said. Her voice carried steady warmth, infused with a quiet loyalty. She liked when Blackburn called her 'little.' Others had spent years calling her big, heavy. Always behind forced smiles or in whispers meant to wound. Blackburn never spoke that way.

Willow's face brightened at the acknowledgment. She settled at Blackburn's feet carefully, arranging herself on the velvet cushions set out earlier. Candlelight warmed the room's edges, casting shadows that shifted with each flicker, holding just enough light for comfort without pretension.

The movie began, credits sliding across the screen in silence. Blackburn lifted her wine glass and took an unhurried sip, the burgundy liquid catching the light. Her eyes followed the movement rather than savoring the taste. She let her shoulders drop, tension easing from her spine. Willow watched every detail, alert to the subtle shifts in Blackburn's posture and breathing.

Blackburn sank back into her leather chair and drew the cashmere blanket over her legs. There was a pause. A silent acknowledgment of Willow's attention to small comforts. The food tray caught Blackburn's eye. She considered the arrangement of cheeses and fruit without comment.

Willow rested her head against Blackburn's knee, the warmth seeping through fabric. Blackburn's fingers found their way into Willow's hair, stroking once before giving a tug on the leather leash.

"Get my gun. And the cleaning kit." Blackburn's voice cut through the quiet, calm but clipped. "I want every trace of that bastard gone from it."

Willow's muscles tensed, breath catching in her throat as the meaning settled. Blackburn released a low laugh that rumbled from her chest.

"He's alive." The words came out with a wry edge. She thought about his broken pride, the tremor in his voice when he had realized she wouldn't let him off easy.

Blackburn looked down at Willow, her eyes turning flat and analytical as she reviewed what had happened.

"When I saw him on you," she said, "I lost it." Her fingers stilled in Willow's hair, grip tightening. "I pulled my weapon." A pause stretched between them while she shaped her hand into a gun and pressed two fingers to Willow's temple. The metal of her rings felt cold against skin.

"Gun to his head," she said, voice even but ice-cold now. Each word landed with precision. "Bam. Bam. Bam." Her fingers recoiled with each count, mimicking the weapon's kick.

Willow's body drew back, eyes searching Blackburn's face for the reassurance she needed.

"But... you didn't shoot," she managed, her voice barely above a whisper.

Blackburn gave a short laugh that echoed against the walls before dying in the corners.

"No shots fired," she said flatly. "I was so far gone I forgot the safety." Her second laugh came quieter. Frustration mixed with relief at her own mistake, the sound catching in her throat.

Willow exhaled, tension draining from her shoulders. The movie flickered on, its dialogue reduced to distant murmurs.

Blackburn traced the rim of her wine glass with steady fingers, the crystal singing faintly under her touch. "I switched from a Severn 22 to an MW1911 over a year ago. The MW has a safety." Her voice carried a clipped edge, each word precise. "I forgot. I don't pull my weapon in the field. Ever. But I forgot this time. That shouldn't happen." She paused, the muscles in her jaw tightening.

Willow watched her, letting silence fill the space. The unspoken consequences settled between them like smoke.

"I'm grateful," Willow said. She shifted closer, the leather couch creaking beneath her, urgency stripped down to its essence. "You could have pulled the trigger. You didn't." Her gaze held Blackburn's, unwavering. "If you had, they'd have locked you away. I'd have lost you."

She pressed her palm against Blackburn's knee, feeling the warmth through worn denim. "I know what that cost." Her voice emerged steadier now, but softer, barely above the hum of the television. The words lingered in the air between them, unresolved.

Chapter 12

Blackburn gazed down at Willow, her hand settling against the warmth of Willow's head. A brief softness displaced the usual hard focus in her eyes. The earlier misstep seemed irrelevant now.

"Get my gun and cleaning kit," Blackburn said. Her tone was level, direct.

Willow rose and crossed the room, her bare feet silent against the cool hardwood. She retrieved the kit from its usual place, the leather case worn smooth from handling, then moved to the table where Blackburn's gun waited. She picked it up with care.

She brought both items back, offering them to Blackburn, who accepted them with a nod.

Willow settled again by Blackburn's side, the carpet rough beneath her knees. The television filled the quiet with clipped lines from an old detective film, the silver light casting shifting patterns across the walls.

Blackburn leaned back, wine glass cradled in her hand. She drank without hurry, the burgundy coating her tongue. It took the edge off a long day.

Willow pressed close against Blackburn's legs, feeling the fabric of her slacks against her cheek. Her gaze moved between the television's flickering images and Blackburn's face, alert for any cue or command.

"Get to the gun, Fawn," Blackburn said. Her voice cut through the dialogue from the screen. "It needs to be clean."

While chaos played out on television, Willow focused only on her work. She handled each component with careful precision, every movement quiet. The solvent she used released a faint scent of citrus and herbs into the air.

Willow dismantled the weapon methodically, laying each part on the soft cloth. Barrel, slide, frame. Each piece received her full attention. Her expression remained calm but intent behind thick glasses as she examined every surface for residue or wear.

The citrus scent sharpened as Willow worked, cutting through the room's dim warmth. It clung to the candles, a clean note riding above the heat and the faint musk of leather from the nearby furniture. Blackburn breathed it in, letting the clarity settle over her nerves. She kept her eyes on Willow, attentive as always.

Willow moved with precision. Each gesture was steady and composed, the cleaning cloth tracing along the gun's cool frame. She pressed solution into the grooves without haste, the liquid seeping into metal crevices with a soft hiss. Her focus never wavered. Blackburn noticed how Willow's brow tightened in concentration, a subtle shift that changed the shape of her face and drew her features into sharper relief. There was an understated beauty in that focus.

The process unfolded quietly. Wipe, check, turn. Willow's hands worked methodically across the steel, her fingertips reading the surface like braille. The gun lay silent under her care, its weight shifting with every small adjustment. Blackburn watched this exchange and felt something build between them in the charged air. The energy was contained but unmistakable.

Blackburn spoke softly, her voice barely disturbing the stillness. "You do this well."

Willow paused just long enough to meet her gaze, her dark eyes catching the candlelight. "Thank you." Her reply was even, colored by respect but not need.

She returned to work without further comment. The room stayed quiet except for the faint whisper of cloth over metal and the occasional pop from a candle wick. Tension gathered between them like static before a storm, a current held under control.

Blackburn's attention lingered on Willow's posture, noting how she settled into her role without hesitation, her spine straight yet relaxed. Each movement was sure, the rhythm of her breathing steady, hinting at a deeper intimacy threaded through routine. The ordinary task took on weight in their silence, every detail heightened by restraint, the air growing thicker with each passing moment.

Blackburn watched Willow move, attentive to the small details. The subtle arch of her back caught the amber lamplight. Her shoulders stayed relaxed but precise. Each motion was deliberate as she disassembled the pistol and wiped down each piece. Shadows slid across Willow's arms and neck, the low light offering only hints of definition. The metallic click of components separating punctuated the silence. Blackburn tracked her progress without speaking.

The mood held steady, quiet but charged. The air between them thickened with unspoken understanding. Blackburn felt acknowledgment build, a warmth spreading through her chest that spoke more of respect than longing. Willow worked with careful hands, every gesture suggesting discipline rather than display. The way she handled the gun said everything: commitment, obedience, a willingness to meet exacting standards. Her fingers moved with the certainty of repetition, each surface cleaned until it gleamed.

When Willow finished, she laid out the cleaned parts for inspection. The components lined up with military precision. She met Blackburn's eyes and tilted her chin up. Pride flickered unspoken in the set of her jaw.

"I hope it's done properly," she said, holding up the polished barrel. Light caught its surface.

"It is," Blackburn answered. "Finish reassembly and secure it."

Willow nodded, quiet confidence in her movements as she put the gun together. Each piece clicked home with satisfying finality. She returned it to its case, the leather creaking softly as she closed the lid. When she came back across the room, her bare feet whispered against the hardwood. Blackburn addressed her in a low tone. "If you want to offer yourself, I'll know you're choosing this. If not, we stop now."

Willow paused. The air between them thickened, acquiring weight and texture. A smile flickered across her mouth, there and gone like a struck match, before she began undressing with the efficiency of someone who'd learned that hesitation was its own kind of lie.

The fabric whispered secrets as it left her skin. She unclasped her bra with the same clinical precision she'd shown dismantling the weapon, folding each piece beside her as if preparing evidence. The drawer's complaint was soft but accusatory as she retrieved the leash. Supple leather worn smooth by use, by need, by the particular arithmetic of their arrangement.

She approached Blackburn and knelt. The floor's chill traveled up through her knees like a confession.

"My leash, Lioness." The words emerged steady, but Willow heard the hairline fracture in her own voice, the place where want leaked through. Her palms opened like an offering, the leather dark against her skin.

Blackburn accepted it with the gravity of a sacrament. The familiar weight settled into her hand like coming home to a place that might kill you. She studied Willow's stillness. Not submission but something more complex, a conscious relinquishing that required its own kind of strength.

"Turn around."

Willow pivoted without hesitation. The lamplight turned her skin to amber and shadow, revealing the architecture of her desire in the subtle tension along her spine, the barely perceptible quickening of breath. She was naked in more ways than the obvious, stripped down to pure intent.

"Spread."

The word landed between them like a dropped stone. Willow's breath caught, a small hitch that betrayed what her posture wouldn't. She reached back, opening herself with the terrible honesty of someone who'd chosen this particular vulnerability. Blackburn leaned close enough that her exhale ghosted across exposed flesh, watching goosebumps rise like braille.

"Only if you want this." Quiet words, but they carried weight.

Willow's nod came sharp and certain. "Yes, Lioness. Please." The please scraped raw from her throat, all pretense abandoned.

Blackburn's mouth found that secret ring of muscle with precision. Willow's gasp fractured the silence. Not surprise but recognition, as if her body had been waiting for exactly this permission to unspool.

"Come here." Blackburn's thighs received the pat like punctuation.

Willow moved to straddle her with liquid grace, settling into the embrace as if into warm water. Their breathing tangled in the narrow space between them. When Blackburn kissed her temple, the gesture carried an unexpected tenderness that made Willow's chest tighten with something dangerously close to emotion.

"You listen well, Fawn." Approval threaded through the words like gold wire. "We're not finished."

The leash's tension sang between them. Willow arced back, her body becoming an instrument Blackburn knew how to play.

"I have a special treat for you." The whisper landed directly against Willow's ear, making her shiver with anticipation that had teeth.

They settled into temporary stillness, but it was the stillness of a held breath, of potential energy coiled tight. The television painted their bodies in shifting light while Willow's hands began their exploration, fingertips reading Blackburn's face like scripture, learning the topography of her with scholarly dedication. When she circled behind the chair, her palms found the locked muscles beneath Blackburn's shoulder blades, working them loose with kisses that felt like prayers.

"Lioness." The word vibrated against skin, a tuning fork struck.

"Yes, Fawn." Control wrapped around Blackburn's voice like armor, but Willow heard what lived beneath it.

"I want to please you. Show me how."

The toys arrayed on the table gleamed like possibilities. Willow's selection was deliberate. The purple vibrator sleek as a weapon. She prepared it with methodical strokes while Blackburn cataloged every movement, filing away the tells: how Willow's breathing changed when aroused, the specific angle of her wrist when she was trying not to tremble.

"Touch your clit with it. Slowly."

Willow's obedience came laced with visible effort. The first contact drew sounds from her throat that she couldn't quite swallow. Blackburn watched with the focused intensity of a chess player, noting how Willow's thighs developed a fine tremor, how her stomach hollowed with each careful breath.

"Inside now. Keep the arm positioned."

The vibrator's hum filled the space between them like a third presence. Willow's spine bowed at the sensation, her head falling back to expose the vulnerable column of her throat, an offering Blackburn filed away for later.

"Don't come yet." The warning carried weight. "You'll earn consequences."

Willow fought her own body with visible determination, riding the edge between control and chaos. Her knuckles blanched where they gripped the sheets, tendons standing out like accusations. When she finally begged, words tumbling over each other in their desperation, Blackburn delivered a precise slap to her thigh. The sound cracked through the room like punctuation.

Then silence. Blackburn killed the vibrator mid-crest, watching Willow's eyes fly open in shock, pupils blown black with interrupted pleasure.

"Ask properly."

"Please, Lioness." Willow's voice emerged roughened, scoured clean of everything but need. "Let me come for you. You decide when I let go. Please."

Another slap for begging, delivered with surgical precision. Then Blackburn was kneeling between Willow's spread thighs, studying the evidence of her arousal with clinical appreciation.

"Keep your eyes on me. I want to see you when you break."

She increased the vibrator's intensity incrementally, talking Willow to the edge with words chosen for their weight, their texture, their ability to sink hooks into flesh. Willow balanced on the precipice like a dancer on a blade, every muscle locked in exquisite tension.

"Come."

The command coincided with Blackburn's mouth finding its target. Willow shattered with the specific violence of something too long contained, her body writing its release across the sheets in a language only they understood.

Afterward, in the amber quiet, Blackburn gathered Willow against her. The silence between them hummed with frequencies only they could hear, promises written in the specific grammar of their need.

"You took that well." Blackburn smoothed damp hair back with unexpected gentleness. "Your control improves."

"This is yours," Willow breathed against her neck, and the words carried more weight than their simplicity suggested.

They existed in that moment like insects trapped in amber, perfectly preserved in their specific hunger, their particular damage, their exquisite understanding of exactly how much the other could bear.

The world beyond their cocoon pressed at the windows: the distant rush of tires on wet asphalt, the low groan of pipes settling in the walls. Morning would come soon enough, with its demands and questions, its cold light revealing everything left unsaid. For now, they lay suspended. Bodies cooling, breath slowing, the city's pulse returning to its usual, indifferent rhythm.

Somewhere, a phone buzzed. A reminder that the night's sanctuary was always temporary.

Chapter 13

Dawn pressed at the newsroom windows, indifferent to whatever kept her awake. Brynn Cassidy sat at her desk, the smooth pen between her teeth warming against her tongue as she turned possibilities over in her mind. The pen stilled. She considered which lead would matter most. Her fingers hovered above the keyboard, the keys cool beneath her fingertips. She pictured the moment a story broke. Her byline crisp in black ink, the ripple spreading across New Dresden like stones thrown in still water, a quiet current of satisfaction flowing through her chest.

She started typing.

The hidden cost of New Dresden's urban renewal: Displacement and gentrification

Corruption inside the department: Uncovering networks of kickbacks and silence

The opioid crisis: Following the supply chain from street corners to boardrooms

She let herself lean back, the chair creaking softly beneath her. These were stories with substance. Work that could shift something tangible, not just for her but for the city. Recognition was less important than getting it right.

A soft notification pulsed at the corner of her screen, its blue glow catching her peripheral vision. She frowned, noting the message labeled with encryption. Adrenaline prickled along her spine. She opened it.

An anonymous file-sharing link waited inside. No details, just a digital trail leading into deeper shadows. Brynn's hand hesitated over the mouse, her palm damp. This could be a tip. It could be provocation. The pull of curiosity won. She clicked through.

A video file loaded. Low resolution, the camera work unsteady and jerking. Around her, the newsroom kept moving, phones ringing and keyboards clattering, oblivious to what flickered on her screen. She plugged in her earphones, the foam tips muffling the ambient noise, before pressing play.

The image sharpened, the frame tightening until everything else fell away except a gloved hand hovering above a blank sheet. Brynn leaned forward, her breath catching. One letter at a time, cut from glossy magazines and pressed onto white paper, arranged with precision. The last piece slid into place. A hard black 'R' torn from newsprint, landing with finality.

The screen went dark. Brynn stared at her reflection in the black glass, searching for the composure she could barely feel beneath her quickening pulse.

The message read:

Brynn,

Enjoing the story? Its far from over. The streets are my playgrond, the cars my puppets. You think you'r clever, but you're just another useless pawn. Watch closely. The next move will be bold. Someone trusted technology to much. Will anyone be fast enough to save them?

The Phantom Driver

Brynn replayed the video, watching as the gloved hand entered the frame. A lighter flicked on, its small flame wavering before holding steady. The flame touched the paper's corner. Edges curled and withered, blackening as the sheet dissolved into ash that drifted like gray snow. In less than a minute, every trace had vanished. Nothing remained to examine or recover.

When the monitor went dark, Brynn caught her reflection in the black screen. Her features had drawn tight, eyes narrowed with a wariness that made her stomach clench. She sat motionless, letting the implications settle like cold water in her chest. The video was a message meant for her alone. Targeted. Personal. She was not a detective or analyst, only a reporter who now found herself standing on ground that shifted beneath her feet.

She released a slow breath, feeling the air leave her lungs as she steadied her tone. "Joseph," she called quietly at first, the name barely disturbing the office air, uncertain whether she wanted him to answer. She gathered herself, then raised her voice.

Joseph appeared at her side, hands buried deep in his pockets and gaze sharp with attention.

"What's wrong?" he asked.

Brynn lowered her voice to a murmur and cast a glance over her shoulder before replying.

"I received something from the autonomous car killer." She hesitated, her tongue touching her upper lip. "He's calling himself the Phantom Driver now. Sent it directly to me."

Joseph's expression tightened, the muscles along his jaw visible, but he waited for more.

Brynn recounted what she had watched: the burning, the message contained in that act. Each word left her mouth clipped and precise, tension pressed beneath every syllable onto her chest.

"We need to keep this safe," she said as her fingers flew across the keyboard to save the file. An error notification flashed red across the screen.

She tried again, jaw clenched hard enough to ache.

"It won't save."

Joseph withdrew his phone without a word, the device appearing smoothly in his hand.

"Play it again," he instructed, holding his camera steady on the monitor.

Brynn complied. Together they watched the sequence unfold once more. The hand destroyed evidence with quiet, methodical control.

When it ended, Joseph lowered his phone and gave a brief nod that barely disturbed the air.

"It's something," he said.

A flicker of relief crossed Brynn's face but faded like smoke.

"If they pull it or swap it later…" she started, then stopped as unease crept up her spine like cold fingers.

She turned to Joseph. Her voice dropped to barely above a whisper but carried an insistent edge.

"Did you hear him? How easily he dismissed everything I've reported?" She leaned close enough that the warmth of her breath would reach only Joseph. "He isn't just making threats. He's pulling us into whatever comes after this."

Joseph nodded, a tight crease cutting across his brow. The air in the newsroom had shifted, grown heavier. He spoke quietly. "The cars as puppets. He's controlling the autonomous vehicles. This is not just a message anymore, Brynn. We need to contact the police before someone gets hurt."

Brynn's fingers froze above her keyboard, suspended in the blue glow of her screen. She weighed the cost of action against instinct. "Hold on, Joseph. If we call them now, we lose our exclusive. Let me get the piece written first, then…"

Joseph's phone was already in his hand, the screen's light catching the hard set of his jaw. His voice carried finality. "This isn't about a story anymore. Someone could die." He dialed without looking at her, his thumb moving with certainty.

The newsroom's ambient chatter dimmed as she listened to the hollow ring of the line. Coffee makers gurgled in the distance. Keyboards clicked. But all of it fell away until only Joseph's voice remained.

"This is Joseph Halperin from New Dresden Today," he said when someone answered. "I need Detective Blackburn in homicide. It's urgent."

Brynn studied the subtle shift in his expression, watching resolve crumble into disappointment as he absorbed whatever came through the receiver.

"Understood," Joseph replied after a pause that stretched too long. "Could you have her call me or Brynn Cassidy when she's available? Yes. Voicemail is fine."

He left a concise message, his words clipped and professional, outlining what they knew while the LED lights hummed overhead.

A small flutter of relief moved through Brynn's chest as he ended the call. Their duty felt discharged, even as her thoughts circled back to what they might lose by moving too fast.

Joseph set his phone on the desk with care and met her eyes. The controlled tone couldn't mask the gravity beneath. "Now we wait."

Brynn nodded once, then turned back to her laptop. Her fingers found the keys again, typing with renewed urgency. The cursor blinked impatiently. She would hold the lead as long as possible, even if circumstances would soon force her hand.

* * *

Blackburn entered the New Dresden Today studios with steady purpose. Her arrival drew immediate attention from the staff, the rhythmic click of her heels cutting through the lively hum of newsroom chatter. The open-plan floor quieted as she passed, people pausing mid-conversation to track her movement across the polished concrete floor.

She found Brynn and Joseph positioned in front of a computer, their focus locked on the screen. Brynn's hands hovered near her keyboard, fingers trembling with barely contained energy. Joseph sat forward, his jaw clenched tight, a deep furrow carved between his brows as he stared at whatever held their attention.

Blackburn stepped into their line of sight. "I got your message, Joseph."

Brynn straightened in her chair, the leather creaking beneath her. "Detective," she said, her greeting clipped but threaded with tension. A few damp strands of hair stuck to her cheek, evidence of nervous fingers raking through it while they waited. The air between them crackled with professional restraint.

Blackburn nodded once, efficient and direct. "Let's see it."

Joseph pulled a second chair closer, its wheels whispering across the floor. His movements were controlled. "Brynn received an email early this morning," he explained. "It contained a link to a video."

Blackburn lowered herself into the seat without softening her posture. Her eyes tracked between the two journalists, cataloging every twitch and gesture, searching for signs of deception or omission.

Brynn positioned her hand on the mouse, leaning toward the monitor's blue glow to click on what should have been an active file. Instead, stark red text flashed across the screen: File not found.

"It was here five minutes ago," Brynn said, her voice dropping to barely above a whisper. She clicked again, the plastic mouse button snapping under her finger. She hammered several keys, each strike sharper than the last.

Blackburn's expression shifted minutely. Just the slightest tightening at the corner of her mouth. "How long was it live?"

Brynn's frustration manifested in white knuckles wrapped around the mouse. She drew in a breath before answering, but Joseph spoke first.

"I recorded it," he said simply. He retrieved his phone and navigated to the saved file with smooth precision.

Blackburn kept her gaze locked on the device as Joseph positioned it between them and tapped play. Her face remained a mask while the video unfolded. A gloved hand arranged cut-out letters beneath harsh LED lighting, each word revealed with calculated slowness. The distorted audio scratched through the phone's speaker, offering no hints about its creator or origin.

She absorbed every frame in silence, filing away details for later analysis. The serif font. The latex texture of the gloves. The grain of particle board visible behind the letterboard.

Her mind sorted through possibilities while her exterior remained stone. No performance here. Only cold observation.

The newsroom's ambient noise gradually filtered back into awareness as conversations resumed their natural flow. Blackburn let the silence stretch for several heartbeats after the video ended, creating space for thought before choosing her next move.

Blackburn sat motionless through the playback, offering nothing as the footage unspooled. Her silence pressed against the walls, thickening the air until each small sound became amplified. The hum of electronics. The creak of Joseph's chair. Brynn and Joseph shared quick, uncertain glances, their shoulders tensing beneath the detective's unwavering attention.

When the video ended on the burning sheet of paper, its edges curling into ash, Blackburn adjusted her position. Casual observation sharpened into something more precise. Her eyes traced the contours of Brynn's face, the nervous tap of Joseph's fingers, before settling back on the darkened screen.

"I'll need a copy," she said, her voice cutting through the quiet like cold water. She reached into her jacket, leather whispering against fabric, and produced a business card. The cardstock landed in Joseph's open palm with careful deliberation. He nodded once and bent to his phone, thumbs moving steadily across the glass surface as he prepared to send the file.

Brynn broke the silence first. The questions she had been holding burst free, tumbling over each other. "What do you make of this, Detective? Is it legitimate? Is there a link to the autonomous car crashes? Do you know who might be targeted next?"

Blackburn's gaze met hers without expression. The smallest movement at the corner of her mouth hinted at a reaction she would not verbalize. A tightening barely visible. "The investigation is active," she said, each word clean. "We're considering every possibility."

Brynn leaned forward, undeterred by the lack of specifics. "But there must be a lead," she insisted, her voice gaining heat with each syllable. "The message calls out technology directly. Is this about the Raider Group? Is someone in tech being singled out?"

Blackburn's spine straightened, her shoulders drawing back. Her tone remained smooth as polished stone. "All angles are under review. Our goal is to prevent any repeat incidents." Her eyes held steady on Brynn, cataloging details. The eager forward lean. The fingers that had danced across keyboards to manipulate GPS systems. The wariness that flickered whenever she mentioned police. All noted. All filed away.

Before Brynn could press again, Blackburn raised a hand. The gesture cut through the space between them with surgical precision. "Thank you for reporting this," she said, her voice cooling another degree. "If anything else comes your way, contact me immediately. We will follow up if there are further questions."

Joseph finished sending the file and lifted his head toward Blackburn. She acknowledged him with a brief nod before turning toward the door, her footsteps deliberate against the floor, each one marking her controlled exit.

Brynn caught the opening and seized it. Her question cut through the newsroom's ambient chatter, crisp and precise. "Detective, is there an ongoing threat to public safety? Should people be cautious with autonomous vehicles?"

Blackburn stopped at the threshold, fingers curling around the cold door handle. She turned her head, eyes flat as slate. "We encourage everyone to remain alert and report anything out of the ordinary," she said, each word measured. The LED lights hummed overhead during her pause. "Do you know how many autonomous vehicles are registered in this state? Take care."

She pushed through the door without another word. The room settled into thick silence as the door swung shut behind her.

Brynn met Joseph's gaze. Both weighed the void Blackburn had left behind.

"We should find out how many autonomous vehicles there actually are," Brynn said, already turning back to her monitor. The screen's blue glow washed over her face.

Joseph lingered beside her desk, coffee mug warm between his palms. His voice dropped to a skeptical murmur. "You think that's more than misdirection? Feels like she's pushing us in circles."

Brynn tightened her jaw and attacked the keyboard. Database windows multiplied across her screen as she hunted through state records.

Joseph shook his head once and drifted away, leaving Brynn bathed in monitor light, fingers flying as she pursued this new lead.

Chapter 14

Blackburn stood at the head of the homicide division's main conference table, her posture still and assured. The detectives arrayed before her waited, some already scratching notes into their pads, eyes tracking her smallest gesture.

She grabbed a pen, and twirled it for moment before dropping it. It rolled behind her. She turned, keeping her back to Sinclair, and bent to retrieve it. The fabric of her pants stretched taut. "Clumsy me," she said without inflection. Behind her, Sinclair coughed.

Willow sat to one side, shoulders curved inward as she worked the laptop, connecting it to the projector. The only sounds in the room were the soft scrape of chair legs against linoleum and the steady mechanical hum of the air system overhead. The LED panels above cast everything in harsh relief: bleached faces, shadowed eyes, nowhere to conceal fatigue or distraction.

"I've called this meeting for a specific reason," Blackburn said. Her voice carried weight without urgency. "You are about to watch a video sent to Brynn Cassidy at New Dresden Today." She held each detective's gaze in turn, noting who tensed and who glanced away. "What you are about to see is not the original. This copy was recorded on Brynn's end after she received a link, but that link is now down."

She crossed to the far wall and clicked off the lights. The room settled into dimness, the projector's blue wash filling the space where daylight had been.

Willow gave a small nod and pressed play. The room stilled. The video spread across the wall in grainy resolution: a gloved hand slid into frame, hovering above a sheet of paper. No distinguishing marks showed through the leather. Nothing suggested gender or age. The background remained deliberately empty, just void and shadow.

The hand held position while text became visible on the page. Then it brought a lighter to the paper's edge and orange flame devoured the words before anyone could read them. The fire bloomed bright for seconds, then left only charred fragments. When the screen finally went dark, the silence stretched taut.

Blackburn switched the overheads back on. The sudden glare revealed little in their faces beyond exhaustion.

"Thoughts?" Her question settled between them without demand.

No one responded immediately. Bodies shifted in seats, each detective turning the footage over privately, separate from their colleagues.

Hayes broke the quiet with a sharp exhale. "We're being baited." He dragged his palm across his scalp, pressing thoughts into order. "If this gets out before we understand what we're facing, every reporter in the city will spin their own version." His jaw tightened, skin flushing pink at the edges.

Blackburn turned to where Willow still hunched over her laptop, the cursor pulsing in an empty search field.

"Any metadata left on that file?"

Willow adjusted her glasses and squinted at the display. "Nothing useful," she said, her voice barely carrying. "Since it's just a recording of Brynn's playback, any original digital signatures are gone." She clicked through directories, checking for overlooked details. "But you said it was accessed twice before vanishing?"

Blackburn nodded once. "First when Brynn opened it, second when her cameraman captured this copy."

Willow's brow creased as she processed this. "That's strange," she murmured. "Most self-deleting links disappear after one view if they're programmed that way." She stilled, hands resting on the keys while she worked through possibilities. "Someone had to remove it manually after that second access."

Hayes leaned forward from his position near the table's far end. "Explain."

Willow lifted her gaze, speaking steadily but low enough that the others shifted closer to hear.

"If you wanted to remain untraceable online, you would never risk returning to your own server." She checked Blackburn's expression before proceeding. "Anyone planning ahead would assume Brynn might copy what she receives or alert us before viewing." She drummed her fingertips lightly against the laptop's edge. "Going back to delete it creates opportunities for accidental exposure. That kind of error doesn't match someone who understands digital concealment."

She trailed off, suddenly aware that every detective had focused on her. They anticipated more or perhaps were startled by the length of her analysis.

"And the video vanishes just as I'm about to view it. Convenient, isn't it?" Blackburn rested her hand on Willow's shoulder. The warmth of her palm seeped through fabric, and the tension knotted in Willow's muscles slowly unwound.

Silence settled over the table like dust. Hayes shifted in his chair, leather creaking beneath him, his discomfort visible in the rigid set of his jaw and the restless twitch threading through his mustache.

Cooper leaned forward, determination carved into every line of his posture. "What concerns me is the risk of another victim," he said. His voice stayed even, but urgency ran beneath it like an underground current. The detectives glanced at one another, weighing his words in the LED-lit quiet.

Reeves cleared his throat, the sound rough in the stillness. A new furrow creased his weathered face as he frowned. "Or it could be a distraction," he said, voice scraped raw by years on the job. "Suppose the killer wants us fixated on the car while something else is in motion?"

Sinclair shifted and hesitated, unease drawing fresh lines around his mouth. He chose his words like a man picking his way across thin ice. "Should we talk about warning people off autonomous vehicles?" Worry colored his tone, quiet but unmistakable.

Blackburn regarded him for a moment before speaking. "It's an option." Her fingers grazed Sinclair's shoulder as she moved past him, the touch brief and grounding.

"No." Hayes cut in before anyone could respond further. His frown carved deeper grooves into his face as he leaned onto the table, elbows planted like stakes. "Not yet." His voice retained its sandpaper authority. "The last thing we need is public panic."

He paused, eyes tracking across the team before adding with exhaustion fraying his edges, "Are we even sure this threat is real?"

Blackburn raised her hand and the room stilled, air growing dense with anticipation. Every face turned toward her like flowers following the sun.

"This is staged," she said. Her tone left no space for doubt. "We're missing key details." She met each gaze with the steadiness of polished stone. "No actual offender sits down to cut out ransom-note letters anymore. It's inefficient. Pure invention for film or television."

A few detectives exchanged glances. Some colored with embarrassment, others sharpened by focus. Sinclair's optimism dimmed beneath a fresh crease etching his brow.

Blackburn continued with surgical precision. "And those misspellings? Whoever wrote this wanted us to believe they're uneducated, but there's nothing sophisticated behind it." Her attention found Willow at the far end of the table. "You called it. Said any script kiddie could pull this off?"

Willow straightened at the prompt, electricity flickering behind her lenses as she found solid technical ground beneath her feet. "Yes," she said, certainty strengthening her voice now that familiar territory had opened before her. "Anyone willing to experiment with search terms could manage it with enough tries."

Blackburn nodded, a trace of approval flickering across her expression. "So why would someone with digital skills bother with an old, conspicuous tactic? It feels unsophisticated for a person capable of scripting all this. The methods do not match the skills supposedly needed to build this from the ground up."

Reeves spoke next, his voice carrying the dryness of old paper. "And why go for such an obvious alias? 'The Phantom Driver' is predictable. If they wanted to stay in line with their strengths, you would expect something like 'Ghost in the Machine.'"

Sinclair leaned forward, the leather of his chair creaking beneath him, eager for a foothold in the discussion. "What's that supposed to mean?" he asked, interest brightening his voice.

Blackburn allowed herself a slight smile, the corners of her mouth barely lifting. "That proves my point," she said. Reeves acknowledged her with a nod, his eyes catching the LED light overhead.

She turned to Willow. "Are you able to work with Brynn on finding the source video? Can you examine the email, trace back to the site it was hosted on?"

The sound of Brynn's name drew a visible reaction from Willow. Her posture stiffened like a wire pulled taut, and her hands shook against the table's cool surface, though she managed a silent nod without looking up. The room quieted. The soft hum of the air conditioning suddenly became audible as others sensed her discomfort.

A memory surfaced in Blackburn's mind: Brynn's dismissive phone call to Willow before any of this had unfolded. The way Willow had been left raw and exposed afterward lingered at the edge of Blackburn's thoughts, an instinctive urge to shield her pressing against her ribs.

Blackburn adjusted her approach, her voice softened like fabric smoothed by careful hands. "Actually, form a team for this. Let Freddie handle Brynn and everything that involves her. You focus strictly on the digital evidence. The email itself, anything technical."

Willow's relief was immediate. She exhaled slowly, the breath leaving her as if she had been holding it underwater, shoulders dropping as she dared a brief look at Blackburn, her eyes glassy with unshed gratitude.

"I'll give it everything I have," Willow said, her voice steadier now, finding its footing. "But these file-sharing sites on the dark web are tough for law enforcement to breach. There may be leads we cannot follow."

"You need to try," Blackburn replied quietly, letting each word settle between them like stones dropped in still water. "What you can do is all I ask." She paused, the silence stretching before adding, "I still think this video is staged." She let that sit for a moment, watching it ripple through the room. "It fits too neatly. A ready-made stunt when our suspect has otherwise been careful and invisible. Why suddenly risk exposure with something so conveniently dramatic?"

Hayes watched her, impatience tightening his features until the lines around his mouth deepened. "If it's not real," he said, his voice low and irritable, scraping like sandpaper, "what's the point of bringing in another tech person? Willow should manage it herself."

Blackburn straightened, her spine aligning as her tone turned clipped and precise. "Willow designed that flowchart behind you." She gestured toward the crowded board on the wall, its surface dense with colored markers and connecting lines. "It gave us our theory that Brynn could be involved." Her gaze held steady on Hayes, unwavering as a locked door. "But Willow isn't an investigator by training and she is not skilled at keeping sensitive information contained." Her words were final, each one placed deliberately. "She should not have any direct contact with Brynn."

Hayes's face darkened, the skin beneath his mustache pulling taut with irritation. He pointed at Blackburn, his voice cutting through the low electrical hum that filled the room. "This is exactly the kind of stunt these people pull. All for attention, all about making us look foolish. We need a real detective on this, not technical support. No offense, Willow."

Willow kept her gaze fixed on the scratched surface of the table. "None taken," she replied, her voice flat.

Blackburn felt quiet relief wash through her, knowing Willow would not have to endure Brynn Cassidy's theatrical posturing. She had no patience for it.

"I'll put Reeves on it," Blackburn said, her eyes moving across her team before settling on him. "He can handle Brynn and the video. It landed in her lap, and frankly, this reeks of imitation or maybe even a ploy for coverage."

Reeves offered a thin smile, shoulders lifting in a casual shrug. "On it."

Hayes looked as if invisible wires had pulled him tighter, his voice fraying at the edges. "You think this reporter cooked up a story? That's a reach. The mayor is pushing to bring in the FBI again." His words tumbled out too fast, betraying the nerves he struggled to conceal.

Blackburn glanced at Willow. Willow hunched over her keyboard, jaw set hard in concentration.

"That Banks guy was useless when he showed up last time," Blackburn said, arms folding tight across her chest. "You don't want more of that circus."

"The mayor wants it," Hayes said, each word bitten off.

Blackburn drew in a slow breath. "How does the mayor already know about this video?" Her words came out calm but carried unmistakable anger.

Hayes hesitated just long enough to betray himself. He cleared his throat, a rough sound in the quiet room, and his eyes slid away. "That's not important right now." His tone had lost its earlier grip.

"Handing this video to the FBI would make us look incompetent," Blackburn replied, her voice steady as stone. "It's a recording sent to a third party who already figures in our case file. It isn't evidence. They'd see right through it."

Hayes shifted in his seat, a thin sheen of sweat breaking along his brow as he met Blackburn's stare for only a heartbeat before his gaze skittered away again.

"It's what the mayor wants," Hayes repeated, uncertainty seeping into every syllable, undermining whatever authority remained.

Blackburn leaned forward across the table, her expression carved from ice. "And what does the mayor think federal agents are going to find in that video?" Her tone stayed flat but carried an edge of dismissal.

Hayes's hand clenched into a fist and struck the table once. The sound cracked through the air, sharp enough to freeze everyone in place but controlled enough to avoid true loss of composure. "To solve the murder!" His shout hung suspended for a moment before dissolving into uncomfortable silence.

Blackburn's eyes tracked him from beneath lowered lids as she eased back, letting a pause stretch between them that nobody rushed to fill.

"You may be onto something, chief." Blackburn's tone shifted, mild and unhurried. "The Bureau could be useful, though I am not sure it's for the reasons we first imagined."

Hayes frowned. The flush drained from his face, giving way to muted curiosity. "Explain."

Blackburn leaned forward, her voice dropping just enough to draw the group closer. The LED lights hummed overhead as she spoke. "They have the resources we lack. Their lab can analyze the gloves, trace the paper stock, identify where that lighter was manufactured. They might narrow it by region and batch. They could even determine the origin point for those letters." She tapped a finger against the polished table surface, slowly. "That kind of detail could reveal where this video came from."

The words settled over the room as everyone absorbed them. Sinclair's eyes brightened with recognition. Cooper and Reeves exchanged brief nods across the table.

"If we identify who sent the video," Blackburn continued, her tone calculated, "we could bring criminal interference charges at minimum. Even if it fails to unravel everything, it would pressure whoever is involved. That alone merits pursuit."

Hayes's shoulders dropped an inch. The rigid line of his jaw softened as he considered her suggestion.

Blackburn edged her voice toward reassurance without losing authority. "You are right, chief. Sending this to the Bureau makes sense. They will know how to handle it." She kept her gaze steady on him, careful not to overplay her hand.

The tension leaked from Hayes's posture. He nodded once. "All right. Yes." His voice found its footing. "Let's get them involved."

Blackburn allowed herself a subtle smile. Nothing more than a slight lift at the corner of her mouth. She noted her team's response. She had maintained control without drawing attention to it.

Blackburn turned to Willow without ceremony. "Find our Bureau contact and ensure this reaches their forensic analysis division directly."

Willow glanced up from her screen, meeting Blackburn's eyes with a flicker of understanding. "I'll handle it," she said.

The meeting dissolved with quiet efficiency. Chairs scraped against linoleum. Notebooks snapped shut. Low voices traded next steps about federal involvement. Hayes rose first, his movements less rigid than they had been that morning.

He paused at the door, fingers curled around the cold metal knob. "One more thing," he said, his voice steadier now. "Banks will not be working this investigation anymore. He had some kind of accident. He'll be out for a while."

Blackburn's gaze dropped to her hands for just a moment. Something flickered behind her eyes. Her expression remained composed.

Cooper reclined in his chair and delivered a dry shrug. "He never contributed much," he said, his voice flat, eyes fixed somewhere above Willow's head. "Spent most of his time watching Willow's computer screen anyway."

At the mention, Willow's fingers tightened against her laptop's edge. The only sign of reaction. She kept her eyes trained on the glowing display.

Blackburn waited for the room to settle before speaking again, her voice as level as glass. "It is for the best," she said simply. "We lack evidence solid enough for terrorism charges regardless."

Hayes departed first, followed by Blackburn and then Reeves. Cooper trailed behind Sinclair through the doorway. Willow closed her laptop with a soft click and followed last. Each exit in order. The hierarchy observed without need for words.

* * *

The auditorium held the sharp scent of floor polish and nervous sweat. Straight-backed chairs lined up before a modest stage where the department's banner hung, its gold and blue dulled by LED overhead lighting. Families and officers filled the rows, their voices an indistinct murmur punctuated by the occasional scrape of chair legs against linoleum.

Paula Court sat with her husband and child. A neat line of stitches traced down her cheek to her jaw, the skin around them still faintly purple. She had saved a boy from a dog attack and was still home on medical leave. Her husband's hand rested on her knee, his thumb moving in small circles while their child wriggled in his seat, too young to understand why people's voices dropped when they passed.

Near the front, Watson and DeForest sat together in freshly pressed uniforms that still carried the chemical tang of dry cleaning. Surrounded by a cadre of other patrol officers all chatting in whispers.

Reeves, Cooper, Sinclair, and Willow sat together on the side, orbiting around Blackburn. Blackburn glanced at her watch. The program was already running late.

Ahmed El-Masir's wife sat rigidly in the center aisle with both children pressed against her sides. The younger one buried his face in her sleeve. The older fixed his gaze straight ahead, his small hands clenched in his lap. She was surrounded by extended family and community members. Older women in modest dress who kept watchful eyes on the children, men in dark suits who had positioned themselves protectively around the group, and several younger couples who leaned forward attentively whenever she shifted or the children moved. No one spoke, but their presence formed a quiet fortress of support around her grief.

A block of seats near the back held a collection of young men and women in crisp business attire: navy suits, pressed shirts, conservative ties and blouses that spoke of corporate dress codes. They sat with the careful posture of people attending a company function, tablets and phones discretely silenced but visible. A few whispered occasionally to each other, gesturing subtly toward the stage. These had to be employees from Halperin's company, here to honor Lilith Halperin and the police who had tried to save her.

A muted ache formed beneath Blackburn's ribs. She shifted in her dress blues, the stiff fabric creaking, and focused on the rows of heads before her.

Ten minutes later, Deputy Chief McLaughlin's heels clicked across the stage as she approached the podium. Her voice cut through the ambient noise, each word precise as she moved efficiently through the formalities. She surveyed the audience without pause or recognition of Blackburn.

The photographer worked: click, move, click, move.

"Our first award recognizes uncommon courage," McLaughlin announced, her tone businesslike. "Detective First Class Morgan Blackburn acted at personal risk to rescue two civilians trapped in a malfunctioning autonomous vehicle."

Blackburn stood and walked down the aisle toward the stage. Her shoes struck the floor in beats. From the platform she caught sight of Ahmed's wife, her composure crumbling as tears tracked down her cheeks. She drew her children closer, their small bodies trembling against hers. Blackburn's jaw tightened. She turned her eyes forward.

McLaughlin revealed a velvet box, the medal inside catching the harsh stage lights, then read the official citation: "For conspicuous bravery and selfless commitment to protecting human life..." The words dissolved into white noise. Blackburn maintained careful poise while memories pressed against the edges of her control.

"Detective Blackburn." McLaughlin extended both hands with the medal.

Blackburn met her gaze directly. Her chin lifted, spine straight. She purposely arched her back, sticking her chest out. Their eyes locked briefly. McLaughlin's mouth tightened with impatience while Blackburn's expression remained steady, almost serene.

After a moment, McLaughlin stepped forward to pin the medal on Blackburn's chest. The pin caught on the thick fabric. "Congratulations, Detective." The words were clipped, professional.

"Thank you, ma'am." Blackburn's response matched the tone as she raised her hand in salute.

Applause swelled through the room. Ahmed's wife wept openly now, her shoulders shaking while her older child reached across to grip her arm. The photographer shifted near Ahmed's family, then quietly redirected his camera toward the stage.

Blackburn gave McLaughlin a single nod before descending to rejoin her colleagues.

Reeves was first to greet her, his applause loose and genuine. Sinclair's fingers brushed her shoulder, the touch brief but warm. Willow offered a small smile while Cooper clapped near her ear, the sharp sound making her wince.

DeForest received his own medal next, followed by Court. Each name brought another wave of applause and the rapid clicking of the camera as families leaned forward or hushed restless children.

Afterward, McLaughlin delivered closing remarks about duty and sacrifice, her words echoing in the high-ceilinged space. The audience gathered belongings, voices rising as families converged around the honored officers.

Blackburn lingered near Reeves and Willow as crowds filtered toward the exits. Ahmed's wife gathered both children, pausing to catch Blackburn's eye. Her lips formed silent words of gratitude before she guided her family away.

"Drinks?" Reeves asked, tugging at his collar. "Feels like we've earned them."

"We?" Blackburn asked with a smile.

"I meant to say we've earned the right to buy them for you," Reeves laughed and stuck his finger up briefly. He could get away with it, once in a while.

Blackburn agreed readily, grateful for something uncomplicated after the weight of the ceremony. "Lead on."

They moved with the crowd toward the doors while Willow walked beside Blackburn, their shoulders nearly touching.

"I saw that," Willow said under her breath.

A brief smile crossed Blackburn's face. "You always do."

They stepped into the afternoon sunlight together, leaving the ordered rows of empty chairs behind.

Chapter 15

Forensic photographs lay scattered across Blackburn's desk. The window caught the hour in its reflection: 4:37 AM. She had stopped marking time. Somewhere after the third autopsy, maybe the seventh crime scene photograph, her sense of chronology dissolved.

Lilith Halperin's face gazed up from a glossy sheet. The 'before' image, cataloged for evidence. Blackburn left the 'after' untouched for now. Even in this frozen moment, Lilith's presence clung to the room. High cheekbones caught the desk lamp's glare, eyes that measured life with joy. She had built her cosmetics empire by promising reinvention; now, that talent for transformation served only as identification.

Blackburn traced the photograph's edge with her fingertip. She remembered Halperin at board meetings, voice cutting through opposition like silk through air, yet privately drawn to submission. Always scripting her own story, until two hundred feet of empty air and unyielding concrete erased it.

Ahmed El-Masri hadn't fared as well. At least Lilith's remains could be called human.

The impact summary pressed cool beneath her palm. Guardrail: twenty-five years old, rust eating through steel like cancer. Soil destabilized long before midnight. Breach at twenty-seven miles per hour. Angle: forty-seven degrees. Three point two seconds from launch to ground.

Numbers reduced catastrophe to calculation.

Fragments of memory surfaced. Tires shrieking against asphalt, brake lights painting the night red, the cab ignoring signals while dispatch crackled through static.

"Unit in pursuit of malfunctioning autonomous vehicle. Requesting backup."

Malfunction sounded clinical enough to contain the fear. But she understood better than most what that word concealed. She had pressed her palm against the chassis where the cab went over the edge. The metal had felt wrong beneath her fingers. This wasn't a mechanic's error. It felt deliberate.

Coffee cups cluttered her workspace, their contents cold at varying depths in their descent from hot to useless. The closest one sat untouched, a skin forming on its surface.

Movement flickered at the door. Cooper entered silently with fresh coffee, steam curling from the cup as he set it beside her keyboard without comment.

"Forensics just posted the Chandworth ballistics," he said, voice low.

She nodded once, gratitude and acknowledgment compressed into the gesture. Three years like this. Early mornings, bitter coffee burning their throats, crime scenes flickering on screens. A routine against disorder.

Cooper retreated to his cubicle beyond the glass wall dividing them from homicide's common floor. She watched his reflection settle in and begin sorting reports as overhead lights stuttered to life across the bullpen. The elevator doors slid open on new arrivals.

Blackburn scrolled through the Event Data Recorder analysis again: acceleration curves climbing like fever charts, GPS tracks threading through city streets, cell ping logs marking final moments. The braking pattern made no more sense than Kendria's case had.

That name sliced through fatigue. She unlocked her drawer and retrieved Kendria's file. The pages felt soft at their edges from weeks of examination, creased where she had pressed too hard searching for answers that refused to surface.

She arranged both EDR reports side by side on her desk.

Two cars had experienced identical failures.

Both transformed from benign machines to instruments of death in seconds.

Their digital footprints defied conventional explanation or mechanical fault.

Her inbox chimed. A new message from Reeves glowed on the screen: *NDCC interview set for 2 PM. Legal bringing two attorneys. Are you joining?*

She typed without hesitation: *I'll review the transcript within an hour of finish time.*

Denials from the cab company's lawyers read no differently than Stan Raider's own script. They would guard their code, shields raised, while women died inside cars built to protect them. The investigation circled, always tight and fruitless. Evidence locked behind corporate walls. Truth stored in servers she could not access. Warrants remained just out of reach.

A Chandworth notification glowed in her inbox. She opened it and watched PDF pages materialize on the screen: ballistics confirmation. Both casings, same weapon. A Trust 19, common enough to mean little on its own. But the second casing, the one she had collected, offered more. A partial print, run through AFIS and narrowing to ninety-eight matches.

Ninety-eight names. Ninety-eight possible suspects.

She scrolled through the list. Each name came with a summary that read like violence distilled into data points. Carjackings, aggravated assaults, rape convictions. Men whose brutality formed patterns, not aberrations. The algorithm sorted them by probability, location history, prior charges. Useful but insufficient. A machine couldn't sense the shift in air when guilt entered a room or catch the flicker behind a suspect's eyes at the sound of his own name.

She pared the list herself, focusing on those whose movements and history intersected with Chandworth's world. Seven names rose to the surface, each one carved onto her legal pad in sharp, precise strokes:

Miguel Flores
Darwin Santana
Carlos Restrepo
Terrell Washington
Isaiah Hutt

Luis Medina

Damon Price

Miguel Flores. Age fifty-two. Armed robbery, distribution, aggravated assault. Blackburn studied his latest booking photo, the harsh LED lighting carving deep shadows beneath his eyes. Out on bail with an ankle monitor and confined to his residence. She exhaled quietly, the sound barely disturbing the stale office air, and dialed his probation officer. The phone rang four times before clicking to voicemail. She left a message requesting the status of any possible violations, her fingers already scratching his name off the list.

She loaded Santana's arrest record. The system churned, pixels assembling slowly into his criminal history: distribution, assault, weapons charges. A predictable progression. Then a line that stilled her hand above the notepad.

Aggravated assault.

Victim: Cole Chandworth. May 15th, two years ago.

Air left her lungs in a controlled release.

Santana had shattered Chandworth's orbital bone with a rock over three thousand dollars in drugs. Eighteen months served. Debt likely never paid. Violence as ledger entry.

She called up Santana's booking photo: thirty-four years old, Hispanic, five foot eleven. An unremarkable face except for the eyes. Flat and accepting, the look of a man who viewed jail time as operating cost.

Recognition settled into her bones with a predator's certainty. This was her man. The partial print would fit. DNA would follow once they had it on file. Science would confirm what her instincts already knew: Chandworth had been marked since that assault. Santana had returned to collect.

Satisfaction arrived cold and clean, sharpening her senses by degrees rather than flooding them. She leaned back in her chair and let the quiet surge of accomplishment spread beneath her skin.

Through the glass wall she caught Sinclair's approach, coffee in hand and intention written in every step. His daily ritual that he mistook for intimacy.

She made her decision as his hand reached for the door.

Her fingers found her shirt's top button and eased it open. Not hurried or coy but deliberate enough to register at twenty feet.

Sinclair entered without waiting for permission, his gaze landing exactly where she had guided it.

"Getting warm in here," she said. Her voice held neither welcome nor warning, just possibility hanging in the space between them.

She watched him swallow, eyes tracking the hand that drifted to his pocket. A reflex. Men always gave themselves away in small movements when instinct outpaced thought. Heat crept up his neck, darkening the skin above his collar.

"Had an odd dream about you last night," she said, shifting just enough for her shirt to pull taut across her chest.

His breathing quickened. The hand in his pocket moved with a familiar rhythm, fingers working against fabric. She could almost taste the shift in his pulse, the sharp edge of arousal cutting through his cologne. Young men never realized how visible their secrets were, each desire telegraphed by a twitch or glance.

"Brought you coffee," he said, extending the cup with forced steadiness.

She nodded toward the other cup beside her monitor. "Already covered."

The words stopped him cold. Jealousy flashed across his face, quick and raw and ugly. Not just rejection, but the knowledge that Cooper had moved first. Cooper had anticipated her needs while Sinclair arrived late and empty-handed in every way that mattered. His jaw tightened as he struggled to compose himself.

He left without another word and dropped the coffee into her waste bin. The sound rang sharp and final through the quiet office.

He disappeared into the washroom. Shoulders rigid, movements clipped by frustration and need. She knew exactly how he would spend the next few minutes, what images he would conjure for relief. The thought settled in her chest like armor. Predictable men powered by hunger and habit.

She smiled, a controlled gesture that never touched her eyes. Let him have his solitary mercy behind a locked door where every fantasy drew him deeper into her orbit. The GPS tracker he had hidden under her car weeks ago had already told its story. His obsession was neither new nor subtle. She wondered how many boundaries he would cross before she decided to intervene.

That question lingered as she returned to the case files. Now it carried more weight than before. He had been following her longer than she realized. Possibly since before Jenna.

Jenna and Kendria for certain. Lilith? If he was still watching, he would have known about Lilith too. The pattern felt less like coincidence than intention.

She pushed the theory aside for now and turned back to the Chandworth paperwork. Darwin Santana's warrants for search, cell records, and arrest were all properly constructed and justified.

She blinked twice and picked up her pen again. EDR data had tracked cell tower pings for cabs from The Roche and New Dresden companies. Routine details she had logged but not examined closely enough.

If Keiran Mott needed to be within twenty feet of his prototype for remote control, what if their killer worked under similar constraints? Maybe it was not some faceless operator halfway across the globe. Maybe it was someone close by.

Her pulse quickened fractionally as she considered it. Every phone near those vehicles at each incident would have pinged the same towers at those times. She just needed to cross-check cell records and find which number appeared at each kill site during every window when a car went rogue.

She could add the car used to kill Jenna Langston. The data was missing, but she had the location and time. The killer hadn't bothered with subtlety. The vehicles broadcast their positions all along.

She drafted cell tower warrants for every site, widening her net through the airwaves for whoever had controlled those cars. The printer whirred to life. Pages slid out warm against her fingertips, edges crisp as new bills. She held each sheet to the light, checking for clarity. A single smudge could stall justice. Any flaw might give someone an escape route.

By now, the courthouse would be running at full speed. Judge Morrison would be between hearings at 10:15. She kept a map of every judge's habits filed in her head. Morrison rarely hesitated when she brought solid evidence wrapped in clean packaging.

The elevator carried her down to street level, cables humming overhead. Four warrants meant four new lines of attack. By nightfall, she expected Santana in custody and more digital evidence to comb through for mistakes.

Outside, New Dresden's morning traffic edged forward in slow, predictable patterns. Autonomous cabs glided past, their chrome surfaces catching fragments of sky. Potential weapons dressed as transport. Each passenger sat cocooned in false safety, whether they knew it or not. Darwin Santana was out there somewhere, moving through his final hours of freedom.

And servers stored everything, humming quietly in climate-controlled rooms with answers about who had taught these machines how to kill.

The courthouse waited on the next block, limestone walls the color of old bones in the gray morning light. Gargoyles perched above, faces smoothed blank after decades of rain and wind. The steps ahead rose steep and official, promising nothing except due process.

Or something colder.

Blackburn tucked the warrants inside her jacket, feeling their weight against her ribs.

Time to collect what was owed.

Chapter 16

Sirens wailed in the distance, their pitch rising and falling in the thin morning air. Arleigh lay motionless, eyes fixed on the ceiling, counting the seconds between bursts of sound. Somewhere nearby, another crash site, another investigation. The city was just hearing ghosts now, jumping at every echo.

The morning light slipped through the thin curtains into the cramped room. Arleigh's eyes fixed on the ceiling where a water stain spread like an old bruise, her thoughts circling in silence. She had been awake since before dawn, caught in that uncertain drift between sleep and waking, her body heavy against sheets that smelled faintly of lavender and sweat. Rest rarely lasted. When it came at all, it was shallow and troubled, leaving her more worn than restored.

She looked in the mirror. Dark circles, recent. Weight loss, five pounds since last month. Fingernails bitten to the quick. Clothes scattered across the floor without care.

Empty mugs gathered along the windowsill, coffee rings overlapping like Venn diagrams. Pages of scribbled notes pressed up against philosophy books stacked on the nightstand, their spines cracked and worn. Nietzsche, Camus, Sartre. Their arguments played on repeat in her mind, each word a stone she turned over endlessly. Absurdity. Finality. Control as illusion.

She pushed herself upright, vertebrae clicking softly in sequence. The shirt slipped down one shoulder, cotton soft against her collarbone as she raked a hand through her hair. Knots pulled at her fingers, small resistances she let remain. Ten o'clock blinked from the old digital clock by the bed, its red numbers harsh in the dimness. She exhaled slowly and rose, feet braced against cold wooden planks that creaked beneath her.

Routine carried her toward the bathroom, each step automatic. In the mirror, she studied a face made unfamiliar by fatigue. Cheeks hollowed out, casting shadows that deepened every angle. Eyes unfocused and rimmed with shadow, the whites threaded with red. Arleigh stood there, fingers pressed to cool porcelain until her knuckles whitened. The question surfaced quietly, rising like a bubble through still water: what was left to find in another day shaped by repetition?

Arleigh studied her reflection in the bathroom mirror. Shadows pooled beneath her eyes, her skin pale and taut across her cheekbones. She took it in with the same dull curiosity she brought to each morning. No makeup. No effort to disguise the fatigue. She splashed cold water over her face, the shock of it barely registering, brushed her teeth, and pulled on a black sweater and jeans that hung loose at her hips.

In the kitchenette, she moved through routine without thought. Coffee grounds tumbled into the filter, water measured and poured. The motions steadied her, gave shape to an otherwise shapeless day.

She reached for her tablet on the counter and opened a news app, letting the shifting headlines occupy her attention. Most of it washed over her: politics, weather, celebrity deaths. Background noise she barely registered.

The bitter scent of coffee filled the cramped space. Once, she might have found comfort in its warmth, but now it only marked time's slow crawl. She scrolled, eyes snagging on each mention of the autonomous car killer. The city's fear was almost palpable, a low thrum beneath every headline, every nervous tweet. The name was everywhere. A cipher, a myth, a threat. She imagined her own name threaded through those stories, imagined the way people would speak it: with awe, with dread, with something like reverence. Someone who mattered. Someone who left a mark.

The articles detailed a string of unexplained autonomous vehicle crashes. Words like sabotage and public panic jumped from the screen. Then a new detail: someone calling themselves "The Phantom Driver" had sent a message to a reporter, taunting authorities and promising more incidents.

She read it twice. The name lingered in her mind. The Phantom Driver. It was calculated and strange, theatrical in a way that touched something deep inside her.

She followed each line of the message intently now, feeling something shift beneath her ribs. The threat wasn't frightening. It stirred an uneasy thrill instead, a thin current of anticipation that prickled along her spine for the first time in months.

Arleigh closed her eyes. She imagined herself sealed inside one of those silent cars, the wheel turning under no one's hands, the city flowing past on the other side of tinted glass. There would be nothing left for her to do but accept whatever happened next.

Her pulse quickened as she held onto that thought: letting go of every decision, leaving herself at the mercy of algorithms and machinery. A kind of surrender that felt almost clean. No choices, no need for control. Only mechanical certainty and whatever waited at the end of the road.

Arleigh blinked, her attention drawn to the glowing tablet screen. The article laid out the public's anxiety and the department's search for the Phantom Driver. None of that registered as fear for her. Something else kindled beneath her ribs. A faint, restless curiosity threaded with longing she had not felt in months.

She didn't want to die, not in the usual way. What she wanted was quieter, more elusive: an end to the dull ache that saturated every hour. Release. Escape. Something different from survival by habit.

She drained her coffee, the bitter dregs cold against her tongue, and left her apartment. Cool air bit at her exposed skin, sharpening her senses for a moment. The city was already churning. People hurried in clusters toward unseen objectives, clutching bags, faces lit by screens or turned toward each other, intent on their own private worlds. Arleigh walked without direction, letting herself dissolve into one more anonymous figure swallowed by movement. No one glanced at her. She preferred it that way. Didn't she? Yet as she passed a bus shelter glowing with a digital warning: REPORT

SUSPICIOUS AUTONOMOUS ACTIVITY. She wondered what it would take for anyone to look up, to see her, not just the outline of a woman moving through space. The Phantom Driver had managed it. A name, a shadow, and suddenly the city was wide awake.

The day unspooled in fragments: rough wood beneath her palms on a park bench by a weathered statue, warmth seeping through a cafe window onto her shoulder, hours marked by drifting thoughts rather than purpose. News of the autonomous cars flickered again behind her eyes. A reminder that there were ways to let go, to step outside the burden of choice. The idea made something loosen inside her chest. What if she just got into one of those cars and let it carry her wherever it wished? No more planning, no more decisions. Just surrender.

At the next intersection, yellow tape cordoned off a stretch of curb where a driverless cab had mounted the sidewalk two days before. The wall still marked the impact, black tire streaks scoring the concrete. Arleigh paused, noting the way pedestrians skirted the scene, eyes averted. The city was learning new routines: avoid the cabs, trust nothing with tinted glass.

Noise pressed in from every side. Engines growled, voices bounced off glass and stone, but none of it penetrated deeply. She slipped through it like water around obstacles, insulated inside herself.

At busier intersections she slowed to watch the driverless cars weave through traffic with silent precision. Their motion pulled at her focus: smooth, calculated, free of human error or hesitation.

Passengers reclined behind tinted glass, faces bathed in blue light from their devices, indifferent to risk or destination.

The thought grew sharper as afternoon shadows lengthened. Almost insistent now. A dangerous fascination tightened its grip each time another quiet vehicle glided past. It would be so simple: step inside, punch in an address or don't, and give up control to something incorruptible and mechanical.

She kept walking. The city blurred at the edges while sleek machines threaded through narrow gaps in traffic, their presence both steadying and ominous. Every one that passed whispered of surrender, offering silence and certainty where nothing else did.

The Phantom Driver kept coming back to her. It was almost perfect. Just enough theatricality to unsettle, not enough to tip into parody. She felt a hot, secret pulse of satisfaction. If it were her, she'd have chosen a different sign-off. Something more final. But maybe that was the point: leave them guessing, always one step behind.

By the time Arleigh unlocked her apartment door, dusk was seeping through the windows and pooling in corners. She sat at the edge of her bed and watched the city transform from amber to bruised violet. Outside, traffic murmured in rhythmic surges. A siren wailed through the distance, then faded into the steady thrum of evening.

Inside, nothing stirred. The silence pressed against her chest, thick and unyielding. It gathered in the shadows and made each breath feel deliberate and strange. She barely noticed the familiar furniture around her. Loneliness collected here like dust on surfaces she had stopped seeing, a residue that clung no matter how often she tried to shake it loose.

She let herself feel it. A dull anger without direction. The hours dissolved into one another, and each day mirrored the last: wake up, venture out, return, repeat. Beneath it all ran a constant strain just to keep moving forward against the emptiness.

When the sun finally slipped below the horizon, she stopped resisting. The idea emerged gradually, then crystallized with startling precision. Being the Phantom Driver meant more than wearing a mask or claiming a name from someone else's story. It meant abandoning ordinary boundaries and transforming into something that compelled people to lift their eyes from their patterns and recognize threat where they once found comfort.

She let that possibility take root in her thoughts. The Phantom Driver challenged everything society promised was protected. That rebellion spoke to something long buried within her: a craving for upheaval, for purpose she could forge with her own hands.

Arleigh cleared her throat and sat at her laptop. She opened a blank email, fingers hovering over the keys. "I am the Phantom Driver," she typed. The words looked strange, almost weightless. She deleted them, then typed them again. Outside, the city's lights blinked on, one by one. Arleigh sat in the growing darkness, waiting.

Chapter 17

The weekend dissolved into silence. Patrol officers still had no leads on Darwin Santana. Thirty-seven media requests glowed in her inbox, each one demanding a statement about the latest homicide. She set up a new BDSMessages account and watched the cursor blink in the empty profile field, but left it unused.

Blackburn worked through the case files at her desk. The kintsugi vase sat to her left, the gun inside it a quiet fact. Banks's fate and the risk of exposure hovered just within arm's reach. She measured the pulse of danger, aware that any misstep could bring everything down.

No one here knew what she carried.

The phone rang. She lifted the receiver, voice flat and professional. "Detective Blackburn."

A man's voice followed, distorted by the tinny rasp of a cheap digital filter. "Hello, Detective. I'm the Phantom Driver. I believe you've seen my video."

The line broke for half a beat. A stutter in his software.

She disconnected, attached an inline recorder with a soft click, then picked up again. Still breathing on the other end, shallow and expectant.

Blackburn allowed herself a slight smile.

"Which video do you mean?"

He tried a laugh that came out hollow and forced, like air through a broken pipe. "I sent it to Brynn Cassidy, the reporter."

"She published that story. You'll have to do better if you want me to believe you're the Phantom Driver," she said. Her thumb hovered over an unsent message to Chief Hayes: Sir, caller on the line claiming to be Phantom Driver. Recording now.

She waited.

"You dare question me?" The words strained for menace but came out theatrical, like a teenager reading Shakespeare.

Blackburn pressed further. "You're not the first to call today with this story. Convince me."

Silence stretched out, thick and telling, before he spoke again. He hadn't prepared for this.

"I cut letters from magazines and glued them to paper. I wore gloves."

Blackburn raised an eyebrow. "That clipboard ransom note? So, you specialize in clichés."

He chuckled again. Fake enthusiasm covering something more fragile, like paint over rust.

"Don't underestimate—"

In that brief flicker, she heard it: lighter tones bleeding through the mechanical distortion. The mask slipped for an instant.

"What exactly shouldn't I underestimate?" Her tone was clinical, cold as stainless steel.

His breath quickened. Not much, but enough. She could almost feel the sweat beading on his palm where he gripped the phone.

"You think this is funny?"

Blackburn kept her gaze on a chipped nail, indifferent. "Someone with actual leverage doesn't bother with children's crafts or cheap theatrics. If you want credibility, show some."

A pause while he recalibrated. She heard the faint rustle of movement, perhaps fingers drumming on a surface. Then came his declaration: "I've brought this city to its knees!" His cadence betrayed him, rising at the end like a question. Uncertainty cracked beneath synthetic bravado like thin ice.

Blackburn listened as the shape of her suspect became clearer: someone hiding behind effects and bluster, straining to project power he didn't possess. Someone trying too hard not to be seen at all.

"To its knees?" Blackburn cut in quietly. A thin smile edged her mouth. "All you've managed is another round of paperwork for me. What do you want? Is it attention? A pat on the head? Or do you just want to boast?"

The voice sharpened, defensive now. "I want respect. I want people to know what I did."

Blackburn tilted her head, the LED lights catching the silver threads in her hair. "Respect isn't given on demand. Anyone can claim credit after the fact. Why should you stand out?"

"I have details that weren't released."

"Details any reporter with half a brain could patch together from interviews." Blackburn's gaze drifted to the wall clock, its second hand ticking through the silence. "You're wasting both our time. If you don't have something real, I'll get back to my work."

"Wait." The plea slipped through the voice modulator, strained and raw beneath the electronic distortion. "I can prove it. I can show you."

"Can you?" Blackburn's calm never faltered. The receiver felt cool against her ear. "That's a confident offer. Though if you're too afraid to meet in person..."

"I'm not afraid of anything."

"Of course," Blackburn answered, letting an edge of amusement color her voice. "Still, relying on remote tricks does suggest hesitation. Understandable. Not everyone handles direct contact well."

"You'd arrest me. It'd be over." The shift was clear through the static; Blackburn recognized a woman behind the distortion now.

"You know my record," Blackburn replied evenly. "My reputation's not a secret. You know I play fair and tell the truth, correct?"

A silence drew out. The office air conditioning hummed softly.

"Yes."

"Then here's my word. I won't arrest you if we talk face to face." Her tone stayed flat, almost bored. She doubted this caller had killed anyone.

Another pause stretched between them.

"All right," the voice said finally. "If you promise."

"I do," Blackburn replied, feigning surprise at this new arrangement. "You'll want somewhere public, I'd imagine?"

"King Street Park," the woman said at last. "One hour."

Blackburn smiled into the receiver, her words soft but precise. "Good choice. Plenty of people around, plenty of ways out if things get tense. You're thinking clearly."

The compliment landed as intended. A sharp intake of breath crackled through the line.

"One hour," the caller said again, the words clipped now. "Don't be late."

"I won't," Blackburn said, already reaching for her coat as the call disconnected.

She stared at the silent phone for a moment, the plastic warm from her grip. No description, no warning about who she should expect.

With a short sigh, she called her team together in her office. As they filed in, watchful and uncertain, Blackburn put Willow on speaker. The conference phone's red light blinked steadily.

"I just got contacted by someone claiming to be the Phantom Driver," she began, voice skeptical. "Though I doubt it. It sounded like a young woman, and our evidence points toward a male suspect." She looked straight at Sinclair as she spoke.

"Still, we follow every lead." She let that settle in the quiet room.

The detectives said nothing at first. Sinclair leaned back against the wall, eyes narrowed in thought. Cooper sat down with his fingers tapping a steady rhythm against the chair's worn armrest while Reeves stood off to one side, arms crossed and listening intently.

Blackburn waited for their reactions before moving ahead.

Willow's voice crackled through the speakerphone. "Did you trace the call?"

"No. But I recorded it," Blackburn said, the digital file already burning in her mind. "She wants to meet in an hour at King Street Park."

Sinclair voiced what hung thick in the air between them. "It could be a trap."

Blackburn's gaze swept across the group, reading each face like evidence at a crime scene. "That's possible. We'll take the chance. If it's nothing, we move on."

"I can follow you there."

She cut him off with a look sharp enough to draw blood. Her decision stood like a closed door. "I'll go to King Street Park alone. The rest of you stay on your current assignments. This doesn't sideline the ongoing cases."

Sinclair shifted, his unease rippling through the room. "Are you sure it's safe, boss? We don't know what's out there."

Before Blackburn could answer, Reeves gave a low chuckle that rumbled from his chest, shaking his head. "If anyone can handle it, it's her."

Cooper shrugged, a faint smile playing at the corners of his mouth. "We could tip off Brynn Cassidy. Let her tail you for free."

Blackburn's reply came flat as old paint, tinged with dark humor. "No need for more complications. The less attention, the better."

She turned back to the phone, its blue light casting shadows across her desk. "Willow, did you get that video? Or the email Brynn received?"

Willow's exhaustion bled through the speaker, frustration sharpening her words. "I have the email but nothing useful from it yet. That's not unusual."

Blackburn kept her voice steady as a metronome. "Alright, keep working on it." She waved the team away with fingers that barely trembled, then ended the call.

The detectives filed out in silence, each carrying their own unspoken concerns as they passed through her office door.

Blackburn sat with her hands pressed flat against the desk, feeling the cool wood beneath her palms while she weighed her options for King Street Park.

She rose and left without hesitation, the lock clicking behind her with metallic finality.

The drive took only minutes through streets that held their breath. Traffic flowed light and indifferent around her. She parked where the exit path beckoned like an escape route.

In the park, she moved with the calm of a predator disguising itself as prey, her eyes cataloguing entry points and sightlines as methodically as if she were drafting a report. Joggers pounded past on the asphalt path, and dog walkers chatted into phones, none registering the careful assessment in her gaze.

Blackburn kept her pace even, her body language revealing nothing while she scanned for danger hidden among the ordinary faces and familiar rhythms of the park.

The park spread out before Blackburn, orderly lawns broken by bursts of late summer flowers. She walked the perimeter, eyes tracking the main paths wide enough for cars and the narrower trails shielded by trees. The scent of cut grass mixed with something sweeter carried on the warm air. Roses, perhaps. Benches and alcoves formed a mental list of exits and cover.

A couple strolled past her, their clasped hands and soft laughter betraying no awareness of her assessment. Blackburn kept moving, gravel crunching softly beneath her shoes, already choosing her ground.

She approached the bench. Ornate metalwork with a wooden seat and back. Blackburn slowed her pace, scanning each face within reach. A jogger circled by, steady breathing audible as he focused on his route. On another bench nearby, an older woman scattered crumbs to pigeons that cooed and fluttered at her feet.

Blackburn's hand brushed her hip, reassurance against her palm. She sat on the bench, near the gazebo, posture relaxed but never careless. To passersby she appeared to be another woman at rest, watching park life unfold. In truth she was charting every arrival within her sightline, filing away movements and faces with automatic precision.

A woman neared the gazebo. Her walk suggested uncertainty. Black hair fell around a pale face marked with worry. Her outfit avoided notice by design: plain black shirt and jeans. As she drew closer, Blackburn marked the taut pull in her shoulders and the way her fingers flexed and curled at her sides.

Without haste, Blackburn pocketed her phone, the smooth surface sliding against fabric. She raised her eyes to meet the woman's gaze, reading the nerves beneath her cautious approach. Fingers twitched against cotton. A sheen of perspiration gleamed at the hairline. Breaths came shallow and quick.

The woman stood at a cautious distance, glancing at the weathered seat as if reconsidering her decision to approach. Blackburn held still, maintaining a posture of patience and understated authority, watching for any crack in composure that might reveal intent.

"Hello," Blackburn said. Her voice gave nothing away. "Have a seat."

She motioned to the space beside her on the bench. After a pause, Arleigh sat down, her body rigid against the wood slats, keeping careful watch on every movement in her peripheral vision.

Chapter 18

Blackburn studied the woman on the bench. A quick, clinical sweep told her what she needed. Not the killer. Possibly the Phantom Driver, but not a murderer. "Morgan Blackburn," she said. "And you are?"

"Arleigh." A pause stretched between them, then, with a tremor threading through her voice: "I'm the Phantom Driver."

Blackburn let the silence settle like dust between them. Arleigh stared back, trying to read the detective's face. Fear crept through her body, slow and visible, until her fingers trembled against her thighs.

"Are you from New Dresden"

Arleigh shook her head. "Sevaston," she said. She looked up at the sky, the ground, anywhere but at Blackburn. Blackburn had never heard of the town, and was not even sure it was real.

"Are you a vegetarian?" Blackburn asked, her tone flat as stone.

The question caught Arleigh like a branch across the path. "Why does that matter?"

"I meet killers all the time." Blackburn kept her eyes steady, unblinking. "Today isn't one of those days. You don't have it in you. I'd guess you don't eat meat at all. Maybe vegan. The sort who helps lost bees find their way to flowers." She leaned back and rested her arm along the weathered wood of the bench. Arleigh's exposed vulnerability pulled something deep and instinctive from Blackburn's core. "You seem kind."

Arleigh dropped her gaze to where her hands lay folded in her lap. Blackburn nudged a dandelion with the toe of her shoe. The small yellow flower stood persistent beside the cracked concrete.

"Dandelions survive anything," she said, pressing her toe against the stem and watching it bend beneath the pressure, then spring upright again.

"You can eat the leaves," Arleigh replied quietly, her eyes tracking the movement. "People make wine from the blossoms. Sugar, yeast, raisins, oranges. Maybe lemon. It tastes good."

Blackburn studied the curve of her face for a moment. "Anyone who gathers dandelions for wine doesn't have it in them to kill strangers." She noted the flicker that passed through Arleigh's eyes before she looked away.

Compassion surfaced just enough to soften the hard lines of Blackburn's features. She recognized women like this. Open, raw-nerved, easy prey for someone assertive enough to steer them. Willow had been like this once.

She scanned the empty park. No witnesses, no interruptions. The afternoon light slanted through bare branches. Her voice dropped lower, settling into the space between them.

"Are you cold-hearted? Did you murder those women?"

"Yes," Arleigh whispered. Too fast this time. Words delivered like lines rehearsed but never learned by heart. "I drove those cars. God."

Heat flooded her face. Her voice went tight and fractured under the lie.

"No." Blackburn's response came pared down and gentle. She dropped her head, making herself smaller, less threatening. "Not you." She waited a beat, letting the truth settle. "Why confess at all?"

"I did it."

"You said you sent a video to a reporter," Blackburn prompted. "What was in it?"

Arleigh explained how she had bought old magazines and spent hours cutting out letters for ransom notes before gluing them onto paper. A trick borrowed from some movie about a kidnapped boy. Burning it at the end was supposed to give it drama, make it memorable.

Blackburn listened without comment, weighing every word against what she already knew about desperation and performance.

"And why the gloves? The letter's burned, and you only sent a video," Blackburn said, her fingers grazing Arleigh's shoulder. "A bug," she explained. "Why the gloves?"

"Fingerprints. I didn't want you to have them." Arleigh nodded, as if convincing herself. "Yeah... I thought maybe you could, I don't know, zoom in or something and pull prints off the paper. Is that possible?"

"No. Technology doesn't work that way. You're not much of a tech person, are you?" Blackburn reached out and touched her hand. The skin was cool, damp.

"I'm not. I didn't do any of it. I don't know how those cars work." Arleigh's words came apart as she picked at the raw skin near her nail. "I was just lying."

Blackburn took her hand, the bones delicate beneath her fingers. "Don't do that. Not right now." She kept her grip light but steady. "What's your name?"

"Arleigh. Arleigh Jenssen."

"That's a good name. I'm Morgan." Blackburn held her gaze. "Does Arleigh mean something?"

Arleigh's eyes lifted, a ghost of warmth crossing her face. "It's about bunnies in a field. Something like that. My mother told me once. I never remembered all of it."

For an instant, Blackburn felt the old hunger shift in her chest. A soft creature drawn close by instinct.

"You seem honest," Blackburn said. "Did you have anything to do with these deaths?"

"No." Arleigh's answer came swift and bewildered. "I couldn't hurt anyone like that... People died, and one woman owned a candle shop." Her brow creased at the memory. "How could someone kill someone who sells candles?" Her hands went slack beneath Blackburn's touch before she drew away.

"Sorry," Arleigh murmured.

"It's fine," Blackburn replied as Arleigh's fingers found her own chin, uncertain.

"They were good people. Happy lives." Blackburn let the words settle, watching. Arleigh's shoulder jerked, confirming what she suspected. "So why say you did it? Why lie?"

Heat bloomed up Arleigh's neck. She shook her head but offered nothing. Blackburn reached for her hand again.

"Sometimes people confess to crimes they didn't commit because they feel guilty about something else," Blackburn said softly, reading the tremor in Arleigh's fingers. That wasn't it. This wasn't about punishment.

"Sometimes it's about wanting to be seen." The moment the words left her lips, Arleigh's muscles locked beneath her hands.

"I see you," Blackburn said gently, pressing once before easing her hold. "Is this alright?"

"Yes." The word barely disturbed the air between them.

"And you're not wasting my time," Blackburn said, releasing her with care. She took in the bright sweep of the park and allowed herself a small smile. "There are worse ways to spend an afternoon than meeting someone new."

Arleigh looked down, color warming her cheeks again. "Maybe."

Blackburn shifted on the bench, turning her body toward Arleigh as she slipped free of her jacket and let the silence stretch between them.

"I see it, you know. The truth. You're beautiful, even if you can't see it. I understand. Killing is ugly, committed by people who are ugly inside. You believe that's you. That's why you confessed to something so dark." Blackburn kept her tone quiet. "But ugliness, real ugliness, I see it every day. That's not who you are."

Arleigh stared at her hands, fingers trembling against each other like leaves in a breeze. "If I'm so beautiful, why is my life the way it is?"

Blackburn considered telling her what a truly terrible life could be. Instead, she held back. No need to spook her. "Maybe you've never stepped into what the world has for you," she said. "Somebody convinced you that beauty wasn't meant for you. But look around." She gestured at the park: a terrier trotting past on its leash, sun catching on weeds and cracked paths, the sweet decay of autumn mulch beneath the benches.

Arleigh's gaze moved from the dandelions to Blackburn's face, lingering there with unspoken questions.

Blackburn met her eyes and tilted her head, resting her chin on her hand as she smiled. The subtle invitation shifted the air between them.

Arleigh hesitated, her breath catching. "I guess... maybe."

"Maybe," Blackburn echoed softly. "Maybe everything is. Maybe you too." She reached out and brushed a stray hair from Arleigh's brow, her fingertips grazing warm skin, pausing just long enough to signal intent before pulling back.

The silence stretched between them as Blackburn watched for that familiar shift in body language. A glance held a fraction longer, a hand that hovered after being released, the subtle lean of a body drawn closer.

She leaned back and let the city's background noise fill the air between them. Traffic hummed in the distance. The sunlight found Arleigh's face and revealed the tentative calm settling there, softening the worry lines around her eyes.

Bit by bit, Arleigh's posture shifted. Her shoulders loosened. Her chin rose half an inch. No one else would have noticed, but Blackburn felt it. A slow thaw, ice giving way to something warmer.

Their eyes met again and held without flinching this time.

"You have striking eyes," Blackburn said, surprising even herself with the softness of it.

Arleigh blinked once in confusion. "Really?"

"They're direct," Blackburn replied, lips barely lifting at the corners. "Honest."

A blush touched Arleigh's cheeks, pink spreading like watercolor on paper. She tucked hair behind her ear, uncertain but emboldened by the attention.

"I never thought of myself that way," Arleigh admitted in a voice barely above a murmur.

"Beauty isn't only what people see." Blackburn tapped her own chest with two fingers and watched as Arleigh mirrored the motion across her sternum. A silent echo Blackburn recognized immediately. The gesture sent a familiar thrill through her.

She felt the tension in herself rise, controlled but insistent, a tightness low in her belly.

"Let's find some shade," she said simply and stood up first. She offered an arm. A brief supportive hold, fingers pressing against the soft fabric of Arleigh's sleeve. Then she let go as soon as Arleigh steadied herself.

They started down the path together at a careful pace away from casual eyes, just enough contact to steady and guide but never forceful. Blackburn could sense how close she might get if she played this right. Deliberate, patient, almost surgical in her restraint. The scent of Arleigh's shampoo drifted between them, something floral and innocent.

She adapted easily. Professional when necessary, predatory when allowed. She matched her stride to Arleigh's as they moved off into quieter corners of the park where the shadows grew deeper and the sounds of the city faded to whispers.

It was nothing serious. Not a hookup, just an idle break in the middle of the day.

There. The gazebo.

Blackburn slipped her arm around Arleigh's waist to guide her in. "Let's go here. The view's better." She released Arleigh as soon as they reached the weathered wooden stairs and let her walk ahead. When Arleigh settled near the rail, her fingers finding the smooth paint, Blackburn approached but kept her distance. She wouldn't trust herself otherwise.

"It's nice, isn't it?" Blackburn leaned into the sun-warmed half-wall, scanning the park where afternoon light filtered through the oaks.

"It is," Arleigh said. She looked at Blackburn longer than she looked at the scenery.

"I like being noticed," Blackburn said, voice even. "People looking at me, it works for me."

Arleigh turned, the breeze catching strands of her hair. "I wouldn't know. People don't look at me much."

Blackburn straightened, her shadow shifting across the gazebo floor. "I'm looking at you now."

Arleigh hesitated, then nodded. "You are."

"Does that bother you? Me paying attention?"

"No." Arleigh glanced away before adding, "You're beautiful."

"So are you."

Arleigh shook her head. "Not really."

Blackburn allowed a slight smile. "I bet sometimes you see yourself in the mirror and think you look good."

"Maybe," Arleigh murmured, turning away again. The wood creaked softly under her.

Blackburn pressed gently, keeping her voice steady. "You are beautiful. You should say it out loud."

Arleigh eyed her, unsure. "Feels strange."

"It's not strange," Blackburn replied. "It's power. Try it. Say 'I am beautiful.'"

A faint smile touched Arleigh's mouth. "You're beautiful."

Blackburn smiled back but didn't let up. "No. Say it about yourself. I want to hear you say it."

With visible effort, Arleigh said, "I am beautiful."

"You are." Blackburn watched her closely. "How does it feel?"

Arleigh shrugged but color rose in her cheeks, warming her skin. "Good, I guess? Hearing you say it helps more."

Blackburn gave a restrained nod, keeping herself contained behind calm. "I mean it. You have striking eyes and good skin." Her gaze lingered only a second too long before she pulled back just enough. "If I were inclined that way, I'd want to kiss you."

Arleigh drew in a quick breath, the sound sharp in the quiet afternoon, and looked away before meeting Blackburn's gaze again. "But you aren't?"

"I believe what I see in the mirror," Blackburn said. "That's all."

"You're still beautiful," Arleigh said.

"So are you." Blackburn traced her own arm with care, her fingertips barely grazing the skin.

Arleigh copied the motion down her own forearm, almost unconsciously. She smiled, but there was hesitation behind it. "Some parts aren't great though. Not really beautiful."

"Not true." Blackburn held her gaze on Arleigh, assessing without apology. "Your hair, your eyes. All of it fits together."

Arleigh flushed deeper now, the color spreading down her neck, and gestured toward her chest with awkwardness.

Blackburn didn't laugh or smile this time; she kept the tone neutral but firm. "Nothing wrong there either." She waited a beat before asking quietly, "Why do you think that matters? Who got that idea in your head?"

"No one," Arleigh muttered quickly. Her eyes dropped to the floorboards of the gazebo, studying the grain in the wood as she spoke again, softer now. "You just see things online and start comparing. Mine seem off."

She started to turn away. Blackburn recognized the moment, knew she was about to slip through her fingers if she didn't act.

"Sit," Blackburn said, taking a place on the weathered wood of the gazebo bench. She kept her voice steady. "Why would someone as sharp as you believe something from the internet is real?"

Arleigh hesitated, then sat beside her and angled in. The bench creaked softly under their combined weight. "You're saying you never did?"

Blackburn let a small smile soften her face. "Not once."

"I doubt yours are anywhere near as messed up." Arleigh folded her arms, the fabric of her jacket rustling.

"Maybe I shouldn't pry. But what makes you think there's anything wrong with you?"

Arleigh crossed her legs and looked away, silent. The distant sound of children playing drifted across the park.

Blackburn leaned in, her gaze steady. "If you want to talk, I'll listen. For what it's worth, you're beautiful. Even the parts you don't know how to see yet."

Arleigh shivered at that. The detective's focus left her exposed but not unwelcome. "I... I don't..."

"Ssshh." Blackburn kept it gentle. "You don't owe me any explanations. Trust me, if it's a contest for secrets, I'd win in a landslide."

A short laugh passed between them, releasing some of the strain. Blackburn kept her posture relaxed but measured every inch of distance, fighting the urge to close it completely.

Arleigh risked another look at her, searching for mockery or dismissal but found only calm interest and something more she couldn't name.

Blackburn shifted, her jacket falling open as if releasing excess heat. The cool air touched her skin. She forced herself back to neutral ground. "Stomachs, arms. Everybody thinks they've got something strange. Do you ever just let yourself be comfortable?"

"Sometimes," Arleigh said. "Usually only when I'm alone." Her eyes lingered on Blackburn's hands.

Blackburn's fingers tapped out a muted pattern against her thigh, the denim rough under her touch, keeping herself anchored.

Silence gathered between them until Arleigh almost spoke again, but held back at the last second. Her cheeks burned with things she wasn't ready to voice.

Blackburn caught the hesitation and wanted to lean in, press further, but held firm instead. She couldn't afford carelessness here.

She rose from the bench, the wood groaning faintly as she stood. "Let's walk."

Arleigh nodded and pulled her jacket tighter across her chest.

They stepped out into sunlight filtered through branches overhead. The warmth touched their faces. The park carried on as usual. No one noticed anything unusual had happened at all.

Arleigh walked more confidently now, her shoulders straighter and her head higher than before, clinging to Blackburn's earlier words as if they might hold up against everything else.

"Do you need a ride?" Blackburn asked without much inflection, hoping for more time together but not betraying it with her tone.

"No, I have a car. I... can I kiss you?" Arleigh asked, her voice steadier than before.

Blackburn shook her head. "No. Not yet." She met Arleigh's gaze, intent. "I want you, but a kiss wouldn't be enough."

Heat bloomed across Arleigh's cheeks. Blackburn let the words settle between them, heavy as smoke in still air.

"I'll call in a few days. Stay out of trouble. And stop confessing," Blackburn said, a faint smile edging her tone.

"I will. Looking forward to it," Arleigh replied, turning toward her car.

"That's your car?"

Blackburn's eyes traced the compact's sleek profile, lingering on the row of sensors that studded its roof like unblinking eyes. The car waited beneath the harsh glare of sunlight, its stillness somehow expectant.

"Nice ride," Blackburn said. The words came out flat against the night air. She recognized the model immediately.

"It's a lease," Arleigh replied. "I like not having to drive. Makes it easier to catch up on reading." She pressed her palm to the door, and the touchscreen bloomed with light beneath her fingers. "The system handles everything."

"Even now?" Blackburn asked.

Arleigh's hand stilled against the cool metal. "What do you mean?"

"The automation," Blackburn said. Her tone remained even, but her gaze returned to those sensors, their dark lenses catching the streetlight. "You just claimed responsibility for deaths tied to self-driving cars. You're not worried?"

Arleigh withdrew her hand from the handle and turned to face Blackburn fully. Uncertainty flickered across her features. "You think it's dangerous?"

"I think you should avoid using it for a while." Blackburn kept her voice measured, almost conversational, but something in the set of her jaw discouraged debate. "Call it a precaution. Those systems aren't as secure as people want to believe."

Arleigh's voice dropped to barely above a whisper. "Do you think someone's targeting the victims? It isn't random?"

"I think someone is angry enough to find a way in." Blackburn's fingers found Arleigh's arm. The touch was brief and decisive. Not comfort. A boundary drawn in the darkness. "Drive yourself for now. Paranoia keeps people alive."

Arleigh's gaze shifted from the dashboard's dormant screens back to Blackburn's face, searching the shadows there for meaning. "You're concerned about me."

"I'm concerned about everyone," Blackburn said without hesitation. The words hung in the cool air between them, solid and immovable. "Take care."

Chapter 19

Blackburn crossed King Street Park, each step measured against the aftertaste of Arleigh's surrender. That particular flavor of naiveté, part trust, part stupidity, had left her blood singing. The morning crowd sprawled across dead grass in their usual configurations: mothers and strollers, joggers making loops, old men feeding pigeons contraband bread. None of them worth a second glance.

The car squatted in the back lot like a diseased animal. Faded blue paint bubbling with rust, mismatched hubcaps, that familiar spiderweb crack across the windshield. Willow's shitbox sedan.

Christ.

The recognition hit somewhere between her ribs and her stomach. Either Willow had gone full stalker or the universe had developed a sick sense of humor about coincidences. Neither option improved Blackburn's morning.

She changed trajectory without breaking stride. Details accumulated: fresh fingerprints on the driver's door, coffee cup balanced on the dash, laptop glow painting Willow's face corpse-pale through the glass. Blackburn's knuckles met the window hard enough to split skin.

Willow convulsed. Coffee erupted across her lap, the laptop, her hands scrambling to save electronics from the flood. Curses tumbled out in a panicked stream while Blackburn watched, blood warming her knuckles, waiting.

The window ground down halfway and stuck.

"What are you doing here?" Blackburn braced one palm against the sun-hot roof, leaning down until their faces aligned.

Willow's mouth worked soundlessly behind rain-spotted glasses.

"Following me?" The question emerged soft as a blade between ribs. "Is that what we're doing now?"

"I can explain—"

"Don't." Blackburn's gaze dropped to the laptop screen. Mapping software bloomed with digital breadcrumbs: her house, the candle shop, the hotel. Color-coded pins marking everywhere she'd been. "Jesus. You're actually tracking me."

The words hung between them like a diagnosis.

"It's not—I was worried." Willow's hands fluttered over the keyboard, closing windows that had already been seen. "The case, you meeting suspects alone—"

"So you decided to go full Sinclair?" Blackburn straightened, her laugh sharp enough to draw blood. "Do you have any idea what this looks like? The IT specialist with server access tracking the lead detective?"

Willow's face drained to match the laptop glow. "You think I'm...? No. God, no."

"What else should I think?" Blackburn's palm cracked against the roof. "Every time I get close to something, there you are. Always knowing where I am, what I'm working on."

"You announced it to the entire team."

"Get out of the car."

The command dropped between them like a stone.

"What?"

"You heard me." Blackburn's voice went subterranean. "Leave the laptop. Get out."

Willow fumbled with the door, legs unsteady as a newborn colt's. Blackburn slid into the driver's seat before the door finished swinging open, pulling the laptop across her thighs.

Consumer-grade GPS app. Nothing sophisticated, just location sharing any idiot could download. The timeline showed Willow's routes in blue, Blackburn's approximate positions in red. Crude as a child's drawing.

"You used the family sharing from my phone." Not a question. Blackburn scrolled through each pathetic screen. "The one I never turned off after we started fucking."

"I didn't touch department systems." Willow's voice came threadbare from outside the door. "Couldn't access field officer data anyway. I just needed to know you were safe."

The addresses glowed: everywhere Blackburn had been, nowhere that mattered. Just the anxious mapping of someone drowning in their own fear.

"The woman today. How?"

"You told everyone at the morning brief." Barely a whisper now. "Said you were meeting her alone."

Blackburn closed the laptop with care. The anger that had been keeping her spine straight dissolved, leaving something raw in its place. When was the last time she'd been wrong about something that mattered?

"You can't—" The words stuck. She tried again. "You can't do this. Follow me like I'm some mark."

Tears tracked down Willow's face, catching parking lot light like broken glass. "I know. God, I know. I just kept thinking something would happen. That you'd disappear, and I'd…"

"What? Kill for me?"

Regret hit as soon as the words left her lips.

"You're not a suspect." The admission scraped out of Blackburn's throat. "I shouldn't have said that."

Willow's head snapped up, hope flickering through the wreckage of her expression. Something in Blackburn's chest twisted at the sight.

"I was scared," Willow whispered. "Not of you. For you."

Blackburn let the silence stretch, cataloging: the tremor in Willow's hands, the shallow breathing, the way she held herself like she expected a blow. Nothing performed. Just misguided love wearing the wrong face.

She stepped out of the car and pulled Willow against her. The contact sparked unexpectedly, both of them rigid with leftover adrenaline until Willow melted into the embrace, shaking.

"Don't follow me again." Blackburn spoke into her hair. "You want to know where I am, you ask."

The anger had metabolized into something else entirely. Heat pooled low in her belly, sudden and demanding. She'd meant to set boundaries. But now...

An empty lot. No witnesses.

She dipped her head to Willow's ear. "Do you want me?"

Willow pulled back enough to meet her eyes, pupils dilated. "Yes."

Blackburn opened the back door and slid inside. "Get in."

The command landed like a struck match. Willow climbed in after her, cheeks flushed with something that wasn't shame anymore. The door clicked shut, sealing them into leather-scented twilight.

Blackburn pressed Willow against the door, using her body like punctuation. The space compressed around them. She wedged her thigh between Willow's legs, pressure calculated to promise without delivering. Yet.

"On the floor."

Willow slid down into the footwell, knees meeting rough carpet. Blackburn stretched across the back seat above her, one leg bent, maintaining altitude. The air between them crackled with ozone.

"You thought you could follow me?" Soft as silk, sharp as wire. Blackburn leaned down until Willow had nowhere to look but up. "Track me like prey?"

She caught Willow's chin, fingers cool against fever-warm skin. Not cruel. Precise. "Eyes up."

Her hand traveled from jaw to throat to collarbone, mapping territory. Each touch left its mark in goosebumps and hitched breath. When she drew Willow's shirt up, the fabric whispered secrets.

"You want to make it right?" Blackburn shifted, knees spreading until they framed the doorway. "Show me."

Blackburn's palm found Willow's breast through cotton that had gone transparent with sweat. Not a caress, an assessment. The way a surgeon might evaluate tissue before the first incision.

"Count." The word dropped between them like a stone in still water.

Willow's "One" emerged already fractured. She knew this arithmetic, had learned it in other rooms. Blackburn's precision was different, clinical in its cruelty, elegant in its restraint. Each slap landed with metronomic accuracy, mapping the geography of permission and trespass across warming flesh.

By five, Willow's breath stuttered like a failing engine. By seven, her body tried to curl away from what it also craved. At ten, Blackburn's hand stilled, fingers splayed possessively over the bloom of heat she'd cultivated. No comfort in the touch, only ownership.

"You followed me." Blackburn's voice carried the particular softness of a blade being cleaned. "Like some lovesick undergraduate who's read too much de Beauvoir and not enough de Sade."

Her fingers drifted to Willow's waistband, a question posed in negative space. The car's recycled air tasted of leather and something chemical: new car smell perverted by their intentions.

"My pants." Not a request. Architecture.

Willow's hands betrayed her with their eagerness. She peeled away the armor of Blackburn's professional life. The wool that demanded dry cleaning, the silk that whispered accusations. Revealed beneath: skin the color of burnt honey, muscles that spoke of Pilates classes and private training.

The black silk triangle of Blackburn's underwear looked like punctuation against her thighs. A full stop. An ending.

"Tell me what you see." Blackburn's tongue traced her own lips. Not seduction, but appetite.

"They're..." Willow's voice cracked. "Beautiful."

"Beautiful." Blackburn tasted the word, found it wanting. "Touch them. Tell me what expensive feels like."

The silk was as cool as morgue sheets under Willow's fingers, a contrast to the fever-heat beneath. She traced the edge where fabric met flesh, that liminal space where want becomes visible. Blackburn's exhale came sharp as breaking glass.

"Now remove them. Slowly. Like you're defusing something."

Perhaps she was. Willow's hands trembled with the concentration of the task, rolling silk down thighs that tensed and released in micro-movements of control. What was revealed gleamed like an open wound. All that careful composure distilled to biological honesty.

"Do you want it?" Blackburn's clinical tone made the question obscene. "This mess you've made of me?"

Willow nodded, mute with recognition. Blackburn traced herself with one finger, a cartographer mapping her own topography. The gesture was performative but not false. She was teaching Willow how to read her like a text.

"If you're very good," Blackburn said, "I'll let you. But you'll work for it. The way you should have worked before following me here like some stray."

She shifted forward, one leg propped against cracked vinyl, pulling Willow down by the nape like scruffing a cat. Willow's glasses clattered aside. She wouldn't need distance vision for this.

The first taste was salt and iron, primal as blood. Willow's technique was eager but unschooled, all enthusiasm and no finesse. Blackburn corrected her with minute adjustments. A shift of hip, fingers twisted in hair like reins. Training her.

"Better," Blackburn murmured. "You're learning."

Encouragement and insult braided together. Willow wrapped her lips around flesh that pulsed against her tongue, working with the focused attention of someone solving an equation. Blackburn's sounds stayed trapped in her throat: small, strangled things that escaped only by accident.

"Harder." The command came raw, control fraying at its edges. "Show me you understand what this is."

Willow slid one finger inside, an intrusion Blackburn's body welcomed with convulsive heat. She found rhythm in the push and pull, tongue and fingers conspiring toward an outcome that would leave them both changed. Or at least one of them.

"Yes." Blackburn's voice had gone thin as wire. "Like that. Like you know your place in this."

The word 'place' carried weight, not just position but purpose. Willow felt it settle over her like a harness as she worked, reading the text of Blackburn's body for signs of approaching climax. The muscles under her tongue went rigid as architecture.

"Now," Blackburn said, and it was neither request nor warning but simple fact. Her orgasm arrived with the same precision she brought to everything. Controlled, deliberate, silent except for one sharp intake of breath. She pulsed against Willow's mouth in waves that seemed almost angry in their intensity.

After, she was immediately composed. As if the preceding minutes had been some brief possession, now exorcised.

"Your shirt," she said. "Use it."

Willow stripped the cotton over her head, using it to clean Blackburn with careful efficiency. The shirt would carry the scent for days. She knew this, and knew that Blackburn knew it too. A marking was as deliberate as any bite.

They dressed in reverse order of undressing, Willow's hands steadier now in their service. The parking lot materialized around them as they exited. Empty spaces and faded lines, a liminal zone for liminal acts.

Blackburn's hand found Willow's throat before she could fully process the transition. Not violence, something more precise. The way one might hold a bird to feel its heartbeat.

"Never follow me again." Each word placed carefully as evidence. "I am not some problem for you to solve with your earnest concern."

Willow nodded against the restraint, feeling the pulse in her carotid kiss Blackburn's palm. When released, the absence of pressure felt like another kind of binding.

"Push-ups," Blackburn said, indicating asphalt that still radiated the day's heat. "Count them aloud. Consider it penance."

Willow dropped without protest. The ground bit through her palms, tiny industrial diamonds embedded in tar. Her form was terrible, all wrong angles and shaking limbs, but she counted through the humiliation: "One... two... three..."

Blackburn walked away before she reached ten, heels marking time against concrete. Willow continued anyway, muscles screaming, counting to nobody but herself and the indifferent sky. When she finally collapsed, cheek pressed to warm stone, she could still taste Blackburn on her lips. Salt and consequence, perfectly measured.

Chapter 20

Blackburn sat at her desk, jaw rigid with tension, frustration burning beneath her composed exterior. She scanned the half-finished report, fingers moving across the touchpad as she clicked to a blank section. The cursor blinked against white space. This was her third draft. Her patience had worn thin as tissue paper.

The computer's soft chime cut through the office silence. An email notification blinked onto the screen. The sender: Physica Smith, Hayes's assistant. The subject line made Blackburn's fingers pause on the keyboard. Notification: Escape of David Jackson.

Blackburn rolled her eyes. She remembered Jackson with crystalline clarity. Five years ago, she had cuffed his wrists while blood pooled beneath his girlfriend's body. He had torn a wooden post from the bed frame and driven it through her chest. The splintered edges had caught flesh and fabric alike. He had entered his not guilty plea with a steady voice, but the jury had returned their verdict in under an hour. Three years into his sentence, guards had dragged him bleeding from the exercise yard after he had shattered another inmate's orbital bone and broken two officers' ribs in a melee.

The timestamp showed he had slipped from Hotion Correctional Facility ten hours ago. Ten hours of darkness between him and the world.

Blackburn typed two words of acknowledgment: Message received. The keys clicked beneath her fingertips as she hit send.

Her patience had evaporated.

The Phantom Driver investigation had spiraled beyond control. After Arleigh's video confession aired, any semblance of order vanished. One week had passed. In that time, chaos bred with mathematical precision. Seventeen more false confessions crowded her inbox, each more absurd than the last. Some claimed to manipulate vehicles through telekinesis. Others whispered of shadow organizations or accused the city council of orchestrating murders through the basketball team. The results read like fever dreams transcribed into police statements.

Pressure flowed down the department's hierarchy like water through cracked pipes. The mayor demanded arrests on a daily schedule, forcing Chief Hayes to call her office with clockwork regularity. Blackburn had nothing solid to offer. Only theories and educated guesses that dissolved under scrutiny.

She replayed her first meeting with Arleigh in the park. Every detail confirmed what her gut had whispered from the start: Arleigh was no killer. She was a lonely woman grasping for attention in whatever form it arrived, even if that meant fabricating crimes beyond her capability. No malice had flickered in Arleigh's eyes. Only desperation and frayed nerves. She had stumbled over basic facts and her gaze had skittered away from direct contact.

These details crystallized now as Blackburn watched reports accumulate on her monitor. Each new false confession smeared the case like wet ink, pulling resources away from leads that pointed toward something tangible.

The coroner's continued refusal to classify the deaths as homicides created another wall. Without that designation, crucial investigative tools remained locked away from Blackburn and her team.

Her fingers hovered above the keyboard as anger constricted her chest. The investigation had devolved into political theater. Every move carried potential exposure and blame.

A soft chime emanated from her phone. She recognized it instantly. The BDSMessages app signaling new activity. She hesitated before touching the screen, reviewing the profile she maintained separate from her official existence: photographs selected for implication rather than revelation, text crafted to establish limits without exposing details. Her face appeared in none of them.

Blackburn scrolled through images and conversations without lingering long enough to feel their warmth. The search for former lovers pressed against her consciousness: Jenna and Lilith claimed by violence, Kendria encountered once in a candle shop. Each name carried fresh regret and accountability.

She had disclosed fragments of these connections to Chief Hayes: Jenna acknowledged, Kendria diminished through strategic omissions that had seemed prudent then but felt precarious now. Lilith remained completely absent from departmental files. That concealment provided scant reassurance.

The prospect of anyone else accessing Lilith's account created a knot of unease in Blackburn's stomach. She couldn't predict what undercurrents might surface if another investigator gained entry to that digital space.

Her focus returned to the cursor pulsing on her unfinished report. The document waited as voices rose beyond her closed door and bureaucratic obligations accumulated in every unopened message.

Blackburn slipped her phone into her pocket, then locked her computer screen with a swift flick of her wrist. She moved to the bathroom, mind already working through her next steps. She understood the risk of using the app, but she was certain that once she closed this case, any unfinished business could wait.

The bathroom offered the privacy she needed. Blackburn checked the light streaming from the high window, positioning herself where the sun carved sharp angles across her body. She angled her phone until only her torso filled the frame. A quick scan of the space confirmed nothing identifying lurked in view.

She set to work with quiet efficiency. Each pose was deliberate. Shoulders squared, chin tipped down just enough, fingers adjusting fabric where necessary. She undid two buttons of her blouse and caught a shot where the sheer fabric clung to damp skin. Her palm pressed against her chest, shaping herself for emphasis, careful not to betray impatience. She moved closer for a tighter angle, then checked each image before taking another. The slight tremor in her grip left a faint blur at the edges of certain photos.

Once finished, Blackburn buttoned up and crossed back into the office area. Sinclair sat hunched at his desk with an open file spread before him, pen suspended mid-sentence. She approached without hesitation.

"Sinclair," she said evenly, letting warmth thread through her tone. "I need your opinion."

He glanced up and froze at her proximity. Blackburn held out her phone, the screen bright with images.

His gaze locked onto the photos. Her body captured in shadow and golden light, nothing explicit but nothing reserved either. Sinclair hesitated before answering, color rising in his face as he struggled to compose himself.

"They're... well," he said, voice catching. "They're impressive."

She tracked his reactions closely. His attention snagged on one shot: a close crop over translucent fabric, the curve of her body unmistakable beneath it.

"And this one?" she asked softly, holding on a particular image where flesh pressed against sheer cloth.

Sinclair swallowed audibly and nodded, though his eyes darted away from hers.

"Could I see another?" He took the phone when she offered it, hands unsteady but eager.

Blackburn leaned in close enough for him to catch the scent of her perfume as he scrolled through each photo with reverent care. She noted how his breathing quickened as he lingered over certain images and traced every reaction. The pulse jumping at his throat, the white knuckles gripping the device. All cataloged.

Blackburn leaned down to retrieve her phone. The fabric of her shirt grazed Sinclair's cheek. She felt him tense beneath her, watched his lips part as he struggled to steady his breath. The muscles in his jaw tightened. He swallowed hard.

"You like them, don't you?" Her voice carried a thread of amusement beneath its quiet surface. She turned away without waiting for an answer, walked into her office, and left the door open just wide enough to catch his reflection in the glass frames on her wall.

Sinclair remained at his desk, one hand hidden beneath its surface. His stare fixed on the impression her body had left in the carpet fibers. After a long moment, he rose unsteadily to his feet and headed for the bathroom with quick, uneven steps.

Blackburn settled into her leather chair, spine straight, breathing controlled. She permitted herself one measured exhale. The familiar rush of control flowed through her veins like electricity, sharpening her focus.

"So easy," she whispered. He might be their killer. He was certainly her stalker. Had his fixation finally pushed him across that boundary? She worked through the possibilities in silence. No new partner meant no more bodies. Willow remained the sole exception.

She opened BDSMessages on her phone and moved through the setup screens with swift precision, creating credentials that led nowhere. For her profile, she chose two photographs from earlier in the week. The first showed her in full uniform, collar buttoned tight, gaze direct and challenging. The second revealed more. Her shirt was open to expose the lace edge of a black bra, shoulders loose, guard lowered.

She tracked each image as it uploaded, aware of an unexpected hollowness as she constructed this fresh identity from nothing. Her previous account had taken months to cultivate. Those followers knew precisely what she provided and never presumed to ask for more. Now she would navigate unfamiliar territory.

A calculated risk. The investigation pressed closer with each homicide update, each new lead that might expose her other life.

The matches page displayed nothing but white space, waiting to populate with names that would emerge gradually. She welcomed the delay. This methodical process restored her equilibrium and gave shape to her intentions.

More tasks demanded her attention today, but Blackburn allowed her screen to fade to black. She sat motionless in the dense quiet of her office, gathering herself for the impending storm.

Chapter 21

Monday afternoon. The phone rang on Blackburn's desk, cutting through the steady hum of keyboards and conversation that filled the precinct. She picked up, her tone calm.

"This is Detective Callahan, Hoggard County." The woman's voice carried a crisp, professional edge. "We had an incident involving an autonomous vehicle. Minor injury this time. Considering what's been happening in your jurisdiction, I thought a conversation might be warranted."

Blackburn settled back in her chair. Her fingers tapped a quiet rhythm against the cool metal desk beside her notepad. "What can you tell me?"

"It's complex," Callahan said. "We don't have an ID on our victim yet, and I don't want to miss anything. I'd appreciate your input."

"I can meet," Blackburn replied. Her mind had already begun cataloging possibilities.

"Good," Callahan said. "If you're willing, I'd ask that you come out to our station. I want to show you the scene itself. You might notice things we haven't."

They settled the details without fuss. Blackburn hung up, her focus sharpening as she rose and looked across the bullpen through the smudged glass of her office window.

She scanned the cluster of detectives. Each had strengths she could list, but only one would suit the demands of unfamiliar ground.

Cooper caught her eye first. His shoulders hunched forward, eyes narrowed at the blue glow of his monitor.

Blackburn crossed to his desk. Her heels clicked against the polished linoleum in a steady cadence.

"Cooper," she said.

He looked up, uncapped pen poised in hand.

"You're with me. Hoggard County had a non-fatal autonomous car hit. We're consulting." She paused just long enough for the information to register in his expression. "On the drive, bring me up to speed on Camilo Lowe and Jane Doe."

Cooper stood at once, sliding into his jacket and tucking his notes beneath his arm.

As they moved toward the exit, Sinclair shot Cooper a glare across the room, raw and unfiltered. Cooper flashed him a casual middle finger in reply. Unexpectedly, Sinclair's scowl melted into a grin.

Blackburn took the wheel for the drive north out of New Dresden. City blocks gave way to stretches of highway bordered by skeletal frames of half-built subdivisions and dense tangles of pine and oak.

After a few miles, with the city noise fading behind them, she spoke. "I know nothing about Hoggard County except that it feels remote."

Cooper nodded and began his update without prompting. "Jane Doe: we recovered clothing. Her DNA was on the inside lining but there's nothing useful from the outer surfaces." He held a folder, photographs paper-clipped to the interior. "Photos went out along with a sketch from the artist, but there's been no response so far."

"She's likely not local," Blackburn said as she guided the car onto an on-ramp.

"I'll send it statewide," Cooper replied, his pen scratching across paper.

Blackburn kept her eyes on the asphalt ribbon ahead as he continued. "It's odd," he admitted after a pause. "No calls at all. Not even mistaken IDs."

"Review the drawing," Blackburn said. "If you use a photo, keep it clean. Nothing that will scare the suburban moms."

"I'll handle it," Cooper replied.

The sedan moved steadily through afternoon light, bands of sun sliding across the hood in regular intervals. Cooper sat beside her, notes spread across his lap, pages rustling softly as he turned them. The suburban landscape gradually thinned. Houses grew farther apart, then fields opened beyond scattered oaks and maples.

"Anything new on Camilo?" Blackburn asked. She kept her eyes fixed on the asphalt ahead. "Saw his name on the board."

Cooper nodded once. "Small detail, but it matters."

"Go on."

He shifted the papers, their edges catching light. "Camilo Lowe, thirty-five. Shot at the northwest corner of National and Rogers, out by that old laundromat with the broken sign. It happened early, seven twenty-eight in the morning. Patrol got the call fast, but he was already gone when they arrived."

"Execution?" she asked.

He traced a finger down his notes. "Single round to the chest, close range. No defensive wounds, no signs of struggle. Cameras caught two figures approaching before he dropped. I think it's Bailey Yaster and Rabya Jones. They walked away after. No rush, no panic. The witness in the bakery next door picked both of them from a photo lineup."

"Solid IDs?"

He nodded again. "As good as we get without the weapon in evidence. Yaster's been easy to spot. Shaved head, walks with a distinct roll to his left side like he favors that knee. The footage matches perfectly."

"And Jones?"

"Medium build, dark hair pulled back," Cooper said, his voice dropping. "She runs with some of Yaster's people. Small-time drugs and sex work mostly. She showed up near Camilo's building two days earlier with Yaster. No prints recovered yet."

The landscape stretched wider outside her window. Cattle stood in distant clusters, their shapes dark against pale grass that rolled toward a horizon softened by heat shimmer.

"Motive?" Blackburn asked.

He adjusted his position, the leather seat creaking beneath him. "Nothing concrete yet. Camilo owed someone. Money or favors, but there's no paper trail. Tox screen came back clean, no fresh charges or priors in the last year." Cooper paused, considering his words. "Might have stumbled into something bigger than he realized."

"You got a location for them?"

"Maybe Florida," Cooper answered, tapping the edge of a photograph. "Yaster's cousin owns property near St. Petersburg. They could be laying low there if they made it that far south." He lifted one shoulder. "The car's stolen, plates stripped. Won't surface easily."

Blackburn glanced at him briefly before returning her attention to the road. "You planning to follow?"

"That depends on Fugitive Division." His tone grew more formal, creating professional distance. "If they hit traffic cameras or dump anything we can trace, we move. Until then, I've only got soft leads and speculation."

Silence settled between them like dust on a windowsill. Both preferred it to unnecessary conversation.

"They'll make a mistake," Blackburn said eventually.

Cooper agreed quietly. "They always do."

A red barn flashed past her window. The color struck deep, immediate as a physical blow.

Blackburn's fingers tightened around the steering wheel until her knuckles showed white.

Cooper continued discussing logistics and warrant procedures, but his voice faded to distant static as memory pulled her under. Twelve years old in brutal summer heat, sweat stinging her eyes as she worked along a sagging fence line. The red farmhouse stood nearby, paint peeling in long strips like sunburned skin.

Her child-sized hands had gripped the hammer's worn handle, driving staples through barbed wire into weathered posts that left splinters in her palms.

Sandy had been there. Last time she had seen her sister breathing.

The details remained vivid. The sweet-sick smell of fresh-cut alfalfa drying in windrows, cicadas thrumming in waves that matched her pulse, the rough texture of sun-bleached wood against her forearms when she leaned in to work.

She blinked hard and focused on the yellow center line unreeling ahead, pushing the images back where they belonged.

Debra checked the line of posts, measuring the tension with a critical eye. The fence remained rough but would serve its purpose. Wire bit into her palm as she made one final adjustment. Her expression stayed tight, mouth set, focus narrowed to the work before her. Wind whispered through the corn behind her, rustling leaves against stalks, but she ignored it. The only thing that mattered was making certain this barrier held. Just as she always had.

She set the last staple with a quick swing, the metallic ring sharp against the quiet fields. Straightening, she flexed stiff fingers and felt blood return to cramped joints, then looked toward the house. Through a dirt-streaked window, Debra caught sight of Sandy watching from her favorite perch. Her sister sat on folded knees, face pressed to the cool glass, afternoon sunlight catching in her pale curls.

Sandy waved, her smile wide and easy. A small flash of happiness untouched by everything outside those walls.

The sight lifted something inside Debra. She allowed herself a brief smile and returned the wave. A moment's warmth, nothing more. For a few heartbeats, work faded and even memory retreated behind the gentle ritual between sisters.

The sun dropped lower, painting deep shadows across the fields and over her scuffed boots. She knew chores waited inside. There were always more tasks waiting. But she let time stretch for a moment longer. She stood quietly at the fence line, breathing in the smell of turned earth and cut wood, holding on to the sense of completion and her sister's distant laughter.

Sandy's voice drifted out through the open window, thin and clear in the late daylight. The sound hollowed something in Debra's chest. She had not crossed that threshold in years. She saw Sandy only as glimpses framed by glass or slivers of movement in passing. There would not be another chance.

The memory slipped away without warning.

Blackburn focused again on the road ahead, hands steady on the warm steering wheel as Cooper sat beside her. A single blink cleared whatever regret lingered from old wounds. She listened for his words, tuning back into their conversation.

"...I said let's go, so we packed up and left," Cooper said from the passenger seat. "My nieces were great but my brother-in-law is impossible."

Blackburn inclined her head once, her features calm though nothing about the trip sounded pleasant. "How long did you stay?" Her voice remained measured, betraying nothing beneath its surface.

"Three days. I—"

The GPS cut him off with a flat announcement that they had reached their destination. Blackburn guided their car into a cracked lot outside Hoggard County Police Station.

She studied the building with clinical detachment as they stepped out onto asphalt still radiating heat from the day. The squat brick station belonged to another era. Its boxy lines and faded red walls suggested it had not changed since construction decades ago. Only a handful of patrol cars marked its presence as law enforcement.

Blackburn surveyed their surroundings. Low hills rose on one side. A cluster of unremarkable businesses scattered down Main Street. Somewhere beyond that, an expanse of farmland stretched to the horizon. The air carried the scent of freshly clipped grass and faint earth instead of city exhaust.

Inside, they crossed worn linoleum that groaned under each step toward an unmanned desk. An officer finally looked up from his glowing screen. A man in middle age with gray threading through his hair and eyes that took them in without surprise or hurry.

"Can I help you?" The officer's voice carried a hint of the local accent, each word measured against the quiet hum of the station.

"We're here for Detective Callahan," Blackburn said, holding up her badge. The leather case caught the overhead light. "Detective Blackburn, New Dresden PD. This is Detective Cooper."

The officer gave a brief nod and lifted the phone, speaking quietly into the receiver. While they waited, Blackburn scanned the lobby. Missing persons flyers covered the walls in overlapping layers, some edges curling with age. A wooden bench hugged one wall, its finish worn to pale patches where countless visitors had shifted and waited. The air carried burnt coffee and the musty scent of old paper, tinged with floor wax.

A door clicked open across the room. Callahan stepped through, her lean frame beneath a crisp white shirt, wire-rimmed glasses catching the LED glare. Her eyes, sharp behind the lenses, assessed them in one smooth sweep.

"Detectives. Thanks for coming," she said, extending a hand with formal efficiency. Her grip was firm, brief. "Let's talk in my office."

Inside, the space pressed close: two chairs wedged beside a desk crowded with paperwork, case files stacked in metal trays that gleamed dully. Callahan motioned them to sit before settling into her own chair, the leather creaking softly.

"We only have footage from two doorbell cameras," Callahan began as she typed. "No one has made a report."

Cooper frowned, shifting forward. "How can you have no complainant?"

Callahan shook her head and turned her monitor toward them. "It's clearer if you see it." She clicked open a file, and grainy video filled the screen.

The footage played in bleached color. A woman sprinted beneath a streetlamp's weak glow, her face lost to shadow and distance. Behind her, a car crept forward, too close, its headlights painting harsh stripes across wet asphalt as it closed the gap.

Blackburn watched without blinking. Something in the runner's movement caught her attention: the particular angle of her shoulders, the rhythm of her stride. Recognition flickered, quickening her heartbeat.

She kept her expression neutral, processing what she saw while the video continued its silent playback.

Callahan spoke without looking away from the screen. "The vehicle isn't a Straight Line model. We ran its signature against local registrations and matched it to a Timbre Day. Cheap semi-autonomous import, common enough around here. Ten registered in town. None with reported damage or incidents."

"Where did this happen?" Blackburn's voice came out steady, controlled.

"Sevaston," Callahan replied, dragging the footage back to replay a crucial moment. "Just ten miles west."

Blackburn filed the name away, maintaining her composure. That's where Arleigh said she lived.

She met Callahan's gaze. "I'd like to visit the location if that's possible."

Callahan nodded immediately. "I hoped you would ask. We can take my car."

Chapter 22

They crossed back through the lobby, emerging into afternoon sun that pressed warm against their faces. Callahan's unmarked sedan sat baking in the lot, heat shimmering off its hood. She unlocked it with a chirp, sliding behind the wheel while Cooper folded himself into the back.

The car pulled onto the main road, tires humming against sun-softened asphalt as they headed toward Sevaston. Callahan's voice rose above the engine noise.

"It happened last night at 10:43 on Yellowstone Road," she said, checking her mirror before glancing at Blackburn. "Quiet neighborhood. Not much happens there after dark."

Cooper leaned forward, the vinyl seat squeaking beneath him. "You only have doorbell camera angles? Nothing from street cameras?"

"No other footage turned up," Callahan answered, her tone clipped and professional. "Neighbors checked their cameras this morning after we contacted them. Two caught pieces of what happened." She let a beat pass. "The first clip shows her walking alone under streetlights. The next one picks her up running hard while that car follows close behind."

Blackburn kept her expression tight. "Do you know what time the car entered the street?"

Callahan shook her head. "No. Doorbell cameras are rare here. Sevaston has a low crime rate, so most people don't bother."

The countryside blurred past their windows as they drove, fields dissolving into hedge rows and scattered farmhouses. Callahan continued, her voice measured. "One of the few homes with a camera is where the alert came from. That footage shows a woman running from the car."

"If we hadn't seen similar autonomous vehicle incidents in New Dresden," Callahan said, "it probably wouldn't have caught our attention. But under the circumstances, we couldn't ignore it."

Cooper nodded, taking in the details. "Have you identified her?"

Callahan's gaze shifted to the rearview mirror, catching Blackburn's reflection. "That's what's odd. She hasn't come forward. Someone in that state would usually contact us."

Blackburn remained silent. She understood something of fear and guilt, how easily self-blame took root in the chest like a weed. If she was right about Arleigh, the woman might feel she deserved what happened, or mistake violence for retribution.

She watched fence posts and fieldstone walls give way to smaller homes and tidy yards as they neared Sevaston, each mile tightening the knot in her stomach. Her unease deepened with every familiar landmark.

Yellowstone Road appeared ahead. Modest houses lined both sides, their porches painted in fading pastels, flowerbeds trimmed with meticulous care. The neighborhood carried an easy calm that belied what had taken place here.

Callahan slowed the car, nodding toward a small bungalow with a wraparound porch. "That's where we found the first video."

Blackburn studied each house as they passed, cataloging every open gate and drawn curtain, the way shadows fell across driveways. She kept her tone even. "Any registered autonomous cars nearby?"

Callahan answered without hesitation. "None."

A block farther on, Callahan pointed to another house at the corner, its brick facade weathered but solid. "This one captured video of the car itself."

They parked at the intersection and stepped out together. The damage to the bus shelter struck Blackburn immediately. Shattered glass glittered across the sidewalk like ice. Metal posts twisted around themselves. Trash scattered across grass still damp with morning dew.

Callahan examined the scene with a methodical eye, her shoes crunching on broken glass. "It looks like the car veered off and struck the bench and garbage can. Not anyone standing nearby," she said. "My guess is that she ran behind the shelter at just the right moment. The driver may not have seen her or this structure at all."

Blackburn listened, standing motionless beside the broken glass. The morning air carried the scent of wet earth and something metallic. Inside, she weighed possibilities and calculated risk, but her face remained a mask. She kept to routine movements. She observed the scatter pattern of debris, cataloged damage, followed procedure while suppressing every impulse not tied directly to this case.

There was more work ahead. Blackburn was determined not to let emotion interfere with what needed to be done next.

"Are you certain there was a driver? I didn't see one on the footage," Cooper said.

"We can't confirm that," Callahan replied. She nudged a piece of plastic with the toe of her boot. The fragment scraped against asphalt.

Blackburn studied the twisted remains of the bus shelter, eyes narrowed against the morning glare. Willow and Sinclair both knew about Arleigh. The detail pressed at her nerves, cold and persistent like a splinter beneath skin. The fact carried weight. She forced it aside.

She crouched and picked up the broken shard. Its edges caught light as she turned it between her fingers. The plastic still held warmth from impact. With a gesture, she handed it to Callahan.

"The priority is locating the car," Blackburn said. Her tone carried the decision, authority quiet but unmistakable. "Have you already processed everything from the scene tied to the vehicle?"

Callahan examined the plastic, her thumb tracing its jagged edge before nodding once. "We've pulled what we can, but without the car itself our options are limited."

Cooper added, "In past cases, we've had one vehicle destroyed on its own, one in a lake, another over a bluff. We need this car found soon."

Blackburn looked past them at the street's edge where tire marks darkened the pavement. Her thoughts moved with precision. "New

Dresden's drones can assist in your search," she said. "They'll cover more ground than foot patrols alone." She paused, letting the words settle. "Also check local garages. Ask your postal workers if they delivered any overnight rush packages around headlamp size or spotted couriers near here."

Callahan's eyes flickered with approval, a subtle shift in her expression.

"A warning," Blackburn said. Her voice remained even, matter-of-fact. "Once our drones launch, media will notice almost immediately. Your story won't stay quiet for long."

Callahan gave a short nod. "I appreciate it. It would help us considerably, but I'll have to go through my chief first. He'll reach out to yours."

"Understood." Blackburn kept her expression unreadable, professional distance intact.

The scene yielded nothing more. They retraced their steps to Callahan's car, gravel crunching beneath their feet, and slid in wordlessly for the return trip to Hoggard County Police Station. Tension wound through the confined space. Uncertainty threaded each silence as they weighed whether this was reckless driving or something aimed.

On the drive back toward New Dresden, Cooper glanced over at Blackburn's set jaw and rigid hands gripping the wheel. Her knuckles showed pale against the leather.

He spoke quietly. "You seem bothered."

Blackburn did not look away from the road ahead. Its surface shimmered with heat. "The autonomous deaths aren't random," she said, voice stripped of excess emotion. "They're connected."

Cooper shifted in his seat to study her profile. The afternoon sun cast sharp shadows across her face. "What makes you so sure these are targeted?"

"When I spoke to Arleigh Jenssen, our so-called Phantom Driver, it was clear she confessed for attention, but not to invite real consequences. We get false confessions now and then, but not like hers. She was shaken by the deaths themselves."

Blackburn kept her eyes on the road as the red barn slipped past, its weathered boards catching the afternoon light. She pushed the distraction aside and pressed forward. "Autonomous cars are impersonal. You can control one from anywhere in the world. But these deaths are different. Messy, public, staged for effect. Whoever did this wants an audience. They're angry. This isn't about eliminating threats or tying up loose ends. It's about forcing someone to witness what they're capable of."

Rows of houses emerged into view, their windows dark against pale siding.

Cooper shifted in his seat, the leather creaking beneath him as he turned toward her. "But who's supposed to see it? What's the point?"

"Whoever's doing this wants us watching," Blackburn said. "Not just murder for its own sake. These victims aren't chosen for who they are, but for how the act affects someone else. That's why standard profiling doesn't work. The motive is provocation."

Cooper frowned and traced a finger along his stubbled jaw. "Provoking someone by killing random people. Who would react to that? Oh." He paused as understanding crossed his features. "It's us, isn't it?"

"Us," Blackburn confirmed quietly. "Someone wants to prove we can't handle this case. Or that cases like this are beyond our capabilities. What better way than to create a series of killings that leave us chasing shadows?"

He studied her profile in the filtered sunlight before speaking. "Are you saying someone's trying to embarrass Homicide? Deliberately?"

"That's one possibility." Her voice remained steady as she developed the thought. "If someone in Traffic Services wanted to highlight our blind spots, they could stage these deaths to resemble technical failures we might overlook. But they wouldn't miss them, since they created them. Or maybe it's closer to home. Someone inside Homicide with their own agenda."

Cooper leaned back, tension visible in his jaw. "You think someone here would go that far? Just for a promotion?"

Blackburn kept her hands steady on the wheel, feeling the road's vibration through her palms as she considered. "Maybe not for my job specifically, but forcing me out would accomplish plenty for certain people."

Doubt crept through her thoughts as she examined the theory piece by piece. It made sense when you traced departmental rivalries and ambition, but something felt wrong at the margins. Especially when she remembered Arleigh living miles beyond city limits, far outside New Dresden's jurisdiction.

Cooper shook his head firmly. "Nobody here wants your job, boss."

She focused on the flat stretch ahead, watching heat shimmer off the asphalt as her certainty wavered.

"Maybe it isn't about taking my job," she said after a moment. "Maybe they just want me gone."

Color drained from Cooper's face as he understood her meaning, his breath catching.

"You out of homicide... that would break you." His voice had dropped to nearly a whisper.

She nodded once, eyes forward.

"It would," Blackburn said flatly.

The car continued past silent houses and manicured lawns, engine noise filling the space neither of them was ready to address yet.

"Who would want to destroy you?" Cooper asked. The unease already crept into his voice, as if he sensed what she might say.

Blackburn let the silence stretch, sorting through possibilities. When she answered, her voice came low. "Sinclair. He would try to ruin me just to play the hero after."

They sat with that thought. The words settled between them until Blackburn spoke again. Her tone remained careful, each word weighed before it left her mouth. "Cooper, there's something else. I think Sinclair might be tracking my car again. I hoped Hayes made it clear last time, but now I'm not so sure."

Cooper's eyes widened behind his glasses. "Tracking you? Why do you think that?"

"I already caught him once," Blackburn said. "Hayes intervened, but maybe he wasn't direct enough." She shook her head, frustration threading through the gesture. "I should have checked sooner, but I let myself believe the GPS incident wouldn't repeat. We should look for one now."

Cooper shifted against the leather seat, restless energy radiating from him. "Actually, there's something about Sinclair I've been hesitating to mention. With this tracking issue, it feels more urgent now." He paused, searching for the right words.

"What is it?" Blackburn asked, her shoulders tensing.

He exhaled slowly, the sound filling the car. "Sinclair's always visiting shady gambling sites at work. A lot of garbage pops up. Ads, strange links." His gaze fixed on the dashboard. "Yesterday I saw what looked like a surveillance feed on his screen. It didn't seem right, but with all the junk he clicks on, I thought maybe it was a virus or some random pop-up."

Blackburn's voice dropped, quiet but firm. "What kind of surveillance feed?"

"A women's washroom," Cooper admitted, the words reluctant but clear. "The angle was from high up, looking down. Couldn't tell which washroom or even if it was inside our building. And Sinclair always claims stuff like that is accidental." His frown deepened as he reached for justification and came up empty.

Cold settled at the base of her spine, spreading upward. "You think he meant to watch?"

"I don't know," Cooper said. "But with him tracking you like this..." He pressed his lips together before finishing. "Boss, I think he's fixated on you with real focus. If someone wanted these murders staged just to pull your attention back to him..."

"It's Sinclair," Blackburn said flatly.

Neither spoke as she turned into a narrow lot beside a small local store, gravel crunching beneath the tires.

"We'll check for the tracker now," she said as the engine ticked into silence.

They stepped out, the afternoon air hitting their faces as they dropped to their haunches beside the wheels. Their hands moved deliberately along cold metal seams and shadowed recesses under the frame.

A minute later Cooper's voice cut through the quiet. He straightened up, a small black device pinched between two fingers.

"Got it," he said after studying the NDPD logo pressed into the plastic casing. "Did he track us all the way to Hoggard County?"

Blackburn stood beside him, her gaze fixed on the device resting in his palm.

"It appears so," she said, her jaw tight with restrained anger.

They got back into the car. Cooper turned the tracker over in his hands, studying it as if it might reveal more secrets. Blackburn kept her eyes on the city ahead, the low hum of traffic filling the silence between them. The knowledge that Sinclair, not Willow, had planted the device shifted something inside her. She felt a muted relief, though it was edged with fresh concern.

Sinclair's fixation had moved from background threat to immediate danger. The prospect that he might have followed her to King Street Park set her jaw tight. She considered the angle he would have chosen, what he might have seen. If he had watched her meeting with Arleigh, then Arleigh herself was at risk now. Exposed by association rather than error.

Blackburn's mind picked quietly through every detail, tension winding slow and dense beneath her skin. She tried to calculate how much she had underestimated Sinclair's reach and found the margin uncomfortably wide.

They pulled into the lot behind headquarters. Summer heat rose from the asphalt in thick, shimmering waves. Blackburn took a breath as she cut the engine, the air conditioning's sudden absence making the heat press closer. She forced stillness onto her face. Control mattered here. Panic would only muddy what came next.

She turned to Cooper, weighing her words. "I'll handle Hayes," she said, voice flat but certain.

Cooper hesitated just outside his door, his fingers gripping the handle. His gaze flicked across the rows of parked cruisers. "Can you leave my name out of it?" His voice carried an edge of unease he could not disguise.

A faint smile tugged at Blackburn's mouth. "You sound like a witness who wants nothing to do with court." Her tone stayed dry, taking some weight out of the air.

He almost smiled in return. "I'd appreciate it."

"I'll do what I can," she replied.

"Thanks, boss." He sounded younger for a moment, almost vulnerable.

Inside, the building's artificial chill raised goosebumps on her arms. They split at the entrance. Cooper disappeared down the hall toward his desk without looking back, his footsteps fading into the everyday murmur of the precinct. Blackburn walked toward Hayes's office, the tracker heavy and cold in her palm. Each step echoed against the linoleum as she rehearsed how she would frame what needed saying and leave nothing unnecessary exposed.

Chapter 23

Blackburn knocked at Hayes's door. Her knuckles struck three times against the wood. Through frosted glass, she saw Hayes on the phone, his head bent, one hand raised to wave her off. She held still for a beat, jaw tightening, then pivoted and walked away.

Her footsteps tracked a line down the corridor to the women's washroom. She pushed through the door, taking inventory in smooth, methodical sweeps of her gaze. The LED lights buzzed overhead, casting harsh shadows in the corners. She scanned each angle systematically. Ceiling, walls, vents. She searched for anything out of order. Nothing obvious emerged, but irritation pressed against her temples like a vise.

She returned to the secretary's desk with the GPS tracker balanced in her palm, its weight heavier than its size suggested.

"Please let me know as soon as Chief Hayes is free," she said, urgency contained behind clipped words. "This can't wait."

The secretary nodded and assured her she would be contacted immediately. Blackburn thanked her and continued down the hall. She cut into the stairwell and paused on the landing, listening for footsteps before slipping the tracker beneath her shirt. The cold metal pressed against her ribs.

Back on her floor, she pulled open the washroom door again. This was familiar territory. The one she used most often. If Sinclair had placed surveillance anywhere inside headquarters, it would be here.

She moved to the first stall and ran her fingers along every surface: the rough plastic of the toilet paper holder, the smooth metal waste bin, even a glance into the porcelain bowl itself. Each stall received the same thorough inspection. Nothing surfaced. At the sinks, she worked methodically. Her fingertips traced beneath cold porcelain edges, eyes following the seams up to mirrors and under towel dispensers.

As she washed her hands with care, something shifted in the mirror's reflection. One ceiling tile sat askew, its edge lifted just enough to catch a careful eye.

Her pulse quickened but her breathing remained steady. Emotion stayed locked beneath composed features. She stared at the reflection for several seconds without moving, memorizing the exact position of the displaced tile.

Then her phone rang. The sharp trill cut through her concentration.

"Detective," the secretary's voice came through crisp and professional, "Chief Hayes is ready for you."

Blackburn raised her phone and captured a single photo. Her face and the crooked ceiling tile appeared clearly in the frame. Evidence, if she needed it later.

She left the washroom in silence and made for Hayes's office with purposeful strides.

Inside his office, she closed the door with a soft click and approached his desk. She set the GPS tracker down between them, the small device landing with a definitive thud.

"Sir," she began evenly, "Cooper and I just got back from Hoggard County on a consult." Her tone remained controlled as she continued. "Cooper found this attached beneath my car this afternoon. I believe Sinclair is responsible." She met his gaze directly. "There's more."

Hayes's mouth tightened into a thin line as he studied her expression. "What did you say to Cooper about it?"

"I told him this was the second time someone had traced my car," Blackburn answered without hesitation.

She waited a moment before continuing, her voice dropping lower but maintaining its directness. "Sir, I have a written report signed by Sinclair himself where he admits to following me."

Hayes's eyebrows rose, disbelief carving deep lines across his forehead. "What? Why am I just hearing about this now?"

"He signed out a police tracker to follow my movements," Blackburn said. The LED lights overhead cast harsh shadows across her face. "He logged it. He also admitted to being outside my house more than once in the past three months." She paused, her jaw muscles tightening visibly. "I didn't mention it before because I wanted to see if the report would be enough to deter him."

Hayes absorbed her words with a slow exhale through his nose, the sound sharp in the quiet office. His expression hardened like cooling metal. "That didn't work."

"No sir." Blackburn kept her tone restrained, though heat simmered beneath each word. "My judgment failed here. I'll forward you his statement right away."

Hayes reached for his phone, the movement swift and decisive. "This is serious, Detective. We need to—"

She cut him off, her own phone already in hand. "There's more."

The metal frame of his chair groaned as Hayes sank back, skepticism flickering across his weathered features.

Blackburn turned her phone screen toward him, the small device heavy with implication. "I believe there's a camera hidden in the women's washroom. Second floor, third stall. It's tucked behind this ceiling tile."

Hayes studied the photo without speaking, the muscles in his jaw working beneath the skin. He set the phone on his desk with care, as if the device itself carried contamination. "Are you certain?"

"I haven't touched it," Blackburn replied, each word precise. "I didn't want to disturb evidence or let anyone know we're aware of it." She held his gaze without wavering. "Along with tracking my car again, it forms a pattern that points directly at Sinclair."

Hayes pressed thick fingers against his temple, the understanding settling across his shoulders. "Do we know how long this has been going on?"

"No." Blackburn shook her head once, a sharp movement. "But that bathroom should be sealed off before he realizes something is wrong."

Hayes's hand hovered above his office phone, suspended in indecision. "We can't close it without a reason. People will notice. And if word spreads about a camera in there, every restroom becomes suspect."

"You'll have to check them all," Blackburn said, her voice dropping to barely above a whisper. "Internal Affairs keeps an RF detector on hand for situations like this." She kept her eyes locked on his. "If there's another device anywhere else and you miss it now, we answer for that later."

Hayes gave a brief nod, then lifted the receiver. The dial tone hummed in the silence. "I'll call IA myself." His hand stilled halfway through dialing, and he looked at her again, the tendons in his neck standing out. "If your suspicions are correct, this goes much deeper than harassment."

"I know." Blackburn's hands curled into tight fists against her thighs as she stared down at the image still glowing on her screen. The ordinary ceiling tile now pulsed with menace.

She kept her gaze lowered when she spoke again. "I keep replaying how this started. The tracking, the surveillance." Her voice dropped lower but remained steady as she finally looked up at Hayes. "I've always been direct with colleagues. Maybe too much so sometimes. Banter, sarcasm. It's how I connect."

Hayes watched her closely, his frown deepening the creases around his mouth. "You think you encouraged this somehow?"

"No." The word came out sharp and definitive. She offered nothing to soften it. "But I wonder if Sinclair misread basic courtesy or humor as something else." She placed her phone on his desk with a soft click that somehow sounded final. "Instead of recognizing I treated everyone that way, he convinced himself it meant something more personal. When reality didn't align with his fantasy—"

"He started acting on it," Hayes said, his voice rough.

"Yes," Blackburn agreed, the single syllable hanging in the air between them. "A reasonable person would back off after a misunderstanding like that." Her spine remained rigid as she continued. "Sinclair decided instead that my confidence was a challenge he had to take control of."

Hayes shook his head. "This isn't on you, Blackburn. That's on him for failing to treat you as an equal."

Blackburn nodded and leaned back in the chair, its worn surface creaking as she gave Hayes room to reach for his phone.

He dialed IA. She listened to his side of the call, his voice pitched low with controlled urgency that made the air in the office feel thinner.

"We have credible grounds to suspect a camera in the women's washroom on the second floor. One of our male detectives may be involved," Hayes said. His free hand curled into a fist on the desk, knuckles whitening against dark wood. "I will send the formal request in writing but this cannot wait. Use an RF detector. Check every washroom in the building. Yes, every one. Because I'm telling you to."

As he spoke, Blackburn opened her phone and forwarded the photo evidence to his inbox, the soft chime of the sent message punctuating his words.

Hayes ended the call and looked at her. "IA will take over. They're shutting that washroom down immediately." His voice had settled but the muscles in his jaw remained tight. "IT will trace any signals if they find a device. We need to know who's receiving those images. If there's even a camera at all. This is ugly."

"I know, sir." She tapped her fingers once against the desk, the sound sharp in the quiet office, measuring her next words. "The fallout from this will hit my own unit."

"Does it matter?"

"It does," she said evenly. "If I'm wrong, I've just accused one of my own in front of Internal Affairs. The rest of them will see the search and draw their own conclusions. I can't have that." She checked her watch without hurrying the motion, the metal band cool against her wrist. "I'll take them to dinner later."

Hayes arched an eyebrow, something like amusement threatening to soften the hard lines around his mouth. "You think that won't attract attention?"

"I buy dinner sometimes," she replied as she reached for the door handle, its brass surface warm from the afternoon sun. "That doesn't make me heartless."

She left without waiting for approval.

Blackburn entered the Homicide office and crossed the bullpen with steady steps, her heels marking a sharp rhythm across worn linoleum. A few heads lifted, curiosity flickering in their eyes before work reclaimed their attention.

In her office, she closed the door quietly behind her and sat down, the familiar scent of old coffee and paper files settling around her. She let herself breathe only when she was out of view.

Through the blinds, she watched Sinclair at his desk across the bullpen. He hunched over his computer screen, the blue glow washing his face pale as he typed with two fingers.

Seeing him there brought anger back in slow currents instead of a rush. He had crossed a line. She felt it settle beneath her skin, cold and unwelcome as winter rain.

She forced herself still. Her hands unclenched on her lap, leaving faint crescent marks in her palms.

Opening a drawer, Blackburn found Sinclair's original report. The one where he had admitted to following her outside work hours. The paper felt brittle between her fingers as she took it out without flinching or hesitation and slipped it into a plain manila folder.

She rose, folder held close at her side, jacket neat across her shoulders, the silk lining whispering against her blouse.

Blackburn left her office and moved toward the stairs without breaking stride or glancing back at the bullpen below.

Chapter 24

Blackburn sat at her desk, eyes tracing the lines of an incident report while sounds from the corridor filtered through her open door. The homicide division felt more restless than usual, conversations pitched just above a murmur, tension sharpening the click of keyboards and the shuffle of papers.

A sudden stir near the second-floor women's washroom drew her attention. Two maintenance workers arrived, tool belts creaking as they headed for the bathroom door. Blackburn watched them pass, noting the way they gripped their equipment, knuckles tight around metal handles. She stayed silent, weighing each detail in her chest.

Cooper noticed as well. He paused mid-sentence in his paperwork, pen hovering above the page as he looked up to catch Blackburn's eye. His brow furrowed in question, but she glanced away, focusing on the worn edge of her desk blotter. She would not risk drawing him into this, not when uncertainty still hung thick in the air between them.

Across the bullpen, Sinclair registered the shift. His gaze lingered on the maintenance crew before sliding back to Blackburn's doorway. He forced a casual posture, hands reorganizing folders that did not need attention, but the tension showed in the rigid set of his jaw and the shallow rise and fall of his chest.

Blackburn rose from her desk with steady intent and crossed to the corridor. Her heels clicked against linoleum tiles in beats. Conversations slowed as she approached, voices dropping to whispers.

She spoke quietly with the lead worker, her instructions clipped and direct. The LED lights overhead cast harsh shadows across her controlled expression, each word chosen for clarity rather than warmth. After a short exchange, she nodded and turned back toward her office, the worker's confused expression following her retreat.

When Blackburn returned to the bullpen, Sinclair's eyes tracked her every movement, suspicion hidden behind the careful arrangement of his features. Cooper's leg bounced beneath his desk, the fabric of his trousers rustling softly, but he kept quiet, waiting for direction.

Sinclair broke first. "Is there a problem with maintenance?" His voice carried forced neutrality, each syllable too precisely formed.

"There's a leak," Blackburn said. Her tone was flat, nearly bored, as if discussing the weather. "The women's washroom is closed until further notice." She did not elaborate. The silence stretched.

Sinclair's fingers tightened on his mouse as he glanced at his monitor with new urgency and began typing. The rapid clicks of his keyboard filled the quiet. Cooper met Blackburn's look, giving a brief nod toward Sinclair before focusing on his own screen again, shoulders tense beneath his jacket.

Blackburn knew Sinclair was likely watching a live feed from inside the closed washroom. A camera he had installed. A camera he monitored. The timeline was narrowing like a closing fist.

She clapped her hands once. The sharp sound broke through the low conversation around her. "Everyone, let's take lunch together."

Cooper and Reeves responded at once, relief softening the lines around their eyes. "Nice. Where to?" Reeves asked, already reaching for his coat.

Sinclair hesitated by his chair, fingers drumming a nervous rhythm along his keyboard as he shifted his gaze between the screens and Blackburn's unreadable face. A bead of sweat caught the light at his temple.

"Come on," Blackburn said simply, her voice carrying the command beneath its casual tone. "We all need a break."

Reeves grinned as he stood up, chair wheels squeaking against the floor. "Did something good happen?"

Blackburn only raised an eyebrow in reply and stepped toward the exit without looking back, her footsteps echoing in the suddenly quiet bullpen.

Blackburn said, "It's part of HR's latest plan. Department heads are supposed to show a little gratitude for the people who keep things running." She let the final word hang, a faint smile touching her mouth. The line drew a few easy laughs.

Reeves played along. "And this has to involve us?"

Blackburn perched on the edge of Dawson's desk, the metal cool beneath her palm. "We've been mired in that car case, and it isn't even listed as a homicide. We're taking confessions from fathers about killing their own kids. We have men shooting wives over breakfast arguments." She shifted, folding one leg over the other, her heel tapping once against the desk leg.

She scanned their faces. "So tonight, leave your files on your desks. I'll take everyone out for dinner. No alcohol on my tab. Just food."

Cooper grinned. "I'm not about to say no to free dinner."

Sinclair still looked uneasy, fingers drumming against his thigh as he crafted excuses before he started. "I should stay back and catch up on reports," he said, voice low.

Blackburn shook her head once. "Reports will wait. Come eat."

She slipped into her office to retrieve her jacket while Reeves and Cooper went for theirs, energy rising among them at the promise of a meal they wouldn't have to pay for. Chair wheels squeaked as they pushed back from their desks.

Reeves called toward Sinclair as he shrugged on his jacket, the fabric rustling, his tone edged with mock impatience. "Come on, man. Leave it for now."

Sinclair paused at his screen, the blue glow reflecting off his glasses, hands hovering over the keyboard before he gave in and powered down. The monitor clicked off. He put on his jacket without comment.

At the door, Cooper's hand on the handle, she remembered someone missing from the group. "Should we ask Willow?"

Blackburn answered without hesitation or apology. "Not today." Her expression softened briefly. "Lunch with just you three."

They filed out together, footsteps echoing against tile as they crossed toward the elevators and into the corridor beyond. The LED lights hummed overhead, casting harsh shadows.

Cooper and Reeves talked easily between themselves about where Blackburn might bring them this time. Sinclair stayed a step behind, still dwelling on whatever had held his attention moments before but following nonetheless, his shoes scuffing against the floor.

Outside, Blackburn led them through crowded sidewalks toward Harvest & Hearth. A small corner restaurant favored by most of the precinct when overtime left little time for anything better than take-out pizza or strong coffee. The striped awning cast shadows across the concrete. Fresh basil and garlic drifted from somewhere near the kitchen window, mixing with exhaust fumes from passing traffic.

Inside, conversation hummed quietly beneath pale pastel walls and mismatched posters collected by owners with eclectic taste. Every table held its own tiny glass vase with cut flowers. Chairs scraped against old wood floors as servers passed with trays of bubbling lasagna and salads bright with vinaigrette. Steam rose from the dishes, carrying the scent of oregano and melted cheese.

They found seats midway along the far wall, the vinyl cushions sighing as they settled into an easy rhythm shaped more by habit than by any real celebration. Blackburn rested her hands lightly on the table edge, the surface sticky beneath her fingers, waiting for menus and watching her detectives begin to unwind under ordinary light and the expectation of something simple. A good meal at someone else's expense.

The restaurant noise filled whatever spaces their conversation left open, each detail grounding them in a moment away from their usual burdens. Silverware clinked against ceramic plates. Ice rattled in glasses. The espresso machine hissed behind the counter, releasing a bitter-sweet cloud of steam.

Blackburn entered first, scanning the dining room with a steady gaze. Her eyes lingered on Sinclair, who clung to the edge of his seat, attention flickering toward the exit every few seconds. His fingers drummed against the polished wood table, knuckles white where they gripped its edge. Cooper and Reeves settled in more easily, shoulders dropping as warmth from the kitchen reached them, carrying notes of roasting garlic and fresh herbs.

The hostess led them to a corner table with clear sightlines across the restaurant. Blackburn took the seat facing the door. Cooper and Reeves reached for menus without hesitation, pages rustling as they compared options, their voices dropping to a comfortable murmur.

Sinclair only pretended to read his menu. The laminated surface caught the overhead light as his hands trembled. He kept glancing at Blackburn, then at the busy entryway where servers weaved between tables. His jaw clenched and released in quick cycles, a muscle jumping beneath the skin. Blackburn watched him over her glasses before returning her attention to the wine list.

Cooper broke the silence first. "What's everybody having?" He tapped a glossy photo of a burger dripping with cheese.

Reeves smiled. "The veggie wrap this time. I promised myself I'd eat better this week." Her tone carried a gentle challenge aimed at Cooper.

Blackburn's lips curved. "No point wasting a real meal on health food." She closed her menu with a decisive snap.

Cooper grinned at her approval. "Artisan burger for me. If you're buying, I'm not holding back."

Sinclair hesitated before mumbling, "Soup of the day." His voice barely carried across the table.

Blackburn studied him for a beat, then spoke clearly to the waitress who had materialized beside them. "I'll have the pasta special."

The waitress made quick notes, her pen scratching across the pad. Pink hair swept into a neat bun, she confirmed their orders with the smooth efficiency of someone who had worked lunch rushes for years.

While they waited, conversation drifted from cases to deadlines. Reeves asked if anyone had caught last night's episode of The Rheinhart Show.

Sinclair straightened, color returning to his face now that the topic offered safer ground. "I still can't believe they killed off Ava." He shook his head, genuine frustration replacing his earlier anxiety.

"Don't tell me anything," Reeves warned, raising her palm like a shield. "I haven't seen it yet."

Blackburn listened quietly, measuring the shift in Sinclair's breathing against his earlier tension.

Cooper shrugged. "You two are way ahead of me. I haven't watched TV in weeks."

The mood softened as food arrived. Their server distributed plates with brisk precision. Steam rose from Cooper's burger as he unwrapped it, juice running down his fingers after the first bite. He made a sound of pure satisfaction. Reeves approached her wrap more deliberately, savoring each combination of crisp vegetables and tangy dressing.

Sinclair lifted spoonsful of soup to his mouth without comment, but the bowl emptied steadily. Blackburn worked through her pasta in neat bites, back straight but shoulders loose.

The air around their table grew thick with competing aromas. Grilled beef mingled with fresh basil, sharp parmesan cut through sweeter tomato sauce. Their corner became its own small world within the restaurant's steady hum.

"This beats eating in the squad room," Cooper said between bites, dabbing grease from his chin.

Reeves murmured agreement while catching Blackburn's eye in silent thanks.

The group found an easy rhythm as everyday sounds filled the spaces between words. Forks clinked against ceramic. Ice rattled in glasses. From a nearby table came bursts of laughter, while behind them servers pushed through swinging doors, releasing brief clouds of steam from the kitchen.

Conversation drifted as they ate, floating from television to local sports. Sinclair's shoulders gradually loosened, his reserved manner melting as laughter replaced the old tension. For a while, his worries dissolved into the warm hum of the restaurant.

When the plates sat empty and streaked with sauce, Blackburn caught the waitress's eye and signaled for the check. The pink-haired server returned, her smile bright against the dim lighting. Blackburn mirrored it, adding a trace of flirtation that sharpened the air between them. Sinclair watched the exchange through narrowed eyes, silent as Blackburn slid her card across the table.

She held the payment device steady for a moment, her fingertips grazing the waitress's knuckles before releasing it.

"Appreciate the service," Blackburn said, her voice low and unhurried.

Color bloomed across the waitress's cheeks as she tucked a strand of hair behind her ear. "Anytime," she replied, her gaze holding Blackburn's a beat too long.

Sinclair's fork clinked against his plate. The ease from earlier had evaporated. Across the table, Cooper and Reeves caught each other's glance, their shared smirk barely contained.

Blackburn rose and collected her jacket, leather creaking softly. "Let's call it a night," she said, each word deliberate. "It's late."

They emerged into air sharp with autumn chill, streetlights casting amber pools on wet pavement. The city hummed low around them as they walked back toward the precinct. Cooper and Reeves strode ahead, their voices bouncing off brick walls as they debated the best meal they had eaten all month. Blackburn hung back with Sinclair, matching his steps.

"That was good," Sinclair said after a stretch of silence. His tone stayed neutral, his profile rigid in the half-light.

Blackburn nodded once. "Every team deserves it now and then," she answered, her words careful, her peripheral vision tracking the tension in his jaw as they moved through the quiet streets.

Chapter 25

Blackburn halted just inside the bullpen. It was Tuesday morning, and the room looked gutted.

Nearly every desk stood bare. Computer towers had vanished. Cables draped over desktops, their copper ends catching the LED light, useless and slack. A few notepads and pens remained scattered across the surfaces, along with two staplers. Nothing else.

Her mind flashed to the gun.

She moved quickly to her office, pulse hammering in her throat. Her computer had disappeared as well. Only pens, paper pads, and her ceramic vase sat on the desk. Her fingers shook as she wrapped them around the vase.

The weight settled solidly in her palms.

Carefully, she tilted it and caught a glimpse of dull metal nestled inside. The gun was still there. She glanced around the hushed room as she adjusted her grip on the cool ceramic. The sense of security she once felt in this space was already evaporating. Sinclair had brought this down on them.

"Boss?" Reeves's voice cut through the stillness. She looked up to find him hovering in the doorframe, his knuckles white against the wood, uncertainty etched across his features. "What happened?"

She set the vase back on her desk with a soft thud and stepped into the bullpen, her palms spread wide. "I don't know," she said. "I just walked in." The words tasted hollow on her tongue, but they were all she could offer right now.

She didn't need a memo to know who'd done this. IA's fingerprints were all over the emptied room. Efficient, impersonal, surgical. She pictured them moving through the bullpen while the detectives were out, stripping away evidence, certainty, safety.

Reeves moved deeper into the bullpen, his footsteps echoing as he examined each workstation, searching for some overlooked detail. He paused at Dawson's desk, fingers brushing the empty surface, before checking the break room.

"The printers are still here," he called out, his voice bouncing off the walls. "Coffee machine too." He re-emerged, his brow creased. "Did someone break in?" Reeves's voice was too loud in the hollow room.

Cooper appeared, eyes flicking from desk to desk, jaw tight. "This some kind of joke?"

Blackburn shook her head, already reaching for her phone. "I'll get Hayes."

Cooper's palm cracked against a dangling cable on his desk. "Where's my computer?"

"I'll call Chief Hayes," Blackburn said, pivoting toward her office as heat crept up her neck. This was not what she had agreed to when Hayes made his promises.

Her detectives trailed behind as she snatched up her phone and dialed Hayes's number, her hip pressed against the desk edge.

Voicemail clicked on immediately.

"Chief, this is Blackburn," she said, her voice flat as old paint. "All our computers are gone from the bullpen. Call me."

She ended the call and dialed again, her thumb jabbing the screen.

"Why would someone take computers? Everything gets saved on our main server," Cooper said as he sank into a chair across from her.

"That's how it should work," Reeves answered quietly as he settled beside Cooper, his shoulders drawn tight.

Blackburn tried Willow next. "Is there an upgrade scheduled for our computers?" she asked when the line connected.

After a stretch of silence that offered no answers, she disconnected and shook her head. "It's not IT."

Reeves dragged his palm down his face and spoke through his fingers. "It's probably IA. When I got pulled during another investigation years ago, they did things like this."

Blackburn tried Hayes again, surrounded by her silent detectives who gathered near her desk like moths to a dying flame, their usual rhythms shattered.

"Shouldn't we get a heads-up if something like this is coming?" Cooper asked, shifting in his seat.

Blackburn's head moved. A bare shake. "Unless it isn't them," she said, her voice dropping low. "Unless someone else took them."

A voice sliced through from behind them. "My apologies for being late."

The office door swung open. A woman entered, her suit so sharply pressed it sliced the air. She moved through the silence, gaze sweeping the room like a searchlight. Blackburn felt the temperature drop.

Of course. IA.

"Detective Blackburn?" The woman's voice was edged with something colder. She offered a hand, but her eyes never left Blackburn's face. "I'm Sergeant Buxton."

Reeves spoke louder than he intended. "Well, fuck me."

Blackburn rose from her seat and extended a hand in greeting. She could not tell whether this visit stemmed from her complaint or from what she had done afterward.

"Detective Morgan Blackburn," she said. She nodded toward her team. "Reeves. Cooper. Where is Sinclair? He should be here by now."

She kept her eyes on Buxton, searching for any flicker of intent behind that professional mask.

Sergeant Kayla Buxton revealed nothing as she shook each detective's hand in turn, her grip firm and brief.

No badge waved. No formal announcement. Just her presence, and the certainty that nothing would be the same after today.

Blackburn met her gaze steadily. She understood.

A shift rippled through the room. Cooper crossed his arms, leather jacket creaking. Reeves bounced his heel against the floor in a nervous rhythm. Dislike for IA never stayed hidden long. It seeped into the air like spilled coffee, bitter and impossible to ignore.

Blackburn kept her spine straight, hands still.

Willow Adler pushed through the door, her voice pitched high with alarm. "What happened? Holy crap, what happened to all the computers?" She wandered into the bullpen, fingers trailing along the exposed cables that snaked across empty desks like dead vines.

"This is Willow Adler, civilian staff." Blackburn watched her carefully. "Information technology support."

Willow did not look up from the tangle of wires. "Did someone break in?"

"Willow! Willow!" Blackburn called again before Willow finally turned and made her way into the office.

Willow approached Buxton and offered a handshake before pushing her glasses up the bridge of her nose. "What's going on?"

Blackburn suppressed a smile. "She takes the job seriously." A sheen of perspiration glistened along Willow's hairline. Even from across the room, Blackburn could see the quick, shallow rise and fall of her chest.

The rest of the team looked no better.

Buxton allowed a trace of warmth into her expression but kept steel beneath it. "Listen up," she said, each word clear. "I will be conducting interviews with each of you, beginning now."

The silence that followed felt heavy as lead.

"I'll go first if you want," Blackburn said, gesturing to an empty chair near Buxton's desk.

"Thank you," Buxton replied without hesitation. She pointed to each person in turn. "You next, then you, then you."

"Me?" Willow's hand fluttered to her chest.

"Yes, unless you prefer to start us off?" Buxton asked, her tone neutral as water.

Willow froze. Color drained from her cheeks.

Blackburn stepped in smoothly. "Might as well get it over with, then head back to your work."

"But I didn't do anything," Willow said, her voice barely above a whisper.

"This is standard," Buxton replied, unmoved.

"She's not sworn." Blackburn directed the words at Buxton while giving Willow a subtle nod toward compliance.

"Oh, okay," Willow managed as she lowered herself onto the edge of a chair, perched like a bird ready to flee.

The detectives shifted, leather shoes scuffing against worn carpet. Reeves tugged at his tie, loosening the knot. Cooper leaned back against the wall as if distance could protect him from what was coming.

"You travel light," Blackburn said, nodding to the stripped desks. "Or maybe you prefer we do."

Buxton's lips twitched in almost a smile. "We like to keep things clean."

"You'll find we're good at cleaning up after ourselves, too," Blackburn replied, not quite meeting Buxton's eyes.

Buxton didn't blink. "We'll see."

A current of unease rippled between the detectives. The silence that followed stretched thin and brittle as old glass.

She could feel Buxton's gaze scraping at her, peeling back layers. Did they know about Willow? Banks? Kendria and Lilith? Every secret felt suddenly exposed, raw and bright under the office lights.

Her chest tightened. She forced herself to breathe, to keep her face still.

She forced a thin smile. "What a mess." She caught herself and pressed her lips together. After a beat, she spoke again. "Excuse my language. Where's Sinclair now?"

Her heart hammered in a careful rhythm, each beat matching Buxton's eyes as they settled on her with judgment.

"We'll start now," Buxton said. She nodded at Willow, signaling for her to step out.

Before Willow could reach the door, Cooper spoke up from across the room. "Whatever this is, we're a team," he said firmly. "We know how to work together."

Buxton offered him a look that barely concealed its skepticism. "Yes," she replied. Her voice was flat and even as poured concrete. "Teamwork is always an option."

* * *

"Which way?" Willow asked, glancing in both directions at the junction.

"This way." Buxton led her right, down a muted corridor toward the stairwell. Willow climbed after her in silence, her breath growing heavier by the time they reached the third floor.

She paused at the landing, taking in the quiet atmosphere. A low hum of distant conversation drifted through the air, but little movement disturbed the stillness.

"First time on three?" Buxton asked over her shoulder.

Willow blinked back into focus and nodded. "Yes. What's up here?"

Buxton guided her past a row of closed doors and private workspaces dotted with nameplates and abandoned coffee mugs. "Administration," she said without elaboration. They passed a glassed-in lounge where afternoon sunlight caught untouched bottles of water stacked beside a small table.

Buxton stopped outside an office and pushed open the door for Willow to enter. "Finance and benefits are managed here," she said simply. "Have a seat. I'll be right back. I need something from my office."

Willow settled into one of the chairs arranged around a pale desk. The room felt orderly, almost generous compared to the homicide unit's cramped interview spaces. No battered furniture or peeling corners marred the pristine surfaces.

When Buxton returned, clipboard in hand, she closed the door with little ceremony and took up position across from Willow beneath LED lights that buzzed faintly overhead.

Buxton clicked her pen, eyes on Willow. "You're the tech."

Willow nodded, mouth dry. "That's me."

"Tell me how you fit in here."

Willow hesitated, then shrugged. "Mostly I fix things. Computers. Sometimes theories."

Buxton looked up, just a flicker. "Theories?"

"They get tangled. Like wires." Willow tried to smile. "I untangle what I can." Willow hesitated. The pause filled with the distant whir of ventilation. "I don't consider myself part of their team."

"You provide technical support for the homicide detectives, correct?"

Willow nodded. Her glance flicked to the door, then back as she shifted against the hard plastic chair.

"Describe how you assist the detectives with their technology," Buxton said.

Willow managed a smile. At least someone seemed to care about her work, now that she was more involved in cases than ever before. "Lately, they've had cases involving autonomous cars, so I've been helping review theories and parse EDR data."

Buxton lifted a hand, palm forward. "I meant general support. Do you handle the computers? Routine problems?"

"Yes, whatever they need." Willow listed examples: filtering data, diagnosing slowdowns, resetting passwords. "Detective Reeves forgets his passwords all the time. He insists on complicated ones, then locks himself out."

"And Detective Sinclair? Do you assist him as well?"

"Yes. Not with passwords. He tends to get viruses instead. When my system alerts me, I go up and clean his computer," Willow said. The air felt thick in her throat. "Could I have some water?"

Buxton's reply came with a quiet laugh. "Of course, help yourself."

"Have you worked with Detective Sinclair on anything visual?" Buxton asked as Willow twisted open a bottle. The plastic crackled. Willow drank deeply, grateful for the relief even from the warm, stale water.

"Visual? Once or twice," she answered, wiping her mouth. "I designed a banner for the squad room once. Maybe you saw it?"

Buxton leaned forward, breath warm. "Anything more personal?"

Willow hesitated, fingers finding a spot behind her ear to scratch as she settled back into her seat. "Personal? No. What do you mean by personal?" The word hung between them a moment too long, triggering her memory of Blackburn's old request about placing images on Sinclair's desktop.

She kept her tone steady. "No, nothing like that. Not photographs or anything private." The water bottle crinkled as she took another long sip.

Buxton's expression stayed pleasant, revealing nothing.

"What kinds of viruses does Detective Sinclair encounter?" Buxton asked after a pause. "All of this remains confidential."

Willow steadied herself with another swallow, the water sliding cool down her throat. "Mostly older types. Adware and Trojans crop up now and then. The antivirus software catches most things, but a few slip through each month."

"Have you helped him with any files related to images or video?" Buxton pressed.

"No ma'am," Willow replied evenly. "If I find malware or questionable files during cleanup, I report it like always. But I don't go looking around anyone's files unless there's cause." She met Buxton's gaze directly, holding it a beat before adding, "I try to respect privacy."

Buxton closed her folder with a soft snap and nodded once. "Thank you for your help today."

Willow twisted the cap back on her bottle and rose. The chair scraped against the floor. "What should I do now?"

"The team is expecting their computers returned today," Buxton said as she stood, smoothing her jacket. "Your assistance would be appreciated setting them up." She paused near the door and lowered her voice just enough to signal importance: "Please do not discuss our conversation."

Willow nodded and stepped into the hallway, LED lights humming overhead.

She made her way back toward homicide, thoughts circling around Sinclair but never quite landing. Her footsteps echoed off the linoleum.

At the next junction she hesitated, weighing whether to stop on the second floor to help with computers or continue down to her own workspace in the basement. The decision came quickly. The day would not move forward until she saw Blackburn.

In the homicide bullpen she found Blackburn at her desk, fingers tapping against a coffee mug.

"Sgt. Buxton wants you on three next," Willow said.

Blackburn stood and left without comment, her chair rolling backward.

As Blackburn's footsteps faded, the others closed in, silent and expectant, their faces hungry for answers Willow didn't have. She hugged her elbows, wishing she could vanish into the wires beneath the floor.

Chapter 26

Sergeant Buxton glanced at her watch. Ten minutes had passed since Willow stepped out. She clicked her pen against the notepad and waited.

Blackburn knocked once on the open door, then entered the interview room. This space was larger than the usual interrogation cells and spared the battered furniture. Sunlight filtered through real windows, warming patches of the polished floor. Bottled water sat neatly arranged on the table next to chairs with intact cushions that did not wobble. The overhead lighting cast sharp shadows but fell short of being hostile.

"Have a seat," Buxton said, settling across from her with a notepad in hand. "Detective Blackburn, thank you for coming. Please state your name and rank for the record."

Blackburn straightened in her chair. "Detective Morgan Blackburn, first class."

Buxton wrote it down, her pen scratching across the paper in quick strokes. "This conversation is confidential and part of an ongoing investigation. Do you have any questions before we start?"

"I do not."

Buxton nodded once, studying the subtle tension in Blackburn's shoulders. "Good. Detective, how would you describe the working relationships within your homicide unit?"

Blackburn leaned back, arms crossed loosely over her lap. The gesture appeared nonchalant, but her fingers pressed too firmly against her sleeves. "I believed our relationships were stable until recently. There are always points of friction when people work under pressure and make decisions that count. We are handling a complicated case now. There have been arguments about direction and theory, but I thought we functioned as a capable team." She met Buxton's gaze without flinching. "Why am I here? I tried Chief Hayes but never got an answer."

Buxton's face remained composed. She ignored the question about Hayes and kept her eyes steady on Blackburn's. "You mentioned stressors in your current case. Can you clarify what those disagreements involved? Who took part? What changed that made you doubt your assessment?"

She leaned forward a fraction. The leather of her chair creaked softly.

Blackburn shifted again, her jaw tight as she chose each word with care. "If this concerns what I reported to Chief Hayes, then standard procedure would call for him to inform me." A bitter edge crept into her voice. "But he isn't fond of routine steps."

Buxton set aside her pen and held Blackburn's stare. The silence stretched between them, filled only by the distant murmur of voices in the hallway.

"Yes," Buxton said. "This review follows from your complaint to Chief Hayes."

She retrieved her pen, fingers precise against the metal. "Since you brought it forward, let's discuss Detective Sinclair directly. How would you describe your working relationship with him over the past few months?"

Blackburn exhaled slowly, allowing a wry tilt at one corner of her mouth though she kept her tone measured. "It has stayed professional, despite headlines suggesting otherwise. We're investigating a series of vehicular assaults. You have seen my name in the news." Blackburn pressed her palms flat against the cool tabletop, steadying herself before continuing in a clipped monotone.

"As for my complaint, it concerns matters outside our current investigation." She paused. The room's air stalled.

"Sinclair is young. Green. Still learning how to keep himself out of his own way." She met Buxton's eyes again before looking down at her hands, studying the faint lines across her knuckles.

"He has trouble separating his personal feelings from his work obligations." Her voice softened just enough to suggest resignation rather than animosity. "He likes me. Everyone knows it. He doesn't bother hiding it most days." She hesitated for half a breath.

"I thought secrecy wasn't his strong suit," she added flatly. "Lately I've realized he can keep some things very well concealed."

Blackburn paused, the muscles along her jawline drawing taut. "I trust you've read the chief's report about the tracker on my car. He used departmental equipment to monitor me."

Buxton's pen scratched across paper, her posture straightening with each detail. "Yes, I have Chief Hayes' statement on the unauthorized tracking. That is a serious breach."

She set the pen down, its weight clicking against the desk. Her gaze held steady, unwavering. "You mentioned before that Sinclair was not good at keeping secrets, then corrected yourself. What changed? What did you find out?"

She shifted forward. Close enough to signal intent without invading Blackburn's space. "And when did you first realize his interest had become inappropriate?"

"He's always been obvious," Blackburn said, her voice carrying the neutrality of someone accustomed to containing reaction. "But about a month ago, I found the tracker myself. It had been there at least two months before that discovery. I didn't know how far it had gone until then. He's made it clear he finds me attractive. I keep it professional, as anyone should. I informed Chief Hayes, but he tends to excuse this sort of attention." The tendons in her neck stood out briefly. "You know what I mean."

Buxton gave a short nod, understanding settling into the lines around her eyes more than her words. She kept her voice deliberate. "So, finding the tracker was the first hard evidence of misconduct on his part. How did you come across it?"

"My neighbor tipped me off," Blackburn replied. Her fingers flexed once against the fabric of her slacks before going still. "She saw someone near my car early one morning. That prompted me to look underneath myself."

Buxton's pen moved across the page in quick strokes, then stopped. Her eyes lifted, unblinking. "When you say he's always looking, what exactly does that entail? Have there been incidents in areas where you were alone or expected privacy? Locker rooms, restrooms?"

The pen hovered, its tip catching the overhead light. "And has Sinclair ever made remarks about your personal life or shown knowledge of things outside work that he shouldn't know?"

Blackburn's shoulders drew back against the chair. Her words emerged precise, each one separate. "He watches from his desk in the bullpen. My office window faces him directly. Most days if I glance up, he's watching until he realizes I see him and looks away."

Air filled her lungs slowly before she continued. "In the past month it has escalated. Twice while we were talking alone about cases, nothing remotely personal or suggestive, he was visibly aroused. Once he actually put his hand in his pocket while it happened. He stood there and didn't bother to hide it until I ordered him out." Her voice remained level, but something harder edged into the spaces between words. "He walked straight into the bathroom after that. The chief is aware."

The LED lights hummed overhead as she continued, each word dropping into the stillness like stones into water. "He also told me he watches my house. But he rushed to clarify it wasn't through my bedroom or bathroom windows." The corners of her mouth pulled downward. Her gaze fixed on the wall behind Buxton's shoulder.

"No one asked about those windows. In homicide work we call that kind of denial its own confession."

Buxton's pen pressed into the paper, the pressure leaving deeper impressions with each word.

"That is deeply troubling," she said. The softness had left her voice entirely. "You're correct. Denials without accusation often signal guilt."

She lifted her eyes from the notepad, her expression carved from professional stone.

"When Sinclair said he had watched your home but denied the bedroom or bathroom windows, do you recall exactly how he phrased it? And how did you respond?"

"This is complicated." Blackburn pressed her fingers to her temple, as if the memory itself carried weight. "I came home one night after dinner with Lilith Halperin. She thought she saw movement in the bushes outside my house. I drew my gun and checked the yard. The air was still, no footsteps in the dirt. Nothing. Later, Sinclair admitted he had been there. He told me, and these were his exact words, 'I never looked into your bedroom or bathroom. I wouldn't cross that line.' I told him he was lucky I hadn't fired, asked how long he had been following me. Willow Adler was present for that conversation. If you haven't spoken to her, she can confirm it took place in my office. At the time, I thought that closed the matter."

"Did you check your house for surveillance devices? Anything unusual after that?"

"No. I assumed it was finished."

Buxton wrote in her notebook, the scratch of her pen steady and deliberate. She circled a phrase before continuing. "So, Willow heard Sinclair admit to watching your home but said he stayed clear of certain windows. That's significant corroboration."

She glanced up, meeting Blackburn's eyes without hesitation. "You said you thought it was over, but something changed. What happened next? What made you realize there was more?"

She brought her pen up again, poised above the paper. "And Detective, I have to ask. Have you found any recording equipment at your residence? Or here in the station?"

Blackburn leaned forward, jaw tight. "I told Detective Cooper about my suspicions while we were returning from Hoggard County on another case. We pulled over so he could examine my car and found another tracker attached to the undercarriage. Cooper also told me he had noticed something disturbing on Sinclair's computer earlier. A washroom camera feed. He didn't know if it was live or not, just said he saw an image that worried him. Since the women's washroom I use is next to Sinclair's office, I went to check myself. I saw that a ceiling tile looked displaced and photographed it immediately before going to Chief Hayes with what I had found and what Cooper had reported to me. I believe Hayes sent you the photo when he contacted you."

Buxton nodded once as she noted details, her focus sharpening with every answer. "Chief Hayes did provide that photo," she said. "You were correct. There was equipment hidden above that ceiling tile."

Her attention stayed fixed on Blackburn now. Professional distance had given way to something more direct. "When Cooper saw the footage on Sinclair's monitor, did he explain exactly what he saw? Was it a static image, video file, live stream?"

"Cooper told me there was no movement in the frame and he couldn't be sure what kind of feed or file it was."

Buxton's pen stilled for a moment before she asked, "Do you have any sense of how long that ceiling tile might have been disturbed? When did you last notice it intact?"

"I don't know how long it had been like that," Blackburn replied evenly. "If there are files or images saved anywhere, their metadata should give you a timeline."

Buxton nodded again and made note of metadata review procedures. "That's exactly right. We've started analyzing all digital evidence for timestamps and related data."

She set her pen aside and looked at Blackburn, her formality settling back into something closer to genuine concern. "Detective, we take these violations seriously. The evidence supports your complaint. Detective Sinclair is suspended while the investigation proceeds."

She paused, then asked, "Is there anything else about Sinclair's conduct that I should hear? Any incidents or remarks, even small details you remember?"

Blackburn's jaw tightened. The professional restraint she had carried into the meeting dissolved. "Sinclair's attention to his cases has deteriorated. This isn't just about wasting time at his desk or scrolling through sports scores. He has ignored key witnesses and failed to secure a scene properly after one of the autonomous vehicle deaths. I told him to disable the car while it was still on site. He stood there and did nothing." Her voice hardened with each word. "There was an arrest last week. He took in the wrong brother for aggravated assault. Used S.W.A.T., no less. Booking ran the prints and told him he had Elijah Malik in custody, not Devon Malik. He kept Elijah anyway, until I intervened and ordered his release." Her tone flattened as she listed each point, the frustration barely contained beneath her delivery. "Those aren't minor errors. Chief Hayes knows every detail."

Buxton's pen moved across the page in silent agreement as she recorded the comments. "That's a clear pattern of negligence," she said, the scratch of pen on paper filling the brief silence. "And the timing of these lapses. Did you notice they began around when Sinclair's behavior toward you escalated?"

Blackburn rubbed her hands together, the skin whispering against itself as she considered. After a moment, she nodded once. "I hadn't made that connection myself," she admitted, her voice dropping lower. "But yes, you're right."

Buxton tapped her pen against the notepad in a rhythm that echoed in the small room. "Do you believe Sinclair's fixation on you impaired his ability to handle casework? Or do you suspect other issues might be contributing? Substance abuse, personal problems. Anything else that might explain this decline?"

Blackburn responded without hesitation. "His attention is fractured because he can't let go of whatever fixation he has developed on me. Every time I raise concerns, someone tells me not to overreact or to wait for more evidence." She pressed her palms flat against the cool surface of the table, the pressure grounding her before she continued, quieter but resolute. "His mistakes put people at risk."

Buxton leaned back in her chair, the leather creaking softly as she regarded Blackburn with clear intent. "I have one last question, Detective: Do you feel safe coming to work? Are you concerned about retaliation or ongoing harassment?"

Blackburn met her gaze directly, unflinching. "Do I feel safe? Most of the time. I carry a sidearm and I know how to use it." She folded her arms across her chest, the fabric of her jacket rustling, before letting them fall again. "My concern is retaliation, absolutely. Sinclair is armed too, and this hasn't stopped with warnings from me or from Chief Hayes. If anything, it's getting worse."

Buxton closed the notepad with a soft thud and shifted into a more decisive stance. "Detective Blackburn, this investigation will be both thorough and conclusive," she said, each word heavy. "We have solid documentation now, and Detective Sinclair will answer for what he has done."

She rose and extended a hand across the table, her grip firm when Blackburn took it. "Your safety remains our priority here," she said steadily. "If there is any contact from Sinclair, direct or indirect, you report it immediately. He has been instructed that all communication with you and with anyone in this office is prohibited."

As they shook hands, Buxton said, "Thank you for bringing this forward. I know it wasn't easy, especially considering how your concerns were handled at first. We'll keep you updated as the investigation moves ahead."

She paused at the door, her hand resting on the handle. "Is there anything you need from us now? Any pressing concerns or questions?"

Blackburn rose and adjusted her jacket, the fabric whispering against her shoulders. "Yes. Since I have reported this to Chief Hayes several times without response, who do I contact next time? I doubt Sinclair will simply walk away."

Buxton's hand left the door handle. She reached into her pocket and produced a card, the paper crisp between her fingers. "You come straight to me now, since this is an active IA matter. My direct number and cell are on the card."

She extended it. Their fingers brushed during the exchange, warm skin against cool paper. "If you cannot reach me immediately, call the IA duty officer. The number's on the back. Someone is always available."

Her jaw tightened, though her voice remained steady. "If you feel you're in any danger, call 911 first and then notify me. Keep a record of everything: times, places, what was said or done, even if it seems unimportant."

She held Blackburn's gaze. One professional acknowledging another. "You did the right thing by coming forward. Don't let anyone make you doubt that."

Blackburn slipped the card into her pocket, the edge pressing against her hip. She lifted her chin. "No one doubts me, Sergeant Buxton. Thank you for your time."

Buxton inclined her head, respect evident in the gesture. "I can see that, Detective. Take care."

She turned the handle, and they stepped into the hallway. The LED lights hummed overhead. Behind closed doors, keyboards clicked and voices murmured.

Blackburn's fingers wrapped around the cold metal of the stairwell door. Her voice carried in the empty corridor. "Do you know how many women in New Dresden are killed each year by men who ignore restraining orders? By men who won't stop?" She turned to face Buxton fully. "Too many, Sergeant. Far too many."

Chapter 27

Blackburn stepped off the plane at Des Moines International. The stale scent of pressurized cabin air clung to her clothes as she moved through the terminal with nothing but her phone and a slim wallet tucked into her jacket. No luggage. She would not be here long.

She found a coffee stand and waited as the espresso machine hissed and gurgled behind the counter. Sunlight cut through the windows, framing the kiosk in hard rectangles that made her squint after so many hours in artificial light. She took her coffee black, the paper cup warm against her palm as she crossed to the rental desk.

The clerk pulled up her reservation and slid over keys to a silver sedan without comment. She signed where required, exchanged two words, and walked outside into the sharp clarity of late morning air.

Once on the highway, Blackburn kept her focus on the white lines unreeling ahead. The city fell away quickly, replaced by subdivisions marked with familiar chain stores and then acres of farmland stretching flat beneath an empty sky. Her headache spread behind her eyes, a dull throb that pulsed with each heartbeat. She drank the coffee anyway, letting its bitter heat seep through the thin cup into her hands.

Fields blurred past in precise rows of corn stubble and soybean remnants, each crop indistinguishable from the last at highway speed. The land where she had spent her childhood was gone now, sold off in pieces and cleared of structures that might have anchored memory or regret. The trust set aside for Debra had evaporated after lawyers took their fees. What remained had vanished quickly.

Brampton appeared on the horizon, more suggestion than place. The flatness pressed in from all sides, familiar enough to make her jaw clench. Each mile closer sharpened old memories to a cutting edge.

She felt it first in her breathing. A tightness she tried to smooth out by counting seconds between inhales. Her knuckles whitened on the steering wheel, but she kept driving.

The smell arrived before any landmark gave warning: manure thickening the air as she passed a collapsing barn. Its roof sagged against the sky while paint peeled from boards that barely held their shape. Not the one from before but close enough for her body to register every detail.

Blackburn forced herself forward, teeth clenched as she watched the road narrow through fields that grew wilder with each passing minute.

A roadside stand appeared ahead: folding table, battered pickup drawn up behind it. She slowed and pulled onto loose gravel that crunched beneath her tires.

A young man hopped down from his truck when he saw her car stop. "Hi there!" His voice carried across the still air with great cheer.

Blackburn matched his tone out of habit. "Hey. How's business today?"

He grinned and reached for a paper sack already filmed with soil. "Can't complain. What are you looking for?"

"Half a dozen sunchokes." Her words came out neutral.

"Sunchokes? Ha, you must be from around here. Not many people call them that," he said as he dug through a wooden bin at his feet. He found six decent roots and brushed dirt from their knobbed surfaces before dropping them into the bag.

"You planting or eating?" he asked, weighing out her order with casual efficiency. "If you're planting, don't go deep. Four inches is plenty or they'll just rot out."

She counted out bills while he spoke, feeling muscle memory guide each movement.

"Six dollars even," he said, holding out both bag and open palm.

Blackburn started to pay, then noticed something near his foot: a horseshoe crusted with rust beside other castoffs aimed at tourists. Bent nails welded into animal shapes, wax candles melting together in mason jars.

She pointed at the horseshoe instead of reaching for the bag right away. "You selling these too?"

"Yep," he said easily and nudged aside dried corn husks to reveal more iron shapes arranged on weathered plywood, waiting for someone to find value in what remained.

"I'll take a horseshoe," she said.

He reached for another paper bag and selected one of the cleaner shoes. "Hang it up, so the luck sticks around," he told her as he handed it over. "That's sixteen altogether."

Blackburn took the bags, passed him a twenty, and left the change behind. She returned to her car, set the bags on the passenger seat, and slid behind the wheel. The metal weighed heavier than the produce.

She started the engine but hesitated. Her hand reached for the bag with the horseshoe. With a swift motion, she pulled it free and let it drop onto the seat with a dull thud. She picked it up, testing its heft in her palm, rolling her wrist to feel the strain in her forearm. The iron felt cold against her skin. A faint smile crossed her lips before she set it back on the seat.

The road cut through trees that shielded farmland from view. Here and there, modern houses appeared alongside farm trucks and rusting equipment tangled with brush. As Brampton drew near, a compact graveyard emerged beside the road. Small, fenced in, overlooked by everyone but time.

Rows of uneven headstones jutted from tangled weeds. The ground looked abandoned, just as it had on her computer screen days before. No flowers marked any of the graves.

She pulled into the narrow gravel drive and stepped out with only the sunchokes in hand. The air carried an undertone of rot and wet earth as she passed through a gate hanging from one hinge.

The plot measured no more than twenty by thirty feet. Reading names came easy; only forty stones stood here. She found it after a few steps. A grass marker.

T. Roth. 1986-2002.

No epitaph. Nothing but a name and dates. He deserved less than that.

Anger pressed tight around her ribs but did not escape into sound or gesture. The inheritance settled in its usual place. Deep and cold.

Memory surfaced with clinical clarity: fourteen years old, crouched behind barn slats on a black night at the edge of family land. The smell of fresh-turned earth filled her nostrils. She watched her father dig by flashlight in hard soil, uneasy certainty rising inside her about what would come next.

She had thought he was making space for her grave.

But she was wrong. Sandy would vanish instead.

Debra doubled over and retched into dead grass, bile burning her throat before she turned away from the sight. Her fists slammed against wire mesh until skin split and blood slicked her knuckles.

She had always planned to save Sandy somehow, holding onto that idea even when it made no sense. That hope was gone now.

Metal sang softly against rust as she punched again.

Her brother's bicycle tires crunched over gravel somewhere behind her. A sound she recognized too well. Every evening before strangers arrived at their house, he came for her. Over five hundred times by Debra's count. Not less, never fewer.

She had convinced herself that endurance would outlast him. That being tough was enough to survive. But now she understood how little toughness mattered.

"You clean?" His voice drifted over as he leaned his bike against wood siding.

She never said yes. It was how she got him to use protection.

"No."

"You're a fucking pig," he said, pulling the key from his pocket. The key. She had seconds to work. Her gaze swept across the packed dirt floor. The cage held nothing useful.

The padlock clicked open. Chain slithered loose, metal links rasping against rusted bars.

She spotted an old horseshoe half-buried in dust just outside the cage. She stretched for it, fingertips grazing pitted iron as her brother's hands clamped onto her waistband and yanked her backward.

She swung the horseshoe with everything she had. The impact rang dull against his skull above the ear.

He staggered sideways, caught off guard, confusion clouding his features. Pure fear flooded her veins, cold and crystalline. She bolted past him without looking back, driving her heel into his cheekbone as she fled.

She sprinted across the yard, through knee-high weeds that whipped at her shins, bursting into open field. Exposed roots caught at her feet, but she pressed forward until her lungs screamed and her thighs burned like acid. Darkness swallowed the landscape on all sides. They would not find her trail tonight. Morning would arrive too late for pursuit.

Night hung thick overhead. No stars pierced the blackness. Every step forward, sometimes running, sometimes stumbling over invisible terrain, was fueled by raw necessity. When exhaustion finally claimed her, she crawled into a cornfield and wedged herself between the stalks, their dry leaves rustling overhead. There she waited, straining for footsteps that never came.

No one followed. No one searched for her that night. Or for nearly two years, until Whitmore arrived.

The memory lodged in her chest like shrapnel, too deep to extract. No one had cared then.

Blackburn stood at his grave now, letting that truth settle into her bones, cold and leaden.

She dropped to her knees and pressed both palms flat against the earth above him. The soil crumbled beneath her fingers as she clawed at stubborn crabgrass and desiccated weeds. The ground yielded nothing. Frustration hummed beneath her ribs. She drove her fist into the dirt once, pain shooting up through her wrist, then forced her breathing to slow as she surveyed the weathered headstones stretching in crooked rows.

She pulled both sets of keys from her pocket: house and rental car. A tight smile tugged at her lips as she slipped one set back into her jacket.

With methodical precision, Blackburn drove the house key into the packed earth and began scratching out a shallow depression. Stab and twist, careful progress by inches. Dirt caked beneath her fingernails and ground into the creases of her knuckles as she hollowed out a rough cavity just deep enough for her purpose.

Her fingers trembled as she upended the bag, spilling sunchokes across the disturbed soil. She pressed each tuber down firmly, then scraped earth over them with shaking hands. Mud streaked her palms. Grit embedded itself under every nail. She pressed the back of one filthy hand against her lips until the wave of nausea receded.

Let go.

The scream tore from her throat before she could swallow it back. A raw sound that split the cemetery's hush. Years of fury poured out while she tilted her face toward the starless void above and waited for the ache in her chest to fade.

Only wind through brittle grass answered.

Blackburn drew in air that tasted of iron and loam and turned toward her car.

At the door she looked back once more at his grave, picturing pale rootlets worming downward through darkness until they found bone, embracing it, never releasing their hold.

The image brought relief. Keen but pure. As though some internal ligature had finally snapped after years of unbearable tension.

She pivoted away from the grave and ground her boot heel into the disturbed earth before sliding behind the wheel. Wind sighed through the headstones at her back with relentless patience.

Ninety seconds spent. No more required.

Home waited somewhere past the horizon's vacant line.

Inside the car Blackburn sealed herself in and absorbed the unfamiliar quiet that pooled in her chest. A tentative peace where fury had always churned.

For this moment, body and mind obeyed together, a strange new harmony settling into her marrow, replacing all that rage had forever demanded.

Chapter 28

Blackburn stepped into the thick heat of late summer, light cutting across the airport parking lot in long, slanting lines. She narrowed her eyes against the glare, the silence out here almost absolute except for the distant pulse of airplanes taking off and landing. She had not told anyone where she was going. She checked her car for another tracker before leaving home; the search had come up empty. Nobody waited for her in this place.

Another jet rose overhead, its roar drowning out her thoughts for an instant. She almost missed it beneath the plane's thunder: a second engine, lower and sharp. Not an airplane. Blackburn turned toward the sound. Tires screamed across hot pavement, a car accelerating fast.

She moved instinctively. Adrenaline hit in a hard rush, flooding her limbs with heat. She bolted right, weaving between rows of parked vehicles, lungs burning with each breath. The car behind her closed in fast, relentless. Her palm slapped the trunk of her own car just as she twisted away.

The oncoming vehicle crashed hard into her parked sedan. Steel groaned and glass shattered in a burst of noise that tore through the quiet afternoon. The impact shuddered through the ground beneath her feet.

For a moment, everything stilled except the ringing that filled her ears. Blackburn forced herself upright, focused on control while scattered voices rose around her.

Sinclair pushed himself from the ruined driver's seat, his movements jerky and uncertain. Blood streaked from his brow down his cheekbone, dark against pale skin. He looked at nothing and everything at once, teetering forward with a gun clutched tight in his right hand.

The crowd kept its distance, drawing back with quick steps as soon as they saw the weapon. Someone's keys jangled as they retreated.

He tried to speak but got only halfway there, voice rough with pain. "Morgan... I just—" The rest collapsed under the confusion and injury.

Blackburn watched his mouth form words she could not hear over the rush of blood in her veins. That did not matter now.

"Adam," she said, forcing steadiness into her tone even as tension crawled beneath her skin. Her hands flexed open and closed at her sides, fingernails pressing into her palms.

"You're hurt," she continued, keeping each word slow and deliberate. "Whatever happened here isn't what you intended." She measured every sentence, trading on memory and shared ground rather than force.

He stood rooted by indecision. Sweat and blood mingled at his temple; the gun trembled but did not move from his grip. His knuckles showed white around the handle.

Blackburn took a shallow step forward, careful to move within his field of vision without sparking alarm. The air between them felt charged and brittle. She could smell motor oil and the sharp tang of antifreeze leaking onto asphalt.

"Adam." Her voice dropped to something gentler, measured rather than pleading. "You know me." The words scrapped out of her dry mouth. She paused long enough for him to register her face in focus again. The sun beat down on both of them, merciless.

She let silence stretch between them before speaking again.

"Let's breathe together," she said simply, tone unwavering. "In through your nose... hold it... let it out."

Each movement, each word, became calculated containment; she asked nothing more than attention while shifting closer by slow degrees. Gravel crunched softly beneath her shoes.

She watched for any flicker of recognition or surrender behind his eyes but kept herself ready for anything else that might come next. Her muscles coiled tight, prepared to move.

"Adam, what you are doing right now isn't who you are." Blackburn kept her tone even, each word steady against the tension that thickened the air between them. "Let's start over. Just us. We can work through this without anyone getting hurt." She watched him closely, tracking the tremor in his hands, the sweat beading at his temples, letting quiet urgency ride just beneath her calm. "I understand what you're feeling," she said, her voice flattening into something cooler. "You care. That's obvious. It doesn't have to end badly. We can figure out another way forward if you put down the gun."

She tasted bile, sharp and acidic at the back of her throat. Men like Adam never changed. She recognized the brittle need twisting his features, the desperate hunger in his eyes, so familiar and so thinly disguised as love.

Blackburn kept her gaze locked on his, holding the charged space between them with a show of empathy she did not feel. Her patience was hollow, a performance refined through years of negotiation, but she maintained it with discipline. The sharp ache behind her eyes pulsed in time with his rattled breathing. She could see the panic working through him, watched it ripple across his face, and she focused on drawing it in her direction, containing it before it broke free.

"Morgan, I don't—can't—" His voice cracked under the strain. The gun wavered in his grip, the barrel catching LED light as it trembled with his conviction.

She stepped closer. Each movement was slow and even, her heels clicking softly against the floor, nothing rushed or reactive. The room contracted around them, her attention narrowing to him alone. "Adam, listen to me," she said. Her words were controlled but not cold, shaped by years of coaxing confessions from guilty men. "If you love me, this isn't how you prove it."

She let his name rest between them again, careful and deliberate, a lifeline cast across dangerous water.

Sinclair's expression flickered. Hope and confusion battled behind his eyes. "Morgan, I don't get it," he said thickly, the words slurring with exhaustion. "Everything I did was so you'd see me. I thought we had something real."

Blackburn spoke softly but with surgical precision. "Love doesn't come with threats or fear, Adam." She kept her gaze steady as she spoke, noting how his pupils dilated with each word. "What you've done is about power, not care." She nodded at his hand, the gesture small but pointed. "You still have a choice here."

He gripped the weapon more tightly, knuckles whitening, jaw clenched until the muscle jumped beneath his skin.

"I never meant for this," he said roughly, his voice scraped raw. "I only wanted to protect you from all of it." He shook his head as if that might shake loose some logic from the chaos he had created.

Blackburn's face settled into a look he would recognize: part understanding, part warning. The expression of someone who had seen too many men mistake obsession for devotion.

"I know your record," she said, her voice carrying the shared history. "Good cops recognize when things have gone too far. They know how to pull back." She gave him a chance to reclaim some dignity without promising more than she could offer.

His features twisted with pain, the professional mask finally cracking as he tried to reconcile their positions.

"It isn't simple for me," he muttered finally, defeat dragging down every syllable. "You just don't understand what it's like to want someone this much and be pushed away every single time."

She waited for him to reach whatever conclusion he needed, understanding that control sometimes came from silence rather than speech. The air between them grew heavy with unspoken truths.

Blackburn advanced another step, closing the gap with calm. Her voice dropped. "You're hurt, Adam. But right now, I need you focused on what's in front of us. There are lives at risk. Ours included. Don't let this get any worse."

She shifted the conversation, making it clear that he still controlled how this ended.

Sinclair's grip on the pistol tightened as he swung it toward the crowd. His voice broke. "They don't get it. They'll never understand what we have, how deep this goes."

Blackburn moved between him and the onlookers, establishing herself as a barrier. Her tone held steady. "They don't have to understand. What matters is that I do. I see your devotion, Adam, and I can help you if you let me."

She watched him for signs of doubt and leaned into his need to be heard.

Sinclair faltered. The gun wavered. She pressed on quietly. "We can work through this together, Adam. We can find a way out without anyone getting hurt. Set down the gun and we'll start there."

His words came in a rush. "I got suspended today. They found those videos. The photos. None of them know what happened, what you said to me. I was only trying to look out for you." His face crumpled as tears threatened, exposing something younger and frightened beneath the anger.

"Watching over me in the bathroom?"

He flinched at her question. "No. Yes. Everywhere! I waited for you all day. After your flight landed, you didn't even see me!" A single shot fired, dust scattering near Blackburn's shoes. Heat flooded her, adrenaline and power. Her nipples hardened against her shirt, a response that enthralled and terrified her even as her body knew how alive the danger made her feel.

Her body tensed but she did not move away or raise her hands in panic. She signaled bystanders back with a firm gesture, keeping her eyes on Sinclair. "Clear out! Give us space," she called without turning away from him. Then quiet again: "Adam, is this what you want? To be here with me?"

His answer came fast and raw. "Yes! That's what I mean. When you told me about Willow. I know you said you're a lesbian. It stung. It had to be a phase, though, right? You wanted to provoke me with the fat girl from IT? Just trying to make me jealous?"

At the insult to Willow, Blackburn's jaw tightened but she let no other sign escape.

"You think making threats is love?" Her tone sharpened but stayed level enough for control. "You're proving nothing except that you can frighten people. Me included." She glanced at his gun and back again. "If any part of this is about how much you care for me, put it down."

He hesitated, breathing quickening.

"You care," Blackburn said, moving closer until only inches separated them. "But jealousy like this isn't love. It's desperation." Her voice lost none of its edge as she moved into his reach. "You say you won't hurt me but look at what's happened here." She nodded toward the ground where dust still lingered from his shot.

"You almost pulled the trigger on me once already."

Blackburn stood calmly, her presence cutting through the noise that pressed in from all sides. She indicated the bullet lodged in the dirt and the ruined shell of her car. Each was a silent ledger of what had already gone wrong.

"This misunderstood lover routine doesn't work for you, Adam," she said, voice precise and unhurried. Each word landed with intention, stripping away his defenses. "You can do better. You should."

She let the words settle between them, using the silence to press against his pride, making it clear he was failing even his own standards.

Blackburn looked up at the crowd clustered at a cautious distance, her gaze unwavering. "None of them will help you, Adam. They're just watching." Her tone remained level. "If you want out of this alive, I am your only option." She made herself necessary to him without ceremony or threat.

Sinclair's hand trembled against the gun. Blackburn saw the quiver and kept her voice steady, weaving authority with something closer to sympathy. "You're not seeing straight right now. This isn't romance. This is a performance for people who don't care what happens to either of us."

The tension rippled across those nearest in the crowd. Their shifting feet scraped against pavement, nervous glances betraying unease more than concern.

From somewhere behind the gathered faces came a shout: "He just loves you!" The speaker sounded almost desperate, as if naming the emotion would drain its danger.

Blackburn ignored it. She stayed focused on Sinclair. "You're asking for something impossible from me. If pointing a gun is how you define love, then you've lost sight of what matters."

Sinclair's reply cracked at the edges. "I could be who you need," he said, eyes darting between her face and the circle of spectators beyond. "Let me prove it. I can protect you."

She watched the tremor run through his shoulders before she spoke again, quiet but clear enough that he could not mistake her meaning. "Look at me, Adam. I haven't moved from your side. Not when things turned bad, not when everybody else pulled back." She angled her body forward by a single step, keeping her movements visible and controlled.

Sirens wailed closer, their pitch rising as they sliced through what little stillness remained. Blackburn felt the clock ticking down behind every word.

She drew another breath, the air thick with exhaust and fear, and closed the space between them by inches rather than feet. "Sinclair," she said softly, restraining any edge from her voice. "I see how far you would go for me. It's more than words." For now, she needed his attention pinned tightly on her alone.

She let her words settle. Each syllable landed with quiet intent, designed to root itself in him and leave no room for doubt. He needed to absorb the narrative she was offering and the shift in their balance.

"Your love is persistent," she said, voice held steady, just sharp enough to keep his attention where she wanted it. "I see that. I see you in a way others haven't."

She leaned closer, her gaze unwavering and direct. The warmth of her breath crossed the narrowing space between them, a deliberate assertion of control. "Most people drift past each other. They pretend to care but never bother to understand." Her tone remained calm, her posture unyielding. The faint scent of her perfume, something dark and floral, filled the air between them.

She waited for any sign in his eyes. A tremor at the edge of restraint or a flicker of hope. She wanted him invested, certain that what lay between them mattered more than the chaos pressing in from all sides.

"This isn't something I could walk away from," she murmured, voice almost too soft to catch. "It's more than ordinary love. It's a force. I feel it too." The lie left her mouth with silken ease, each word tasting of necessity.

Every syllable reinforced the illusion of unity, each reassurance calculated to draw him deeper into her orbit. She mirrored his longing, turning his need into an instrument she could play with precision.

"We can handle this together," she said, her tone even and composed as pressure mounted around them. The distant whine of sirens grew louder, threading through the air. "You and me, Sinclair. We outlast the storm and set our own course."

He hesitated. Doubt lingered in his expression. The moment fractured just enough for her to press further. "If we get married," she said, "all of this ends. I'd be your wife then." Power surged through her veins, electric and immediate, as soon as the promise left her lips.

His eyes searched hers, desperate for confirmation. "You would do that?" His voice broke, rough with disbelief, as if reality had shifted beneath him.

"I would," she replied, keeping her voice steady and controlled. Nothing wavered in her face or posture as she delivered each word with careful precision. "We're stronger together than apart. Think about everything you've done for me."

The thrum of tension grew heavier as police vehicles eased in nearby, engines purring low. Blue uniforms moved silently behind open doors, their movements fluid and purposeful, scanning the scene with trained focus. The smell of hot asphalt and exhaust mingled in the air.

The confusion of the airport parking lot faded until only their locked gazes remained. Car doors clicked shut. Radios crackled with static.

Blackburn drew a slow breath, tasting the metallic edge of anticipation on her tongue. Her eyes fixed on Sinclair's face.

"Tell me why," she asked, voice low and level. "Jenna, Kendria, Lilith. Was it all for me?"

Her question struck clean through the silence.

Sinclair looked stunned. Confusion rippled across his features before indignation settled in its place. The muscles in his jaw tightened.

"I didn't kill anybody, Morgan," he said. "Why would you think that?" He shook his head once, every muscle tense with disbelief and exhaustion, his shoulders drawing back as if bracing against an unseen weight.

"Because I was sleeping with them," she said, stepping closer, her brows drawing together in irritation. "You fixate on me, on my personal life. Is that it? I am a lesbian. Is that what you wanted to hear?"

"I didn't know you were involved with anyone but Willow." His voice cracked upward, the desperation sharp in every syllable.

"Don't start lying now, Adam. You even saw me with Jenna at my home. You knew," she said with a shake of her head.

"You think I'd do something like that? I'm a man. I could show you what real love is. I love you. You're the only one I care about." The words dropped between them like stones of need.

Blackburn caught herself wanting to push harder, but something in Sinclair's eyes stopped her. For a moment, he looked stripped bare, all pretense dissolved.

"All right," she said. Her tone gentled by a degree. "I believe you."

Sinclair nodded and released a breath that shuddered through him. Relief mapped itself across his face in uneven patches. "You believe me? You know I love you."

She weighed his words, felt the tension coil tight beneath her ribs.

Ice flooded through her veins, but she kept her expression steady. If he sensed anything, the balance would tip. "Look at me, Sinclair," she said evenly. "I need you to trust me now."

He nodded again, slower this time, worry carving deeper grooves into his features. "I just want to be with you," he admitted, letting himself settle into the brief comfort she offered.

The noise outside sharpened suddenly as a new voice cut through. Decisive and unyielding. "Drop the gun! Police! Drop the gun!"

The moment shattered. Blackburn saw it happen across Sinclair's face: shock blooming first, then understanding bleeding into panic as his gaze darted from her to the space beyond. She remained motionless, careful to suppress any trace of relief, though he caught the glint of calculation in her eyes. It was enough for him to know he had already lost.

His hesitation lasted a heartbeat. He jerked the gun upward in one violent arc. Her pulse hammered as she registered the threat and tensed.

"Adam, don't," she said quickly. "You don't have to do this."

A shot cracked through the air, obliterating everything else and plunging the room into chaos.

Chapter 29

The sun slipped down without ceremony, orange and red streaks catching on the wings of passing planes. Blackburn watched activity unfold from her place beyond the tape. Officers barked orders to clear the scene. She noted each command, cataloguing every movement as paramedics loaded Sinclair into the ambulance and a flight attendant soothed a crying child nearby, the girl's wails cutting through the diesel rumble of emergency vehicles.

A white sedan coasted up, its brakes squealing softly as it stopped just short of the perimeter. There would be no end to the paperwork this time. Internal Affairs, Professional Standards, Officer-Involved Shootings, Major Crimes. The unions would be circling already.

Reporters gathered at a distance, cameras trained on the flashing lights. Blackburn felt their attention like heat pressing against her back. This would be her third public incident: first, the slap she had delivered to Clyde Mullen; then the failed rescue of Lilith and Ahmed; now, survivor status in an attempted murder.

She pressed her tongue to her teeth and exhaled slowly, tasting copper where she had bitten her cheek. Brynn Cassidy was already hovering too close, her perfume sharp against the acrid smell of jet fuel. She would go deeper now, past boundaries that had held until tonight.

"Detective Blackburn?"

She looked up. "Sergeant Buxton." Blackburn sat on the ambulance bumper, back stiff against the cold metal edge, a dull ache curling above her left hip. She had texted Willow already. Short and direct. So, Willow would not learn from breaking news or rumor. Reeves had needed no update; word moved fast enough that he called first. Cooper's call had steadied him, or as close as he allowed.

Her phone buzzed against her thigh. "Chief Hayes," she said for Buxton's benefit.

"Please don't—"

Blackburn answered anyway. "Sir." She held the phone away as Hayes' voice cracked through the speaker, loud enough to draw looks from nearby EMTs. Without comment she hit speaker so Buxton could hear the tinny echo of his shouting.

"Sir, you are on speaker with Sergeant Buxton from Internal Affairs," she said, voice flat but steady. "I'm uninjured and cooperating fully." She kept her tone measured, almost bored, while sirens wailed in the distance.

Hayes hesitated before responding with something clipped and official. "Good. Glad to hear it." Buxton nodded at Blackburn in acknowledgment, her badge catching the strobe of emergency lights.

"You take care," Hayes finished before disconnecting. Blackburn set the phone aside with a flicker of irritation and tried rolling her neck. The muscles held tight as wire.

"How are you holding up?" Buxton asked as she joined Blackburn on the edge of the bumper. The rig dipped, springs creaking.

Blackburn shook her head once, absently raking fingers through sweat-damp hair that clung to her temples. "I haven't decided yet," she said. "This wasn't on my list for today."

Buxton allowed herself a small smile that faded quickly. "We'll need statements for a few units. Doing what we can to streamline it."

Blackburn appreciated the effort but kept it brief. "When does it start?"

"Now." Buxton raised a hand before Blackburn could react further. "Standard procedure. We'll get you checked by a doctor."

Blackburn pushed herself upright despite protest from strained muscles. She forced out a dry laugh when movement sent a sharp twinge across her lower back. "Didn't think dodging bullets would leave me sorer than running laps."

She settled into the front seat of Buxton's sedan, leather still radiating leftover sunlight that warmed her legs through thin suit fabric. In the side mirror, airport chaos receded behind shifting red and blue lights that painted the tarmac in alternating colors.

Riding in another officer's car always grated on Blackburn's nerves. Old habit made her right foot tense at every corner or stop sign even though she was not in control. The unfamiliar dashboard smelled of stale coffee and vinyl cleaner.

Buxton drove without comment other than an occasional glance over to check Blackburn's composure. The radio flickered with static and then news headlines until Buxton shut it off mid-sentence, leaving only the hum of tires on asphalt.

Neither said anything as they left airport property behind them and darkness gathered outside the windows, streetlights beginning their nightly vigil.

"Can't taint the witness, hmm?" Blackburn asked.

"No."

"Can you tell me how he is?"

"No."

Blackburn let silence settle. The city slid by outside her window, New Dresden's blocks familiar but distorted, as if seen through water. Her hands had steadied, though the adrenaline still pulsed beneath her skin like a second heartbeat. Every detail felt sharpened yet oddly remote.

* * *

Dr. Curry's office projected an artificial calm. Soft lighting washed across beige upholstery and bland landscape prints, while vanilla air freshener fought a losing battle with the sharp chemical bite of disinfectant underneath. Blackburn sat upright in the cushioned chair opposite the department psychologist, maintaining professional composure despite the pressure behind her eyes.

Dr. Curry watched her closely, the fine lines around her mouth deepening as she studied Blackburn's face.

"How are you feeling right now, Detective?" she asked, her voice carrying both warmth and clinical distance.

"Tired," Blackburn replied. She kept her tone measured. "Otherwise, fine."

The session unfolded with mechanical precision. Questions about sleep, appetite, flashbacks. Each one pulled from the standard playbook. Blackburn drew on her training to answer in careful phrases. She was grateful to be alive. Her actions had been driven by instinct. She understood the event's gravity.

"Any lingering physical reactions? Hypervigilance? Startled easily?" Dr. Curry's stylus whispered across her tablet, marking each response.

Blackburn thought of the adrenaline that had surged through her veins in crisis and the hollow it left behind. She kept that observation to herself. "Nothing unusual for what happened," she said.

Overhead, a ceiling fan turned in lazy circles while outside the narrow window officers crossed the parking lot with purposeful strides. The world continued its rhythm as Blackburn found herself caught in procedural limbo.

"I'd like you to come back in a few days," Dr. Curry said as she placed her tablet on the side table. "Just so we can check in again." Her tone balanced genuine concern with departmental requirement. "This was a serious incident for anyone."

Blackburn nodded once. Compliance would expedite her return to active duty. She knew these steps as intimately as any case protocol. The investigation would not pause while she sat here parsing her reactions to nearly dying in uniform.

* * *

She checked her watch. Home should have meant a glass of wine and vinyl records by now, not harsh LEDs and government-issue furniture. A brief stop at the hospital had led straight into a wordless drive with Buxton and delivered her here to IA's most unforgiving interview room.

Blackburn cleared her throat. "Could I get some cold water? The temperature isn't great." She studied the faces before her. Buxton from Internal Affairs, Peck from OIS, Cox from the union. Each one wore their discomfort like an ill-fitting suit.

Cox stood, his movements deliberate in the cramped space. "Of course, detective." He shot a pointed look at Peck. "Lieutenant Peck, would you mind? I can't leave our member unattended."

Peck rose with visible reluctance then smoothed his jacket before departing without acknowledgment. His designer frames caught the unforgiving light as the door clicked shut behind him.

The questions had not yet begun.

Peck set a cold bottle of water before Blackburn, his fingers steady and precise, nails trimmed flat against clean skin. Condensation beaded on the plastic, pooling in a perfect ring on the scarred tabletop. She thanked him, her gaze catching on the LED tubes overhead. Their harsh light carved hollows beneath every eye, turned skin sallow, left no corner untouched.

She knew this room too well. Windowless walls painted institutional beige, air thick with disinfectant fighting old coffee and sweat. The ventilation system rattled to life every few minutes, pushing stale air in circles. The table bore its history in scratches and gouges.

Handcuff scrapes, pen marks driven deep by frustrated fists, spots where fingernails had worried the veneer thin. Today she sat on the wrong side of it, hands folded, waiting.

Peck settled across from her and nudged his glasses higher on the bridge of his nose. His pen found paper with a soft scratch. The clicking of its mechanism punctuated each pause. "We're going to need some background," he said, voice neutral as tap water. "Describe your relationship with Mr. Sinclair."

A predictable opening. Blackburn's eyes found Cox across the table. He sat motionless, watching with that particular stillness she had learned to read over years of partnership. His chin dipped once.

"We worked together in homicide," she said. "That was all."

Peck's pen moved across the page, then stilled. His eyes lifted. "When did you notice any change in his behavior?"

Cox nodded again, slower this time.

She kept her account clinical, echoing what she had told Buxton earlier. Sinclair's lingering stares that lasted beats too long, comments calibrated to unsettle, the crawling sensation of being watched during ordinary moments. Peck pressed for dates and specifics she deliberately blurred. The air conditioning shuddered on, its drone loud enough to force a pause.

Buxton shifted forward, chair creaking. "If you knew he had a weapon, why didn't you get out immediately?"

"She did," Cox interrupted, words crisp. "She moved between parked cars."

Peck redirected smoothly. "But then you turned around and engaged him. Why didn't you keep fleeing?"

Blackburn waited. Cox's nod came reluctantly, accompanied by a tightening around his eyes.

"He was bleeding from a head wound," she said, measuring each word. "He appeared disoriented. Possibly concussed from the impact." The LED hum filled the gap before she continued. "There were civilians nearby. I needed to avoid escalating the situation."

Peck's pen froze mid-stroke. "So, you made an assessment to de-escalate?"

Cox's head snapped toward Blackburn in warning. "Don't answer that," he told Peck, voice hardening. "That's putting words in her mouth about intent."

Peck pressed on, rephrasing. "Did your choices contribute to officers needing to use deadly force later?"

Cox's chair scraped linoleum as he leaned in. "No one is assigning fault here except you."

Blackburn spoke before the tension could spiral further, addressing Peck directly.

"The victim was ordered by police to drop his weapon," she stated, each word precise. "He refused and aimed at me." No embellishment. No interpretation. "His refusal created an immediate threat requiring response."

Buxton's throat clearing drew focus. "What exactly did Sinclair say to you during this encounter?"

Cox's hand lifted from the table. "Only what you recall verbatim."

Blackburn reached for the water bottle. The cold shocked her throat, cut through the recycled air and building pressure.

"He called me by my first name repeatedly," she said, voice dropping but remaining steady. "He said he loved me." The words came out flat, drained of their original heat. "He mentioned his suspension." She selected the next facts carefully. "I asked if he killed Jenna Langston, Kendria Chaplin, or Lilith Halperin because of me. If he wanted my attention."

Buxton lifted her eyes from the notepad.

"Why?"

Blackburn waited.

"Don't answer that. It goes to his state of mind."

"And his response?"

"He denied it," Blackburn said, steady. "Appeared confused I had even suggested it." She met Buxton's gaze. "I pressed him about having seen Jenna at my house. He had already admitted as much to you. Still denied everything."

Peck shifted closer across the table. "Did you believe him?"

Cox raised a hand in quiet objection, but Blackburn only leaned back, mouth set flat.

"So, we're looking at someone else for your cases?" Buxton asked, voice careful.

"Let's not speculate on active investigations," Cox warned. His words were formal, but he sounded tired rather than forceful.

Blackburn kept her reply to a silent stare at the wood grain of the table.

Peck tried again, forward in his chair. "Did he threaten you directly?"

"Don't answer that."

"What about the timing of the shooting?"

"Don't answer that either."

"State of mind assessment?"

"Same answer."

Peck's questions came faster now, each one blocked by Cox before it could land. Blackburn steadied herself with slow circles traced on her thigh beneath the table, using the small movement to settle the flutter in her chest.

At last Peck tossed his pen down and exhaled hard through his nose. "Tell me this: why did we find a horseshoe in your possession?"

The question caught even Blackburn off guard. The tension eased a fraction. She allowed herself a brief smile. "That one's simple," she said. "I bought it in Des Moines when I went to visit my brother's grave. The kid who sold it claimed it would bring good luck."

Her voice was unhurried, matter-of-fact. With that sparse detail, some of the pressure in the room receded. Peck picked up his pen again, turning it over between his fingers instead of clicking it against the wood.

He straightened his notepad with his thumb and said, "That covers what we need for now." The words landed flat but final.

Chapter 30

The airport parking lot stretched out under morning light, the yellow flicker of security lamps overhead casting uneven shadows between rows of vehicles. Parked cars sat in quiet lines, metal shells waiting for their owners' return. Blackburn stood beside her battered sedan and surveyed the buckled door without comment. Sinclair had been moving just fast enough. Two other vehicles caught before hers bore lesser scars from his passage. The left rear door caved inward, the wheel well bent at an angle that made her stomach tighten with remembered impact.

Willow circled the damage, hands buried deep in her jacket pockets. She shook her head once, voice low. "You were lucky."

Blackburn ran her fingers through Willow's hair, the gesture absent but gentle. "Thanks for driving me."

Willow traced the length of a fresh gouge along the fender with one finger, metal rough beneath her touch. "You're going to take this thing home?"

"Office first," Blackburn answered quietly, fishing keys from her pocket. The metal edges bit cold against her palm.

"Office?" Willow watched her, wariness creeping into her voice.

A short laugh escaped Blackburn as she unlocked the car with familiar ease. "Would you expect anything different? There are more interviews waiting at headquarters." She paused to scan an alert on her phone. The EDR report and cell location data had come through overnight, and she needed confirmation on Darwin Santana's whereabouts during Chandworth's murder.

She noticed a chip in the rear glass. A fractional break that separated ordinary chance from disaster by inches.

"It's back to work for you," she said as she leaned close enough for Willow to feel the warmth of her breath against her cheek.

Willow caught Blackburn's hand before she could move away and held tight for a moment longer than usual. Her fingers pressed firm against Blackburn's palm. "Are you sure you're all right? I'm worried."

Blackburn let herself offer a thin smile. Nothing added or concealed. "I'm fine," she said. "Sinclair is unconscious in intensive care now. Whatever threat he posed is done."

For an instant it looked like Willow would protest or press further, but she only tightened her grip once before letting go.

She brought Blackburn's hand to her lips and kissed it softly. A simple gesture. Then she turned away and headed across the shimmering asphalt toward her own car without another word.

Blackburn watched until Willow disappeared behind rows of parked vehicles before turning back to study the damage again, jaw set against what waited next.

She watched Willow drive away. Only now did her mind clear enough to replay the encounter with Sinclair.

The drive to the station unfolded quietly, radio murmuring static and voices in the background. Headlights slid across faded lane markers as she took familiar streets into the heart of New Dresden. She preferred starting early. It bought her time before the building filled with tension and expectation.

The city appeared unchanged, but Blackburn felt the aftermath of violence settling around her like morning fog. Safety always felt provisional after incidents like last night.

She noted the car's subtle pull to the left, a mechanical reminder of damage suffered and not yet addressed. The steering wheel vibrated faintly under her hands. She considered how much worse the department had fared, fractured and uneasy, Chief Hayes scrambling to manage containment.

Hayes deserved his share of responsibility for this mess. He had received repeated warnings about Sinclair and did nothing until she forced his hand.

Blackburn lingered outside the precinct, keys pressed deep into her palm until the edges left marks. The building remained its impassive self, concrete and tinted glass reflecting the morning sun, but nothing inside followed suit. Not since she had stared down a gun pointed at her chest, not since Sinclair had been shot by fellow officers in an instant that changed everything.

Exhaust fumes mingled with the sharp scent of coffee from a vendor cart nearby. She let herself breathe it in, grounding against city noise and diesel before entering through the spinning door.

The security guard straightened at her approach. His greeting carried respect tempered by disbelief, as if television reports failed to bridge the gap between story and fact.

"Detective." He nodded with more formality than usual.

"Any reporters?"

"Cassidy came by earlier. I turned her away."

A brief smile touched Blackburn's lips. "Good."

She climbed one flight of stairs, feeling her legs stretch and strain against yesterday's tension. Enough to collect herself before facing everyone else.

The homicide division looked unchanged but carried a charge in the air like static before a storm. Each conversation faltered as she entered. People glanced up, then quickly away. Too much had gone unsaid for too long.

Cooper spotted her first from Dawson's old desk, fingers arrested above the keyboard, eyes wide behind thick glasses. A visible swallow moved down Cooper's throat. Blackburn gave a slight nod: permission to proceed, routine preserved on the surface.

Reeves hovered by the coffee machine, mug halfway raised. His shirt showed deep creases, and exhaustion lined his face. He met Blackburn's gaze and set his cup aside with care.

"Boss." His words cut through the silence lingering in the squad room.

"Reeves." Her tone remained steady as she crossed to him, steps precise. None of it betrayed what churned beneath her skin. "Anything new?"

"Bullshit." He opened his hands, not quite reaching for an embrace but leaving space for her choice. Blackburn stepped in for a quick hug, brief contact acknowledged and ended. His shirt smelled of stale coffee and sleepless hours.

"Hey," Cooper called from behind them. She turned for another half-embrace before gesturing Cooper over for something longer. A proper hug this time, deserved and grounding. Cooper's arms wrapped tight around her shoulders.

"How is everyone?" she asked when it finished.

Reeves exhaled hard, air rushing between his teeth. "Fucked up," he said. "How are you?"

Blackburn allowed a short smile. "Fucked up." Internal Affairs commanded every conversation now, boundaries drawn tight around what anyone dared say aloud. She accepted those lines without protest.

"What's the latest?" Blackburn asked, settling onto the edge of Dawson's desk. Her fingers drummed once against the cool metal surface. "Are those new machines?"

Willow kept her eyes fixed on the monitor's glow in front of her. "Yes. I'm finishing the setup, configuring security and transfer protocols. This one's almost done."

Blackburn let her gaze drift toward her own office, where a new terminal waited on her desk, its black screen reflecting the overhead lights. "Mine included?"

She wanted to know not just about the computer but whether Willow had spotted the EDR from Roche's car again. Willow had already accessed it, handed over a report. Blackburn did not want her catching on that she was running second checks, not after Sinclair's near-confession.

"Yours is last," Willow said without lifting her head. "I'll get to it after this."

That meant time to remove the device and USB before Willow entered.

Cooper arrived, sliding into his seat with a weary thud that shook the desk partition. "Zhang filed a lawsuit." His voice carried no inflection. "His lawyer called twice already today."

The room stilled under that name. Zhang had been accused of orchestrating the first autonomous car crash, but if Sinclair was responsible for all four deaths as Blackburn now believed, then dropped charges were only the beginning of what Zhang should have received.

"That belongs to Hayes," Blackburn said, her words barely above a murmur. "He booked Zhang against clear advice."

Her gaze traveled to Sinclair's empty workstation. The desk looked preserved: pens scattered across the surface, notebooks half-opened with pages exposed, screen aligned perfectly with his chair. Only Willow organized things that precisely.

"How do we access case files?" she asked Willow, studying her for any pause or shift.

Willow answered smoothly. "You'll need a senior tech, or use the desk phones. Star seven seven reaches admin security."

Reeves raised an eyebrow. "Since when?"

"At least three years." Willow shrugged and turned back to the glowing screen.

Cooper smirked at Reeves. "Real cutting-edge stuff." Reeves flicked a pen at him, missing by inches.

Blackburn's fingers pressed hard into the leather chair back as something sparked behind her eyes. Sinclair's face twisted by something darker than rage as he raised the gun. His words cut through the roar of jet engines: Everything I did was so you'd notice me. Officers shouting from somewhere beyond her peripheral vision. Sinclair's eyes locked on hers until two sharp cracks ended it.

"We're not supposed to touch his workspace," Cooper reminded her softly, tracking where she looked. "IA sealed it pending review."

Blackburn nodded once, the movement sharp. "Anything they pulled worth mentioning?"

Cooper hesitated, exchanging a glance with Reeves, who shifted forward in his chair.

"Officially? Nothing," Reeves said, his voice dropping to a tired monotone. "Unofficially, they took external drives and a journal."

"And unofficially." Blackburn caught herself, shaking her head. She would not risk drawing them into wrongdoing now. "Forget it. I didn't ask."

Reeves cleared his throat and straightened in his seat. "You're not technically supposed to be here anyway, boss."

"I know." Blackburn drew herself taller, keeping her tone measured. "I only needed a few things from my office and wanted to check in on everyone." She moved toward her door, her eyes sweeping each desk for fresh signs of disturbance.

Inside her office she closed the door and stood motionless in the sudden quiet. Traces of strangers hung in the air. An unfamiliar cologne with sharp notes, something sour lurking beneath. Evidence of whoever had rifled through her space since she had last stood here.

Her stomach tightened, muscles contracting. She swallowed, tasting the metallic edge of adrenaline, and steadied herself. When she reached for the vase, its ceramic surface felt cool and reassuring beneath her fingertips, as solid as ever.

A glance at the bullpen confirmed no one was watching. The usual hum of conversation and keyboard clicks continued undisturbed. Blackburn lowered the vase beneath her desk, using the wooden barrier to shield her movements. She tipped it carefully, feeling the shift inside.

Banks's gun slid into her palm with a whisper of metal against ceramic. The grip settled naturally into her hand before she moved it to her pocket in one smooth motion, quick and precise.

The vase returned to its place, its base meeting the desk with a soft thud. Next came the EDR. She pressed her palm against the scanner, feeling the slight warmth of the reader, and listened for the cabinet's mechanical click. Another look confirmed Willow's back was still turned, her attention absorbed by her screen.

Blackburn lifted the EDR, its plastic casing heavier than she remembered, then set it down again. Too heavy. Removing it would leave a trace. A broken chain of custody she wanted to avoid. Willow did not have clearance for this cabinet anyway. Instead, Blackburn took the USB stick holding the case files, its small weight barely registering as she slipped it into her pocket alongside the gun.

She needed proof that Sinclair's phone had pinged off the same towers as Roche's car. The case had passed beyond her reach now, but she accepted that with the resignation of someone who understood jurisdictional boundaries.

Investigating another cop was never easy to admit on paper. Suspicion floated like smoke, shapeless and deniable; signing your name and submitting evidence made it permanent in ways that left scars on careers and friendships alike. Major Crimes or Internal Affairs could handle it from here.

She tucked her laptop close, using its bulk to obscure the telltale outline of the gun in her jacket, and stepped out of her office. The bullpen's LED lights seemed brighter after the dimness of her workspace.

"I'm off until they clear me," she told them, keeping her tone light enough to sound routine. The words tasted false on her tongue. "I'll try not to get in your way."

"See you next week," Reeves called over with a short laugh that echoed off the walls.

* * *

At home, Blackburn placed her laptop on the kitchen counter. She poured herself a glass of wine, the bottle's neck clinking softly against the rim. Her actions were measured, each step part of an old routine that brought comfort through repetition. The only sounds came from the refrigerator's steady hum and the distant whisper of traffic filtering through her window.

Tomorrow would mean insurance calls crackling with static, maybe arranging a rental car that would smell of artificial pine, booking time with Dr. Curry in her office that always carried the faint scent of lavender. Each task another small hurdle in a long line of aftermaths she knew by heart.

She reminded herself this was nothing new, though her hands trembled around the wine glass. Sinclair's fixation had nearly killed her, left her with the phantom taste of fear, but now he sat at the center of every theory about the autonomous car deaths.

Chapter 31

Morning light angled across Blackburn's living room, falling through the blinds and breaking into stripes on the sofa. Her laptop glowed faintly in the shadowed room. She shifted, her knee cracking as she opened the next file.

Darwin Santana's cell phone records. She scanned columns of cell tower pings, searching for one time, one date that would hold.

She found it after a minute.

Reeves, attached please find the file. Shows Darwin Santana was at the Chandworth crime scene at the time of the murder. See the file on the network. Evidence folder. Put together a warrant with the fingerprint evidence and get that bastard arrested. Please.

~ B.

It was ten in the morning, and she had one arrest lined up. She closed her email and released a slow breath that fogged briefly in the cool air.

Now for Sinclair.

There were simpler ways to pull EDR data from Kendria's, Lilith's, and Ahmed's attacks, or from Stan Raider's logs in Jenna's case. It did not matter. They had started tracking department cars unofficially, now officially, and when that broke public it would be someone else's scandal to manage.

Phone company data filled one half of her screen, listing every tower in New Dresden and each phone that pinged within a fifteen-minute window of each attack. The system took seven minutes to open the file. On the right: car locations narrowed to just the relevant cell tower hits, stripped of everything else.

She focused on the column labeled CH26_CELL_TOWER_ID.

It came down to matching car tower hits with Sinclair's phone tower hits.

Her coffee sat untouched beside her elbow, the ceramic rim stained with old lipstick marks, cold and stale. She barely noticed. Each data point flickered across her vision. Accusations in numbers, waiting for her verdict. She muttered, "He won't walk on a technicality."

Sinclair had done real damage. She felt nothing for his condition now, still ventilated, the mechanical wheeze of machines keeping him alive, and nothing for his shooting either.

She flexed her hand once, the joints stiff from gripping the mouse, before continuing.

Another search: Ctrl+F, 555-1783, Enter. A match returned. She cross-checked that cell tower ID against the vehicle data. Another match lined up cleanly.

Her skin tingled as she leaned closer to the screen, the pixels sharp enough to make her eyes water. Sinclair's phone had pinged the Oak Street tower at exactly the same time Roche's car struck Kendria.

She wrote it down in neat print on her notepad, the pen scratching against paper, and paused with the pen balanced between her fingers. He had been seen after the incident. She needed proof he was there beforehand too, before any first response could explain his presence away.

Blackburn drew a controlled breath, tasting the stale air of the closed room, and pressed forward.

Her eyes stung from staring at rows of numbers but she refused to look away. The answer was somewhere in this monotony. If she kept going long enough, it would reveal itself.

A discrepancy caught her eye. She narrowed her focus on the screen, the blue glow harsh against her tired retinas. Sinclair's phone had connected to a Westside tower at nine forty-seven in the morning, the same day Kendria was nearly killed. But Oak Street, where Kendria's near miss occurred, lay clear across the city.

Her working theory had depended on proximity. Sinclair would need to be near the vehicle, just as Keiran Moss had operated his own from no more than twenty feet away.

This data put Sinclair far from the scene at the critical moment.

"No," she said, shaking her head. The words tasted wrong in her mouth. "It doesn't add up." Not unless the Oak Street incident was unrelated to Kendria's case. A coincidence, and another coincidence that Roche's car showed impact marks consistent with scraping a wall.

She did not trust coincidences.

Blackburn pressed her teeth together until her jaw ached. The simplest answer was some technical error in the report. She opened a new window and checked Lilith's incident data. Again, Sinclair's phone placed him miles away.

A cold unease crept into her gut, spreading like ice water through her veins. She slid her laptop down to her knees and rubbed at her temples, eyes shut against the headache that pulsed behind her forehead. The certainty she had carried minutes before fell away, replaced by something brittle and uncertain.

She forced herself back to work, intent on locating the error. There had to be a reasonable explanation, some technical failure or overlooked variable in the records. If she checked everything again, perhaps it would fall into place. Blackburn refused to let herself consider the alternative: that she might have misjudged Sinclair entirely.

Sunlight shifted across the room, lengthening into dull amber stripes along the floorboards and sofa arm. The air grew thick and warm. She barely noticed, focused on cross-checking columns of numbers and location stamps. The longer she worked, the more frustration bled into each movement, her fingers growing stiff against the keyboard, accompanied by dread that grew steadily heavier.

Reviewing Jenna's report, she found it again: Sinclair's phone far from the attack site at the necessary time. Her hand came down hard on the couch cushion. A muted thud that failed to push back against the wave of panic gathering behind her ribs.

"This can't be right." Her voice sounded small in the still room, swallowed by the afternoon quiet. She pulled her fingers through her hair until her scalp throbbed with sharp pain, hoping for clarity that did not come. The computer screen glowed steady blue, cold and unforgiving as she scrolled back through data points for any slip or hidden clue that might save her theory.

The pattern held firm. Every entry confirmed what she least wanted to believe. Sinclair could not have orchestrated these attacks as she had thought.

A sour bitterness rose at the back of her throat as she absorbed the truth, coating her tongue with the taste of failure. If not Sinclair, then who? How had she missed what now seemed obvious? Questions circled without answers, unsettled and pressing closer with each breath that came too shallow.

Her gaze found a mug abandoned on the table beside her laptop: coffee cooled to a slick brown film at its rim. She drank anyway, wincing at its chill and acrid taste as it settled against her tongue, leaving behind the flavor of stale grounds.

Setting down the cup with more force than necessary, ceramic clicking against wood, Blackburn leaned back and closed her eyes tight against the weight pressing down on her chest. Her conviction about Sinclair had been so complete that it felt like armor. Now it lay broken around her in pieces too sharp to ignore.

Her eyes settled on the last unchecked number. She recognized it at once, the digits familiar and intimate, a presence that had quickened her pulse every time it lit up her phone. Blackburn's fingers hovered above the keyboard before she entered it. For a moment, she sat very still.

The screen processed her search in silence. She watched, barely breathing, as if her restraint could keep the results from arriving. Then the data appeared.

One heartbeat. Another.

The search stopped. A highlighted entry glowed at her in yellow. Below it, another. Then another. Willow's number threaded through Kendria's records again and again.

There was no way to excuse it or look away.

Blackburn blinked hard, certain her mind was playing tricks on her. "Fuck," she muttered, voice rough.

She ran the cab logs next. More yellow blocks scattered across the display, each one undeniable. The same pattern, unbroken and obvious. She hurled her mug across the room without thinking. Coffee splattered across the floor in a dark arc, ceramic shards skittering against the wall. She did not flinch.

Blackburn stared at the evidence as understanding settled in like cold water filling her lungs. Willow had lied to her face. She had manipulated every move, rewritten every rule between them. All this time, control had been an illusion.

Her jaw tightened as she stood over the laptop, heat flooding through her chest in sharp waves of humiliation and anger. She felt stripped bare. The authority she wore so carefully had become a mask for weakness she never intended to show anyone, least of all Willow.

The pattern was too precise to ignore now. Willow's calculated performances for sympathy. Her subtle shifts of focus during team meetings, sending everyone in pointless circles, humiliating them all by implication but targeting Blackburn most of all.

It would not just end her career if this became public. It would erase everything she had built.

She scrolled further through the data with care, though her stomach twisted tighter each time another timestamp lined up perfectly with the attacks. Every crime scene mapped out like coordinates on a private road only Willow traveled.

Blackburn felt her breath catch and release in shallow bursts as she tried to make sense of it. The evidence offered no reprieve, just cold certainty. That Willow had been present was undeniable. That she might be responsible seemed suddenly unavoidable.

Nausea rose sharp and metallic, different from anything she had felt standing over bodies or chasing suspects through rain-slicked alleyways at midnight. This was personal. A violation measured in trust rather than blood.

She forced herself upright from the couch and gripped the armrest until her legs stopped trembling beneath her. The walls pressed closer than before, air thick with disappointment and rage that did not dissipate but crystallized with each breath.

Her steps traced restless circles across the coffee-stained floor until the bitter scent filled every corner of the room.

She punched at empty air once to release what would not move any other way.

Then she looked back at the screen for something that could explain away what she saw laid out so plainly before her. Those unforgiving yellow marks remained unmoved.

Willow had not just hidden secrets. She had outplayed everyone involved. Clever was not strong enough for this kind of deception. Cunning fit better.

Blackburn's hand went to her phone automatically, thumb brushing over Willow's contact without pressing down. The need to call surged hot and demanding within her. A demand for answers or maybe just to hear some trace of guilt in Willow's voice. But she held herself back by force of will alone. If Willow was involved this deeply, any warning now would make things worse.

She realized then that Reeves had had his suspicions too. Written plainly across his face. But no one else knew what they were dealing with yet.

Willow had fooled them all.

Very cunning indeed.

She set the phone on the table, her fingers curling slowly against her palm. She leaned back and released a breath.

She recalled Willow beneath her hand. The faint tremor in Willow's exhale. The wordless plea that filled her eyes, seeking permission. For two years, she had studied every subtlety of Willow's body, reading each shift of muscle, each flicker of fear. Through all that time, Willow had harbored the capacity for violence somewhere deep within, hidden even as she sought absolution for lesser transgressions.

They shared more than she had once imagined.

Blackburn composed the message with care.

Come over. 10pm.<

Her thumb hovered above the screen.

Good girl<

She deleted that lie. Now she would see if Willow would answer when called.

Chapter 32

Headlights swept across the curb and dimmed in the drive. Willow was early by ten minutes.

Blackburn waited until darkness reclaimed the room, then rose to face the door. Her black suit hung perfectly tailored against her frame, the white shirt beneath still crisp and fresh, shoes catching the hallway's amber glow.

She drew on black nitrile gloves, the material whispering against her skin.

A soft knock echoed through the quiet.

"Come in."

The door opened slowly. Willow lingered on the threshold, her gaze fixed on Blackburn through the dim light. "I said, come in. Lock it behind you."

Willow crossed the threshold and turned the lock, the click sharp in the silence. Her fingers trembled around a ribbon-wrapped box of chocolates. She stilled herself, drawing in a breath that lifted her shoulders.

She extended the box. "I brought these for you, Lioness."

Blackburn took them with a slight nod, the box cool through her gloves. "Thank you, Fawn." Her voice carried its usual restraint. She thought for a moment and decided she could use these. "They suit tonight's plan."

Willow's eyes sparked with carefully contained anticipation. "My special night?"

"Most special," Blackburn said. She observed the subtle shifts in Willow's expression. "Are you ready?"

Willow's chin dipped once. "Yes, Lioness."

Blackburn examined her face more closely. "Why are you crying?"

Willow's fingertips brushed the wetness on her cheeks. "You've carried so much," she said, her voice barely above a whisper.

Blackburn permitted herself a fleeting smile. "Yes." She gestured toward Willow's shoes. "Take those off and follow me."

They passed into the bedroom where lamplight cast warm shadows across the walls, illuminating the charged space between them.

Blackburn halted mere inches from Willow, close enough to feel the warmth radiating from her skin. She traced gloved fingers along Willow's arm, watching the flesh prickle in response.

"Impatient?" The question carried a subtle warning. Willow had no idea what was in store tonight.

Willow's lips parted to respond but Blackburn seized her shirt and yanked. The cotton split to expose the black lace beneath.

The fabric tore with a sharp whisper. Willow's breath hitched as cool air kissed newly bared skin, her pulse visible at the hollow of her throat.

Willow's gaze dropped to the gloves, her throat working. "Gloves tonight?"

Blackburn held her eyes a beat longer before gliding her fingers across the exposed flesh, pausing to feel each quickened breath beneath her touch.

"Yes," she said. "Do you trust me to try something new?"

"Yes, Lioness."

Of course she did.

Blackburn crossed to the chest beside the bed and lifted its lid, withdrawing two metal clamps. She displayed them on her open palm, the lamplight glinting off their surfaces.

"Do you want these?"

"I am for your pleasure, Lioness," Willow whispered, her voice catching on the last word.

Blackburn eased the bra straps from Willow's shoulders and let them fall. She did not linger on the reveal, only traced a line with her fingertips down the soft skin of Willow's arm. At the gentle touch across her chest, Willow's breath hitched.

"You put them on," Blackburn said, nodding to the clamps that lay cold in Willow's palm. She wanted Willow to take control of just one pleasurable pain.

Willow's fingers trembled as she dragged the chain across her skin, the metal links raising goosebumps in their wake. She fixed one clamp in place. The pressure bit down without mercy. Her mouth fell open around a sharp gasp.

"Now the other," Blackburn said, her voice calm but with intent.

Willow completed the task. She swallowed back another sound as pain bloomed into arousal. Her pulse hammered in response to those two small points of cold metal pressing into tender flesh.

Blackburn surveyed her, head tilted. "Beautiful." Her tone stayed level, but something tightened in the line of her jaw. "You wear them well, my Fawn."

The constant ache at Willow's nipples pulled her attention inward. Her body responded to every slight movement with fresh waves of heat.

"Undress," Blackburn instructed.

Willow reached for her zipper too quickly and felt the sharp tug at the chain between the clamps. A warning that made her stomach clench.

"Slowly," Blackburn said, drawing out each syllable with control. She needed to draw this out.

Willow complied, sliding the denim down her thighs and letting it pool at her feet. The tattered remains of her T-shirt followed, then her bra. She peeled off her socks last and stood at the edge of the bed in only thin cotton panties.

Blackburn studied her for a moment longer before settling onto the mattress. She used one bare foot to nudge a roll of PVC across the hardwood floor toward Willow.

"Blow it up."

Willow bent for the heavy bundle, her movements careful to avoid jarring the chain. She unfolded it into a flat sheet that smelled of new plastic. When she closed her lips around the air valve, she kept her eyes locked on Blackburn. Each breath came slow but determined, filling the mattress inch by careful inch.

With every other breath, Blackburn let a fingertip graze against the chain. The sting shot through Willow's chest and refocused her when she faltered or moved too quickly.

The room filled with intimate sounds: the rush of air from Willow's lungs, the faint creak of metal pressing and releasing over sensitive skin, Blackburn's steady breathing as she watched without expression. Routine action took on new weight inside their silent negotiation for power.

As the mattress expanded beneath Willow's knees, fresh color bloomed across her chest and throat. Stray hair clung to damp skin as she worked. The effort left her dizzy but obedient.

When Blackburn rose again, she reached forward and lifted both chains between her thumb and forefinger before releasing them at once. The bite vanished. Sensation flooded back in a sharp rush that pulled a low, helpless moan from Willow's throat.

Blackburn did not smile or offer comfort. She watched carefully as pleasure tangled with pain across Willow's features and waited for her to find her balance before continuing. Willow had to be fully present tonight.

Blackburn traced her fingertips across Willow's bare skin, working with attention. She pinched and rolled each nipple between her fingers, drawing brief, involuntary sounds from Willow. The small reactions registered as confirmation more than invitation: shallow breaths catching in her throat, the tightening of her jaw beneath pale skin. Blackburn watched without hurry.

"You've been difficult lately, Fawn," she said, opening the buttons of her own shirt to reveal black lace beneath. Her tone carried no warmth, no real anger.

"Naughty?" Willow's question barely rose above a whisper. Something tense flickered behind the word.

"Oh, I know what you did," Blackburn replied. She met Willow's gaze with a look that suggested amusement more than reproach. "You tried to keep things from me."

She leaned in close enough for Willow to feel the heat radiating from her skin, then pressed her lips to Willow's forehead. The kiss lasted only a moment. Not comfort, but control. "Face the wall," Blackburn said. "Do not move until I say."

Willow obeyed quickly. She took her place in the corner, shoulders drawn back, hands straight at her sides. The air felt cooler against her exposed skin.

Blackburn stepped in behind her and slipped off Willow's glasses with steady fingers. "Do you remember our first meeting?"

"Yes, Lioness," Willow answered. Her voice had lost its edge of bravado and sounded stripped down. Vulnerable without sight.

Without ceremony, Blackburn pressed two fingers against the soft curve of Willow's waist, then traced upward along exposed skin. She punctuated each touch with calculated pressure. Enough for discomfort but not pain. Each sharp intake of breath told her exactly what she needed.

A memory surfaced. Blackburn walking into that windowless meeting room, LED lights buzzing overhead. Willow sat hunched over a laptop screen, thick glasses catching the harsh light. Without asking, Blackburn had reached down and removed them. No protest had come. Just stillness and something like trust in the gesture. Or perhaps resignation. Blackburn had wiped each lens clean with her shirt before placing them back on Willow's face, noting how essential they were to her composure.

It had been obvious then: Willow needed structure as much as she needed oxygen.

Returning to the present, Blackburn spoke quietly so only Willow could hear. "You didn't argue that day either."

Willow stood rigid for a moment. She shifted from one foot to the other. "Almost good enough?" she asked.

"Nearly," Blackburn replied. She could not give Willow the perfection she craved. She drew a silk blindfold from her pocket and positioned it across Willow's eyes, smoothing the fabric until it sat just right. The movement was gentle but left no room for vision.

"Yes," Willow whispered after a pause.

"Will you follow every instruction tonight?"

"Yes." Smaller this time.

Blackburn let silence settle between them and took a step back. She watched without comment as Willow remained motionless in the corner. The quiet pressed in on them both. Deliberate. Heavy. Intended to reveal what words would not betray.

Willow waited, muscles coiled beneath her skin, every nerve singing with alertness. Blackburn let the silence thicken between them, watching her partner's chest rise and fall as each second stretched like pulled wire.

It was time.

"Kneel by the mattress, Fawn. Take off my shoes," Blackburn commanded. Her voice carried the weight of stone dropped into still water. "Come here."

Willow obeyed, crawling forward with careful hands that swept the floor until they found the bed's edge. The blindfold pressed against her eyelashes, sealing out every trace of light. She located Blackburn's feet through touch alone, pressing her lips to the smooth leather before her fingers sought the laces. Her hands trembled, but she drew in small, controlled breaths that tasted of anticipation.

"Good girl. Obedient." Blackburn's approval came measured and distant.

Willow allowed herself the smallest curve of a smile. "Yes. Anything you want."

Blackburn leaned forward to begin the spanking. Each strike landed with deliberate rhythm, neither rushed nor hesitant. Willow's fingers dug into the mattress edge near Blackburn's thighs, her jaw clenched against the sounds that wanted to escape as heat bloomed across her skin.

"I know what you're doing, Fawn." Blackburn's tone carried a thread of amusement wrapped in steel. "Dragging it out just to get more attention."

Willow shook her head frantically, but words scattered under another precise strike that sent sparks racing along her nerves.

"No, Lioness! It's just the blindfold." Her protest dissolved into a sharp intake of breath.

Another slap connected with surgical accuracy. "Don't lie," Blackburn said, each word falling like a hammer strike. "You forget how well I read you."

The next strike caught Willow's thigh. She jerked, then redoubled her efforts with the shoes until the leather finally released its hold.

"That's better." Blackburn rose and stepped around her. "Hands on the bed. Back arched."

Willow shifted immediately, her pulse thundering against her ribs.

Blackburn's palms traveled up Willow's legs, fingertips barely grazing skin. She paused at the hips just long enough for goosebumps to scatter across exposed flesh. The blindfold disappeared without warning. Light crashed back, making Willow squint against the sudden brightness.

Blackburn loomed above her, every line of her body radiating control.

Neither spoke. The air between them crackled.

Then Blackburn guided Willow onto her back. The air mattress whispered beneath their shifting weight.

"I want you looking at me," Blackburn murmured, sliding Willow's glasses into place with care.

"I can see you," Willow breathed.

Blackburn reached for the box of chocolates waiting on the nightstand. Her voice carried a fraction more warmth as she issued her next command.

"Knees up. Legs apart."

"Yes, Lioness." Willow arranged herself instantly, breath coming in short bursts while her hands remained perfectly still at her sides.

Blackburn knelt between Willow's spread thighs and selected a chocolate. She placed it against sensitive skin, nestling it between labia with one smooth motion.

"These last two months have changed me," Blackburn said as she pressed another piece into the hollow of Willow's navel. The words emerged steady and inexorable, though tension pulled at her shoulders. "Those deaths. I had someone torn away by one of those cars right in front of me."

Her palm rested against Willow's waist a moment longer than the action required.

"One nearly took me too."

Willow's throat worked as she swallowed, searching for equilibrium before responding. "I'm glad you made it back." The words emerged thin but unwavering.

A third chocolate found its place. Willow squirmed beneath its cool presence and released a brief laugh that held more electricity than mirth.

"That tickles."

"Careful." Blackburn's voice stayed even as she set a chocolate on Willow's left nipple. The cool sweetness pressed against warm skin.

"Keep still, Fawn. Don't let them fall." The words hung in the air with quiet authority. She looked down at Willow, her gaze steady. "It has been chaos. All those women. And the cab driver. Ahmed El-Masri. He had children."

Blackburn placed another chocolate, this time on Willow's right nipple. The slight weight made Willow's breath catch. "I followed them fast that night. Faster than I should have. Every turn in the road sharpened my focus." Her tone remained reserved, each sentence measured. "When they stopped at Dunbar Bluffs, I caught up to their car. My heart was pushing against my ribs, but my hands stayed steady on the wheel. Lilith screamed when she saw me coming. She kept crying, louder every second." Blackburn paused to lift a chocolate and rest it against Willow's forehead. The scent of cocoa mingled with perfume. "And I felt something I shouldn't have felt, Fawn. Excitement instead of fear."

For a moment, Blackburn watched her, expression unreadable. "I watched her go over that edge." Her voice fell lower and lost none of its precision. "The ground shifted under me too." A trace of satisfaction flickered behind her eyes.

She pressed the last piece of chocolate to Willow's lips and studied her reaction in silence. The bitter edge of dark chocolate spread across Willow's tongue. "That night changed something in me," she said. "It opened up a hunger I can barely control."

Willow did not move. Her breath quickened as she kept her focus on Blackburn, the chocolates balanced and trembling where they lay. The shifts against sensitive skin demanded her complete attention.

The silence thickened, interrupted only by their breathing and the faint hum of traffic from outside the window. Blackburn traced her fingers through Willow's hair, her touch unexpectedly gentle after so much control.

"You're a good Fawn." The words were soft, almost tender.

Blackburn's hand lingered at Willow's jaw before moving down her cheek in a controlled sweep. The warmth of her palm sent a fine tremor through Willow's body.

The spell broke as Blackburn leaned in. She knelt with careful intent between Willow's legs, letting her tongue find heat and sweetness where chocolate had begun to melt against flushed skin.

She worked with efficiency, gathering every trace from Willow's skin without haste or flourish. The contrast of cool chocolate and warm tongue made Willow's muscles tighten. The taste was secondary to Willow herself. Her tension. Her stillness.

"Oh, Fawn," she murmured against flesh, voice roughened by desire but controlled by habit. Her breath ghosted across damp skin. "You're sweet tonight."

Willow gripped the edge of the mattress tightly, the cotton sheets bunching beneath her fingers as she tried to keep from shifting beneath the attention.

Blackburn kept her movements deliberate as she circled and pressed with her tongue. Each action was precise rather than frantic. The wet heat of her mouth contrasted with the cool air of the room until Willow shook with the effort of restraint.

"You're wet," Blackburn remarked without embellishment, her chin damp as she paused for a breath. The scent of arousal mixed with chocolate filled the space between them.

Willow could not manage words. Her throat tightened around silence as she gave herself over to sensation and let the moment stretch out between them.

Above all there was control: measured, ruthless, and necessary for both of them as dawn crept toward the edges of the blackout curtains. The room held their heat like a secret. Neither woman dared break the silence further while pleasure built in small increments under Blackburn's steady hands and tongue.

The chocolates threatened to slip from their places, but Willow held still, muscles trembling with effort. She was determined not to disappoint as heat pressed in close around them both.

"Come for me, Fawn," Blackburn said, her tone resolute. "Let go. Show me you're mine."

Willow obeyed. The orgasm struck with sudden force. She pressed her body flat against the cool sheets, lips parted but silent, swallowing back the cry that threatened to spill out. Her breath came in sharp, shallow gasps. She blinked hard, eyes wide, anchoring herself against the waves of sensation that rolled through her. She willed her muscles to stay still. Two pieces of dark chocolate balanced on her skin. She had nearly forgotten.

Blackburn watched closely. She withdrew her mouth and replaced it with her fingers, moving with clinical precision. Willow trembled as she climaxed again, body arching taut before gravity pulled her back to the mattress. One chocolate slipped from the curve of her breast and tumbled onto the rumpled sheets. Neither woman reached for it.

Blackburn's expression shifted. Satisfaction flickered across her face in the slight tightening at the corner of her mouth. She reached for the damp cloth on the bedside table and cleaned Willow methodically, the cool fabric gliding over heated skin, ensuring no residue remained. Without haste, she lifted the remaining chocolate from Willow's navel and placed it between her own teeth. She chewed slowly, her gaze never leaving Willow's face.

She stood beside the bed for a moment, eyes assessing. "You're irresistible tonight," she said. Her gaze swept over Willow's flushed chest and tangled hair. "The way you listen so well." The words carried both approval and warning. Blackburn gestured toward the fallen chocolates scattered on the coverlet. "You moved."

She climbed onto the bed, knees framing Willow's hips, her leather-gloved hand resting flat against Willow's sternum to feel each rapid heartbeat beneath her palm.

"But you've done worse than that before," she continued, voice dropping low as she leaned forward until her breath warmed Willow's ear. "Eat."

Willow did as told, lifting the last piece of chocolate between trembling fingers. The candy had softened against her skin, melting slightly at the edges. She pressed it past her lips as Blackburn watched from above. The sweetness spread across her tongue, simple and rich compared to the heat still thrumming beneath her ribs.

Blackburn dipped down and pressed her lips to Willow's forehead. "Thank you," she said softly, the words carrying genuine gratitude that felt rare between them.

Willow looked away for a moment before meeting Blackburn's gaze again. Pride warmed through her chest at having pleased her lover so thoroughly.

"I want to obey you," Willow said.

Blackburn kissed her then, slowly at first, without urgency or ceremony. Her gloved fingertips brushed along the curve of Willow's cheek in a controlled gesture of affection.

When they parted, Blackburn lingered near, holding Willow's gaze through the amber bedroom light.

"You look beautiful when you surrender," Willow whispered.

A brief smile crossed Blackburn's lips. Not quite gentle but more real than most ever saw from her. "There are no angels here," she replied evenly. Her voice never lost its edge of command.

She traced a single line across Willow's brow and down to her jaw with one fingertip, careful and almost surgical in its precision. She paused to watch every small reaction play across Willow's features.

"If I were capable of love," Blackburn said very softly, "I might have loved you."

Willow's eyelids fell as she lifted a hand, reaching for connection without words. "I can help you." Her voice wavered and broke.

Blackburn pressed two fingers to Willow's lips and silenced her. "No talking. No resisting. Let it happen." She traced her hand down the curve of Willow's jaw, then along the smooth line of her throat.

Willow settled back against the mattress, the sheets cool beneath her shoulders. She understood what was expected of her. With Blackburn, surrender came as naturally as breathing.

Blackburn worked in silence, her touch controlled. Each movement carried purpose. Willow gave herself over to the sensations, letting the knots of tension unravel from her muscles.

"I know you killed them," Blackburn said. Her fingers tightened where they rested against Willow's neck.

Willow's eyes snapped open, pupils dilating. "What?"

Blackburn held her more firmly, though not cruelly. The pressure remained measured. "I won't see you locked away, Fawn, but this cannot pass without consequence."

Fear flickered across Willow's face, shadowed by something more complicated. She shifted beneath Blackburn's hold, muscles tensing, but stilled when Blackburn spoke again, her voice perfectly level.

"Stay still. Let me do this." She caught a tear with her thumb before tightening her grip enough to make each breath a conscious effort. "This is my offering. You will take it."

Her hands remained steady as she restricted Willow's airflow, her gaze calm and focused. Willow's eyes fluttered with the strain. Her body trembled as she tried to speak but could only shape soundless words.

"Please..." The plea barely escaped.

As Blackburn watched Willow's features soften toward release, she felt moisture slide down Willow's cheek. Then she realized the tear was her own. Her hands shook. She released Willow's throat immediately.

Chapter 33

Blackburn sat rigidly, muscles aching with the effort of stillness. The chair's vinyl stung her thighs, heat blooming where she pressed down too hard. The hallway's churn faded to a blue. White coats, blue scrubs, faces pinched by their own emergencies. None of them saw her. She liked it that way. Her hands rested in her lap, fingers flexing, as if testing the strength left in them.

She lowered her gaze to her hands. The creases across her palms stood out in sharp relief under the LED glare. She flexed her fingers slowly, watching skin stretch taut and tendons rise like cables beneath the surface. Power lived there, coiled and waiting beneath each movement. When she lifted her eyes, the closed door opposite commanded her attention: a flat expanse of institutional beige, its surface cool and impenetrable. She measured her patience against its silence.

To her left, a young security guard shifted on a matching chair, the vinyl creaking beneath him. The brass nameplate on his chest read "Finnegan." His gaze darted across the corridor's traffic in nervous sweeps. Perspiration beaded along his upper lip despite the hospital's aggressive air conditioning. His palm drifted near his belt, fingers twitching inches from the holster.

She recognized Finnegan's discomfort instantly. A rookie's tell. His orders, clipped and impersonal, were her own legacy. She'd written this protocol, never imagining she'd be the stranger under suspicion. The irony tasted metallic in her mouth.

The corridor thrummed with competing sounds. Rubber soles squealed against worn linoleum. Monitors chirped their electronic warnings from unseen rooms. The antiseptic smell of floor cleaner mixed with something sharper, medicinal. For Blackburn, these sensations compressed into white noise as she waited for movement behind that door.

She rose without preamble. The abrupt motion jerked Finnegan upright, his hand dropping to his holster before he caught himself and froze.

"I'm not waiting here like a suspect," Blackburn said, already on her feet. She didn't look back to see if Finnegan followed. She knew he would. "If the doctor has a problem, he can take it up with me." Her voice was ice, all edges.

Finnegan quickened his stride to match hers, tension radiating from his shoulders as they navigated the hospital's warren of hallways and emerged into morning light.

Sirens split the morning, too late to matter. Blackburn watched the patrol car glide in, blue lights painting her reflection across the glass. She measured the officers as they stepped out. Fast, oblivious to the real threat standing just outside.

Finnegan stuttered to a halt. "Uh, guys?" The words came out reedy against the ambient noise.

Blackburn tracked the officers' movements, a subtle shift in her expression the only sign of interest. She pivoted toward the parking lot's far edge and continued walking.

"The issue with the new autonomous car system is that the officers do not know why they have been called," Blackburn said, her tone flat as old paint. "Give it time. They will."

She broke from the group without waiting for a reply and walked to her own car. The trunk thudded open, releasing a whiff of leather and gun oil, then shut again after she retrieved a book. She tucked it beneath her arm and started toward the hospital entrance, her heels clicking against the asphalt. Finnegan lingered a moment, uncertain, then followed.

Blackburn returned to the white door outside Willow's hospital room. Her posture remained rigid, shoulders squared. Two uniformed officers stood beside the entrance. Their faces shifted from alertness to vague recognition when they saw her.

"Detective Blackburn?" Officer Holden asked, his voice carrying the particular pitch of confusion. "Is this a homicide investigation?"

Finnegan looked at him, baffled. "Homicide? What are you talking about?"

The second officer, Sowels, answered Finnegan without looking at him. "This is Detective Blackburn from homicide. She has jurisdiction here." He glanced at Blackburn, his badge catching the LED light. "Did she not tell you?"

Blackburn gave a brief laugh that died in her throat. "No, I didn't."

Understanding dawned across Finnegan's face too late to matter. He turned to her and started an apology he never finished.

She brushed it aside with a small movement of her hand. "You did your job," she said simply.

She took her seat near the door again, the book's leather cover cool beneath her fingertips. The officers waited for direction, their uniforms rustling with each shift.

"You want my statement?" Blackburn's lips curled at the edge. She could make this easy for them, or she could make them sweat. "Let's get it over with." The lie came smooth, practiced, almost boring. She wondered if they could see the effort it took to keep her hands steady.

She kept her voice even and avoided their gaze, focusing instead on the scuffed tile beneath her feet. "Willow Adler works for me in a technical role. We had plans tonight and I came to pick her up at her apartment. The door was open and Willow was on the floor. I put her in my car and called 911 while driving here."

Holden's pen scratched across paper. "What's the address?"

"Apartment 406 at 47 Williams Street."

He nodded once with recognition. "Blankship Apartments has its share of calls."

The hospital door opened with a soft pneumatic hiss. The doctor stepped out into the corridor, his eyes flicking over each officer before landing on Blackburn.

She stood immediately, hands steady at her sides despite the tension that pulled tight around her ribs.

The doctor spoke quietly to Holden and Sowels while Blackburn waited motionless nearby, the antiseptic smell of the hospital sharp in her nostrils.

A few strained moments passed before he turned to address her directly, his expression awkward behind wire-rimmed glasses.

"I apologize for bringing in law enforcement," he said.

"There's nothing to apologize for," Blackburn replied, her voice carrying exhaustion beneath its calm surface. "I wrote most of your current protocols myself."

He relaxed and adjusted his glasses. "Do you want an update on Ms. Adler's condition?"

"Yes." Her voice held no tremor.

He kept his words clinical, each syllable precise. "Ms. Adler was strangled but survived due to rapid intervention." He lowered his voice further, although everyone could hear him in the narrow hallway. "She arrived unclothed so we assumed sexual assault. We found no injuries consistent with penetration."

Blackburn's jaw tensed. The word "unclothed" scraped raw against her nerves. Even the clinical chill of the doctor's voice couldn't bleach away the image: gloved hands, impersonal and methodical, skimming over Willow's skin. Hers. The urge to snatch Willow back, to cover her and reclaim her, flared so hot it threatened to burn right through her composure.

Finnegan shifted away from the group as if the words themselves carried contagion.

"I don't need any more details," he muttered as he walked down the corridor, his shoes squeaking against linoleum tiles that gleamed under harsh hospital lighting.

Blackburn waited as the officer left the room before turning back to the doctor. "Is Willow talking?" Her voice carried no inflection.

The doctor answered with clinical calm. "Yes. She claims she doesn't remember what happened or how she ended up here."

"Can I see her?"

A moment of hesitation passed before the doctor nodded. "Briefly. She's been through significant trauma. Only after the officers have finished their questions."

Officers Holden and Sowels entered, the door clicking shut behind them. Blackburn sat, composed, certain that Willow would say nothing to implicate her. There had never been any doubt. Willow was not only responsible for three deaths but had drawn Blackburn further than she once thought possible.

She glanced at the book in her lap. The Darkest Harvest, Whitmore's signature neatly inscribed inside the cover. She found no comfort in blaming Willow for what she herself carried. That darkness predated Willow by decades.

After several minutes, Sowels opened the door and addressed her. "She asked if you were here, ma'am." Blackburn gave a nod and followed him into the hospital room as protocol required.

Willow lay motionless in a narrow bed, her face pale against bleached linen, eyes closed beneath heavy glasses set askew on her nose. An oxygen tube rested beneath her nostrils. Monitor beeps marked each second in cold regularity. Deep purple bruises circled her throat. Evidence more eloquent than any report.

Blackburn crossed to her side, leaned down, and pressed a brief kiss against Willow's forehead. At the touch, Willow's eyes shot open, wide behind thick lenses.

"You made me cry," Blackburn murmured against her ear and placed the book into Willow's hands.

She left without another word.

* * *

Willow whimpered between ragged breaths while the doctor murmured empty assurances nearby. When her tears did not subside, he motioned for the officers to step out and dimmed the lights as he exited.

Alone now, Willow coughed and drew air deep into her chest. The aftermath made little sense. Her Lioness had walked away as if none of it mattered. After everything that had happened.

After almost dying by those hands. Gloved fingers wrapped around her neck with precise intent.

She let her head sink back into the pillow but flinched when an alarm sounded down the hall. Code Blue crackled over the speakers. A reminder of how quickly life could stop if help did not arrive in time.

Willow touched the brace fastened at her neck, fingertips exploring tender skin above dark bruises. The memories remained with perfect clarity: heat and betrayal tangled with something that still felt dangerously close to love.

'If I could love it would be you,' Blackburn had said.

She lowered her gaze to the book resting on the blanket where Blackburn had left it: The Darkest Harvest: A Farmhouse of Horror.

Turning it over in trembling hands, she absorbed its details. The author's name printed starkly across the cover: Whitmore. The front depicted an abandoned farmhouse graying beneath an indifferent sun, a lone figure standing silhouetted at its edge. A promise of secrets locked within decaying walls.

She traced each letter of the title with slow precision while a chill ran through her fingers. On the back cover, a synopsis waited for her to read.

"In the isolated farmland of rural Iowa, a dark secret festered within the walls of a decrepit farmhouse. The Roth family, led by a tyrannical and demented patriarch and supported by his vile, treacherous wife, inflicted unspeakable horrors upon their own flesh and blood. From incest and imprisonment to rape and murder, no member was spared from the cruel grasp of this twisted family tree. This detailed account, penned by the head of the FBI Behavioral Division, delves into the darkest corners of their dilapidated homestead, unraveling a legacy of evil that shocked the nation."

Willow traced the edge of the cover, feeling its slick surface beneath her fingertips. She was not a reader. Certainly not of books like this.

She opened it without haste. A line of blue ink greeted her on the first page. 'To whomever receives this book... she trusts you ~ Whitmore.' The inscription blurred behind her glasses. She trusts you. The words circled, their meaning just out of reach. Was the "she" Blackburn? Someone else?

Blackburn had handed over the book with an odd confession. You made me cry.

The phrase lingered in the hospital room, filling the space that antiseptic air could not cleanse. Willow had killed four people, yet Blackburn had been gentle afterward.

Her neck brace forced her gaze upward. She turned pages awkwardly. Crime scene photographs stared back at her. Floor plans of a weathered farmhouse followed, then police reports streaked with blacked-out lines. This was not a standard true crime book. It was an FBI case file reconstructed with painstaking detail.

The front cover offered nothing more.

She studied the back cover's description: flat, factual language that could not conceal what lay beneath. The violence inside rendered her own actions small by comparison.

Almost small.

Willow's hands trembled as she returned to the inscription. Someone had survived this story long enough to share it with federal agents.

The message on that page felt heavier now. Not a passing note, but something chosen specifically for her.

She moved to the photo section and absorbed each image under the harsh LED light. The farmhouse appeared sunken and tired, its roof sagging beneath decades of neglect, windows smashed into jagged teeth, weeds strangling the porch boards. Interior photos showed cramped spaces closer to cells than rooms. Numbered evidence markers scattered across grimy floors bore stains she did not want to identify.

Among police forms and witness testimony came transcripts from a single survivor's interviews. Most statements were redacted nearly to silence. What remained sketched the girl's ordeal in fragments: a teenager enduring years of calculated torment until she carved out her own escape.

Willow read every surviving line with care. Even reduced and filtered through official language, the survivor's voice held steady. A tone shaped by long observation and necessary silence.

She let the book rest against her chest for a moment, pressing into her ribs through the thin hospital gown. Life passed as usual beyond the window, but here everything had shifted. The same woman who had nearly strangled her, who might have been justified in finishing it, had chosen to give her this instead.

Not just a book, but proof that survival mattered.

Willow opened to the first page again and began reading from the start. If someone believed she could be trusted with this story, if Blackburn did, maybe there was a reason for it buried somewhere within herself.

Even if she could not find it on her own yet.

Chapter 34

The Sunday morning light filtered through the slats of Blackburn's blinds, casting thin bars of shadow across the hardwood floor. She lay back on her leather sofa, one knee bent, a book balanced in her lap. The title, Gaming the Irrational Mind, rested warm against her fingers as she read, unmoving except for the small tightening at the corner of her mouth when she reached an argument that interested her. The quiet in the apartment settled around her like dust until the phone rang, sharp and insistent, cutting through the stillness.

She let it ring twice before checking the display. New Dresden Hospital. A pause, then she answered with, "Blackburn."

Willow's voice came across faint but steady, threaded with exhaustion. "It's me. They're letting me go today. I need clothes. And a ride. Room 305."

Blackburn listened to the shallow rhythm of her breathing for half a second before answering. "I'll be there in an hour." Her tone made it clear she was not asking.

When the call ended, Blackburn closed the book over her finger and finished reading to the chapter's end. She stood. Clearing breakfast dishes took only minutes. She set plates into place with soft clicks, wiped the granite counter clean, rinsed and dried each glass with movements that left no water spots.

A new bag waited by the door, filled with clothes she had chosen for Willow: soft fabrics that wouldn't irritate healing skin, subdued colors, no patterns loud enough to draw attention. She had spent too long weighing options in cold store aisles while other shoppers drifted past, their carts rattling on linoleum.

She dressed herself in a burgundy cashmere sweater she had bought on impulse late last night. It held a muted richness against her pale skin. She ran her palm over one sleeve and let herself feel the difference. The gentle weight, the warmth rising from within the fibers.

She set Willow's bags on the passenger seat, their paper rustling against leather, and started her car. She paused only to check her watch before pulling out into traffic. If every light stayed green, she would arrive early. Timing mattered more than distance.

At the hospital, Blackburn parked at the far edge of the lot where no one lingered. She shut off the engine and waited in silence with both hands on the steering wheel, feeling its texture beneath her palms, until twenty minutes had passed.

Inside, she rode the elevator up through nine slow floors, arms full of neat paper bags that smelled faintly of new fabric. When the doors opened with a soft chime, she walked without hesitation to the nurses' desk.

"I'm looking for Adam Sinclair's room," she said through her mask, her voice muffled.

The nurse looked up from her monitor, LED light reflecting off her glasses, and gestured down the hallway. "Room 1008 is just there. Next to where those officers are posted."

Blackburn thanked her quietly and continued down the hall, her footsteps absorbed by industrial carpet. Two uniformed officers sat outside a closed door, their posture loose but alert, coffee cups cooling on the floor beside their chairs.

She stopped beside them. "Officers," she said evenly.

Both men straightened as she showed her badge, the metal catching the overhead lights. "I'm Detective Blackburn with homicide."

One officer squinted at her above his mask. Jones was printed on his tag in neat block letters. "Wait. Aren't you..."

She met his eyes but did not answer at first. "Officer Jones?"

He nodded, his hand moving unconsciously to his duty belt.

The other officer checked his own ID badge so she did not have to ask his name aloud.

"Did you clear this visit with Chief Hayes?" he asked, his voice carrying a note of uncertainty.

Blackburn shook her head once but kept eye contact. "No, Officer Cloud," she told him quietly, reading his badge as well. "I'm here about another patient." Her words hung between them for a moment, heavy as hospital air.

Jones lifted his chin uncertainly. "Didn't he...?" He seemed unable to finish his thought, the words dying in the antiseptic-scented hallway.

"Yes, sir. He tried to kill me. But he was still one of ours. An injured colleague deserves a measure of dignity," Blackburn said. She had not come here out of respect. Curiosity, cool and detached, had drawn her to this room. If he died, the autonomous car case might die with him.

Jones glanced at Cloud. "Just a few minutes. You'll need to leave your bag." He gestured toward the leather strap crossing her shoulder.

Blackburn nodded, set the bag against the wall near the chair, and spread her fingers wide for inspection.

"I appreciate this," she said. "If there's fallout, blame me. Which of you will supervise?"

Cloud stepped forward, his shoes clicking against the linoleum as he opened the door. "I will."

"Don't touch him or get too close to the monitors," he said as she entered.

The room's only light came from monitors casting a green glow across the walls. Sinclair lay beneath thin hospital sheets that barely moved with his breathing. His face looked washed out and slack, skin nearly translucent where it stretched over the sharp angles of his cheekbones. Tubes snaked from purple-bruised arms into machines that beeped in steady rhythm, tracking each faltering heartbeat.

Blackburn paused just inside the doorway. The antiseptic smell hung thick in the air. He had chosen this path.

"How is he?" she asked.

Cloud's jaw tightened before he answered. "Not well. I heard the physicians briefing his parents. A sad thing." His voice dropped until she could barely hear it over the ventilator's mechanical breathing.

Blackburn gave him a brief nod. She kept her features still as marble. Without a word, she left the room and retrieved her bag from where it rested against the cool wall.

"Thank you both," she said before stepping away down the hall. Her footsteps echoed as she left them to oversee a man whose consciousness would never return.

She pressed the elevator button and waited, arms folded tight across her chest. The doors parted with a soft chime. She entered, alone in the metallic box as it descended. The LED lights hummed overhead. The silence felt clinical rather than comforting.

When she stepped onto the third floor, she checked her watch and moved at a pace through the corridor. She passed the nurses' station where monitors blinked and phones rang softly. Willow's room appeared ahead.

She opened the door without knocking.

Willow looked up the instant Blackburn crossed the threshold. Her voice came out rough and low from strain but brightened immediately. "You came."

Blackburn's eyes softened just slightly. "And I hope to again." She crossed to Willow's bed and held her close for a moment. She felt the tremor that ran through Willow's body, the way her breath caught and released unevenly against Blackburn's shoulder.

"Ready to go?" Blackburn asked when Willow's grip loosened.

Willow nodded, glancing down at the thin hospital gown that hung loose around her shoulders. A flush of embarrassment colored her cheeks. It didn't quite reach her eyes. "Did you bring anything for me to wear?"

Blackburn smiled gently and brushed a strand of hair from Willow's forehead with two fingers. "Yes." Her voice stayed even as she reached into the canvas bag beside them. The zipper rasped softly.

"I thought we could try something different tonight." She pulled free a folded blue polo shirt. The cotton felt soft between her fingers but held enough structure to keep its shape. She glanced up at Willow again. "No more t-shirts."

"I didn't bring a bra," she added quietly as she helped Willow pull off the gown and slip into the new clothes with careful hands. Her movements stayed efficient but gentle. Her attention focused entirely on Willow's comfort as she eased the fabric over pale skin marked by fading bruises and fresh white bandages that caught the overhead light.

"There," Blackburn said once she finished. She smoothed down the collar one last time, feeling the warmth of Willow's skin beneath the cotton before letting her hands fall away.

Blackburn handed Willow the underwear and khakis. "These will do. They're more formal than jeans," she said. "Leather loafers. No laces this time."

Willow slipped on the shoes and flexed her toes against the soft leather interior. "They fit," she said. She hesitated, her fingers reaching for the edge of the foam neck brace.

Blackburn kissed her, lips grazing the exposed skin above the collar. "I know your body," she said. Her fingertips traced the contour of the brace, checking where foam met flesh. "Is it hurting?"

Willow blinked. "Only when I swallow."

Blackburn surveyed the room. The book she had left was missing from the bedside table, absent from the neat stack of paperwork and the untouched cup of water that caught the afternoon light.

"Where's your book?" Blackburn asked, keeping her tone even.

Willow tugged at her shirt hem, her gaze fixed on the speckled tile floor. "I tore out your note and threw out the rest." Her voice came thin but clear through the quiet air.

She looked up, meeting Blackburn's eyes across the sterile room. "I'm sorry about your gift. I read what you wrote, but I couldn't get through it. I already know you're strong. I don't need to see proof."

Blackburn's expression softened at that. "Why keep just the inscription?"

Willow managed a smile and pulled a folded slip of paper from beneath her pillow, the edges worn from handling. "'She trusts you.' I needed to hold onto something good," she said. "I'm going to frame it." She coughed. Pain flickered across her features.

Blackburn's hand settled in Willow's hair, fingers moving slowly through the loose strands. The gesture held both reassurance and possession.

"I want to go home," Willow said after a moment, her voice carrying enough firmness to matter. "If I stay any longer, they'll charge me for more than what insurance covers."

Blackburn nodded once and released Willow's hair. They left together, Willow keeping the torn page pressed between her fingers as they stepped into the LED hallway.

* * *

At home, Blackburn guided Willow with a warm palm at her lower back into the living room. She studied Willow's figure in the familiar light, noting the bruises that circled her throat like a necklace of shadows, uneven in color and shape.

"We've been through enough," Blackburn said as she sank onto the couch, stretching out along one armrest with her legs parted for space. She tapped her thigh in invitation. "Sit here. We need to talk."

Willow moved quickly into position, fitting herself between Blackburn's legs and settling back against her chest. The steady rhythm of Blackburn's heartbeat pressed through fabric, anchoring her breathing.

Pressing a kiss to Willow's crown, Blackburn reached into her pocket for a metal tin of Farmer's Rescue balm, its surface cool and unadorned. She slid off the lid with a soft click.

"Lift your shirt."

Willow obeyed without hesitation. With care, Blackburn gathered the waxy balm on her fingertips and stroked it over Willow's nipples with pressure. Her touch remained precise, methodical. Each circle and stroke both soothed damaged skin and marked territory.

Willow exhaled softly and melted further into Blackburn's hold, enveloped by warmth and the faint herbal scent of the balm, surrounded by purpose in each motion.

Two days had passed, but the need for aftercare lingered. The balm spread cool across Willow's skin as Blackburn worked it in with strokes. Willow pressed closer, her body seeking reassurance through touch.

"I'm going to touch your neck. Rub some balm in. Is that alright?" Blackburn held up her fingertips, slick and glistening, and waited. A tremor ran through Willow's shoulders.

"We have to rebuild trust. This is where it starts. I know my own strength now. Can you trust me to touch your neck?" Her words emerged steady, almost formal, though her fingers betrayed the slightest quiver.

Willow's breath caught before she answered. "Yes."

Blackburn traced the rigid edge of the neck brace with two fingers, gliding over purple-tinged skin for just a heartbeat before drawing back. She pressed her lips into Willow's hair, inhaling the faint scent of lavender shampoo, then dipped her fingers into the balm again and returned to her task.

Her strokes remained feather-light, her movements measured. The only sounds were their breathing and the subtle whisper of skin against skin.

When she finished, Blackburn wiped her hand clean on a tissue. The paper crinkled as it dropped onto the table. "I put you in a position where you felt desperate enough to do this. That will not happen again." Her tone remained level.

Willow shifted, tilting her face upward. "Thank you." Blackburn's pulse maintained its steady rhythm.

"But you have to promise me. Never again. No more killing." She threaded her fingers through Willow's hair. The strands slipped like silk between her fingers, no longer trembling.

Heat bloomed across Willow's cheeks as her eyelids fluttered.

"No shame," Blackburn said, her thumb grazing the curve of Willow's cheekbone with careful tenderness. "But that promise is not optional."

"I promise," Willow whispered, her voice breaking. "I promise."

"And I will protect you from whoever takes over homicide." Blackburn's words carried quiet certainty.

A sob broke free as Willow's grip tightened. "Thank you," she managed. Tears slid silently down her face as she let out a cough.

"You will have to be punished, little one. That is my responsibility. And you will have to atone for what you've done. That is your responsibility." Blackburn drew small circles on Willow's chest, a little touch of ownership.

"How?"

"We need time and space to decide what is best. What is just and fair. I won't bring you so close to death, ever again. But why?" Blackburn put her hand over Willow's.

"Tell me, Fawn," Blackburn said. She rested her palm against Willow's cheek, the warmth of her touch steady against cool skin.

Willow's breath caught and stuttered. "Brynn Cassidy called. She told me no one ever loved me, that my foster family took me for the money." Her voice thinned to a whisper, each word growing smaller. "I believe it."

Blackburn's thumb traced the curve of Willow's jaw, following the delicate line of bone beneath silk skin. "I remember," she said, her voice measured and low. The pattern revealed itself clearly. Most killers had a catalyst, that single moment that shifted their course forever. For Willow, Brynn Cassidy had been that moment. Blackburn would ensure that Brynn answered for it.

Willow's body shook as she tried to stifle another cough.

"Do you want tea? Honey and lemon?" Blackburn kept her voice soft, allowing routine to seep back into the moment.

Willow's body convulsed with another rough cough before she managed to steady her breathing. She pressed her palm to the rigid edge of her neck brace and winced. The plastic felt cool against her fevered skin.

"I'll make you honey lemon tea," Blackburn said, untangling herself from their embrace and rising from the couch. She moved toward the kitchen, her knees protesting with a dull ache. Willow followed. Each step was careful.

Blackburn filled the kettle at the sink, water rushing cold from the tap, and set it on its base with a soft click. She kept her voice level. "How did you pull it off?" Her attention shifted fully to Willow, who lowered herself onto a stool at the island, gripping the counter's edge. "High-level version. Talk me through it."

Willow cleared her throat again. The sound was raw and scratchy, her voice thin but steady. "Mesh network access for the first two cars."

Blackburn pulled a ceramic mug from the cabinet. It felt familiar in her hand. "That's a proximity exploit. You needed to be close by."

Willow nodded, brow furrowed as she focused on the memory, fingers drumming silently on the granite. "I used my department laptop. It has the police band, so I could broadcast malformed emergency packets. Most vehicles filter those out, but if I drove around enough, eventually one would connect."

Blackburn took lemon juice from the fridge and squeezed it into the mug. The plastic bottle was cold against her palm, the citrus scent sharp in the air.

"So, you needed line of sight to run that attack," she said. Behind her, the kettle snapped off with a metallic click.

"About two hundred feet was as far as I could get away with," Willow said.

Blackburn poured boiling water over the lemon. Steam rose to warm her face. She reached for the Manuka honey, its amber thickness catching the light as she measured out a spoonful with care.

"Jenna and Kendria. Were you following them directly?"

Willow shifted on her seat. The leather creaked beneath her. Another cough escaped as she adjusted her brace. "Yes. I couldn't lose you."

Blackburn stirred honey into the tea, the metal spoon clinking against ceramic, and glanced over her shoulder. "And with Lilith's cab? How did you know to target that one?"

"That was different." Willow's hands traced idle circles on the cool countertop while she spoke. "Lilith never traveled on foot if she could help it. Her car was manual transmission and not connected to any automated network. So I followed her. She always drove herself. When I saw her arrive in a cab at that lot, everything changed."

"You followed me there that night," Blackburn said, carrying the steaming mug back toward the living room. Its warmth seeped through to her fingers.

Willow trailed after her, footsteps soft on the hardwood, gaze downcast but focused.

"Yes," Willow replied, lowering herself beside Blackburn on the sofa once more. The cushions sighed.

Blackburn rested back against the warm fabric and let Willow settle in close. She felt the heat radiating from Willow's body.

"How did you know Lilith would take a cab?"

"I didn't." Willow spoke softly now, breath warm against Blackburn's shoulder, tone measured as she drew comfort from their proximity. "But by then I had adapted what I was doing. That idea came from something you said."

Blackburn tensed under Willow's weight. Her muscles tightened. A flash of irritation passed through her words. "From me?"

"One meeting with the team. Reeves said sold Straight Lines are still connected to company servers. You asked if I could break into their cloud."

Blackburn smiled at that and handed over the steaming mug. Their fingers brushed in the exchange. "You told me it wasn't possible without crossing a legal line."

Willow clasped both hands around the ceramic warmth. Steam curled up to fog her glasses as she blew over its surface before sipping cautiously. "Turned out it was easier than expected once I tried it outside official channels. Range wasn't an issue anymore. I didn't have to follow anyone."

"Every Straight Line model is exposed," Blackburn murmured as she locked an arm around Willow's waist and drew her closer. She felt the subtle tremor that ran through the younger woman's frame.

"Yes. If their security protocols are still old. I read about it online from Keiran Mott's write-ups. He explained that you could compromise the cars by linking to them, sending data through the Raider cloud, and then you had a way in. I used AI to create an app on my phone to scan for cars as they passed. It sent out handshake requests and pinged when a car answered. Once I found one, I connected. I tested it," she said, pausing to take a steady sip of her honey lemon tea. The warmth spread across her tongue, sweet citrus cutting through the tension.

"I could switch off the lights or honk the horn. But I got better. When I saw the cab stop and you saw it, I noticed how straight your back was, how you ran your tongue over your lips." Willow's voice softened along the edges, like fabric worn smooth. "That was how I knew it was her in the car. I turned on the interior lights to be certain, then routed into the cab and into the cloud and sent a new set of commands straight back down. I gave the car GPS coordinates fifty feet out into Lake Canada, off Dunbar Bluffs. Once those were locked in with a 'no override' tag attached, it wouldn't respond to anyone else. When you all chased after it, I took my phone and went home."

Blackburn blinked once, maybe twice, releasing a breath that stirred the steam rising between them. Her hand settled on Willow's thigh, tracing a slow line with her fingertip. "You didn't know she would be in an autonomous cab?"

Willow shook her head. "No. I just took advantage. I know what I did broke something between us," Willow said, her voice thinning as she spoke, like thread pulled too tight. "You can't trust me anymore."

Blackburn raised her finger once in warning. "No theatrics. You're far tougher than you let on. And trust? You're holding boiling water between my legs right now. What do you think that means?"

Willow studied her cup, watching the surface ripple in her grip before allowing herself a small smile.

Blackburn lifted Willow's chin between her fingers until their gazes locked. "There's work ahead of us, Fawn. You'll have to make amends for what happened, but I'll stay with you." Her words fell gently yet absolute. "We recommit when you're ready."

"When we're both ready," Willow replied, her voice barely audible. She accepted the tissue Blackburn offered and dabbed at her damp cheeks.

She released a long breath as Blackburn resumed tracing slow circles between her shoulder blades.

Quiet stretched between them until Willow's eyes found hers again. "How did you know it was me?"

Blackburn unscrewed the lid and pressed more balm into Willow's skin. Her fingers moved with surgical precision, the cool cream warming instantly against heated flesh. "I reviewed the EDR data myself," she said. The words hung between them as her hands stilled, her gaze unfocusing toward some middle distance. "Accessing it was straightforward once I decided to stop relying on your summaries. We have work ahead of us, Willow, but not tonight. Sinclair is our focus now. That gives us breathing room." Blackburn's eyes traveled the length of Willow's body stretched between her legs, her approval settling like silk across bare skin.

"You look beautiful." The words emerged low and controlled, vibrating with restrained power.

Heat bloomed across Willow's cheeks, spreading down her throat. She dropped her gaze to the sheets. "Thank you, Lioness."

Blackburn's eyebrow lifted a fraction, the ghost of humor flickering in her eyes. "About your name. Fawn might not fit anymore."

Willow's muscles locked tight. The words tumbled out, breathless and urgent. "No, please, Lioness. I want to keep it."

Blackburn's gaze held steady, weighing. "There are no killer fawns."

Willow shook her head, her voice climbing. "Wait. Give me your phone, please, Lioness. Let me show you." Her fingers stretched upward, trembling.

Blackburn placed the phone in her palm, curiosity softening the corners of her mouth.

Willow's thumbs flew across the screen, her bottom lip caught between her teeth. The soft glow illuminated her face as she searched. After several heartbeats, she turned the display toward Blackburn.

Blackburn leaned in, her breath warming Willow's shoulder. Her brow furrowed. "What is that? Is this legitimate?"

The screen revealed a delicate creature. A small deer with two curved tusks descended from its jaw like ivory daggers.

"Yes," Willow said, her voice brightening with hope. "It's called a water deer. They use those tusks for fighting and defense. See? I can still be your Fawn."

Blackburn studied the image, the silence stretching taut before she nodded once. A smile ghosted across her lips as she drew Willow closer, solid warmth against her side.

"That is a brutal little creature," she murmured against Willow's temple. "You can keep the name." Her arm tightened, anchoring them both in the quiet moment.

"And you have my permission to call me Morgan."